CW00554895

TO
KILL
—A—
KING

Also By David Gilman

Master of War series
MASTER OF WAR
DEFIANT UNTO DEATH
GATE OF THE DEAD
VIPER'S BLOOD
SCOURGE OF WOLVES
CROSS OF FIRE
SHADOW OF THE HAWK
TO KILL A KING

The Englishman series
THE ENGLISHMAN
BETRAYAL
RESURRECTION

Dangerzone series
THE DEVIL'S BREATH
ICE CLAW
BLOOD SUN

Standalone novels
THE LAST HORSEMAN
NIGHT FLIGHT TO PARIS

Children's stories
MONKEY AND ME

DAVID GILMAN

MASTER OF WAR

TO KILL A KING

An Aries Book

First published in the UK in 2024 by Head of Zeus,
part of Bloomsbury Publishing Plc

Copyright © David Gilman, 2024

The moral right of David Gilman to be identified
as the author of this work has been asserted in accordance with
the Copyright, Designs and Patents Act of 1988.

All rights reserved. No part of this publication may be reproduced,
stored in a retrieval system, or transmitted in any form or by any means,
electronic, mechanical, photocopying, recording, or otherwise,
without the prior permission of both the copyright owner
and the above publisher of this book.

This is a work of fiction. All characters, organizations, and events
portrayed in this novel are either products of the author's
imagination or are used fictitiously.

9 7 5 3 1 2 4 6 8

A catalogue record for this book is available from the British Library.

ISBN (HB): 9781801108096
ISBN (E): 9781801108126

Typeset by Divaddict Publishing Solutions Ltd.

Cover design: Simon Michele
Map design: Vanessa Periam

Printed and bound in Great Britain by
CPI Group (UK) Ltd, Croydon CR0 4YY

Head of Zeus
First Floor East
5–8 Hardwick Street
London EC1R 4RG

WWW.HEADOFZEUS.COM

For Suzy, my wife, with love

CHARACTER LIST

*Sir Thomas Blackstone
*Henry Blackstone

THOMAS BLACKSTONE'S MEN
*Sir Gilbert Killbere
*Meulon: Norman captain
*John Jacob: Blackstone's squire and captain
*Renfred: German man-at-arms and captain
*Will Longdon: veteran archer and centenar
*Jack Halfpenny: archer and ventenar
*William Ashford: man-at-arms and captain
*Aicart: Gascon captain
*Rosslyn: Renfred's scout
*Dene: Renfred's scout
*Bartholomew: Renfred's scout
*Tricart: Renfred's scout
*Walter Root: archer
*Roger Fairfoot: archer
*Bullard: man-at-arms

HENRY BLACKSTONE'S MEN
*Hugh Gifford: man-at-arms and Henry's guardian
*Walter Mallin: mercenary
*Robert Helyer: mercenary
*Raymond Vachon: French mercenary

*Arnald Bezián: Gascon mercenary
*Eckehart Brun: German mercenary
*John Terrel: mercenary

BRETON MEN-AT-ARMS AND OTHERS
Bertrand du Guesclin: commander
*Jean de Soissons, la Griffe/the Claw: routier
*Pellan: routier
*Le Bourc: captain of Josselin
*Yagu: fisherman

GASCON MEN-AT-ARMS, MERCENARIES AND NOBILITY
*Galhard de Prato: commander of the
   Château de Langoiran
Garciot du Châtel: mercenary commander
Bertucat d'Albret: mercenary commander
Jean de Grailly: Captal de Buch

ENGLISH ROYALTY
Edward of Woodstock: Prince of Wales and Aquitaine
John of Gaunt: Duke of Lancaster

ENGLISH OFFICIALS, ALLIES, MERCENARIES, MEN-AT-ARMS
AND OTHERS
Sir John Chandos: Constable of Aquitaine
Sir Nigel Loring: the Prince's chamberlain
Steven Cusington: Marshal of the Army
Guichard d'Angle: Marshal of the Army
John, Count d'Armagnac
James IV: exiled King of Majorca
Eustache d'Aubricourt: Hainault mercenary

Sir Hugh Calveley: mercenary commander
Sir William Felton: knight
*Flemyng: man-at-arms
*Alfred Vaisey: routier
William Durant: Warden of Merton College,
    Oxford
*Clara: Durant's niece

FRENCH ROYALTY
Charles V: King of France

FRENCH OFFICIALS, NOBILITY, MERCENARIES,
MEN-AT-ARMS AND OTHERS
Simon Bucy: counsellor to the French King
Arnoul d'Audrehem: Marshal of France
Gaston Phoebus: Count de Foix
*Alphonse: Count de Foix's steward
*Garnier: routier
Hélie 'Petit' Meschin: mercenary
*Bernard de Lagny: man-at-arms
*Hugo Muset: man-at-arms
*Nicholas de Mitry: man-at-arms
*Gautier de Fleur: knight
*Louis de Roche: knight
*Père Éraste: priest

SPANISH ROYALTY
Pedro I: King of Castile and León
Henry of Trastámara: Don Pedro's half-brother and
    claimant to his throne
Charles II: King of Navarre

SPANISH OFFICIALS, NOBILITY AND OTHERS

*High Steward to King Pedro I

*Sancha Ferrandes of Castile

*Don Fernando Ferrandes of Castile

Martín Henríquez de Lacarra: Navarrese knight

Count de Osona: Aragonese ally of King Pedro

*Abbess of the Convent of Santo Domingo de Estella, Navarre

*Abraam Abroz: leader of the Jewish community in Estella

*Indicates fictional characters

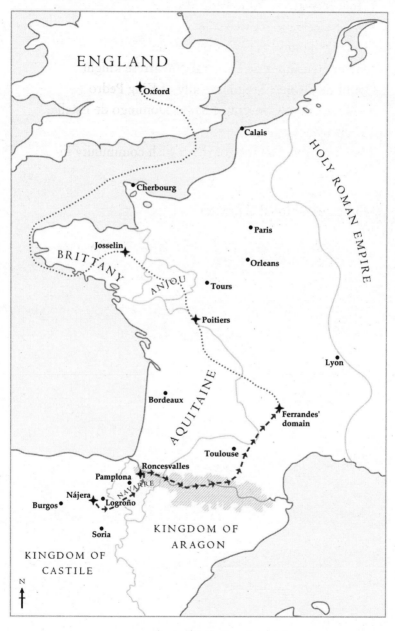

1367

BLACKSTONE AND HENRY'S ROUTES THROUGH FRANCE

ENGLAND

Oxford

Calais

HOLY ROMAN EMPIRE

Cherbourg

Paris

Josselin

BRITTANY

ANJOU

Orleans

Tours

Poitiers

Lyon

Bordeaux

AQUITAINE

Ferrandes'
domain

Toulouse

Roncesvalles

Pamplona

NAVARRE

Nájera

Burgos

Logroño

Soria

KINGDOM OF
ARAGON

KINGDOM OF
CASTILE

N

BLACKSTONE'S ROUTE   ➝➝➝

HENRY'S ROUTE   ·······

THE PRINCE OF WALES'S ROUTE TO THE BATTLE OF NÁJERA

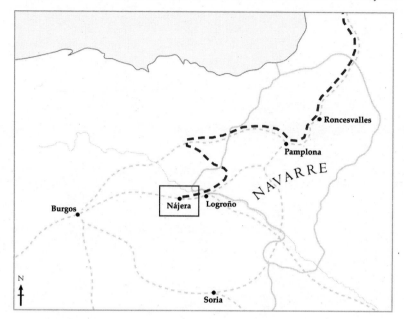

THE BATTLE OF NÁJERA

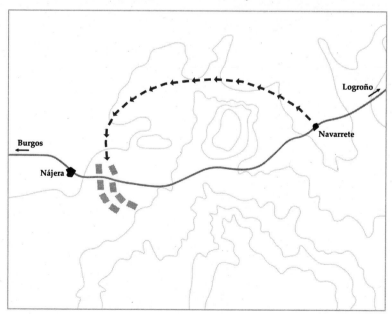

THE PRINCE OF WALES'S ROUTE   – ◆ –

HENRY OF TRASTÁMARA'S ARMY   ▓

MAIN ROAD   ――――

Ignis aurum probat, miseria fortes viros.

As fire tests gold, so adversity tests brave men.

Seneca

PROLOGUE

For seventeen years the High Steward to King Don Pedro I of Castile and León was a silent witness to the depraved violence of the Spanish King. And he had lived in fear since Thomas Blackstone had returned from Galicia where he had slain the King's favourite, Velasquita Alcón de Lugo. There was no doubt in the steward's mind that the woman was a creature of the devil. At Pedro's behest, she had murdered his young Queen, using her skill with poisons to make it seem like suicide. She had sided with the murderous Ronec le Bête, the beast who had slaughtered Blackstone's Gascon captain, Beyard, and a boy witness who had identified Velasquita as the young Queen's killer.

And Blackstone had killed the poisoner and the beast who served her.

How had the scar-faced English knight done so? It should not have been possible. No one had ever survived her poison. No one. And yet... and yet Blackstone had. Had God favoured Blackstone? Or had the devil found a stronger ally than even the woman? The High Steward recalled the terror instilled in him by the poisoner when she asked him to choose between

God and the devil: which of them did he fear the most? And after he confessed to her that he feared the devil more, he had agreed to administer her poison to Blackstone. Had he refused, Lucifer would have torn his soul from his body. And so he had been a party to murder and further encumbered his soul's burden by poisoning Blackstone's wine before he set off in search of the woman killer. Who was the most aggrieved by the High Steward's action? God or the devil? If only he could banish his doubt about which entity waited to wreak vengeance on him. Every day in the small hours the Castilian King's trusted servant slipped away from the royal chambers at the Archbishop's palace adjoining the northern perimeter of the Cathédrale Saint-André and made his way to the cathedral itself, where he would kneel in penance.

Blackstone had returned to Bordeaux months ago and reported to the Prince of Wales all that he knew of the murders and what he had done in the name of justice. Pedro had condemned the Master of War, insisting Blackstone be punished for the wilful slaying of a member of Pedro's court. There was no proof of Velasquita being a witch, he had insisted: Blackstone had killed her to satisfy his thirst for revenge. Worse still, Blackstone had threatened Pedro. Insulted and treated with contempt a God-chosen king. A king the Prince of Wales had sent Blackstone to rescue.

And Blackstone had not denied it.

To appease the Spanish King, Blackstone was banished from the court and imprisoned. Common men do not threaten royalty and escape punishment. That had put him beyond the city, confined in a castle, separated from his men and guarded day and night.

The High Steward replayed in his mind's eye the confrontation between Prince, King and Master of War. He exhaled the tension held in his chest, his breath cold on the air. His knees ached from the pain of spending so much time on them. The cathedral's flickering candles cast him into a half-world of darkness and light. Shadows lifted the priest's monotonous incantations into a mere whisper high in the vaulted roof arching above his bowed head. His tightly clasped hands turned his knuckles white as his mind berated him. Was he afraid of Blackstone or the Lord Jesus? Surely it was the latter: he feared the Almighty's condemnation, not any physical threat from the Englishman. He was safe. He was protected. Blackstone would never dare harm him. The Prince of Wales had commanded it. Blackstone's name had not been uttered in months. He was as a ghost in the Prince's court. The English King had decreed that the Prince must return Pedro to his rightful place in Castile. An army was being prepared. The French must not be allowed to usurp a vital ally on Aquitaine's southern flank across the Pyrenees. And Pedro, despite his cruelty and violence, was that ally. There had been no mention of Thomas Blackstone when his master had discussed plans with the Prince of Wales. Doubt about waging war without the renowned knight was not even touched on. For all the High Steward knew, Thomas Blackstone would never be favoured in the English Prince's court again.

As his tormented mind raced through the purgatory of doubt, a small miracle enveloped him: a God-given moment of warmth seeped into his aching bones. The cathedral's deathly cold chill had stiffened his ageing muscles, but now he felt the comfort of spiritual forgiveness embrace him. A tear trickled down his cheek in gratitude. The Lord had accepted his penance.

He gathered his cloak around him. It would not be long before they recrossed the Pyrenees and returned home. All would soon be well.

★

The High Steward scurried along the cloisters leading to the cobbled passage that would return him to the servants' entrance to the palace. His survival instinct these past months made him avoid the main public thoroughfares, seeking different ways to reach the cathedral's side door. A single lantern burned in the distance. He hugged the darkness, focusing on the lamp's glow. A beacon guiding him back to a warm bed for the scant few hours before dawn when his master would be roused for morning prayers.

Then he faltered and turned to face the darkness behind him. He had heard someone moving in the distance. He waited, breath held tightly. Shadows moved beyond the cloisters. His tension eased. It was only a handful of worshippers leaving the cathedral's main entrance, silent except for shoe leather scuffing cobbles. He did not berate himself for his caution – better to be wary. A servant holding the lantern was waiting for him. The High Steward struck out across the courtyard as the hooded man raised the oil lamp above his shoulder, showing the King's steward the way.

'All is well?' the High Steward called.

'Aye, my lord. The night watch has passed by. There is no one else abroad at this hour. Only the righteous.'

The High Steward nodded and gestured the man to lead the way. He followed in his wake. They turned a corner. A sliver of light entered the passageway from a high window: a narrow slit in the rough-hewn walls. A servant lighting a lamp, no doubt after having slept in a stairwell or wherever a humble resting place could be found. The High Steward's gaze returned to the lamp carrier, who had stopped half a dozen paces ahead of him.

'Get on,' he ordered the man.

The lantern bearer made no response. He stood still, gazing down. The High Steward reached him and saw what the man was looking at. It was the crumpled body of a servant. His servant. He took a rapid pace backwards as the man in front of him turned and pulled back his hood. The High Steward stared at him. He thought he recognized the face, but could put no name to it. He gasped as his retreat brought him up against a second man. He whirled around, pressing his back against the wall. Two cloaked men barred the way. One close, the other several paces and to one side behind him. A block against any escape attempt should he manage to get past the hulking figure who stared faceless from the darkness of his hood.

'All right, Will,' said a voice from behind the lantern bearer, who handed the lamp to the voice's owner, a fourth man who stepped out of the darkness and pulled back his cowl.

King Pedro's steward lurched forward, heart pounding as he gasped for breath. The blood drained from his face as he stared at Thomas Blackstone. 'It cannot be you. You are banished.'

'I am,' said Blackstone.

'Then, how...?' The question died on his lips. His throat was dry with fear. It made no difference how Blackstone had found him.

But Blackstone answered anyway. 'We waited. My men watched for weeks. The huddled beggars in the doorway; the street seller sleeping beneath his cart. The spy from the window up there,' he said. 'We were in no hurry. Your servant is not dead. My archer struck him but he will recover from the blow.'

The steward blinked rapidly, his mind racing. Ever cautious, he had altered his journey to the cathedral every time he went to pray. Some nights one door, the next another. They had still tracked him. It made sense. They were hunters.

He fell to his knees. 'I have begged forgiveness from our blessed Lord Jesus. I have done penance. Sir Thomas, I had no choice in what I did to you. None.'

'You poisoned me to protect yourself and the King you serve.'

The steward shook his head, his hands clasped in front of him as if he were facing the very wrath of God Himself. 'I bore you no ill will. I swear it. It was the woman. She turned my bowels to water with her threats.'

'You remained silent. You kept the secrets of a murderess. You protected a foul king. You allowed a child to be slain and my loyal captain to die trying to save him. They were killed in a cathedral in Spain not unlike this one. You knew everything.' Blackstone stared down at him. 'But you remained silent. And then tried to kill me. There must be a reckoning for their sake.'

The High Steward spread his hands in supplication. 'Do not kill me, Sir Thomas. I beg you. I will pay whatever restitution you ask. My lord, I beg you with all my heart.'

His upturned face looked at the scarred features of the man gazing down at him. 'I won't kill you,' said Blackstone.

The High Steward felt tears sting his eyes. He clasped his hands again. He was saved. For a moment, he was not aware of Meulon's honed blade sliding across his neck. The bite was so sharp it felt little more than a wasp sting. And then he choked. His lungs filled with blood. By the time his head hit the cobbled street, the cloaked men had stepped away into the darkness. All except one. His dying eyes saw Blackstone crouch and gaze at him.

'Hell awaits you,' said Blackstone.

The steward blinked as Blackstone turned away. As he died, a single thought tormented him. He had been right. Blackstone was the devil's disciple.

PART ONE

THE ROAD TO WAR

CHAPTER ONE

Duchy of Aquitaine
1367

The Prince of Wales rode hard and fast. His stallion's flanks were flecked with sweat despite the crisp morning air. His entourage of a dozen men-at-arms could barely keep pace with a prince fired with anger. His inconsolable fury was penetrated only by persistent cries of alarm from the captain of his guard that he would kill his horse if he did not slow down. The thought of losing his favourite stallion drove sense into him and Edward of Woodstock, Prince of Wales and Aquitaine, pulled up his horse. Dismounting, he strode across the open meadow as a servant grabbed the reins. The courser, its lungs heaving, trembled from its effort. The men-at-arms held back. Better to let the Prince exhaust his temper. Edward turned to his captain. 'We will banish him, I swear. Not to a fortress château within three hours' ride of our palace, but there!' He gestured wildly to nowhere in particular. 'Across the damned Alps. We will send him to Italy. Again!'

The captain remained silent.

'Well? Are we not too lenient already with his imprisonment?'

The captain had served the Prince since the great victory at Poitiers a year short of a dozen years back. If he was asked a question, he was expected to answer. 'Highness, there is no evidence it was Sir Thomas.'

'Is there not? Who else would render the man's servant unconscious and lure his master to his death below our palace walls? Are we held in such contempt?'

'The steward's purse was taken, highness. A simple robbery would explain it.'

The Prince gazed across the distant landscape; his breathing settled. He looked back to where his horse was tended by the servant. He nodded. 'Perhaps,' he said. He strode back to his mount. 'But I'll wager a gold leopard it was Blackstone.'

The formidable tiered defences of the Château de Langoiran clawed up a rugged hillside, its battlements affording an unobstructed view across the valley to a bend in the River Garonne a mile or so away. The Prince and his men rode up the winding approach and galloped across the bridge into the outer yard. The fortress was manned by Gascon men-at-arms loyal to the Prince. Their captain, Galhard de Prato, was no stranger to the Prince. He had been chosen to watch over the English King's Master of War. Thomas Blackstone was to have anything he required to keep him comfortable. This was no harsh prison environment. It was a confinement more in name than reality, but one that restricted Blackstone's movement. A place where he would be watched and guarded. It was politics. A gesture to assuage the Spanish King's fury at having been insulted and threatened by Blackstone those months ago despite the Englishman saving the King's life.

The Prince followed de Prato onto the steps leading up to the walls.

'Has Sir Thomas left the château? He is kept here? He has not been allowed to ride?'

'No, my lord. He is confined within the walls, as you commanded. His horse was grazed in the outer yard and then stabled and fed. It took several men to hobble him for the farrier. If Sir Thomas had made any attempt to leave the stables, we would have known.'

'Is there any way he could have slipped out? To have reached the city?'

'I have sentries patrolling and a night watch checking every door. I have men on the road and at the Pont de Langoiran. He could not have crossed the river. No one could get there and back on foot in the hours of darkness.'

The higher up the steps they climbed the louder became the clash of steel.

'And food?'

'Brought to the gate by villagers, checked and paid for and taken to the kitchens. Served by the cook. One man takes it to Blackstone's squire.'

'No one else? No visitors?'

'None, highness, only the priest from the Église Saint-Léonce and the local fishermen from Langoiran.'

'Priest? Sir Thomas needed a priest only once and that was when he lay close to death at Crécy.'

'It was for his squire, John Jacob, lord. The sacrament.'

'You saw Sir Thomas throughout last night?'

'His squire attended him. The candles burned in his quarters. John Jacob took bathing water and food to him.'

The Prince stopped at the last turn of the steps and gazed across the valley to the river. 'How is the fish brought here?'

'In salted barrels and rundlets.'

'And the old barrels returned?'

'Yes, lord. They are brought, and then several days later the empty ones collected when the cook and kitchen servants have taken what they need.'

'How many fishermen enter the kitchens?'

'Three, my lord.'

'And three return?'

'Aye, my lord.'

The Prince looked beyond the walls. If Blackstone had been responsible for the High Steward's murder, was that how he had escaped the fortress? It would take more than a fisherman's barrel for Blackstone to be smuggled out of the fortress, but a man hefting such a barrel on his shoulder, a cowl hiding his face, would be allowed to leave. How, though, would he have returned unseen before daylight – if, as he suspected, the Master of War had committed murder?

He gazed hard at the glistening breadth of the River Garonne. 'The tides could take a man in a boat to the city in a few hours. And bring him back.' He looked at the Gascon man-at-arms, who shrugged. The Prince took the steps two at a time. There was little more to be gained from the interrogation. Reaching the walls overlooking the inner yard, he saw Blackstone and his squire John Jacob stripped to their shirts despite the biting cold, striking hard as they honed their sword-fighting skills. Blackstone wielded Wolf Sword with ferocious strength, causing the Prince to grip the wall when it looked as if Blackstone had forgotten it was his squire he fought. The Prince and his trusted Gascon watched as John Jacob retaliated and forced Blackstone onto the back foot, then kicked his legs from beneath him. For a breathless moment, it looked as though he had beaten him. The Gascon drew a sharp breath and muttered to himself. 'By God, neither man gives quarter.'

The Prince turned to him. 'Thomas Blackstone would have it no other way. He expects his men to best him.'

As he uttered the words Blackstone twisted away, deflected Jacob's sword and deftly disarmed his squire, throwing him to the ground, sword at his throat. A lesson learned.

'Though they have yet to succeed,' said the Prince. 'Attend to your duties. I have business with him,' he told de Prato. The Gascon obeyed as the Prince leaned across the wall and bellowed. 'Thomas!'

Blackstone hauled John Jacob to his feet. They looked up and then took the knee.

CHAPTER TWO

The Prince swept into the courtyard, ordering his men-at-arms to stay with the horses. What he needed to say to the man who had shadowed his life since they were both sixteen-year-old boys at Crécy, when both had been blooded in battle and Blackstone had saved the Prince's life, would be uttered in private.

'Thomas!'

'Highness,' said Blackstone, still on one knee.

'Get up, for God's sake. You too, Master Jacob. Courtly respect has its place. It is acknowledged.'

Blackstone and John Jacob got to their feet. The Prince studied Blackstone, who returned his gaze. 'All right, Thomas. There's much to discuss.'

John Jacob needed no invitation to leave. He bowed and turned away.

When he was out of earshot, the Prince took a step closer, his voice low with constrained anger. 'You dishonour me, Thomas. You come into our city and kill a royal servant. King Pedro's steward had his throat cut last night. We are not to be treated like a court jester. Even a fool knows when he has been shat upon.'

'I did not kill him, my Prince.'

'So you say. Would we expect you to own the murder? How did you do it? The roads and bridges are guarded. A fast boat and a willing accomplice would have you in the city in a few hours. The tide turns by dawn and brings you back. But how did you get back in here? That is what tantalizes me.'

8

'I did not kill that man,' said Blackstone.

The Prince turned and paced, a fist clenched. 'We are obliged to deal with Pedro. We are aghast at his vile behaviour, but he is an ally. There is a treaty. We have a duty. We have to protect our borders. He must be mollified.'

'You have incarcerated me here these months, lord. Has he not been mollified?'

'Do not spar with us. It will not be tolerated.'

'Highness, I am held here at your pleasure while Sir Gilbert and my men remain outside the city limits. And I have—'

'Has it been so hard a time to serve?' the Prince interrupted. 'Did we not allow you the freedom of visitors? Did we have you flogged or starved? Cast in a dungeon? It was a gesture, Thomas. To calm a vicious king you had threatened. It is your doing. Your actions brought you here. It is a temporary measure. Nothing more.' The Prince calmed himself. 'All right, all right. The man poisoned you. We are thankful he failed. But did you have to kill him outside our palace walls? Yards from the cathedral? His blood still stains the street where he fell.'

Blackstone remained silent.

'Are we still your Prince or are we to be ridiculed?'

'You are until I die, highness, and no, you are not.'

The Prince turned his back. His cloak disguising the rapid drawing of his sword, Edward released the tie on his cloak, letting it fall into the dirt. He pivoted, the blade threshing the air. Blackstone was no longer where he had been a moment before. Blackstone took two paces back, his sword still held low. Expressionless, he stood his ground as the Prince attacked. Blackstone defended himself. He felt the man's strength in the sword strikes and let his sword arm yield. The two blades slid free, forcing the Prince to half turn. Blackstone shouldered him hard. It was unexpected. The Prince stumbled. Blackstone backed away.

'I am sworn to protect you,' he said. 'I will not fight you.'

'Defend yourself,' the Prince answered, and struck out with the ferocity of old, the muscular strength of a seasoned fighter and expert swordsman, relentless in his attack.

Blackstone parried but made no attempt to break the Prince's guard. Several minutes passed and still the Prince pressed on with his unrelenting assault. Blackstone felt the man's strength diminishing. He allowed a high-guard strike to cast Wolf Sword from his grip. The tip of the Prince's sword hovered at Blackstone's throat.

'Swear to me, Thomas. Did your hand kill the High Steward?'

'I swear to you on my life and yours it did not.'

Sweat glistened on the Prince's face. He lowered his sword, fought for breath and staggered. Blackstone grabbed him before his knees buckled. The exertion had left the Prince racked with coughing. Blackstone half carried him to a low wall where his tunic and wineskin hung. Blackstone uncorked the wine and held it for the Prince, who drank and steadied his breathing. Blackstone remained silent. The Prince had been unwell before they had gone into Castile to rescue Pedro. Clearly, the malady lingered; the Prince's stature suddenly diminished by an unseen enemy.

The Prince raised a hand to gesture he was all right. 'It comes and goes, Thomas. It is what it is.'

'Who knows that you suffer?' said Blackstone.

'Those who need to.'

'Your father, the King?'

'No.'

'Then the Lady Joan must know.'

The Prince smiled. 'Thomas, we are blessed with the Lady Joan who would have me in her chamber day and night if we permitted it. There are days we wish it could be so. Our father sent us to govern and protect the duchy. It takes more than a strong arm. Politics, Thomas: it leeches a warrior's spirit. Perhaps it is that which ails us. She suspects but does not know – she is soon to give birth. The less she knows and the more we conceal the malady the better.'

The Prince stood. Blackstone retrieved his cloak and shook it free of dirt and did not belittle him by draping it around his shoulders. Edward of Woodstock, Prince of Wales and Aquitaine, understood his Master of War only too well. 'I came to challenge you, Thomas. To see if you would confess to the killing. Perhaps even to challenge your loyalty. It was obvious you could have disarmed me at any point.' He tugged the cloak around his neck and sheathed his sword. 'I believe you. If it was not your hand that did the murder, it was another's. Someone close to you. But I can now face King Pedro and proclaim in all good faith that it was not you.'

'I would never raise my hand against you,' said Blackstone. 'I swore to the Queen all those years ago that I would protect you.'

The Prince appeared to be his old self once more. 'And irritate our conscience like a stone in a boot rubs flesh. Your time here is over, Thomas. We have need of you.'

Blackstone and John Jacob watched the Prince and his escort ride clear of the fortress.

'Does he know?' said the squire.

'He knows,' said Blackstone. 'What he didn't know was how I got back inside.'

'If he had seen Will Longdon playing the role of cook these past months, he'd have known. The postern gate is only a few yards from the kitchen.'

Blackstone nodded, keeping his gaze on the now distant

figure of the man Fate had bound to him. 'Thank God we no longer have to eat what he offers. We leave for Bordeaux and the men.'

'And then, Sir Thomas?'

'We lead the Prince and his army through the mountains back to Castile. We go to war.'

CHAPTER THREE

During Blackstone's token banishment from the city, Sir Gilbert Killbere and Blackstone's men had camped outside Bordeaux's walls, close to one of the city gates at Port Judaea. It was where they had previously been billeted before setting off to Spain to rescue Pedro the Cruel of Castile. Jews were not persecuted by the English Prince but were still forbidden to live within the city walls; the old Jewish quarter accommodated moneylenders, tradesmen, merchants, herbalists and doctors. Those doctors attended to the men's ailments without charge, in recognition of Blackstone's kindness to and protection of one of their own during the Master of War's previous journey south. Killbere made certain their generosity was not abused or their lives intruded upon. The hulking figure of Meulon, head and shoulders above all others who packed the narrow alleyways and streets, became a beacon of protection should any outsiders enter the Jewish quarter and cause insult or threaten violence. Blackstone's horses were shod, stabled and fed at the Prince's command and paid for from his own purse.

Killbere had kept the fighting men busy during Blackstone's absence. Days spent in the surrounding countryside kept horse and man fit for war. Long-held skills in defence and attack were honed further. Killbere ran them until, sweat-soaked and exhausted, they faltered. And then he ran them again, for the ability to move rapidly on foot from one place to another, as a shifting battle might demand, was critical.

Fishermen had carried messages from Blackstone to the city

so that planning the High Steward's death could be done with care and without haste. When the hooded figure of the King's Master of War appeared before the poisoner that night, Killbere ensured those men not involved were raising hell in a tavern far from the killing place. The night watch was summoned to deal with the distraction, and the veteran knight assured them that his men would return to their quarters without causing further disturbance. By then, the High Steward lay choking on his own blood in a shadowed corner of the city walls.

'You had everything you needed?' said Blackstone when he returned to his men. 'The Prince honoured his pledge to reward you for what we did?'

'Good food and wine enough,' said Killbere. 'Our horses had the best grain that could be had. Aye, he played his part.'

'And bushels of arrows with the best goose-feather fletchings I've seen in a long time, Sir Thomas,' said Jack Halfpenny. He served as ventenar to twenty archers, but in Longdon's absence had taken on Longdon's role of centenar and kept the bowmen as taut in readiness as their waxed bowstrings. 'I had the lads on the butts every day. Now that Will's back from his cooking duties, he can see for himself.'

'We're going to war. We'll have no need of yard-long arrows or hardened steel. We'll send them pots of Will's cooking,' said Blackstone.

Longdon scowled. 'It stuck to your ribs and kept the guards distracted so we could sneak out.'

'Will, they had to spend time in the latrines, which is how we slipped away.'

'You know, Thomas, I look forward to returning to my scab-arsed, whore-mongering archers where any food is devoured with thanks, no matter how bad.'

Halfpenny smiled. 'Like I said, Will, we had good food and wine while you served Sir Thomas. No complaints at all.'

'Aye,' said Meulon. 'In fact, I doubt your lads noticed you were gone.' He looked at the archers around them. They nodded and murmured their agreement. 'Maybe you could find work in our enemy's kitchens. That would save us from killing them,' he said.

Will Longdon glared at the man towering above him. 'Meulon, the next time you hunger for fresh meat when I go out and kill it for the pot, I'll make sure you choke on its gristle.'

Meulon shrugged. 'Then that would be an improvement.'

Longdon knew the leadership of even his hard-bitten Welsh archers was best served with jibes between the men. He turned to address them. 'All right, before I give you rations of horse cake, I will see if Jack Halfpenny has kept a tight enough rein on you in my absence. The wind is freshening from the east, the air is cold, there'll be snow soon enough. A day without food or drink standing in the butts will see how prepared you are for a battle line.' He glanced at Blackstone. 'We'll be facing an enemy soon enough.'

'Soon enough,' said Blackstone.

The Prince of Wales and Aquitaine stood at the palace walls gazing over forest and village and across the breadth of the River Garonne beyond the flat countryside. Out of sight, two hundred miles south, lay the Pyrenees, his gateway to Spain. Blackstone and Killbere had been summoned and waited respectfully at the far end of the walkway until the Prince broke his reverie, glanced their way and smiled. Blackstone saw his cloak was wrapped closely around him. Whatever ailed the Prince had its claws into him more than the biting wind. The Prince beckoned them to join him. Blackstone felt a warm sense of welcome.

'You are to go back to Castile, Thomas. Our father wishes it.'

'To seize back the throne for Pedro?' said Killbere.

The Prince sighed. 'Aye.'

'Highness, he is not worthy of your efforts,' said the veteran knight.

'We know. But he is a rightful king; his half-brother is a bastard usurper.'

'Lord, this cruel and vindictive man will ruin you,' said Blackstone.

'Pedro is an ally,' said the Prince. 'We must honour our treaties.'

Blackstone shook his head. 'You risk everything. For this man.'

'Are you suggesting we will fail to win against Henry of Trastámara?'

'If he is foolish enough to meet us face to face on the battleground, you will defeat him.'

'Then,' said the Prince, irritation creeping into his voice, 'there is nothing more to discuss.'

Blackstone dared to block his path as he turned for the palace.

'Highness, you open a door to a future fraught with danger for you and for Aquitaine. Gascony is not rich; the taxes you can raise will not cover the cost of an army. Can you not see how this will unfold?'

'Thomas, do not lecture your Prince! Damn you. What do you know of our business?'

Blackstone did not back down. 'I know my men will die and you risk more than the loss of a battle.'

Killbere grabbed Blackstone's arm to restrain him. Blackstone tugged free. His head was up, his eyes challenging the Prince.

'Pedro has agreed to pay for the cost of the war. For everything,' insisted the Prince.

'And you believe him?' said Blackstone. 'How? We brought him out of Castile with the clothes on his back and the jewellery he carried. He has no wealth. Castile is already wounded and war-weary. Sire, you will pay for this war and he will betray you.'

'And you are now a fortune teller?' said the Prince.

'I speak out of loyalty. You will lose because you will have to pay thousands of men to do your bidding. Your own and those of the routiers. The French will send Henry troops, and when you are ruined, you will raise taxes and your loyal noblemen will object. And that is when the French King will strike against you. You will be weak. And he will declare war. All that you have gained here might be lost.'

The Prince turned away, controlling his temper. No one other than Thomas Blackstone would dare challenge him in such a defiant manner; and everything Blackstone had said was nothing more than he had already considered. 'We have our duty, Thomas. You must lead us across the mountains.' His eyes stung in the wind. His voice softened. 'Come, we'll talk in the warmth.'

Killbere gave Blackstone a wary look as they followed. If the Prince was this determined then nothing Blackstone could say would deter him from his course of action. He touched Blackstone's arm.

'I love a good fight as much as the next man, Thomas. He won't be swayed.'

'I know,' said Blackstone. 'But he's wrong.'

CHAPTER FOUR

Blackstone and Killbere followed the Prince as a heavily studded chestnut door swung open. A servant stepped back as the Prince and his guests swept into an antechamber. Men-at-arms stood at strategic points in the corridors. The high office of the Prince's chamberlain belonged to Sir Nigel Loring, not only an honoured Knight of the Garter and adviser to the Prince, but also the man responsible for the Prince's safety. Blackstone caught sight of the tall, sallow-faced chamberlain at the far end of the corridor, standing ramrod straight, obviously waiting for his master to return. He bowed when he saw the Prince and ordered more doors to be opened; then he led the approaching men deeper into the palace.

The further they went, the more extravagant became the surroundings. Gold and silver plate; richly embroidered tapestries; silk coverings over windows rustling in the river's breeze; fine wood tables the length of a room to seat a hundred guests; benches decorated with hand-carved birds; ceilings painted in varying colours: the skilled hands of craftsmen were evident everywhere. Blackstone had visited the Prince at Bordeaux before, but the palace's furnishings were now even more magnificent. The Château de Langoiran had held Blackstone at the Prince's pleasure: no dismal prison, it had sufficient comfort for any lord of a manor, but nothing could compare to this splendour. No wonder the Prince of Wales and Aquitaine was renowned for his lavish entertainment and extravagant generosity.

'We fight and die for this,' said Killbere under his breath.

'We fight and die for the King and his son the Prince,' Blackstone answered quietly.

Sir Nigel led the Prince into a room more intimate in scale than the others, yet the fireplace burning split logs was large enough that six men could stand shoulder to shoulder inside its opening. The Prince shrugged free of his cloak.

'There is nothing more to discuss. You take us through the mountains, Thomas. You know the route. We put the King back on the throne at Burgos.'

Killbere glanced out of the window towards the Pyrenees he could not see. 'Highness, at this time of year? Another month or two, perhaps, when the thaw begins further south.'

The Prince smiled. 'When have we ever shied away from the difficult, Gilbert? Not once since we shared the battlefield at Crécy. We will not delay our duty to our father. We know our enemy. Who did you fight to get the King here?'

'The Breton, du Guesclin. He was their best commander. The French paid for enough routiers to kick Pedro's arse hard. If we hadn't dragged him out of Burgos, he'd've been skinned and fed to the crows,' said Blackstone.

'Aye, but don't forget Hugh Calveley,' said Killbere. 'He made a damned fortune fighting against Pedro.'

'But he never raised a blade against us,' said Blackstone. 'Had he done so, we would be crow bait. He had a right to sell his sword.'

'Sir Hugh is now fighting with us again,' said the Prince.

Killbere snorted. 'He helps puts the bastard half-brother on the throne, makes his fortune and then returns to serve you, highness?'

Blackstone levelled his gaze at the Prince. 'An English knight who has defied his Prince. Can he ever be trusted?'

'The order not to support Pedro's brother was received

too late to stop him. So, this is why we must strike back now, Thomas. Henry of Trastámara holds Castile, but he has paid off the Bretons and the routiers and now he is isolated. He has too few troops to muster against us. Calveley and others now sell themselves to my cause, Thomas. We are all soldiers of fortune.'

'But Trastámara will soon have reinforcements,' said Blackstone. 'The moment we start through the mountains, the French will make sure he is supported.'

The Prince leaned against the mantelpiece and pushed the heel of his boot against a log. Sparks flew. 'Before your return to our good favour and need of you, Thomas, our brother John sailed from Portsmouth. He leads five hundred men, mostly archers. He will await us at Dax.'

Blackstone glanced at Killbere, who shrugged. The Prince's younger brother John of Gaunt might be travelling the length of western France through the extended territory now held by the English, but his archers were still too few to wage war. Were their numbers nothing more than a gesture from the English King to his son, the Prince?

'Highness, five hundred bowmen?' said Blackstone. 'We would be fortunate to hold one flank against a concerted attack. We cannot retake Castile with only them and the men-at-arms you have here. Man and horse will die in the passes, snow and ice will lose us supplies—'

The Prince's raised hand silenced Blackstone's complaint. 'Our own retinue accompanies us, and we have drawn Gascons and English captains to us. Eustache d'Aubricourt brings his men; Sir John Chandos has recruited more from the east. Loyal Gascons and Bretons already approach Dax as the rallying point. We have the men, Thomas.'

'Aye, lord, but what kind of men? I have loyal Gascons among my own, but who is it that Chandos brings with him?' said Blackstone.

'Garciot du Châtel, Bertucat d'Albret, among others. They have hundreds with them.'

'Murdering bastards, them and their followers,' Killbere blurted, followed by a look of remorse at his outburst.

The Prince showed no sign of irritation. 'Gilbert, we have need of battle-hardened men. They will be commanded by us, our brother and Chandos. You and Thomas will lead and do what is necessary when the time comes. But now is the time to strike.'

'But at this time of year we will make slow progress through the passes, lord,' said Killbere.

'How long to breach the mountains?' said the Prince.

'How many men?' said Blackstone.

The Prince hesitated. 'Seven, perhaps eight thousand or more.'

Blackstone's mind's eye saw the snaking column of men and horses laden for war, encumbered by royal servants. They would have to move through the King of Navarre's territory and if he had been bought off by the enemy, then blocking passes before they reached Castile would require only a handful of men at every turn in the road.

The Prince read his thoughts. 'Charles of Navarre has agreed not to contest the passes. We made our feelings clear to him. Better for him not to stand in our way. He had struck a deal with Henry of Trastámara to deny us access but that deal is no more. He will not fight with us, but he will not impede our approach.'

'How did you convince him?' said Blackstone. 'We have no men near Pamplona.'

'It is well known now that you are the only man who can threaten a king. We told him we would send you.'

So, the Prince was one step ahead and had secured the route through the untrustworthy Navarre's territory. Yet Blackstone knew the self-serving King Charles would protect those passes in word, not deed, no matter what threat was levelled. And the new King Henry of Castile would trust Charles of Navarre as little as did Blackstone. There would be raiders waiting to ambush them; not as many, perhaps, as the Castilian would like, but enough to hamper and kill. Once again, it would be Blackstone's men who would root them out. And then, once past Pamplona, they could strike at Burgos. It was a wretched business to put a vile king back on his throne.

Blackstone saw the flush of blood on the Prince's face. Was it the heat of the fire or the prospect of battle that invigorated the warrior prince? His spirits had lifted, his demeanour now more like the fighting man Blackstone knew. Despite his reservations about the campaign, Blackstone felt it too. The surge of aggression that flung men into war fuelled their very existence.

'Thomas?' said the Prince. 'How long to get through the mountains and reach Pamplona?'

'With good fortune on our side, ten days.'

'Then we tread the pilgrim's route and I shall pray to God to embrace our cause and bless us with good fortune.'

Killbere snorted snot back into his throat and spat, then wiped an arm across his mouth. 'Let us hope He has time to listen. There's many a voice needing him when the killing starts.'

CHAPTER FIVE

Blackstone and his captains looked across the landscape to where pennons and banners fluttered in the stiffening breeze. Flecks of cold rain, the advance guard of threatening snow, swept across the gathered army.

'God's tears, Sir Thomas, we're leading an army as large as the Prince had at Poitiers,' said John Jacob. 'There must be near enough eight thousand gathered here.'

Blackstone grinned. 'And more. Closer to ten. And better that we are in the vanguard to make the choices needed to put that evil bastard back on his throne, John. The less we have to do with him, the better.' He turned in the saddle. 'William, you served in the Prince's guard. He would be pleased to greet you if you care to ride to his pavilion and rouse him and the murdering dog turd of a king. Tell him we advance for Saint-Jean-Pied-de-Port and he is to follow. Be sure to say, "at his pleasure".'

'At his leisure, more like,' said Killbere.

William Ashford spurred his horse forward from where he rode with the other captains, Renfred, Meulon and the Gascon, Aicart. 'With respect, Sir Thomas, would the Prince not prefer to be told by you?'

'I dare say, but he has already advised against me being too close to Pedro, who remains convinced I killed his High Steward.'

'Even though it has been firmly denied by the Prince,' said Killbere. 'Pedro was barely placated by his insistence on our innocence in the matter.'

'Which proves he is not as stupid as he looks,' said Will Longdon.

'It's a pity you could not have cut Pedro's throat that night,' said Killbere, 'but that would have dishonoured the good men we lost in his rescue. William, he would not take kindly to being so close to Thomas and if the fool lost his head and there was bloodletting, then the King's Master of War would rot in a dungeon never to be seen again.'

William Ashford smiled. 'Then best I deliver the message. Is there an order of march, Sir Thomas?'

'Tell him we lead, and our scouts will be three hours ahead. Chandos follows – we'll need men-at-arms at our back if there's fighting in the passes. Then the Prince with his brother John and his archers at his rear, and finally d'Aubricourt and any of the other skinners.'

Ashford needed no further command and spurred his horse towards the heights and the Prince's pavilion.

Killbere sighed as he gathered his reins. 'Well, Thomas, if I thought we could convince Henry of Trastámara not to side with the French, I would happily arrange for Pedro to have an accident as we cross the mountains and beg the forgiveness of those we lost. Then no blame can be laid at our door.'

Blackstone heeled the bastard horse forward. 'Do you not see it yet, Gilbert? Our time with the Prince is drawing to a close. Getting Pedro back to Burgos will be only a small part in our lives, as surely as what ails the Prince will eventually take him back to England and then... then the French will declare war. And if the Prince abandons Aquitaine then he has no need for us. This is a fool's errand. We endure it while thinking beyond Pedro of Castile.'

★

Aquitaine's coast lay shimmering in the distant west as Blackstone led the army higher. They had little time to traverse the mountains. Daylight hours were short. The Prince had gambled and amended Blackstone's order of march by splitting the army into separate groups over two separate days for the crossing. Blackstone led the vanguard, followed by Sir John Chandos and John of Gaunt. Once they were across, backmarkers would guide the Prince. The decision risked missing what was at the moment undemanding weather. Three miles beyond Saint-Jean-Pied-de-Port's town gate, the road climbed uphill and several miles further became little more than a track. Heavily laden men in full armour with their weapons would soon have to negotiate a narrow passage where a wrong-footed horse could send man and beast plummeting to their death.

'Chandos and Gaunt's men move slowly, Sir Thomas,' said John Jacob. 'Waiting through December and January for his brother to arrive was hard for them, and made them unfit – and we're barely through the foothills. Steeper ground will slow them even more.'

The veteran knight grunted. 'He's right, Thomas. And every guide who has ever taken pilgrims through the mountains to Compostela warns not to travel in winter. That knowledge has been passed down for a hundred years and more. And here we are barely out of Saint-Jean and half of them have not yet reached the town. We are not even six hundred feet up and they drag their arses. How will it be when we scale four thousand? Thomas, we have only a few daylight hours to travel in. This plan is going to go wrong. I feel it in my water.'

'You piss too often,' said Blackstone. 'We press on and they follow. There can be no other way. It is a simple plan. It's the only plan. Seventeen miles and nine hours of daylight to get through the pass. It is what it is.'

The veteran knight cleared his throat and spat. 'I look ahead, Thomas, and can't see the peaks for the mist. Rain, hail, snow and treachery await us.'

'And?' said Blackstone.

'And? There's nothing more to be said.'

'Then we are blessed with the chance of silence,' said Blackstone. 'Spur them on, Gilbert, I need to see matters for myself. Will? John? With me.'

Blackstone heeled the bastard horse as John Jacob and Will Longdon followed.

Meulon rode alongside Killbere. 'Sir Thomas doesn't see any honour in this venture. He's anxious to sniff out the murdering scum who lie in wait,' he said. 'He has better skills than a hunting dog.'

Killbere sighed. 'After what we endured getting Pedro to safety, he's right. And the Prince knows it as well. It's the King who demanded we put the vile creature back on his throne. I fancy I would rather be in bed with a big-hipped woman than shrinking my balls atop a freezing cold mountain.'

'Like Sir Thomas said, it is what it is, Sir Gilbert.'

'Aye. That never changes.'

CHAPTER SIX

The higher they climbed, the colder it became. Stinging rain turned to sleet. Blackstone's bastard horse was as surefooted as a mountain goat, but its uneven gait had Blackstone come close to leaving the saddle as it forged ahead around a tight bend on the narrow track. Had he not adjusted his weight and yanked hard to pull the horse's misshapen head closer to the rock face, he would have tumbled over the edge and fallen two thousand feet to the gorge below. Heart pounding from the sudden lurch, he slowed the beast who might, for all he knew, be trying to unseat him. Such was its temperament.

Blackstone saw horses ahead. They were hobbled and attended by one of Renfred's men, who had created a temporary corral using a length of rope between two rock outcrops. Sacking covered the horse's heads as insurance to stop them panicking. And Blackstone knew there must be a reason for such precautions. John Jacob and Will Longdon followed four lengths behind, their mounts not as reckless as Blackstone's: that creature thought to have been sired by the devil. Blackstone dismounted and led it forward – but not too close, lest the scent of the other horses stirred the bastard horse's instinct to exert its dominance. He secured the reins to a jagged piece of rock and threw his cloak over its head, pulling it into a narrow defile. The biting wind immediately made itself known through his gambeson. John Jacob and Longdon followed his lead.

Blackstone strode through the veil of sleet. Beyond the next turn in the track, he could see a darker sky whose tumbling clouds were buffeted across the peaks. How long did they have before the rain and sleet worsened? Blackstone recognized the man tending the corralled horses as one of Renfred's scouts.

'Where are the others?'

The man bent his head against the wind-driven sleet. One hand settled on the nearest horse's neck, calming the nervous animal. If one panicked, the others would break free. 'Ahead, Sir Thomas. He's trying to find a way past some men who hold the track.'

Blackstone's instincts had not failed him. Henry of Trastámara was suspicious of the duplicitous Charles of Navarre, as was anyone who had dealings with him. Navarre would play both sides, but he would not interfere. He was already skulking, pretending to be held against his will in Pamplona. The coward's absence suited Trastámara. It allowed him to send men into the mountains of Navarre without challenge. The French King had offered his support in removing Pedro and now urged the usurper to learn from French mistakes when they fought the English. Do not stand and fight a pitched battle. English bowmen will slaughter cavalry, and English knights and men-at-arms will engage with such violent fury that the shock will rock an opposing army back on its heels. There is only one way to defeat the English. Starve them out. Wear them down. Cut their supply routes. Harass and hit them with lightning strikes. Kill stragglers and slow-moving elements of an overburdened column. By day and night send men into the English camps to burn, kill and wage terror. Make the English fear men who come from nowhere, only to disappear as quickly as they appear. Such men now waited along the treacherous route.

John Jacob and Will Longdon nodded their greeting to the man, then followed Blackstone. They rounded a bend, saw

Renfred and twenty of his men crouched behind cover among the uneven rock face. Scattered crossbow bolts littered the track. A man lay dead four yards ahead with a bolt in his chest. Blackstone pressed himself tight against the wall.

'Renfred?'

The German captain, who always led Blackstone's scouts, pointed further along the defile. 'Thirty men, Sir Thomas. Their horses must be further along the track. You see where it widens after the narrow? I had Rosslyn there'—he nodded towards the dead man—'move ahead on foot. It just didn't feel right, so I held the men back with the horses.'

'Your instincts saved the others,' said Blackstone.

The huddled men who had laid the ambush were concealed behind a low barricade of rocks and, behind that, their shields. They covered the breadth of the track.

'We can't rush them on foot, Sir Thomas,' said John Jacob. 'They'd bring us down like Rosslyn. And up to where they span the track it's barely wide enough for a horse even if we could get a mount to jump their barricade. A horse refuses and man and horse go over the edge.'

Renfred squatted, turning his back against the wind, and rubbed a grubby hand across his beard. 'I thought of rushing them on foot behind a shield wall but they could fall back a step at a time and cut us down.'

'And they have the wind at their backs. It gives them an edge with their range,' said Longdon.

Blackstone squinted against the sleet. 'Will, I make them to be two hundred and twenty yards.'

Longdon pressed close to Blackstone's shoulder and peered past. 'Aye, well, you can add another fifteen to that.'

Blackstone looked at the jagged outcrops at his shoulder that rose up to the higher peaks. 'We have thousands of men at our backs and if they are forced to stop here we will have men and horses falling to their deaths. The weather is closing in. Those few men can stop the army.' He peered again at the huddled enemy. 'We need to get behind them.'

Renfred, John Jacob and Longdon let Blackstone's words sink in.

'All right,' said Renfred. There was obviously only one way to do that.

'A mountain goat of a climb,' said John Jacob.

Blackstone nodded. 'The visibility will get worse. Will, you have to make them think we are going to try and breach from the front. Place your shots when John and I get high enough to make our way across to get behind them.'

'I'll climb with you,' said Renfred.

'No. You lead your men hard and fast when we attack them from their rear,' Blackstone told him.

'Thomas, you make one wrong move up those cliffs and we'll be waving goodbye to you and John when you fall into the gorge,' said Will Longdon, pulling his war bow from its greased bag. He took his bowstring from beneath his cap and nocked the bow.

Blackstone crouched and edged away. He unbuckled his sword belt. Pressed his lips to Wolf Sword's pommel with its embedded silver penny, a permanent reminder of his murdered wife, and put the belt around his shoulders. The sword nestled in its scabbard against his back. 'They won't see us if we start our climb back there. Shoot when we get beyond them, Will, and then space your shots to give us time to climb down.'

John Jacob followed him.

Will Longdon selected his first twelve arrows and settled them neatly, the shafts with their goose-feather fletchings resting against the protection of the rock face. He rubbed his hands together and blew warm air into them. 'Renfred, I'll need room to draw. Have your lads get behind me. You watch and tell me when they start their climb. Let them get as high as they're going and then tell me when they're beyond those bastards. I need to see how my shafts fly in this wind.'

Renfred did as Blackstone's centenar asked. He herded his men back a few paces to give the bowman room and then turned his back to the wind and sleet to watch Blackstone and John Jacob clamber up the broken rock face. They were already being swallowed by the swirling storm.

CHAPTER SEVEN

Blackstone turned his face from the stinging sleet as he hauled himself up to the next foothold. His hands stiffened from the wind's cold onslaught. He moved slowly, searching for a fingertip grip. His hose were already torn at the knee, the skin scraped. His eyes stung. How long had it taken to get this far? He looked down. John Jacob was ten feet below, following his lead. Blackstone knew the slow, demanding climb would take its toll on both of them. There was no point in going higher. They had barely climbed fifty feet and time was running out. The column would soon be halted if he and John Jacob did not take a greater risk.

'John!'

His squire peered up, eyes narrowed against the sleet.

'Get alongside me. We can't go any higher.'

Jacob nodded, reached up, found his grip and slowly heaved himself closer. Blackstone saw that his squire's hands were already bloodied. He looked across to where they had to traverse along the rock face to get behind the enemy. His hands gripping the rocks were no different from his squire's, but at least the cold air numbed the pain. John Jacob had almost reached him when the rock he was gripping came away. He lurched backwards. Blackstone snatched at his flailing arm. His grip slipped until it reached his wrist. Blackstone squeezed. His shoulder muscles felt as if they were tearing. His fingers were weakening. John Jacob was mid-air. He had no hand or foothold. He peered up. Shook his head.

'Let me go or I'll take you with me. Let me go. Do it!'

Blackstone shook his head. 'The rock face! Reach!'

The squire extended his arm, his fingers tantalizingly close. Blackstone bunched his back muscles. His grip was slipping again. They only had one chance. He heaved, pressing himself against the mountain, hauling John Jacob into the wall. The trailing man squirmed, twisted, put even more pressure on Blackstone, who felt his wet hand slide from Jacob's wrist, his squire's fingers slipping through his own. John Jacob clung to the rocks, face pressed hard against stone; he sucked in life, breath pluming as he exhaled fear.

He looked at Blackstone and nodded.

Blackstone edged along the rock face. Impossible to know how long it would take to traverse the two hundred and more yards to get behind the enemy.

'I've lost sight of Sir Thomas,' Renfred shouted.

'How far along did he get?' Longdon asked, his eyes focused on the men blockading the track.

'Halfway. Perhaps more.' Renfred crouched next to the archer. 'Will, we need to halve the distance between us and them. The weather might cover us. You shoot, we run, find what cover we can. Then we wait until Sir Thomas gets behind them.'

Longdon pulled another handful of arrows from his bag. 'Have your men ready.'

Mist swirled from the gorge below, churning into the sleet and wind. Despite the distance, blurred outlines of the men behind the barricade and shield wall were visible as the wind blew the white curtain clear for a moment. One man dared raise himself. In a swift movement, the arrow shaft in Longdon's hand that had not yet been nocked suddenly flew. The wind made the arrow stray from the target; it glanced off the rock barricade, barely missing the man's head. He ducked.

Longdon cursed but wasted no time damning the fickle wind. Nock, draw, loose. Nock, draw, loose. His rapid delivery of the first twelve arrows punched through the enemy shields. He heard a scream carry on the wind. At least one defender had been hit. As the twelfth yard-long arrow left his bow, he bellowed to the men.

'Now!'

Renfred ran ahead of his men. They needed to find a cleft in the rock wall for protection.

There was none.

A hundred and ten yards from Will Longdon's position, Renfred dropped to the ground, face pressed into the dirt. His men flattened themselves behind him, hoping that if the crossbowmen had seen their run that they would not dare stand up to angle their bows down to shoot at the prostrate and helpless men.

Renfred squirmed, looked back and saw Will Longdon with a handful of arrows tucked into his belt, another nocked on the bow cord. He was crouching. Ready to make his own run. Waiting for when he could kill the unsuspecting defenders. Waiting for Blackstone.

John Jacob was only three paces behind Blackstone. A narrow seam of rock acted as a ledge. Shuffling as fast as they dare without losing their footing, they pressed their chests to the rock wall and grasped any tenuous hand hold that presented itself. They heard voices drifting upwards. Cries of alarm. Men shouting that some were wounded. That an unseen bowman was among the attackers. The sleet had turned to snow. The wind freshened even more. Blackstone went another twenty yards past the huddled men below and began the torturous climb down. Leg and arm muscles complained. He slipped. Held on. Cursed as skin tore from his leg and hand. It was nothing. A wound in battle brought its own kind of pain. This was little more than a scratch.

He dropped the last six feet, took the fall with legs bent, his bloodied hand reaching for Wolf Sword. There was no need for words. There was killing to be done. They ran.

A dozen fast strides brought them behind the defenders. A man suddenly loomed out of the snowstorm. His jaw opened and then the scar-faced ghost cleaved him from shoulder to breastbone. John Jacob was already past the dead man. Steel clashed. Men screamed. Blackstone was at his shoulder. They slashed and parried, each covering the other's killing arc, but the defenders whirled and struck back with fierce determination. The two of them would soon be overwhelmed. The snowstorm obscured one man from the next. It was impossible to see where the next attack would come from. Then a scream of defiance defeated the howling wind as Renfred led his men over the barricade.

The narrow road constrained the fight. Men were too close to even swing their swords. They grappled with knife, axe and mace. Fists beat opponents senseless. Others were forced back, split from the main group. Pushed ever closer to the edge. Those who lost their footing stumbled over the brink, their screams devoured by the beast howling through the gorge, pushing the snow before it.

And then Fate rewarded Blackstone's daring. It stopped snowing. Clouds tumbled away over peaks, briefly exposing the sky. The stark scene revealed blood-soaked ground. Bodies lay scattered. Some of the enemy were crawling in agony.

Will Longdon sat on the barricade, wiping his archer's bastard sword across the tunic of a dead defender. 'Thomas, for once my war bow was of little use. There are times when honed steel is better.'

Blackstone looked at the seven bodies lying pierced with arrows. It was a formidable kill given the conditions.

Renfred's men finished off the enemy wounded and tipped their bodies along with their dead comrades over the edge.

'How many men did we lose in the attack?' Blackstone asked Renfred.

'Three.'

'Who?'

'Bartholomew, Dene and Tricart.'

'Good men wasted for a poor cause,' said Blackstone. They had served with Renfred's scouting group for three years and more. The German captain would feel their loss.

'We'll strap them to their horses and bury them when we get across the mountains,' said Blackstone.

The men cleared the barricade as Will Longdon retrieved what arrows he could. The sky had darkened again. In the distance, leaden clouds moved nearer. Blackstone felt the wind freshen on his face. A trickle of blood ran down his forehead into his beard from a head wound. The wind swept it from his face.

'Aye, Thomas, I can see I'll need my needle and thread again.'

'You only killed seven with the bow, Will. You spent too long in the kitchens at Château de Langoiran.'

'I was shooting blind.'

Blackstone scooped a handful of snow and pressed it against the cut on his head. 'Then when you get your eye back, I'll let you stitch my wound.'

CHAPTER EIGHT

The column following Blackstone clung to the narrow track. Killbere arrived with Blackstone's men, who led their horses on foot, pressed between beast and rock face. If a horse shied, better for it to go over the edge than take its rider with it. Killbere looked at the bloodstained snow, which told its own story.

'How many did we lose?' said Killbere, voice raised against the wind.

'Four,' said Blackstone.

'How many did we kill?'

'Twenty-six. Likely a few more. Some went over the edge when we attacked.'

Killbere wiped an arm across the snot running from his nose. 'A bargain,' he said. 'How bad is it ahead?'

'Renfred has gone on. Another two hours and we are at the highest point. The track widens from here. They chose their ambush site well.'

'Chandos and John of Gaunt are following,' said Killbere, hunched against the biting cold and swirling snow. 'The Prince will stay on the French side of the pass until the weather clears.'

'He'll be waiting days,' said Blackstone. 'Snow and ice won't stop overnight. That means I'll have to go back for him. Damn! I never thought the day would come when I had to wet-nurse him.'

'Thomas, my balls ache. My breath is like broken glass. I

can barely see with this infernal wind. It's churning the snow like a devil's cauldron. Can we discuss this when I am brought back from near death?'

Blackstone pointed to where John Jacob and Will Longdon waited with their horses. 'We'll go over and down into the valley. We've lost valuable daylight time dealing with the ambush.'

Killbere was too disgruntled to praise Blackstone's success. He tugged his horse after him. 'Then you took too long, Thomas. You must be getting old.'

Four hours of daylight remained. Blackstone increased the pace so the men who followed would reach the far side of the mountains before nightfall.

The keening wind howled like tormented souls: baleful cries of lost spirits terrifying horses and causing men to offer muttered prayers as they fought the weather and their laden beasts. Men stumbled on the ankle-breaking ground, losing control of their mounts that shied and fell blindly, whinnying pitifully as they tumbled into space. Those men who collapsed, injured, were left to face their lonely death. The column could not be stopped. They crested the highest point where, thankfully, the track widened. Now the men stood in the lee of their horses, letting the great beasts shield them from the buffeting wind and snow. On the jagged rocks below could be seen the deformed, shattered bodies of the dead from the ambush. The lower the soldiers descended, the calmer the weather became. The mist-laden peaks had been a challenging, hostile terrain, and those who looked over their shoulders at the winding column of exhausted men saw the mountain gods release ghostly, exhausted figures from their grasp.

The lower slopes became less barren as boulders merged into softer, rolling forested hills. Snow gave way to rain, and as the bedraggled men remounted, they took heart from having survived the passage. When they filtered down onto the valley floor, Blackstone's men went up and down the line, urging the column to keep moving. To stop now meant the hundreds of men still to descend would become log jammed.

'Thomas!' Will Longdon called, cantering towards him. 'Riders. Hundreds of them.' He hauled on the reins. 'Renfred says they've banners and pennons flying. If it's Trastámara, he has us in the open. And we're like a gaggle of belly-gripped peasants looking for a latrine.'

'How far?' said Blackstone.

'They'll be here before dark.'

'Fifty archers and as many men-at-arms won't stop them, Thomas. They'll ride through us and around us. We're in disarray.'

'Gilbert! No matter. Form up our men. Will, ride with me. Halfpenny knows what to do.' Blackstone wheeled the bastard horse and galloped back with Longdon to the straggling column where Chandos and John of Gaunt rode at the head of their men. The two commanders looked as if they had not slept for a week, their strained features reflecting the fearful passage.

'My lord, I need your archers. Armed men are riding hard towards us,' Blackstone said abruptly.

The Prince's younger brother grimaced. It was difficult for Blackstone to tell whether it was from his request or the wet saddle. 'I command my archers. I and I alone.'

Blackstone fought the bastard horse that lunged and snapped its yellow teeth at John of Gaunt's magnificent courser. It shied. The Prince's brother swayed in the saddle but didn't fall.

'My brother warned me about you. You are disrespectful. Your horse is ill tempered and needs thrashing.'

'Any man lays a hand on my horse and he will lose that hand. I need your archers now. If the riders approaching are hostile, we do not have time to form battle lines. My men can hold for only a few minutes. Ride with me or give me your men.'

John of Gaunt was known for his love of pomp and splendour, and that bred arrogance. His position in the royal family firmly established him as the next fighting prince after Edward. His jaw gaped at Blackstone's insolence. Before he gathered his wits, Sir John Chandos nudged his horse between him and Blackstone.

'My lord, I would trust Sir Thomas with my life, and have done so on more than one occasion. And if this is another such time, then I'd yield to his request. Give him your archers.'

'Request, Sir John? A demand more like.'

John of Gaunt barely had time to look from the renowned commander back to Blackstone and nod his assent. Will Longdon had already spurred his horse towards the straggling line of archers coming down off the mountain.

Blackstone offered no thanks but wheeled his belligerent beast back to join Killbere.

Twenty minutes later, Longdon returned with the first two hundred archers who had reached the base of the mountain. They hobbled their horses, then ran to where Blackstone and his men formed a line of defence. The wind had eased its constant buffeting and now pushed against the men's backs. It would give the archers' arrows extra distance.

Longdon ordered the two centenars who had brought their men down to take up position. A hundred men on each flank.

His own archers stood between Blackstone's men. There was no argument from the Cheshire bowmen who had followed John of Gaunt. Blackstone's name was held in high regard by the common fighting man.

'There're Renfred and his men,' Jack Halfpenny called.

Killbere squinted in the half-light. 'Feel that, Thomas? The earth is trembling. There's more than Renfred and his patrol returning.'

Renfred swung his men behind Blackstone's battle lines. 'I couldn't see who they were, Sir Thomas. They ride at the canter.'

The valley stretched before them for several hundred yards and then curved behind a promontory. The approaching men would soon appear. Blackstone looked back. Chandos and John of Gaunt were still a long way to the rear as they formed up their men. It took time to bring an army together and even though this was only two commanders and their men, they would not be ready in time should the enemy launch an assault. Suddenly the wind veered, sweeping mist down from the mountains. Visibility had dropped to five hundred yards and would soon envelop the waiting men.

'Will!' Blackstone bellowed. 'Shoot when you can. Whoever comes around that corner will slow if they see a forest of arrows planted in the ground.'

Grey ghosts appeared in the distance. Horsemen swept around the blind mountainside into full view, fifty wide and six ranks deep. Pennons and banners flew, the wind fluttering them so they could not be identified. Blackstone saw Will Longdon step beyond the front ranks so he could be seen and heard by the archers. 'Nock! Draw!'

Bowmen bent their backs, muscled arms hauling back their bow's heavy draw weights.

'Loose!'

The sight of an arrow storm climbing high before falling to earth always held fighting men's attention. Blackstone and Killbere craned their necks, watching the whisper of arrow shafts. Blackstone felt the spittle on his tongue. It was no different from the lust a man felt for a woman. Its taste took his memory back to when he stood in line as an archer and fear had mingled with the desire to kill and live. Without thinking, he reached for the archer's talisman around his neck, Arianrhod, Goddess of the Silver Wheel: a simple figure of a woman, captured in a wheel of silver, whose curved arms met above her head. She was the protector of archers in this life and would carry their soul across to the other side when the time came. A dying archer had gifted the medallion to him when Blackstone was a sixteen-year-old bowman fighting through the streets of Caen. Blackstone's dead wife's small crucifix nestled next to the pagan goddess. He brought it to his lips. The past never left him. Neither had his love for her.

The horsemen were five hundred yards away when the arrows seeded themselves. Blackstone's men swore they could hear the strike from where they stood. The leading horsemen reined in hard. Riders bellowed orders to halt. Confusion overtook man and mount. The second-rank horses broke through those who had been pulled up, then their riders also sawed their reins and yanked their horse's heads to stop them. The charge had been halted, and they were still out of range.

Blackstone watched the chaos. The horsemen wore surcoats over mail, and as they turned this way and that, their banners showed themselves to the waiting men.

'God's tears,' said Killbere and spat. 'A pity they hadn't come into range.'

'And then we would be in the shit pit,' said Blackstone. He strode forward, arm raised to show no violent intent to the horsemen. Killbere and John Jacob accompanied him. 'Because our Prince would not be well pleased if we killed the King of Navarre.'

CHAPTER NINE

Charles, King of Navarre, urged his horse forward as his cavalry quietened their mounts, bringing them under control. A knight rode alongside the King, bearing Navarre's standard. The duplicitous ruler squinted into the wind and rain, raising a hand to cover his eyes. His breath came first in the cold air, as Blackstone realized the man had sighed, then came his name.

'Blackstone. Sir Thomas Blackstone,' he corrected himself. 'You are Edward's Master of War. I should have known that if death was close by, then it would be wielded by your hand. You have archers shoot at a king?'

'Highness, I have my bowmen shoot at fast-approaching horsemen who have neither the wit nor courtesy to announce themselves.'

The King's chin raised at the affront, but Blackstone continued speaking before Navarre, or any of the knights who rode with him, raised an objection. They should have known that riding with such force against the Prince's army was not a good idea. Perhaps, Blackstone thought, their stunned silence meant they had followed the King blindly. Perhaps in their arrogance they knew no better. 'Your show of strength with such renowned lords, knights and men-at-arms would surely have made my Prince's enemy turn and run. We are not such men. And, uncertain of who might approach, we laid a warning ahead of you. It gave you enough time to pull up.' He paused. 'No one fell off their horse and was injured, I hope?'

The barbed comment could have been taken as a genuine enquiry. Either way, the King ignored it.

'We came to secure the pass. We heard that Henry of Trastámara had men blocking the route.'

'You are too late, my lord,' said Blackstone. 'That matter has been resolved. And I fear your horsemen would not have been effective. So many on so narrow a path.' His smile was as insulting as his tone of voice, but the King of Navarre had scant experience of Blackstone's dismissive taunts.

'Where is the Prince? I came to offer support for his venture.'

'He waits at Saint-Jean-Pied-de-Port for the weather to improve. His younger brother John of Gaunt is the one you see riding forward to greet you. Sir John Chandos accompanies him.'

John Chandos and the Prince's brother slowed their horses, nudging past Blackstone and Killbere.

'A royal greets a royal,' said Killbere under his breath. 'Two popinjays nodding like stuffed birds at a feast.'

'Careful, Sir Gilbert,' said John Jacob just as quietly. 'The wind will carry your words.'

'Then I wonder if he'll kiss his ring,' said the veteran knight. 'Providing he gets off his horse and bends over.'

Blackstone and John Jacob swallowed their grins. Chandos heard the muted comment and glared at Killbere, but Blackstone also saw the edge of his lips twitch in a suppressed smile. The greetings were complete and John of Gaunt was invited to share the King's pavilion.'

'My camp is two leagues from here. I offer warmth and food.'

John of Gaunt addressed Chandos. 'Sir John, you will see to it that the men are settled and that my archers'—he glanced at Blackstone—'are returned to my command.'

The King of Navarre turned his horse. The men parted and then closed ranks behind him and his royal guest.

'Thomas, he's an ally,' said Chandos.

'Who thinks he's at a tournament, John.'

Chandos nodded. Rain dripped from his nose, and his beard, like every other man's, glistened with droplets. 'Aye, well, he looked... uncomfortable. You might have loosened his bowels with that arrow strike.'

'As long he stays downwind from me, I don't care. His perfume is stench enough. The man's an untrustworthy ass who makes a pledge with whoever next walks through his door. I hope the Prince's brother doesn't wake up in Henry of Trastámara's camp.'

'Navarre isn't that big a fool,' said Chandos, his horse at Blackstone's side as they went back to his men, who remained in their battle lines. 'Send Gaunt's archers back to his ranks, Thomas, and let's get the men out of this icy rain and food into their bellies.' He spurred his horse.

'Thanks to God that we have Chandos with us,' said Killbere. 'We'll need his counsel on our side. Too many royals going to war can make a man yearn for the uncomplicated life of a monastery.'

Blackstone put an arm around his friend's shoulder. 'And such a life has its rewards. It's times like these we need some cheer, Gilbert. Didn't you once bed a nun?'

As darkness fell, the remaining men of that first column spilled onto the valley floor. Horses were hobbled, fires lit and tents erected. Despite the rain, men went about the business of feeding themselves pottage and bread, and finding what comfort they could in the cold, wet night beneath woollen cloaks and blankets. Blackstone's captains organized pickets even though the King of Navarre's three hundred were only a few miles away and might be thought to provide some security for the newly arrived men.

'Sir Thomas? Where are you going?' said John Jacob. Blackstone had thrown off his blanket and tugged his cloak around him. It had stopped raining, but the biting wind's cries still haunted the peaks.

'Go back to sleep, John,' said Blackstone quietly, not wishing to risk waking Killbere, whose muffled snores were swallowed by his blanket.

His squire immediately got to his feet. 'Who can sleep with Sir Gilbert next to them?'

It was useless to argue with the devoted squire. Blackstone nodded. 'All right.'

Their horses were tied to a picket line, their saddles still on their backs in case an attack came in the night. The bastard horse was separate, tied to a stake, a feed bag on his muzzle. It had already raised its head, ears pricked forward, before Blackstone was in sight. What little light there was from the sentries' windswept burning torches showed the beast's outline. It watched his approach, eyes focused on him. A shiver went along its withers and it scraped a front hoof on the ground. Always alert. It was a war horse bred for belligerence. While John Jacob untied his mount, Blackstone eased off his horse's nosebag. It made no attempt, as he would expect, to snap at his hand with its yellow teeth. Instead, as he reached to secure the opposite rein and pull its head away so he could not be bitten, it swung its misshapen head. The beast's huge neck and head caught Blackstone's side and sent him sprawling. As he landed close to its back legs it stamped an iron-shod hoof close to his face. Blackstone rolled clear. The bastard horse looked back at him. It seemed content, now, to let him mount.

'One day that horse will kill you,' said John Jacob.

'If I don't kill it first,' said Blackstone.

The horse trotted on as if it were a well-behaved pony trained to carry a child.

CHAPTER TEN

The ancient landscape was hauntingly beautiful beneath the clear night sky as the stars glistened in the cold air. Flames from the King of Navarre's campfires fluttered in the wind. The tents and pavilions were pitched behind a sheltered rock face. Their backs to the mountain, their flanks cocooned by rising ground, forested and boulder-strewn, it was a safe haven from the open valley.

'One way in, one way out,' said John Jacob as the two men crouched in the shadows. 'If an enemy force came from inland, they'd all be dead in their fur-lined bed rolls.'

'And if they are going to fight with us then we need to make sure they don't think they're on a boar hunt. Too much wine, rich food and a warm bed in a pavilion makes men slow in thought and action.'

'Best we can hope for, Sir Thomas, is that the Prince puts them in the rearguard.'

'Would you want them protecting our back?'

John Jacob sighed. 'You're right. Better we should throw them at the enemy in the vanguard.'

Blackstone saw Jacob's flash of teeth when he smiled in the moonlight.

'John, let's see how far we can get before the alarm is raised. We're going to war and they're sleeping the sleep of the dead. And if they go on like this they soon will be – once Henry of Trastámara gets among them.'

Blackstone edged along the shadows afforded by the rock

face. They got within thirty yards of the first campfire and the pitched tents. No one moved in the camp. The tethered horses were unguarded on the far side of the enclave.

'Sir Thomas, I've half a mind to release their mounts and let them wake up bare-arsed and horseless,' John Jacob whispered.

Blackstone put a restraining hand on his squire's arm. They had reached the middle of the camp. 'We'll take what we can to show them how easy it would be to have their throats cut. They'll sleep with their weapons so we can't steal those, but they need to be taught a lesson. Take their pennons and flags.'

Every knight and lord had their heraldic blazon hoisted outside their tent. Blackstone and John Jacob split up. It was a simple enough task to remove them. The wind flapping against the tents covered any sound of the two men's activities. It took little more than an hour to pull down sixty pennons and flags from the most important knights and lords of Castile. It was enough to make the point of there being no security. It was also an insult to every knight. John Jacob pointed to where individual knight's shields stood against their tent entrance. Blackstone nodded.

By the time they had taken as many shields as they had pennons and flags, the moon's arc had moved across the sky and balanced precariously on the tip of a mountain peak. The shields were stacked like sheaves of wheat; the flags dumped unceremoniously beside them as crumpled as old washing. Blackstone and John Jacob stood looking at the still slumbering camp.

'Let's get back,' said Blackstone. 'We might still get an hour's sleep before first light.'

Forty yards away, a tent flap opened. A stooped figure emerged, dropped the flap on his hose and urinated in the gap between the tents. He finished, raised his face to the stars, yawned, shivered and turned to stare directly at the two intruders. Blackstone raised a hand in greeting. The half-asleep man made a feeble gesture of acknowledgement and returned to the warmth of his bed.

John Jacob sighed. 'I fear we have already lost the war.'

Two hours after Blackstone's men rose at first light, John Jacob waited at the horses as Killbere accompanied Blackstone to where the bastard horse watched their approach.

'Thomas,' said Killbere. 'Don't fall off that mountain bringing the Prince here. We need you.'

'I wish I could arrange a landslide and have the wretched Don Pedro smashed on the rocks. It pains me more taking him back than the suffering we endured getting him out.' Blackstone turned as horsemen appeared. 'Here comes an agitated royal son,' he said.

John of Gaunt rode in with his personal retinue. He was accompanied by a Navarrese captain Blackstone recognized. Martín Henríquez de Lacarra had fought with the English in France. Fifty knights were with him. De Lacarra kept a respectful distance to the rear of John of Gaunt. The Prince's brother eased his horse to where Blackstone stood with Killbere.

'You come like a thief in the night and humiliate a king?' he said. 'Lords and knights of Castile and Navarre now wish to be anywhere except by our side. And do not deny that it was you. No one else would dare.'

'I went into the camp of an ally who is supposed to help us and offer protection as we ride into hostile territory. If I were one of Trastámara's men, my lord, you would not be sitting on your horse breathing clean mountain air. Your throat would be cut.'

'I do not have my brother's tolerance for those who show such disrespect to those of higher rank,' said John of Gaunt.

'Then it's just as well I don't serve under your command, lord. I serve your father the King and am sworn to protect the Prince. And if I am to test our defences at the risk of making a fool more foolish, then I consider my duty done. Perhaps next time you will insist that pickets are placed. A lesson learned, my lord, is one well remembered.'

'When my brother crosses the mountains, I will inform him of your insolence personally.'

'Then I will forewarn him. I'm leaving now to bring him through the pass.'

John of Gaunt looked as though he had a lump of meat gristle in his throat. He swallowed hard, glared at Blackstone, then spurred his horse away to where Sir John Chandos bivouacked with his men.

De Lacarra followed but pulled up next to Blackstone. 'Sir Thomas, I am obliged to ride with Gaunt. Those are the wishes of my King.'

'And who will King Charles be riding with?' said Blackstone.

De Lacarra leaned down from the saddle so only Blackstone could hear. 'The King will not fight. He has made a pact with French routiers to seize him and hold him until the battle is over. No one has yet learned of this. He is a bigger fool than you thought. How easy it is to bring shame and dishonour on fighting men. Perhaps you would tell the Prince?'

'I will. And a man's honour is his own. Yours cannot be impugned.'

De Lacarra dipped his head, acknowledging the compliment. 'When the situation permits I hope you will allow me and my men the privilege of fighting with you.' The Navarrese captain extended his hand. Blackstone gripped it.

'Consider it done.'

De Lacarra spurred his horse to follow John of Gaunt.

Killbere sighed. 'Merciful Christ, Thomas. Does Navarre not think his subterfuge will be known for what it is? He'll be the laughing stock of Europe once that news gets out. Papal decrees might deny marriage between those sharing degrees of affinity but I swear incestuous breeding abounds. I weary of fighting for village idiots.'

'Then let's fight for ourselves and the Prince. We need to be ready to leave Spain. Do you think the King of France is a village idiot? No. He's watching what we do here like that buzzard circling up there. He watches and he plans. Mark my words, Gilbert. We fight here today and tomorrow we fight him. And we must be ready because I fear our King and the Prince are not.'

PART TWO

SINS OF THE FATHER

CHAPTER ELEVEN

Oxford
1367

Man-at-arms Hugh Gifford was a loyal subject to his lord, Thomas Beauchamp, Earl of Warwick, long-time friend and confidant of King Edward. For the past two years, Gifford had been a guardian shadow to Henry de Sainteny. Gifford was there on the Earl's orders, a command passed down by the King himself. A command to protect the Oxford University student. He was not told of the reason and he never raised the question. It was honour enough to be chosen, an expression of trust from Warwick. The scholar he protected was currently locked behind the door of his attic room in a cold, unheated, half-timbered Oxford townhouse with his protector outside on the landing. Gifford sat precariously on a three-legged stool, his back against the wall, his boots raised onto the stair's banister. Boredom was a part of every fighting man's life. And Gifford was bored. He had studied the vertical crack in the wall, imagining it to be a cleft in a hillside, a meandering river, a crooked path through cornfields. The splintered plaster revealed images in his mind's eye, allowing him to recall the campaigns where he had followed Warwick. Places he had trudged along to war. A door slammed below, followed by urgent footfalls ascending. Without haste, Gifford lowered his feet to the floor and peered over the banister into the stairwell, his hand moving to his sword's hilt. The laboured breathing of the man thudding up the stairs told him there was no threat. No assassin would announce his intent thus. It was a clerk. The breathless man stopped on the half-landing, leaned on the handrail for support, wiped his brow and struggled on upwards.

Head down, he turned onto the final dozen stairs and came face to face with Gifford's boots. He raised his eyes, a brief shadow of doubt crossing his face when he saw Gifford's surly look.

'I mean no harm,' he gasped.

'If I thought a clerk was capable, I'd become a monk. What do you want?'

'Warden Durant instructs me to fetch de Sainteny.'

'Why?'

'Why?' The clerk might have been no physical match for the man-at-arms, but he carried the authority of the Warden of the college. 'He's late. He was expected an hour past. Now get out of my way unless you wish him to hear of this.'

'My charge is studying.'

The clerk stayed three steps down, leaned against the wall and dragged off his cap to pull a hand through his sweat-soaked hair. He had run all the way from Merton College. 'Studying the arse and tits of a town whore is my guess.' He knew he had no choice but to return once he had delivered the message. 'All right, my part is done.' He resettled his cap. 'Warden Durant has the lad's report from his tutors which might determine his future here. I care not if he's absent.' The clerk turned back down the stairs.

'Tell the Warden he'll be there shortly. Once I get his head out of the books.'

The clerk did not look back. He raised a hand. 'Out from between her legs, more like.'

Gifford waited until the front door slammed closed. He beat the side of his fist against the door. 'Master Henry! You're in a shit pit. You're supposed to be at the college!'

He listened at the door. There was a scurry of activity. A curse, and then moments later the door was unlocked and swung open as Henry de Sainteny tucked in his shirt with one hand, handed his cloak to Gifford with the other. His bodyguard held it open, draped it around him as Henry turned back into the room, leaned to kiss the young woman on his bed, who tucked the blanket around her.

Gifford held back his impatience. Henry joined him, then lingered in the doorway a moment too long for Gifford's liking. He grabbed Henry and forced him onto the stairs. 'Even the damned clerks know your reputation. I'm not here to wet-nurse you in your studies. I don't give a damn. My job is to keep you alive, not to lie for you while you bed a whore.'

'Clara is no whore. She's the Warden's niece.'

Gifford grabbed Henry's shoulder. 'Even a dog doesn't shit where it sleeps. You're asking for trouble. When he finds out, the bailiffs will arrest you on some trumped-up charge and then you're banished from Oxford.'

They reached the cobbled street. 'Hugh, she is as much a prisoner as am I. You think a university town like Oxford isn't a place of confinement behind its walls? She beds me as much as I bed her. Her servant girl watches out for her the way you watch out for me. It's a mutually happy arrangement. Now, let's get to college and discover my academic fate.'

Gifford was, by his calculation, several years older than the tall nineteen-year-old he followed through the slop and detritus of Magpie Lane. The man ahead strode quickly and, being head and shoulders taller than Gifford, it caused the fighting man to extend his stride.

When Gifford was first appointed the student's custodian he'd kept his distance, as neither he nor the mysterious Henry de Sainteny liked the arrangement or his permanent presence. Within weeks, however, both men had softened their objections. It came more easily for Gifford once Henry insisted on spending time in taverns, interrogating the broken-nosed fighter about the battles he had fought in. Gifford described those conflicts modestly, heaping praise on those who fought at his shoulder. And when Henry learned that Gifford had taken part in the Breton War he made no mention of his father's involvement but asked him to teach him the Breton language.

Gifford was pleased to be of more value than simply a bodyguard, and the young scholar, who was already well versed in other languages, learned quickly.

And then, eating and drinking in the back-street alehouses, Henry de Sainteny also showed himself to be someone who would not back away from a fight. The 'town and gown' antagonism between the townsmen and scholars had gone on for years. Civil authority and the university were virtually one and the same and Hugh Gifford had, much to his surprise, managed to calm potential violence before it escalated into bloodshed. Yet still he knew nothing of his charge other than he was to be protected by order of Edward, King of England. And Hugh Gifford was not about to defy a king by being lax in his duty.

The lad called. 'Hugh! You're lagging behind. A beggar's crutch would move quicker.'

'Perhaps I am in no hurry to be scolded by the Warden of your college. Whenever you find trouble, I get a tongue-lashing for allowing it.'

'I never seek trouble, Hugh. It is drawn to me like a physician's leech to a man's skin.'

'And I'm the one who has to pull its suckers from you,' said Gifford, pushing a basket-carrying tradesman out of his way.

CHAPTER TWELVE

Henry's pace quickened into a narrow lane. After the years in Oxford the shortcuts and back alleys were familiar to the student and his guardian. Hugh Gifford used them as escape routes for his charge when trouble flared and the odds suggested the lad would suffer serious injury; no matter how willing Henry was to fight. Ten minutes after leaving the naked girl at his quarters in Queen's Lane he entered Merton College.

A clerk peered out of a doorway at the sound of their approach. He raised a hand. 'Wait here.'

'If this goes badly your arse will be thrown in the castle dungeons,' said Gifford. 'The protection afforded by my Lord Warwick and the King will be of no help if the Warden learns you have been bedding his niece.'

'How would he know?'

'Perhaps the girl's servant told him. A servant betraying their mistress may well get a reward.'

'Then you must think of an escape plan, Hugh. If the bailiffs are in the room waiting I suggest we escape over the city wall and strike out across the meadow and find a place to cross the river.' Henry de Sainteny smiled. 'Hugh, there is nothing to worry about. It's my tutors' reports. Nothing more.'

Before Gifford could say anything else the door opened and the two were called inside.

The Warden of Merton College looked up from behind his desk. It had been understood since de Sainteny had been placed at the college that his armed guardian was to be in attendance at all times. It was questioned but all the Warden had been told was that the lad had suffered an assassination attempt in Avignon and, now recovered from his wounds, needed protection. Even in the Warden's presence? he had asked. Even then. It denoted the boy was someone of importance. Warden Durant cared little. The fees were being paid. It made no difference if the broken-nosed man-at-arms stood back against the wall as de Sainteny was beckoned forward. It was customary for all communication to be done in Latin and William Durant knew that Gifford had no knowledge of the language. De Sainteny had been able to speak it from before he arrived at Oxford, and proceeded to make his apology accordingly.

Henry bowed his head. 'Master Durant, my apologies for my lateness.'

'I am told you were studying,' said Durant, laying out the reports across his desk, glancing up briefly from them to the bowed head. 'Studying what, Master de Sainteny?'

'Ptolomy's *Almagest*, Warden.'

Durant stared at him. Henry felt a frisson of doubt. Instinct alone was enough to tell him that Durant didn't believe him. Had his answer been too glib? Too quick?

'I continue to hear your interests lie elsewhere,' said Durant. 'Beyond learned works. And I am not pleased.'

Henry didn't blink as he stared at the stern-faced Warden, but his anxiety was short-lived.

'You continue to spend too much time in taverns, Master de Sainteny. Increasingly so. And you and your guardian continue to practise swordsmanship as you have done these past few years. It is unbecoming of a scholar.'

'Master Durant, it is forbidden to bear swords within the town walls so we go outside into the fields and woods.'

Durant's eyes continued to scan the sheaf of papers written by Henry's tutors. 'You are suspected of brawling with townsmen, spilling out of alehouses and engaging in running fights through the back streets. The bailiffs have no definite proof but you are becoming recognized. You run the risk of arrest. I warn you, that will not be tolerated.'

Henry bowed his head in an appropriate gesture of submission.

William Durant tidied the reports beneath his fingertips. 'That said, your tutors once again speak highly of your grasp of your subjects, but we are agreed you are over-confident. And it is felt you only exert minimal effort, which is enough to place you near the top-achieving students.' He sighed. Henry's studies at the university from the previous years until now told a familiar story. 'Grammar, rhetoric, dialectic, arithmetic, astronomy.' He sighed again. 'Always just enough. Extra effort would result in excellence.'

'Thank you, Master Durant. I find the study hard enough,' Henry lied.

The Warden leaned forward. 'We had hoped since you came to us from the papal seat at Avignon that you would have been attracted to the study of theological or canonical law, but the Church is unlikely to be as welcoming as this place. We see it is common secular law that might offer you a future. Opportunity awaits for those who focus their talents. You could travel to Bologna. Their university is renowned for legal scholars. Perhaps, though, if you remain here and apply yourself more, you may well become a regent master and lecture here for two years. Or you could be retained as a steward in a lord's household and preside over court and administer his estate. A prestigious position and a worthy outcome for those who support you being here.'

'Thank you, Master Durant. I have not yet seen where Fate will take me.'

William Durant nodded his dismissal. Henry reached the door. Gifford stepped into the corridor.

'Master de Sainteny,' Durant called.

Henry turned.

Gifford heard Durant say something to Henry, who nodded at the Warden and closed the door behind him.

'Trouble? What was all that about in there?'

'Too much drinking and swordplay. I need to work harder. Said I could become a lord's steward. I cannot imagine anything worse.'

'Nothing about the girl?'

Henry shook his head.

'He called you back. What did he say?'

'*Fato prudentia major.*'

Gifford's brow furrowed.

'Wisdom is stronger than Fate,' Henry explained.

'Then perhaps he has your measure and is warning you. You need to think about that girl before Fate shoves a dagger in your back. Assassins can easily be bought.'

'No, it's not that. He means for me to find my destiny through study and logical thought.'

'Well, what does that mean?'

'It means, Hugh, that I am thirsty and my destiny is to drink in the Bear.'

CHAPTER THIRTEEN

The Bear Inn was packed tight. Curs begged, scraps were thrown, drunken men bellowed, the shimmering lamp- and tallow candlelight twisted faces mouthing joy into gargoyles. A dog yelped, kicked hard by a belligerent drunkard who was complaining about the weakness of the ale. The innkeeper, broad shoulders and huge girth, booted aside the man's stool, sending him sprawling. An open-handed slap across the head from a meaty fist rendered the drunk unconscious. The innkeeper dragged him to the door and threw him into the narrow street with minimal effort.

Meat, bread and cheese were shared among those at the tables. Henry's table nestled in a corner, giving his guardian a clear view of the room. They had eaten, but they had been at the inn for the better part of the afternoon and Henry leaned on the table, resting his head on his arms. Daylight was fading as the inn's door swung open and a table of four men hailed a late arrival. Their raised voices caused Henry to lift his head. He saw that his companion recognized the latecomer. 'You know him?'

Gifford nodded. 'He served Warwick. I can't remember his name. He's trouble.'

Henry looked from the stranger to his companion. 'Why?'

Gifford shrugged and sipped his ale. Henry sighed, head lolled back. Drinking was a serious business. 'You're not staying the course, Hugh. Ale is to be drunk, not sipped.'

'And you drink enough for both of us.'

'I am a loyal servant to my boredom. I drink to accommodate it. My studies are demanding but not difficult.' With that, he ordered more ale.

They ignored the raucous men for the next hour as Henry kept drinking and became more insistent on trying to convince Gifford, as he had done these past months, to learn to read and write and that he would teach him.

Gifford sighed. 'Every time you drink too much, you start wanting to make me someone I am not. Or wish to be. I see no point in reading or writing. I follow the command of my sworn lord. If I fight, I follow the drum and trumpet. Church bells tell me when I need to rise, to sleep, to pray. What use are words on parchment? What use a book to a man like me who could never afford to buy one? They are there for the likes of you. You're a scholar.'

Henry supped the ale. He cast a pensive glance into the candle flame, its glow not as clear as it had been two hours ago. 'I am no genuine scholar. Yes, I have always loved books. That passion was gifted to me by my mother.' Henry's face creased at the memory of his mother's murder all those years ago, a recollection that would never leave him.

Gifford studied him for a moment. He knew nothing about the strapping young man who sat next to him. Where had a scholar learned his skill with a sword? Or the stamina to trade blade strokes with a fighting man like himself?

'Your father? Where is he?' said Gifford. He had always suspected the boy had been orphaned young and taken into a lord's household and taught his skills; he had also asked the question often enough before. He asked again now because whenever the lad was relaxed with drink, he thought Henry might reveal more about himself. A chance to unfold the mystery of the one he protected. But the question was never answered.

Henry was distracted, listening to something the group of men were discussing. Gifford knew Henry had had one drink too many and gave up his probing.

'Master Henry, enough of this place. The stench of tallow candles and men's farts is too much.'

Henry was squinting towards the loudmouth stranger. 'He likes the sound of his own voice.'

'I remember him now. His name is Flemyng. He left Warwick's service and sold his sword. Not always to those who fought with us.'

'Men do such things. When wars end, fighting men must find employment.'

Gifford swallowed the last of his drink. 'Aye, but Flemyng held a small town for a French lord and betrayed them to a routier. They had sport sewing townsmen in a sack and drowning them. The French have a price on his head. He's trouble. Let's go.'

Henry's eyes stayed focused on the braggart, head jutted forward as if trying to catch the latecomer's words. 'Did you hear what he said?' Henry muttered, lurching to his feet, leaning on the table for support.

Gifford reached out a restraining arm. It wouldn't be the first time that Henry had started an argument in an alehouse that resulted in a fight. 'It doesn't matter what he said.'

'It does to me, Hugh. When scum like him spew falsehoods, it's like breathing poison as vile as the plague.'

He shouted across to the men's table. 'I heard you say you fought with Thomas Blackstone?' he shouted. 'The King's Master of War?'

The men fell silent as they turned to face him. They looked him up and down, seeing his black cloak and cap on the table. A student.

'You eavesdrop on other men's talk?' said one of them.

Gifford sensed danger. He knew some of the men at the table – they drank regularly in the taverns around town – and if Flemyng was known to them, then they would side with him. Gifford placed a hand on Henry's arm, but he stepped away, drink in hand, leaning back against the table.

'I couldn't help but hear. Your friend wants everyone to know he served with Sir Thomas.' He drank from the beaker, but his eyes stayed on the men.

'Leave it,' said Gifford.

Henry glanced back. 'Hugh, this man says he knows Blackstone. How many men can say they have stood at his side?'

The storyteller stood and glared at Henry. 'You call me a liar?'

'I'm fascinated. I may be only a humble scholar, but I've heard of Thomas Blackstone's exploits.' He paused. 'And his men.'

'Aye, I know them all. Like brothers.'

'I have heard of a man who serves with him, a Will Longdon. They say he's as tall and strong as Blackstone.'

'As tall and well regarded, yes,' the man said confidently. 'Second only to Blackstone himself with a sword.'

Henry looked impressed, coming across as an eager admirer. 'There is another, a Norman. Been with Sir Thomas for many years. I heard he is called Meulon.'

'I know of no such man. The last time I saw Sir Thomas, he was fighting off a dozen Moors in Castile. He slew twenty or thirty of them.'

'One man did this?' said Henry.

'Aye, a giant of a man is Thomas Blackstone.'

'And yet you survived when I suppose many died.'

'Many. I was fortunate.'

'Fortunate your lies were not discovered,' Henry said calmly.

Flemyng rose from the bench, but a companion grabbed his arm as the landlord shouted across the room. 'Not here. You take your argument outside,' he said, keeping his distance. These were no mere drunkards like the last man he struck. These were mean in spirit and intoxicated enough to exercise their ill humour.

Flemyng nodded. A fight in the Bear would bring the town watch. 'You're a scholar and you call a man-at-arms who fought at Poitiers with the Prince, who served Warwick, a liar. You guttersnipe. You're not worth the trouble of gutting.'

Gifford swore beneath his breath. It was about to get violent. Henry took a step forward, still holding his beaker, but his guardian knew the beaker would be slung hard and then Henry's knife would be in his free hand. He stepped around the table.

'Flemyng. I am Hugh Gifford. We both served Warwick. Let the matter go. This lad has had too much to drink.'

The man squinted in the dimly lit room at Gifford. 'I don't know you.'

'It was a time ago.'

'You know this boy?'

'I do. We'll leave. With your permission, Flemyng. He means no harm.'

Henry had not moved or looked at Gifford. His eyes rested on the liar. 'My friend is right, Master Flemyng. I shall apologize for insulting you.'

The man grunted. His friend tugged his arm. 'Let it rest. The lad has apologized.'

'No,' said Henry. 'I said I'll apologize, but there is a caveat. A proviso. I will apologize when he admits his lies. To even stand in the shadow of a man like the King's Master of War bathes a liar in glory.'

The man took a stride forward, but was held by his friends as Gifford stepped between the two.

Henry had not moved. 'Will Longdon is an archer. He is short and stocky. A favourite of Thomas Blackstone, a man who has served with him since Crécy. Before I was born. And the Norman's name is Meulon. A big man. A throat-cutter. A devoted friend of the man you claim to know.'

Henry's words caused the man's friends to look questioningly at Flemyng.

'You cannot know this,' the man blustered.

'I know it because I know those men.'

'You hear rumours is how you know. And if you did, you would know that Blackstone has been imprisoned by the Prince because he threatened King Pedro of Castile. Imprisoned, aye,' said the man, seeing doubt crease Henry's face. 'Imprisoned in Aquitaine outside Bordeaux. He'll rot there no matter how favoured he is. A common man does not threaten a king. I returned from Aquitaine a month back and that's the truth.'

Everyone was rapt, looking from Flemyng to Henry and back.

'Sad news. Five years ago, I was a boy in Avignon. An assassin killed my friend, thinking it was me. I was wounded when I took my revenge, but I recovered and was brought here for my safety. Thomas Blackstone nearly lost his son that day and now I must suffer the indignity of hearing a coward spread his lies.'

Flemyng strode forward. 'You son of a whore. I'll gut you.' He stopped at arm's length as Gifford raised a hand to stop him.

'Then real trouble would visit you because my father would

hear of it and seek you out.' Henry smiled. 'My father. I am Henry Blackstone,' he said, dipping his head in greeting.

Gifford looked as though he had been punched. The liar's jaw dropped, but his hand reached for his knife. He was too slow. Henry sidestepped Gifford and his restraining arm, threw the clay beaker into the man's face and kicked him hard between the legs. He fell to his knees. Henry was on him, a handful of the man's beard in one hand, twisting hard, pulling flesh, hauling the man's head back, his knife at his throat. It happened too quickly for Gifford or the other men to stop it.

'No!' snapped Henry to everyone, before they could move. Then he glared at Flemyng. 'You never fought at my father's side.'

His knife's point pressed hard enough to cause a trickle of blood. Flemyng was hurting, his eyes watering, breathing hard to dull the pain. 'I did not,' he gasped.

Henry nodded, satisfied, and sliced a handful of the man's beard away. 'Next time, it will be your lying tongue.' He kicked him away into the men.

Flemyng was being dragged to his feet by the time Gifford hustled Henry to the door, turning to leave them with a threat. 'Let it be. You step through this door after us and you'll find my knife in your throat.'

The liar's parting words followed them: 'If you are his son, then know that he rots. That much is true.'

Gifford slammed closed the hefty door and pushed Henry up the cobbled alleyway.

'By the Blessed Virgin! Is it true? You're Henry Blackstone?'

'It is,' said Henry. 'And I am.'

'Sweet merciful Jesu, no wonder you have the King's protection. Now the word will spread like the pestilence. The King's Master of War, legend that he is, has many enemies, and there are Frenchmen here in Oxford who would like nothing better than to kill his son. The sins of the father are gifted to a son.'

'I use my mother's name and I honour her, but it's time I stood on my own two feet. I am Henry Blackstone.'

'And a damned fool who drinks too much and lays a scent for a pack of hounds to hunt us down.'

'You don't need to be here. Tell your master that your charge has gone his own way.'

Gifford stood in Henry's path. 'You're an idiot. If nothing else, Flemyng will sell your whereabouts. There will be no alehouse, tavern or alley safe for you now.'

'I can look after myself!' Henry insisted.

'You're a scholar. Why else would you be sent here?'

'I can fight!' said Henry, and made the mistake of trying to push Gifford away. The man-at-arms blocked his arm and struck him in the face, splitting his lip. Henry fell back against the wall. Instinctively he went for his knife, but Gifford struck his shoulder with a punch so hard it numbed Henry's arm. Henry winced in pain as Gifford followed up with a head butt that floored him.

Dazed, Henry rolled onto his side. He was sober now.

'You have skills, Master Henry, and I have seen you brawl in a tavern before now, but you are no street fighter, nor do you have the instinct to stand on a battlefield and embrace the madness needed when the enemy comes close. That is why you are here, studying, not at your father's side.'

Henry spat blood. 'Mother of God, you sound no different from him. All I have ever wanted was to be at his side.'

'But he must have seen you were better than the likes of us.' He extended his hand and hauled Henry to his feet. He pressed his palm against Henry's cut lip and smeared away the blood. Gifford sighed. There was forgiveness and a note of understanding in his voice. 'Now your pride has changed everything.'

Henry was sufficiently chastised. He had been foolish to try to best Gifford. 'You'll forgive me, I hope. I meant no disrespect.'

'What's done is done, lad. There is no ill will between us.'

'Then we had best hurry before those who wish to cause *me* harm find my lodgings.'

'Hurry?' said Gifford.

'To France,' said Henry.

'I cannot abandon England. My duty is here.'

Henry smiled. 'Your duty is to protect me. We must get through the town gates before the curfew bell and along Dead Man's Walk into the meadow. The bridge across the river will soon be closed by the night watch.'

As Henry strode away, Hugh Gifford stood rooted to the spot. His mind swirled. He was caught in a bear pit and there was no escape. He had been commanded to protect a scholar who turned out to be the son of the King's Master of War. He glared into the fading light. Henry was already out of sight. He began to run.

'Wait for me, dammit.'

CHAPTER FOURTEEN

The full force of a North Atlantic storm had struck the thirty-ton cog *Nicholas* as it rounded Finistère. The small ship battled against the shrieking gale, its fifteen crewmen hauling down the iron-hard sail. Four men were lost overboard when the ship was almost knocked down by a rogue wave. Confused seas tossed the helpless ship ever closer to the rugged shore. Men's screams were swallowed by the howling wind and blood flowed across the heaving deck as sailors were crushed by the falling spars. Henry and Gifford had strapped their swords across their backs when the first swells lifted the tub of a boat and showed them the top of a wave and then plunged them into the trough. They had also lashed themselves down with rope but when the cog ran onto some sawtooth rocks with a terrifying lurch and unencumbered men were thrown into the boiling waves, they realized the ropes would seal their fate – they would drown when the cog's death knell came.

Cutting themselves free, they clung to whatever handhold was available. They were still half a mile from shore when the deck lifted again, rolled and threw them into the water. Gifford saw the young man he was to protect hurled through the air and disappear into the white-flecked turmoil. Then he, too, was sucked down. He rolled and twisted, helpless against the power of the sea. His legs caught a rock, then his shoulder. He kicked hard, broke the surface, gasped a lungful of air, saw through salt-stung eyes the bobbing figure of Henry Blackstone face down. A wave lifted Henry's body and Gifford lunged, ignoring his wounds, and caught Henry's belt, used his fighting man's strength to drag him upright from the water, then embraced him like a child so that the two were buffeted together towards the shore. Chest deep, the surge pushed Gifford against tide-worn boulders. He found a cranny; the swell pressed against his legs, but the force of the water was bypassing them now, the boulders offering some respite. He forced Henry upright, slapped his face, and then again. Henry's head snapped back. His eyes opened. He vomited salt water over his rescuer. Deafened by the roaring waves crashing on the shore, he saw Gifford's mouth open and close. He shook his head.

'Breathe, lad! Breathe!'

Henry finally heard his guardian, nodded, sucked in air, pressed a hand against the boulder. 'I'm all right. All right.' He nodded.

He clung onto Gifford as a swell lifted the stocky man-at-arms, threatening to sweep him away towards the rocks guarding the shoreline where, beyond the beach, sand dunes rose showing a track leading through the tufts of spiked grass. Henry was about to push on towards the shore when Gifford stopped him.

'No!' He pointed.

Beyond a fishing skiff hauled onto the beach, flotsam was washing up into the shallows. Peasants were scurrying down the sand dunes onto the beach, salvaging whatever they could. Had the cog been returning from Bayonne, it would have been filled with barrels of Gascon wine. Now, though, there would be little in the way of booty. Three of the merchant crewmen staggered ashore two hundred yards from Henry's place behind the boulders. The peasants struck the injured men down and beat them to death with clubs and a falchion. Women stripped their bodies as their menfolk hauled away ropes and timber and whatever else could be seized from the wreck.

Henry and Gifford waited, shivering in the ice-cold sea and wind. Rain swept over them, pockmarking the dunes. The renewed storm flattened the sky, depriving it of the last vestige of light. When the moon broke through behind the scudding clouds, its cold light showed the last of the men dragging their spoils up the track.

'Come on,' said Henry. 'There's a village up there somewhere.'

They waded ashore, each holding on to the other through the backwash. Gifford's skin had been scraped from his legs. Blood oozed into his boots. His back muscles had taken a hefty blow, but there was nothing broken. Henry had no visible injuries and seemed the stronger of the two as they finally reached the beach.

The rain lashed them, but they were thankful for its icy sting that sluiced the salt from them. They turned their faces to the rain and let it trickle into their mouths. As clouds raced, the moon came and went. The three sailors lay naked in its glow, and were then quickly hidden.

'We have the wind and rain at our back,' said Henry. 'We'll need food and drink and to bind those cuts on your legs. I feel no generosity in my heart towards those villagers,' he said, strapping his sword back onto his waist. 'You can keep up?' he said, nodding at Gifford's lacerations.

'You lead, I'll follow, Master Henry.'

Clambering up the sandy track, they crested the dunes and saw firelight from a brazier several hundred yards away. A dozen huts, safe from the wind, huddled close to each other in the lee of the land. Torchlight lit the area where men were sorting what they had salvaged.

'Poor-as-dirt peasants,' said Gifford. 'A few pigs and not

much else. Barely anything will grow around here. They'll barter what they've salvaged for food.'

'You pity them?' said Henry.

'I understand their need,' Gifford answered.

'They could have helped those sailors instead of killing them.'

Gifford shrugged. 'There is that. Do we kill them all?'

'Only those who want to die,' said Henry and strode down, sword in hand, towards the hamlet.

CHAPTER FIFTEEN

The villagers did not see the two survivors walk out of the darkness of the storm. A couple of village dogs, ribs showing, growled and barked as they raised themselves from where they sheltered next to a hut. Three men had their backs to Henry and Gifford. They turned. Henry punched the closest man as Gifford levelled his sword against the two men at his side. Henry's blow knocked the man flying. He was unconscious before he hit the ground. The sudden attack shocked the others into immobility.

'You kill innocent men. Victims of the sea. Do not expect mercy here,' said Henry. 'Help us and you'll live to see another day. Turn against us and we will kill you, your women, your children and even these snarling dogs.' Memories of his father leapt into his mind, and it seemed, his throat. The use of a violent warning with the promise of death came from being in the company of fighting men when he was a boy.

The men backed away. A young woman, wrapped in layers of rags, stepped out from a pile of dirt-clad turnips next to her hut. She stood frozen, her arms full, toothless mouth gaping at the intruders.

Gifford gestured with his sword. She came closer.

'How many live here?' said Henry to the nearest man.

'Sir, we are nine men – those you see here – and seven women who bear children, of which there are eleven.'

The cowed man was as wiry and strong-looking as his companions. If they thought the intruder's clothing and weapons could be seized, Henry knew they could be rushed and overwhelmed. A hut's wicker door showed a light behind it. Other doors had stretched pigskin across their frame. Smoke drifted from holes in the huts' roofs. Drying racks of fish swayed as the wind shifted. Henry smelled food. A woodshed stacked with fuel offered shelter from the rain.

'Bring us food and drink. There's a crone here who heals wounds?'

The man nodded.

'See to it. Bring her and the food to the woodshed. Every man stands out here so he can be seen.'

The men backed further away as Henry and Gifford circled the brazier and found a chopping log to sit on with their backs against the stacked wood, which allowed them to keep a clear view of the compound. There was sufficient overhang to offer some protection from the rain. The men stood watching, seemingly unconcerned about the chilling squalls. The dogs crouched, inching forward to sniff the newcomers. Gifford hurled a piece of wood and scattered them.

'They'll serve a lord somewhere in these parts. Not that I know where we are,' said Gifford. 'But if there are more than nine of them and they run for help, we could have armed horsemen here come daylight.'

'They scavenge from the sea, Hugh. They are worthless to any lord. Somewhere there'll be a field where they grow something. Those turnips didn't get sent by any lord of the manor.'

The toothless woman re-emerged carrying two bowls of pottage and dark rye bread on a tray made from a hewn piece of wood. Nervously she stood off from the men until they beckoned her forward. She knelt, placing the tray on the ground, then hurried back to her hut. Henry and Gifford ate hungrily. By the time an old woman was ushered forward with a pail of water and a wooden mixing bowl, they had finished eating. The older woman was less fearful of the two men. If they needed her help, they were unlikely to harm her. She bent and sniffed Gifford's leg.

'She likes the smell of you, Hugh,' said Henry.

Gifford gently pushed her head away. 'She gets any closer and her breath will rot my wounds.'

The old woman put the pail down.

'You wash, master, and then we treat the cuts,' she said.

Gifford pulled a rag from his tunic and washed away the grime and salt encrusting his wounds. The crone nodded as he dabbed them dry. Her filthy hands were about to dip into the bowl to scoop out the ointment when Henry grabbed her wrist.

'You let those hands near your cuts and they'll be poisoned in days. Wash your hands and put it on yourself.'

'You know about such things?'

'My father met a herbalist woman once, and his bowman, Will Longdon, learned from her. Do as I say.' He looked at the woman. 'What is this?' he said, meaning the mixture in the bowl.

'Plantain and herbs, lord.'

'Get back to your hut, woman,' he told her. He pulled off his tunic and took his knife to the bottom of his shirt, cutting a broad enough strip to be used as bandaging. 'My arse will freeze, but your leg will heal.'

Gifford spread the potion across the lacerations on his thigh, then took the strip of linen and bound it. 'I'm supposed to be looking after you, Master Henry, and here you are nursing me.'

'I need you strong and at my back, Hugh. If we are in de Montfort territory, then we are safe, for my father helped secure Brittany for him.'

'Aye, but I fear we may be a long way from safety. There are still strongholds of skinners. Even when we set out tomorrow, these men could get ahead of us and sell us to a routier. A skinner likes nothing better than ransoming men to a French lord, and then they like nothing better than a public execution. I've seen it before.' He tapped his leg with the palm of his hand. 'I'm ready.'

'Sleep. I'll stand watch. I'll wake you, then I'll rest before daybreak. We have food in our belly and we'll need our strength for tomorrow.' He looked up at the shifting clouds. 'Wind's shifting. With luck there'll be less rain by then.'

The wind flicked rain against Henry's face as Gifford slept, curled on the earth, back resting against the woodpile. They needed rest after their ordeal and the uncomfortable ground posed no hardship for the man-at-arms. Sleep was a gift wherever it could be found. Henry had no sense of time passing by. A woman fed the brazier with dried and withered salt-laden sticks from the beach, blue flames jumping like the devil's imps. Men returned to their womenfolk and the houses fell silent. The beaten man had slunk away. The wind shifted, chasing clouds and their smattering of rain. Henry's eyes closed as the night wore on. His chin dropped onto his chest.

He jerked awake, stared into the night. The brazier had settled into a dull glow. The burning torches still flickered in the night wind. He looked around, stood and stretched, yawned and shook his head to clear away the fatigue. It was quiet. Only the wind whispered across the bullrush roofs. Even the dogs had found refuge somewhere. He sat again on the woodpile, folded his arms, keeping his attention on the darkened huts. Images in his mind recounted the storm at sea and the fight for survival as he went overboard, cracking his head on the bulwark, then the strange, disconnected sense of lying face down in the water. Floating. Rising with the tide. Rocked like a child. A lullaby. Asleep.

Behind his closed eyes a shadow interrupted the torchlight. Instinct jerked him awake. The men were storming towards them, wielding clubs, knives and axes. The nearest was barely twenty paces away, axe raised high.

'Hugh! To arms!' Henry bellowed and stepped forward to meet the attack, pulling his knife free with one hand, sword in the other. He sensed rather than saw Gifford kick free from the woodpile behind him. Blood surged through him, the sharp focus of impending violence hurling him out of his torpor. Keeping the protection of the woodshed a few paces at his back, he sidestepped the savage attack and cut through the man's thigh with his knife, let him fall, half turned to finish him. No need. Gifford plunged his sword into the man's chest, then took three paces to Henry's side, so they offered two defensive positions. The fishermen would have to split their attack. Two came for Henry, who parried a hurled piece of wood with his arm, bent low and let the man run onto his sword. The second man sidestepped into Gifford's slashing knife hand; blood spurted from his neck as Gifford moved aside, drawing in the next man.

Henry and Gifford stood their ground, forcing their enemy to stand off, ducking and weaving in their uncertainty, shouting to each other, fear and false courage driving them on, determined to finish what they had started. They dared not surrender now. Henry and Gifford let them come, those years of practice on the Oxford meadow now a seamless and efficient exercise in killing. Henry feinted; a man faltered, chest exposed; Henry's sword plunged through him. The torchlight's glare distorted men's features. Etched shadows scarred their faces, mouths gaping, eyes wide as they sought the best way to kill the strangers in their midst. Gifford hamstrung one man, turned his sword hilt and plunged its guard into his companion's eye. The blinded man dropped his knife and fell to his knees as Henry plunged his knife down into the man's skull.

Four men backed away. Their attack had failed. Henry and Gifford stepped over the bodies.

'Throw down your weapons!' he demanded.

The survivors turned and ran. It was only when they raced towards the track down to the beach that Henry saw the women and children huddled behind the largest dune. Even the cur dogs cowered with them. The sky was clearing, the moon illuminating a shimmering sea and the abandoned families. A baby cried. Then another. Howls carried on the wind. The women backed further away, edging down the beach path to follow their cowardly men.

The rush that had surged through him subsided. It had been years since he had been forced to kill a man. Back then, he was only a boy; now he had reacted with the same instinct. This was no tavern brawl; this was life or death. His hand trembled. His stomach knotted. The pounding in his chest was a mixture of regret and fear. He clenched his fist, drew in a deep breath, and let the tension escape into the night.

Gifford checked the nearest hut. Then another. 'They're empty.'

'Check the rest,' said Henry, focusing again on what danger might still present itself. He followed Gifford's example by pulling free the wicker doors and looking inside.

'They've gone. No one hiding,' Gifford said.

They stood in the clearing, looking around them, checking that no other attack could come from another direction.

'We should leave before daylight, Master Henry.'

'Search the huts. Find whatever food we can.'

'And we let these men live?'

'We've more than halved their numbers. It's enough. They won't pursue us now.' Henry didn't know why but his heart felt the cold grip of vengeance, a desire to punish those who wanted them dead. 'Burn their huts,' he said.

The torches soon set the hovels ablaze. Sparks flew high into the night sky as the wind whipped the flames. The two men stood back, each with a small sack of scavenged food.

'Time to go, Hugh. We'll need angels on our shoulders to find a safe haven.'

'The Almighty didn't bring us out of that sea to die like dogs,' said Gifford. He settled his eyes on the dead bodies. 'That's not to say He won't find a more gruesome death for us, though.'

PART THREE

TO KILL A KING

CHAPTER SIXTEEN

Blackstone and John Jacob brought the Prince and the rest of the army through the pass and, days later, led him onto the plains around Pamplona. It was only when they paused to rest the army before going into Castile that the Prince told Blackstone his son had gone missing.

'Left Oxford?' said Killbere when Blackstone related what scant news there was.

'He wrote a letter to the Warden of his college saying he had considered what had been said – whatever that was – and that he was travelling to Bologna to study law.'

'Henry said that?'

'That's what I was told. A messenger reached the Prince at Dax. He held off from telling me, he said, because he did not want my thoughts distracted as we came over the pass.'

Blackstone and Killbere were sharing a fire and a cooking pot with John Jacob. The squire ladled out pottage into bowls.

'John?' said Blackstone. 'You think it's true?'

John Jacob had once acted as guardian to Blackstone's family when his children were young and before his wife was murdered. He took a moment to think. He shrugged. 'He's always been headstrong, Sir Thomas, you know that. He has the wit and intelligence to make his own decisions. He's no longer the boy who nearly lost his life in Avignon, is he? And he killed the assassin who went after him. So, he has the skill to defend himself, the brains to think things through and the ability to pull it off.'

'That's not what I asked, John,' said Blackstone.

His squire smiled. 'Henry volunteering to go to another classroom? No.'

'Damn,' said Blackstone. 'That's what I thought.'

'If he's coming back to France, he'd do what? Get into Normandy? Travel down through the Prince's territory? Is that his plan? To get to you?' said Killbere, spooning in food.

'Me? Why would he come to me? He knows I'll never let him fight. He had the King's protection. Damn the boy. He causes trouble. Always has done. Why can't he do as he's told?'

'Like his father does?' said Killbere.

'Gilbert, do not side with the lad. His life was as threatened as my own. He was given sanctuary. An education. Paid for by the King.'

'Thomas, I'm surprised he lasted this long cooped up in a tutor's room. He hungers for something more. He has your blood in his veins. Let him find his way to wherever he goes. I've always said he would play his part if he stood shoulder to shoulder with us in a fight.'

Blackstone laid the bowl of food aside, his hunger gone. 'We are bred for what we do, Gilbert. He had his mother's love and wisdom, a tenderness far beyond what I could give him. He could be a lawyer. A learned man using rhetoric to argue against war, who could defuse men's anger and reconcile them. He is different.'

'Not if he seeks honour on the battlefield, Thomas. Not if he wants to be seen as your son. If he is to become all that you would wish for him, then I wager he'll want to walk through fire first.'

Blackstone stood and grabbed his belted sword and scabbard, his irritation plain to see. 'Hasn't he already done that? He was little more than a child when he killed to protect his mother; he was wounded and close to death when he tried to save the lad in Avignon. Wounded so that he could have died. Is that not fire enough? Are the soles of his feet not sufficiently singed? Damn him! I had him kept safe.' Blackstone stormed off.

Killbere sighed and settled down, pulling a blanket over himself. 'John, best feed the fire. His temper'll keep him warm for now but the night's chill will soon cool him down.'

'You think so, Sir Gilbert? That anger will last at least until Castile. Heaven help any man who stands in his way until then. He loves Henry more than he admits. He wants him kept out of harm's way. I'll wager the lad wants to win his spurs, and if that's his reason for leaving Oxford, better he does it with us.'

Killbere groaned and belched. 'The Blackstone family. Nothing but trouble since I first took them to war.'

The hidden moon starved the camp of light, but the burning torches and fires cast enough of their glow for Blackstone to meander among his men. Some raised a hand or nodded in his direction as they recognized the size and height of the dark shadow that stalked among them. Perhaps it was instinct that kept them silent. Blackstone looked like the grim reaper. Most of the men had eaten and bedded themselves down against the chill wind. His captains had posted pickets on their own perimeter and, with his thoughts full of Henry's absconding, Blackstone soon found himself near the entrance to King Pedro's pavilion, where loyal Castilians stood sentinel.

Blackstone watched as the guards changed over. One of the new men brought a fresh torch to replace one that flickered low; another opened and closed a lantern to replace its oil-soaked wick which was now smouldering. Neither torch nor lantern offered sufficient light to see more than two arrow lengths beyond each man's station. And even if the men had not been distracted, there was not enough light to see the shadow that flitted quickly between the King's pavilion and the one next to it.

Blackstone strode past the men and turned next to the gently flapping canvas wall. He edged around the side and saw the back of a crouched figure slowly cutting a slit in the pavilion's rear. Blackstone guessed Pedro's sleeping mattress and pillows would lie behind it. The assassin was taking his time. Blackstone watched without moving. If Pedro was killed in his bed, it would save other men's lives in the battle to come. A worthless king's life seemed a good exchange. Blackstone was content to let the assassin do his work – apart from one nagging doubt: the cost already paid by his own men in bringing Pedro to safety. Their lives would have been surrendered in vain if he allowed the killer to murder a man who deserved little better. Still he hesitated. The assassin eased a shoulder through the cut he had made. It was a small incision; a bigger cut would have flapped in the night wind. The figure was half inside the tent when Blackstone surrendered to his doubts. He took four fast strides and snatched the smaller man's shoulder. He yanked, spun the assassin around; his bunched fist clubbed the cowled head. The assassin's body barged into the pavilion's wall, then hit the ground. In the few seconds it took for Blackstone to bend down and drag the unconscious man around the side of the tent to the torchlight, the alarm was raised. The guards who appeared faltered when they saw it was Blackstone who dropped the body unceremoniously outside Pedro's entrance.

As Blackstone went down on one knee to uncover the assassin's identity, the tent flap was flung aside by a guard and King Pedro of Castile and León appeared in his night attire. His full-length silk nightgown was covered by an ermine-lined cloak. Wide-eyed, he glared down at the Master of War. Blackstone saw Pedro's hand – a bejewelled hand gripping a stiletto – was trembling. Was it bloodlust or fear that caused his tremor?

The King nodded to his guards, who came forward to expose the assassin. Blackstone stepped aside. They dragged the semi-conscious man to his feet, punched him in the kidneys and tore away the cowl and cloth tied across his face. The assassin sagged for a moment, still reeling from Blackstone's blow and winded by the guard's punch, then began to struggle, apparently determined to resist. Head back, she howled.

Blackstone was as surprised as the guards when the black-haired woman bared her teeth and hurled insults at them. The soldiers gripped her tighter. One grabbed a handful of her hair and yanked back her head. She writhed, but was helpless in their grasp. She spat, her phlegm splattering the King. A guard slapped her; the blow split her lip. The mouthful of rapid curses that followed was too fast for Blackstone to understand. She glared, seemingly daring the King to kill her. She didn't flinch when Pedro stepped forward, knife ready to plunge in her throat.

Blackstone reached out, grabbed the King's wrist, his strength forcing Pedro to drop the weapon. Pedro bellowed like a wounded beast. Not in fear, but in rage, and then through gritted teeth challenged Blackstone.

'You do not strike a king! Never! No one strikes me!'

Blackstone allowed him to shake free his wrist. It must have hurt because he nursed it with his free hand.

Blackstone stood between Pedro and the woman. 'You need to control your rage. A king should kill an enemy only once they know why the enemy wants them dead.' Blackstone spoke without deference.

Pedro looked sharply at his men, a signal for them to force

the woman to her knees. He sneered at Blackstone without looking at his victim. 'Kill her.'

Before the first guard could draw his knife, Blackstone turned and struck him, sending him flying backwards; he lost his grip on the woman, scattering the other guards who had gathered behind him. The second man used one hand to hold the assassin, went for the knife at his belt, and felt the vicious impact of Blackstone's elbow in his face. His nose split, he dropped to the ground.

The woman squirmed, trying to escape, but Blackstone held her, his arms easily embracing her.

'Stay still or you will die. Listen to me and you might live,' he told her.

Pedro's men had rallied. They blocked any escape.

A voice called out. 'Stand aside. Stand aside!' It was Sir John Chandos. He strode into view, pushing through the men. Killbere was at his side and, following him, John Jacob, William Ashford, Longdon and Halfpenny; Meulon towered at the rear.

'Sir John!' Pedro commanded. 'Arrest Thomas Blackstone for assaulting me and hand that woman to my men. She attempted to kill me.'

'Of course. One moment, highness,' said John Chandos, ever the diplomat. He raised his eyes to Blackstone and lowered his voice in supplication. 'Merciful suffering Christ. What now, Thomas?'

'I've just saved the King's life.' He faced Pedro. 'Again.'

CHAPTER SEVENTEEN

Lanterns glowed in the Prince's pavilion as he sat before a brazier wrapped in his fur-lined cloak, with John of Gaunt and the Spanish King sitting either side of him. The assassin, hands bound, stood in front of them. Blackstone and Killbere and Sir John Chandos stood to one side with Martín Henríquez de Lacarra and Pedro's Aragonese ally, the noble Count de Osona, while the woman was condemned by the Prince.

'You attempted to kill a king of the house of Castile and León. There is no possible verdict other than death. We do not know why you were brought before us. There is no reason to hear you speak.'

'Highness,' said Blackstone. 'This woman risked coming into your camp to commit murder. Perhaps she believes she is the instrument of God's vengeance for a wrong committed against her by King Pedro.'

Killbere glanced at Blackstone. It wasn't like him to bring God into a defence of the indefensible. An assassin had to die, and that was an end to it.

'I will kill her,' said Pedro. 'And then I will find her family and kill them also.'

Blackstone looked from the snarling King to his Prince. His appeal had baited the King. Pedro the Cruel's viciousness and bloodthirsty behaviour offended the Prince's sense of justice and honour and his deeply held belief that God guided men in their actions. Or in this instance a woman.

'Our holy fathers tell us that women are Satan's Gate.

Through them, men fall prey to lust and commit foul deeds that dishonour them. What cause could possibly exonerate someone who has embraced the devil and tried to kill a king?' said the Prince, glaring at Blackstone, knowing all too well that his Master of War had used Pedro's character to draw him in.

'Let the woman speak in her own defence, lord,' said Blackstone.

'There *is* no defence for killing a king!' John of Gaunt said. 'We would hang, draw and quarter any man who tried. Such a man should not live.'

'I tried to kill a king,' said Blackstone.

The intake of breath was as noticeable as the sudden slap of canvas in the wind.

'At Poitiers, I came close to killing King John. He had slain my friends, and I vowed vengeance.'

'And you were banished for it,' said the Prince. 'It is not the same thing at all.'

'Then banish this woman, lord. Show your mercy and your justice. She did not succeed, and neither did I. Let the punishment be lenient. Let her tell you why she risked everything to come here with a knife in her hand.'

King Pedro raised himself and pointed at the Prince, spittle on his lips. 'You do not have jurisdiction here. You are an English prince not a Spanish king. *I* will decide her fate.'

Colour seeped into the Prince's cheeks. His pale and sickly skin flushed with constrained anger. His measured response left no doubt in Pedro's mind who it was that commanded.

'My lord, with respect, you forget where you are. Our father sanctioned your return. We see to it that his wish is honoured. Sir Thomas risked everything to take you to safety and bring you into our hospitality. If you wish to seize your throne alone, then we will turn back with our army and leave you to do so.'

Pedro's outburst and insult had given the woman the audience she needed.

'Woman, tell us who you are and why you did what you did,' said the Prince.

Her back straightened. Her chin lifted and her dark eyes focused on the man who would have her executed. 'My lord, I am Sancha Ferrandes of Castile.'

Those present witnessed Pedro flinch at her name.

She turned her gaze to the stricken-looking King. 'This man had my family tortured and killed in order to seize their wealth and land. My father and thirteen-year-old brother were mutilated in front of my mother and sister and kept alive long enough to witness the soldiers rape my mother and sister, who was only eleven years old. My infant brother was thrown from a cliff. Then they cut my mother and my sister's throats. Every servant was slain so they would not be witnesses. I was returning home and hid from sight. Last year, I found his captain and killed him.' She addressed the Prince once more. 'When I learned that the English Prince was returning King Pedro I disguised myself as a washerwoman with the men from Navarre to get close to the camp.' She fell to her knees. 'I know I will die by your command, good Prince. Your justice is fair, I have heard that said. You must do what you must. My only regret is that I failed. You are a royal prince, son of a noble father. It is impossible for you to imagine seeing your beloved mother, wife or child slaughtered so cruelly. I ask our blessed Mother of God, who cradled her only son on his death, to forgive me.' She made the sign of the cross.

So did the Prince.

Blackstone knew she had been clever. By appealing directly to the Prince's heart, she had given herself her only chance of avoiding execution. Edward would have seen in his mind's eye his own infant son being cast into a ravine, and his mother and sister being treated in the same manner as this woman's.

No one spoke. Sancha stayed on her knees, hands clasped as if in prayer before the English Prince.

'Thomas,' said the Prince. 'See that this woman is held securely. We will sleep on it.'

Pedro's anger was barely contained as he stood to challenge the Prince but John of Gaunt blocked him. 'Enough has been said, highness. Let my brother spend what hours of darkness remain in prayer.'

Pedro stepped forward and looked down at the woman. 'I will garrotte you myself,' he whispered, and then left the pavilion.

The Prince nodded to Blackstone, who brought the woman to her feet and guided her outside with Killbere at his side.

'Thomas, you challenge the devil himself.'

Blackstone smiled. 'Where the devil lurks, angels hover, Gilbert.' He touched the Goddess of the Silver Wheel at his throat. 'We need all the help we can get.'

CHAPTER EIGHTEEN

The woman was bound and held under guard for the night and then brought to the Prince, John of Gaunt and Pedro the next morning when the Prince and his brother had finished their morning prayers. Sir John Chandos stood to one side next to Pedro's ally, Osona, and the Spanish King. Blackstone stood with Sancha Ferrandes of Castile as the Prince gave his verdict on the woman's fate.

'We have considered the matter,' said the Prince, 'and our deliberation took us through the night. This woman was driven to seek vengeance for a wrong done to her.'

Don Pedro's shoulders straightened; his head turned to face the accusation levelled against him by the Prince, who ignored him and remained focused on the accused. 'A wrong we have no proof of,' he said by way of appeasing the Spaniard. 'But a wrong that she does not doubt. Such passion can turn the heart and mind of the innocent. We deem this woman should live the rest of her life with the nuns at the convent at Roncesvalles, where she will labour in service to holy pilgrims who travel the Way of St James.'

Blackstone saw Sancha's head drop to her chest. She fell to her knees, bound hands clasped in gratitude. Blackstone lifted her back to her feet.

'Sir Thomas, you will have one of your captains and his men escort her there. And then you will scout the road ahead to Pamplona.' The Prince looked directly at Blackstone, who did not question the unusual command. It was Renfred who usually rode ahead while Blackstone led the army.

'Sir John and our brother will lead the army onwards with Sir William Felton. This matter is closed,' said the Prince. He stood; those present bowed, except for Pedro, who glared at the woman who tried to kill him.

Blackstone led the woman out to where Killbere waited. 'Does she live or die?' said the veteran knight.

'Spared. She's to serve pilgrims on the way to Compostela.'

Killbere picked his nose and examined the contents, then wiped his finger on his tunic. 'The workings of the royal mind continue to baffle me, Thomas.' He grabbed the woman's arm. 'Am I to take her?'

'No, send William Ashford to me. And have her guarded.'

'And what of us?' said Killbere.

'I don't know. It seems the Prince has another duty in mind for us.'

Killbere shrugged. 'Then we await his pleasure and do his bidding.'

The veteran knight turned away. 'Gilbert, keep her clear of Pedro's men.'

The warning was not lost on Killbere. He nodded and took the woman away to where Blackstone's men were camped.

One of the Prince's clerks came out of the pavilion and beckoned him. 'Sir Thomas?'

Blackstone followed him back inside. The Prince was alone except for another clerk who sat writing a document. He dried the ink, presented it to the Prince who read it, nodded, handed it back, watched it being folded and then had his seal press into hot wax to close the fold.

The Prince dismissed the two clerks and handed the folded document to Blackstone. 'Thomas, whom do you send with the woman?'

'One of my captains, William Ashford, highness.'

'Good choice. He served us well when he was in our guard. We are changing our orders, Thomas. Our command was to take her to Roncesvalles away from anyone who wishes her harm but we now fear she is in danger. Can you find another convent to take her to?'

'Yes, highness. When I brought Pedro out of Spain, my route took me through Estella. It's another half-day's ride south. I returned an old Jew to his home there. Christian and Jew share the town, and the convent is known for its care of pilgrims.'

'Then have Ashford turn south of Roncesvalles and take her there. Our request to the abbess is in your hand. She will be rewarded.'

'Very well, lord. And what of me?'

The Prince smiled. 'We need others to see you leave with a small detachment of your men. But yours is no scouting party. You will shadow William Ashford. Don Pedro has routiers in his pay. It would be easy for him to blame any attack against Ashford and the woman on them. If he has ordered her killed so that she may never testify against him, then he will make the attempt before Ashford reaches Roncesvalles. See to it she arrives safely in Estella, then you and Ashford turn back to Pamplona and meet us there. And after that we shall strike into Castile.'

Blackstone had stopped her killing Pedro and now the Prince had taken the woman's side, and for that he was grateful.

'Thomas, we cannot condone an assassin, but we are under no illusion as to the character of the King of Castile. We must make allowances for those he treated so brutally. We place our trust in God that this is the right decision.'

CHAPTER NINETEEN

Throughout the woman's ordeal Blackstone had kept the shock he'd felt at seeing her to himself. When her identity as a woman had been exposed, her dark-eyed glare of defiance, her feisty attempt at resisting Pedro's men and her ability to smother the pain from their blows had caught him unawares, reminding him painfully of another young woman, slight of build, strong in character, willing to risk death as she escaped Bohemian horsemen in a forest across the ford at Blanchetaque before the Battle of Crécy. As a sixteen-year-old archer, he had gone to rescue her. Had been willing to die for her. Christiana. Lover, wife and mother to his children. And for a brief, heart-stopping moment when Sancha's eyes challenged him, he'd seen his beloved again. That missed heartbeat had given him the determination to challenge the Prince and give the woman a chance to live.

His efforts were not appreciated.

'Do not expect gratitude from me,' she said when he told her his men would escort her to safety. 'I will hate you as long as I live. I was prepared to die rather than let that monster take another breath. I despise you for saving him.'

Her admonishment stung. A stab as sharp as the jolt he'd felt when he saw her. The reality, of course, was that this was not Christiana. Her anger was that of a highborn woman thwarted by the English King's Master of War who, in her eyes, was nothing more than a common soldier. Blackstone let the moment pass quickly.

'Pedro's cruelty will not go unpunished,' said Blackstone. 'Eventually a man like him will be killed. It was my duty to do my Prince's bidding. Once Henry of Trastámara is defeated and Pedro is back on the throne at Burgos, then Fate will turn on him.'

'And hundreds of men will die long before it does.'

'True. But you forget, my lady, that the French favour Trastámara, and my King needs an ally in Castile.'

'Well, my kin side with Pedro's brother.'

'Half-brother. A bastard.'

'But they will fight your Prince and nothing will change until Pedro is dead. If you see a blazon bearing a black-headed griffin holding a sword, then you are facing my uncle, Don Fernando. He will kill you if you face him. And if you kill him, I will never rest until you are dead.'

'You have given your word to serve in the convent. If you escape and are captured, then no one can save you.'

'I am a noblewoman of Castile. I do not break my pledge. But one day someone will find me and rescue me.'

'Then you should hope that Pedro is already dead because if he is not, then I will be the one sent to hunt you down.'

'If you live long enough,' she said and turned her back, dismissing him.

Despite her antagonism towards him, Blackstone would ensure she reached safety with the Prince's blessing.

'You lead the men, Gilbert. Stay in the vanguard. John of Gaunt and William Felton are behind you, then John Chandos and the Prince.'

'Aye, I'll do that. You'll take no archers with you? Will and a half-dozen could give you an advantage.'

'No. If Pedro has plans to kill the woman, it will be a mounted attack from cover. It will be close-quarter killing.'

Killbere looked at the sprawling mass of men and to where Sir William Felton's pavilion was being struck. 'Felton has no cause to like us. Remember when he was Seneschal of Poitou and demanded we pay for a resupply of arrows? If he takes it into his head that he wants to lead the army instead of us, he will have John of Gaunt's ear.'

'But we have the Prince's. If Felton is looking for glory, he can find it elsewhere. Keep no more than a mile between you and the column. Henry of Trastámara will not face us yet. If he does attack us – and he'll have to ignore the fact that he is in Navarre's domain – it will be to harass our supply lines and pick off stragglers.'

'Right enough, Thomas.' He paused. 'This woman – she means something to you? Enough to challenge the Prince in her defence?'

'She reminded me of Christiana.'

'Ah. Well, that explains it. Don't get yourself killed for her. She would never forgive you.'

'The woman?'

'Christiana, you oaf. You're the one who believes in angels.'

The Prince's camp lay east of Roncesvalles, a place that could accommodate the thousands of men and their supply train. Chandos and John of Gaunt's captains easily spread the word that the Master of War had been commanded to scout ahead while the army struck camp for its march to Pamplona. Blackstone, John Jacob, Meulon and the Gascon captain Aicart, accompanied by Renfred and his dozen scouts, rode south of the Prince's camp an hour after William Ashford headed north-west with Sancha Ferrandes. His small escort of several men had been briefed by Blackstone without her learning of the suspected threat. If Don Pedro stayed true to his character, he would have already sent killers from the camp before first light, slipping away in the darkness; they would have at least three hours' start on William Ashford's escort. Once Blackstone and his men cleared the foothills that shielded them from the army, they were out of sight and spurred their mounts as they changed direction to follow William Ashford.

The slower-moving Ashford came into view as the soaring mountains dipped and then rose into foothills that offered Blackstone easy-to-navigate contour paths. Forests and grassland shielded them from Ashford's steady progress in the valley below. When they eventually drew parallel with Ashford's escort, there was no sign that he knew Blackstone's men were so close.

By midday, the swirling mist on the peaks had sunk lower, swept by the wind pushing at their backs. Sparkling droplets clung to men's beards and clothing. The damp air cushioned sound. Blackstone and his men had ridden ahead using the cloud-laden hillsides as cover. Renfred emerged from the murkiness after reconnoitring the way ahead.

'Thirty men, perhaps more, waiting in a forest a mile down the track,' said the German captain. 'They look like skinners. If they are Pedro's men, they have stripped off his blazon.'

'He won't risk his own followers. They'll be routiers he's promised to pay when he retakes the throne. Do they have lookouts?'

'No, they're too far down the slope, about forty yards into the trees. They'll attack the road when William reaches them.'

'Can we get behind them? Close enough to be on their heels when they attack?'

Renfred nodded. 'There's a goat track leading down. Fallen

trees and bracken will keep us out of sight. When they strike, we could be as close as fifty yards behind them.'

Blackstone turned to his squire. 'John, pass the word back. We move quietly behind skinners lying in ambush in a forest not far ahead.'

Once the men reached the treeline, they dismounted and followed Renfred's lead. The creak of saddles and scuff of footfall were swallowed by the groaning trees swaying in the wind. Ghostly shrouds of mist clung to branches. Blackstone peered through the murk, unable at first to see the waiting enemy. As mist shifted and a horse adjusted its weight, its rider was obliged to correct his balance. The movement drew Blackstone's eye. From that one man, he let his gaze go from one tree trunk to another, penetrating ever deeper into the dense forest, seeing the shadows that were routiers who waited quietly.

Blackstone's men settled their horses with a tight rein, a hand on their muzzles. It was not long before they heard rather than saw William Ashford's escort approach. A voice asked where they would rest for food. It was time to mount while Ashford's approach held the routiers' attention. Blackstone stood in his stirrups, peered through the low branches, and through the stubborn mist saw an indistinct movement on the track below. It was enough to tell him Ashford was about to be attacked. He drew Wolf Sword and felt the comfort of its grip, then tightened its blood knot on his wrist. The bastard horse raised its misshapen head, ears forward, nostrils flared, smelling the air. Tension rippled through its muscles. Blackstone took another turn of rein in his left hand. If the malevolent beast plunged forward, it would cause havoc.

The bastard horse's senses were keener even than Blackstone's. A moment before the horsemen further down the slope spurred their horses to attack, the beast launched itself forward. Blackstone felt the warning as power gathered in its haunches. He cursed, fought the rein, gripped with his legs. The war horse leapt a fallen tree and charged through the undergrowth of saplings, fern and brush. Blackstone ducked and weaved to avoid low-lying branches. The rush of horsemen at his back were barely seconds behind him. An avalanche of horseflesh and fighting men thundered down on the unsuspecting routiers, who tried to turn in the tight confines of the trees. Defeated by their own ranks, with cries of panic they spurred down onto the road where William Ashford's men, already alerted by Blackstone's unplanned assault, spurred their mounts another twenty yards down the track, then turned to face the enemy, barricading Sancha Ferrandes in their midst for safety.

The routiers plunged down the bank onto the track in disarray. Yanking reins and raking spurs, they saw their intended victims armed and ready, blocking the road. They were trapped. They whirled to face the enemy at their rear as sudden violence burst from the trees.

Blackstone's beast barged the first horse as Blackstone swung a lethal blow that severed its rider's arm below the shoulder. Blood gushed; the horse fell, crushing its fatally wounded rider. Its hooves lashed other horses, which panicked and reared as their riders fought to control them, giving Blackstone's men a lethal advantage.

Meulon swung a flanged mace, crushing bone and rendering men helpless, slumping from useless shattered sword arms, easy prey for the swordsmen swirling around them. It was carnage, the pitiful whinnying of wounded horses outdone by men's screams as hardened steel buried itself into chest and stomach. Innards spilled across one man's saddle as his desperate hands tried to scoop them back. Sancha Ferrandes screamed at the gruesome horror as the man's horse trampled his guts. John Jacob put the man out of his misery.

Renfred and two of his men gave chase to four mercenaries who tried to escape. Their mounts were stronger and faster than the routiers', who were struck down from behind, unable to pivot their horses on the narrow road. The ambush site was a slaughterhouse. Bodies lay scattered. Riderless horses cantered free and then stopped, uncertain where to go, their saddles and flanks sluiced with their riders' blood. Four horses lay mortally wounded. Some of Blackstone's men dismounted and cut the horses' throats, then went among those routiers writhing in pain and despatched them also.

Blackstone nudged the beast that had begun the attack towards Ashford, whose escort had remained as a cut-off group to box their enemy on the track.

'William, all is well?'

'They didn't even get close, Sir Thomas.'

'Then the woman is unharmed?' said Blackstone, peering past his captain to where the slim figure of Sancha Ferrandes waited with her guardians.

'I am unharmed,' she called.

'Good. Then we ride on.'

'My lord,' she said. 'The convent at Roncesvalles might not be so welcoming to men covered in their enemy's blood. Or their own.'

Her eyes told him he was wounded. He reached around to the back of his left shoulder with his sword arm. His fingers came away bloody. 'It's nothing. And we are not going to Roncesvalles. There is another place that cares for pilgrims on the Way of St James. You will be safe there. You are now under the protection of the Prince of Wales and Aquitaine.' He heeled the bastard horse closer to her. 'And me.'

CHAPTER TWENTY

Convent of Santo Domingo de Estella
Navarre

The Sierra de Santiago de Lóquiz rose up from the valley where the convent nestled in the small town of Estella. Blackstone had led the men across the Río Ega at Puente de la Cárcel half a mile north of the convent.

The booming thud from Meulon's curled fist echoed as he beat three times on the arched timber doors.

'Not too hard, Meulon,' said Blackstone, leaning on the bastard horse's withers. 'We don't want them to hear us in the next town.'

'Or the French King in Paris,' said Renfred.

Sancha Ferrandes did not understand the men's banter. She looked from one to the other. William Ashford gave her a reassuring smile.

'And we don't want to pay for damages,' said Aicart.

The throat-cutter grinned and took a step back as the door was opened by a monk. He stood uncertainly as he faced the phalanx of dirt-encrusted men staring down at him from horseback. His trepidation was not eased by the size of the man in whose shadow he stood.

His nervousness was added to by the brusque manner of the scar-faced man who led the soldiers.

'You speak French?'

The monk looked uncertain for a moment. He nodded. 'We have many French pilgrims who come this way. Yes.'

'Who's in charge here?' said Blackstone.

'We are at our studies,' said the monk.

'That's not what I asked. Is there an abbess? An abbot? Who?'

'Yes, yes, we... we are a place of learning. We teach Latin and Arabic. We have both nuns and monks – a few brothers only – in separate houses of course, and so it depends on who... I mean... for what reason... you, er... you wish to speak...'

Blackstone dismounted. 'The good Lord was a patient man. I am not. Who serves the pilgrims? Who attends to their needs on their way to Compostela?'

The monk backed away, looked at the door and spread his arms across the entrance defiantly. 'No soldiers or weapons are permitted.'

Blackstone, spoke calmly, offering no threat. 'You offer sanctuary?'

'Yes.'

'I need sanctuary.'

The stricken monk had no time to think as Blackstone eased him out of his way. He signalled John Jacob. 'Bring her.' He nudged the monk. 'Lead the way.'

He followed the monk into a near-dark passage and then stepped into the light of the inner cloisters that framed a kitchen garden. His squire and Sancha Ferrandes of Castile followed.

'Is that the abbess?' said Blackstone to the monk, pointing at an elderly nun bent double, attending to a basket of gathered food.

'Yes.'

'All right, you can go.'

The monk seemed uncertain, but Blackstone's glare made him scurry away to disappear behind another door. Blackstone gestured John Jacob to go no further and then approached the elderly abbess, who was dressed in a brown tunic with a white headdress covered by black cloth.

'Mother Abbess,' said Blackstone as the woman straightened to face him. He looked at her gnarled hands, hands that were used to hard work, fingertips ink-stained. Her face, despite her obvious age, had a smoothness to its skin. It was a complexion bathed in devotion and prayer.

She nodded.

'You care for pilgrims who are sick or injured on the Way of St James?'

'Of course. Are you in need of help, my son?'

'No, but there is someone in need of sanctuary and who will gladly serve you for that privilege.'

The abbess looked to where Jacob waited with Sancha Ferrandes. She frowned.

'Is she here under duress?'

'Here instead of death.'

The abbess looked uncertain. 'We take no woman of poor virtue here.'

'Then you will welcome this Christian lady with open arms. Treat her with kindness and she will share your burden.' He took a step closer, stooped so only she could hear. Cloisters could carry even a whisper. 'Treat her unkindly and I will hear of it.'

No further explanation was needed.

The abbess led Blackstone through the cloisters to an adjoining building.

'We house laywomen here in the *beaterio*,' she said. 'She will be treated as a lay sister.'

Blackstone nodded. It was suitable in its simplicity. Little in the way of creature comforts.

He followed the abbess to a small room. A modest, wooden-hewn crucifix hung on the wall behind a table, edges worn smooth where her arms had rested over the years. She sat down, opened a ledger, picked up a quill and dipped its sharpened point into an inkwell and looked up at the rough-hewn man who loomed over her.

'It would be a courtesy to know who you are and who it is you have brought into our care,' said the abbess. 'We keep a record of all those who enter and stay within our walls. We do not divulge their names to anyone.'

'Then why keep a record?' said Blackstone. He felt out of place in the small room. He was too big for the space. It was meant for slightly built women, nuns and novices who would stand hands clasped before the abbess. Blackstone had already had to bend low to get through the door and now, looking down on the elderly woman, felt obliged to remain stooped like a chastised child in front of a teacher.

'You may walk to the rear of the convent and look at the names we place on the graves. Many served here for most of their lives. Their names were long forgotten when they embraced Christ and took a name of our, or their, choosing. It is fitting that they are remembered.'

'My name is unimportant, and as for the woman, it is up to her to tell you how she wishes to be known. If a record must be kept, then have her written down as a lady of Castile.'

The abbess's beatific smile never wavered. Blackstone wondered if it was a mask that hid intent to do harm. He had little trust in the Church and those who called down the wrath of God on fighting men.

She nodded. 'Very well. As you wish. Do you know when you will return for her?'

'No. I might have to send others to take her to the next place of safety.'

'Then how will I know who it is that I can trust?'

'They will say I sent them.'

'But you do not wish to disclose your name.'

Blackstone fell silent. It was an obvious problem the abbess had raised.

'To tell you my name might place her in jeopardy if anyone came looking for her.'

The woman's apparently kindly demeanour considered him for a moment. 'Then should you send another in your place shall we agree on a message that indicates they are your men?'

'Yes, a word or a phrase.'

The abbess paused and then wrote four words. Tearing the scrap of parchment, she handed it to him.

'I don't understand Latin,' said Blackstone.

'There is no need. Send that with your messenger and we will let the lady go with whomever you send.'

'But its meaning?'

She extended her hand for him to return it. '*Res est sacra miser.* A person in distress is a sacred object,' she said. 'That's what it means. It is appropriate. But we will not release her from our care without this.' She rolled the scrap and slid it into a small, boiled-leather cylinder, hard like iron, which had a strip of leather holding a cap to seal it. She gave it back to him. He slipped its leather thong over his neck and tucked the cylinder, no bigger than his little finger, under his collar.

'She will attend to the pilgrims and undertake whatever duties you ask of her. She is strong and uncomplaining,' said Blackstone.

The abbess stood and faced him. 'And until you return,

she will be embraced and protected.' She looked at his bloodstained gambeson. 'And what of your wounds?'

Blackstone glanced at his shoulder. 'A cut, nothing more.'

'Do you intend to return for this lady of Castile?'

'I've said so, haven't I?' he said, irritation sharpening his answer. The wound was nagging him as the torn flesh was rubbed raw by his shirt, coarse now from dried blood and sweat.

'Then you will let me take you to the infirmary and have your wound cleaned. If it is not attended to poison can seep into flesh and then you will never see that lady again.' Her questioning look suggested she knew Blackstone was more than the woman's escort. That his threat against the convent should she be mistreated spoke more of the man's feelings than his duty.

Sancha Ferrandes was shown to her cell. Light from the small high window flooded the stone walls. There was a cot with a straw mattress covered with a blanket. A bowl and jug of water for washing rested on a simple wooden stand. The abbess instructed a novice to bring a simple linen chemise and head covering which were dutifully laid on the cot. Blackstone waited until the girl had left and Sancha Ferrandes took stock of where she was to live.

'It will not be forever,' said Blackstone.

'That is not what your Prince said.'

'It's what I am saying. When the time is right, I will bring you out of this place, and if I cannot, then I will send someone. You will be returned to your home.'

'I have no home. Do you forget so easily?'

'Your family are landowners. Are there not places that lie beyond Pedro's grasp?'

She nodded. 'An estate in France. But it is not where my heart is.'

'Then you make that place your home until the war ends and you can reclaim your lands in Castile. Don Pedro will not live forever. He has too many enemies.'

'Would you kill him?' she said.

'I am obliged to save him,' Blackstone said.

'And if you were not under such an obligation?'

'Then vultures would already have picked his carcass clean. I lost good men, men close to my heart, and an innocent child on his orders. I have taken what revenge I can.'

He was about to leave when she touched his arm. 'Sir Thomas, the Prince cannot know that Henry of Trastámara has twelve thousand men behind him. There are many knights. Renowned families, the Knights of la Banda – the Order of the Sash, their finest – they have joined him. Three crusading orders, Calatrava, Santiago and St John, will also be at his side.' She lifted a beaded crucifix from her around her neck. 'I spoke harshly before. I ask your forgiveness. Take this so that Our good Lord and his angels will protect you.'

He curled her fingers back into her hand. 'You keep it. I have my own talisman.'

'We are all in need of a guardian angel, Sir Thomas. Belief is what protects us.'

'My dead wife is my guardian angel. Belief I leave to those who need my sword for protection.'

She studied him for a moment, nodded, kissed the small crucifix and replaced it. 'Then how long must I stay here?'

'Months, a year, no more.'

She dipped her head in acceptance. Blackstone reached inside his tunic and took out a black-handled knife. Its guard was half-curved; the hilt was inlaid with a thin filigree of ivory curling like a growing vine. It was delicate work from a skilled craftsman. The blade sat snugly in a plain scabbard. It was the knife Sancha Ferrandes had used in her assassination attempt. Blackstone laid it in his palm, hilt forward, offering it to her.

'Keep this concealed. In case it is needed.'

She looked concerned. 'Am I not safe here?'

'As safe as can be. It is always better to put your faith in something other than the Almighty.'

She held it, closing both hands over it. 'It was my father's and his father's before him. Thank you.'

Despite the cell's cool walls, Blackstone felt warmth spread through him. The longer he gazed at the woman from Castile, the more his skin prickled. He nodded, turned on his heel for the door and stopped without looking back when she called his name.

'Sir Thomas. I owe you my life. I shall never forget.'

Blackstone closed the cell door behind him.

PART FOUR

THE CLAW

CHAPTER TWENTY-ONE

Henry Blackstone and Hugh Gifford walked twenty miles inland. There was no sign of village or town settlement. A road through a dense forest beckoned, but they avoided it, wary of finding woodcutters who might see them as easy prey, as did the fishermen. Their salt-laden clothes chafed and the food they had taken from the hamlet in the dunes would be gone in another day.

'I say we find a river and wash these clothes. Darkness will protect us.'

'I've no desire to be caught in my braies, Master Blackstone. Let's walk on and find another village. These Bretons should be loyal to de Montfort.'

'And if those we find serve a master who did not fight on our side they might harbour resentment and then we'll have more than untrained fishermen to deal with. No, we stop, wash the sea from us, eat and sleep. You're limping. Another mile and your leg will not hold.'

Gifford looked to the horizon and the sky. 'All right, but I smell woodsmoke.'

Henry raised his face to the breeze. At first, he could smell only the salt marshes that stagnated in mires, and then the breeze shifted. 'Over there,' he said. 'But do we approach or keep our distance? For all we know, we are in a viper's nest of hostile peasants.'

Gifford let Henry weigh the odds.

'You think we should go and I think we should pass them by.'

'I think you need to decide, Master Blackstone.'

'I yield to your experience, Hugh. I'm not the one to lead us, I know that.'

'Aye, well, you've not done too badly so far. If we go in, we go in one at a time. That at least gives the other a chance to help if help is needed.'

'Then I will go forward once we have sight of the village.'

'Well said, but you can see that if you are attacked, then with this leg, I'll be slow off the mark to come to your aid; meanwhile, I offer a tempting opportunity for any peasant with an eye to taking my sword and boots.'

Henry considered the alternative. 'Then I am happy for you to take the risk and hope I can get to you in time if you need me.'

Gifford shook his head. 'God's tears, for an educated man you have a poor way of offering comfort.'

'It was your argument that convinced me. I studied law, Hugh. Facts don't show compassion.'

Gifford sighed, spat and trudged on. 'Lawyers and priests. Had you gone into the Church, at least I would have had a blessing.'

Henry laid a hand on his guardian's shoulder. 'Hugh, my sword is my blessing.'

A mile further on they skirted a copse of woodland beyond a stream whose bulrushes gave them cover. Through the swaying stems and bare trees they could make out a dozen huts, smoke curling from their roof holes. A child was milking a tethered goat; the sound of axe splitting wood carried on the breeze, as did the smell of hot food. Women's voices called to each other. Boys no older than five or six stacked firewood.

Henry and Gifford crouched in a ditch studying the handful of huts.

'There are other shacks deeper in the trees – more dwellings or shelter for animals?' said Henry. He scanned the copse. 'No sign of any men.'

'They'll be woodcutters, but the nearest woodland is back where we came from. And they would have likely seen us before we saw them, yet they haven't shown themselves.'

'All right,' Gifford continued, 'watch and listen for any trouble. I'll declare myself one of John de Montfort's men-at-arms and hope I've chosen the right side. We need to find horses but we must keep whatever coin we have between us out of sight until we find out where we are and where their loyalties lie.'

Gifford clambered out of the ditch and limped to where a stout plank crossed the stream. From there he was a hundred yards from the huts. Henry bent double and edged along the ditch to keep Gifford in sight, pushing himself deeper into the bulrushes. He kept his head low, peering across the top of the bank, daring to raise himself only when the boys stacking firewood turned back into the settlement. Gifford walked into the clearing and stopped. He raised a hand to show he was no threat. The women attending to their chores stopped what they were doing. Henry couldn't hear what Gifford said over the rustle of the bulrushes, but the women looked from one to the other and seemed undecided. One woman dared to take a pace forward, pointing an accusing finger. Her challenge made Gifford raise his hands as if to press back an unseen force as the women stepped closer together, forming a protective pack; one who was holding a fire iron levelled it like a sword and shouted something at Gifford. The wind was at Henry's back so the woman's words were carried away. Gifford retreated a step and then dared to cast a glance towards where Henry might be watching. It looked as though the women had the courage to attack and overwhelm the intruder in their midst, despite Gifford showing no sign of aggression. The women shuffled closer to him. Henry saw that at least two of them held knives from cutting food.

'Damn it, Hugh, draw your sword,' Henry muttered to himself.

It looked as though Gifford was retreating; he was stepping backwards slowly, watching the women spread out on his flanks like a wolf pack circling their prey.

Henry cursed, his hand reaching for his sword. He stood up, ready to ford the stream and clamber into the village. The shadow to one side blurred as it lunged forward, its approach concealed by the wind in the reed bed. Henry spun; three men glared at him, knives and axes in hand. They faltered; he saw their eyes dart past him and in that instant knew there were others behind him.

The thought was his last. Pain streaked through him and he fell face down into the water.

CHAPTER TWENTY-TWO

Clara was kissing Henry in his room in Oxford, running her tongue over his face and neck in her hunger for him. He groaned. She persisted. And then he shook himself free from her demands and the dream. A village dog lurched back, afraid of his sudden move. It cowered as he sat up painfully, hands bound behind him. He was barefoot. His boots stolen. Dried blood had attracted the dog's tongue to his face and neck. It encrusted his collar, droplets staining the front of his shirt from the blow to his head. His ankles were tied as firmly as his wrists. He stared into the gloom, focusing on his surroundings. The hut stank of goat droppings and the moving shadow tethered to a stake told him he had been thrown into an animal shelter.

Twisting around, he saw Gifford lying on his side facing him, similarly tied, with one eye swollen and closed, blood-matted beard and -encrusted lips. His chest rattled when he coughed and he spat out phlegm and blood.

'Just as well I went in first so you could move fast and rescue me,' he said. Then he fell into a wheezing coughing fit, causing him to groan in pain. 'Bastards have broken a rib, I reckon.'

Hugh Gifford could have slain a dozen women and the mange-ridden cur that darted in, jaws snapping at his legs, but when the men appeared dragging an unconscious Henry, he knew he had no choice but to surrender if he was to save young Blackstone's life. If the lad were already dead, they wouldn't be hauling him into the village. Fighting every instinct bred into him to stand his ground and make an enemy pay dearly before being killed, he unbuckled his sword and waited for the beating he knew would follow.

'They came up behind me,' Henry said lamely.

'Aye, well, I should hope that if they'd attacked from the front you might have killed at least a couple of them.'

Henry had let Gifford down and he knew it. Now their fate was in the hands of woodcutters. 'You only had women to face,' he said defensively.

'And you'd have me hack them down? Merciful Christ, you had one thing to do and one thing only.'

'All right! I'm sorry. I was in the bulrushes when they jumped me.'

'Moses did a better job of escaping Herod's men, and he was a babe. I thought you had your father's instincts.' He coughed and sighed. Talking was taking its toll. 'All right, lad. No need for me to chastise you. They knew their ground and you were watching me. It is what it is.'

The man-at-arms's admonishment had found its mark. Henry did not have his father's ability or instincts. Few did. And as much as he thought himself to have courage enough to stand his ground and kill if he had to, he had not honed his fighting skills to the point where his senses were as keen as those of a wild animal. He fell silent. The rope's bite on his wrists was a welcome distraction from the shame he felt.

'They think we're skinners,' said Gifford. He rolled, grunting with effort, so that he could sit upright, back pressed against the wall. 'And they've been raided and suffered from them over the years. They don't know who John de Montfort is or that he and the English control Brittany. They're peasants. They know who's in the next village and which lord takes their taxes.'

'Then if we can speak to their local lord, we will be freed.'

Gifford spat a globule of blood from his mouth. 'You think so, Master Henry?' he said sarcastically. 'There are Breton and Norman lords who pay for captured skinners. No matter who they are, English, Gascon, German. Routier companies scorch the earth. If they're caught, they're executed. We could be dragged out of here and taken to the nearest town. It's good entertainment to see mercenaries killed in a public square.'

Fear and regret crawled in Henry's belly. His actions had brought them to this place. But there was no time to make any plan to escape. Men came into the goat shed and hauled Gifford away, then came back for Henry. He saw his guardian had not resisted. That made sense. They were helpless and would only invite another beating if they struggled. If there *was* any chance of escape, they would need their strength.

At first glance there were thirty men, women and children gathered in the clearing. Henry's captors threw him on the ground next to Gifford. Thirty yards away on the track, two men-at-arms sat on their horses talking to one of the villagers. A cart stood behind the two horsemen. The village spokesman was too far away for Henry to hear what was being said, but it obviously concerned him and Gifford. Another villager ran up with Gifford and Henry's swords. The horseman nodded and signalled for the two prisoners to be brought forward. They were manhandled to the cart where half a dozen other men were bound and looked to have suffered a similar beating to that Henry and Gifford had endured. Scraps of half-eaten rotting fruit on the wagon's floor told Henry these men had been on the road for days.

One man lay huddled, a bound hand clasped to a wound in his side. There was barely enough room for Henry and Gifford as they were punched and kicked to scramble up into the cart. The cart's driver stood ready with shackles and chain, locking each man's legs and passing the chain through a restraining bolt on the cart's floor. Once secured, their weapons were pushed into the space behind the driver's seat.

The cart jolted forward. The villagers ran alongside, jeering, and spat at the prisoners. One of the men, hair and beard matted with dirt and blood, half raised himself and gave a snarling roar of defiance. The villagers fell back. The man roared with laughter.

'You are sheep,' he bellowed at them. 'That's why we kill you.'

His outburst made the other men in the cart smile, but, once they had trundled away from the village, they let their heads drop onto their chests. The uneven road made the cart bounce and sway, a creaking, slow-moving land boat that rocked men to sleep. Exhaustion and pain lulled Henry into his own escape.

What sun could be seen behind the clouds had moved across the sky by the time he awoke. The man opposite him had kicked his foot. Henry shivered. He was thirsty and cold. Blearily, he studied the black-eyed man with his gaunt features and hollow cheeks. Henry had seen this look before, on men who had endured days of battle. It spoke of suffering but also of cruel indifference.

'You're no skinner, you've barely whiskers.' He was an Englishman.

'I'm not,' said Henry. 'We were shipwrecked.'

'A sailor, then?' said the mercenary, clearly unconcerned about his fate.

'No, a passenger,' Henry said.

The mercenary seemed bemused. The others waited to see what the man had to say next.

'Not a soldier, not a sailor, a traveller. A man who has money to pay for a ship's passage.'

'I had only a little money. I was a student.'

'A student? Of what?'

'Many things.'

'A wise man, then. Someone who knows the world through books, off on a big adventure.' His sarcasm made the others snigger.

Henry nodded towards the wounded man slumped on the floor of the cart. 'Wise enough to smell your friend's wound is turning bad and you could help him.'

'Help him? He's a dead man.'

'Is that how you treat men who fight at your side?' Henry didn't wait for an answer. 'Pick maggots out of those apples and put them on the wound. He'll have a chance.'

The mercenary's mouth gaped in disbelief and then he laughed. 'You'd have the maggots eat him before he gets put in the ground?'

'Open his shirt, put the maggots on the wound and they eat the bad flesh.'

One of the other men leaned forward and scooped a handful of rotten apple, fingering out the maggots. His companion did the same. 'It's worth a try. He's dead anyway if we don't,' said the older of the two men. His beard had been scraped down to bristles and his short hair was shot through iron and silver.

'Tear a length of shirt and put it over the wound once you've put the maggots in there. Press them into the pus,' Henry told him.

The wounded man groaned. 'All right, Robert,' said the older man attending to the wound. 'You're not dead yet. Stop yer complaining. Like a bloody old woman who's fallen out of bed.'

The grizzled-looking man did exactly as Henry had instructed.

'All right, lad. You seem to know what you're talking about. I am Walter Mallin.' He fussed over the dressing on the wound. 'This is my friend, Robert Helyer. He took a blade meant for me.' He pointed to the men in the cart. 'The big-nosed Frenchman there is Raymond Vachon, man next to him is a Gascon, Arnald Bezián, and the ugly bastard with half a shaved head is Eckehart Brun. He's the only German we had riding with us.'

'And who are you?' said Henry, looking away from Mallin towards the antagonist who had scorned the villagers.

'If you can smell a man's rotting guts then you should smell trouble when it looks you in the face. I don't trust strangers, and I don't answer to a snot-nosed brat with barely a whisker on his face. You're going to be hanged along with the rest of us. Your hacked limbs will swing on meat hooks at a crossroads. Clever bastards like you die no different than the likes of us.'

'You mercenary scum deserve what you get. He's an innocent in all of this,' said Gifford.

'And you're his pet guard dog, are you?' said the routier.

'Keep your mouth shut and leave us alone,' Gifford warned him.

'Or what? You'll lick your balls and fart, then beg for a bone?'

The men laughed.

Gifford lunged with his bound feet for the man's face. The mercenary reared back. The strike was halted by the restraining bolt on the floor. The failed assault was meaningless: a gesture from one fighting man to another. It was ignored, meriting no further verbal threats, but both knew that if the opportunity arose, they would face each other.

'Hugh, leave it be,' said Henry. He addressed the belligerent mercenary. 'I was trying to get to Bordeaux. My father is there. He serves the Prince.'

'Bordeaux? Aye, we heard they're heading into Spain. We decided there was better picking to be had here.' He nodded towards the other prisoners. 'We ran into a spot of bother though.' Then he turned his attention back to Henry. 'Going to join the war, were you? Was that your plan?' He snorted and spat over the side of the cart. 'Looking for glory?' He leered at the others, who all knew the truth. 'No glory in war, boy. Blood and spilled guts, men with arms and legs hacked off. Men screaming. There's your glory. Some looting, maybe some rape.'

'My father hangs rapists,' said Henry.

Henry's comment lifted men's heads from their chests to glare at him. A man who could order other men's deaths was either of high birth or a routier captain with a reputation. Either way, it made Henry's interrogator regard him with cautious respect.

'He does, does he? Then he'd be a man of rank.'

'Why are you afraid to tell my friend and me your name?' said Henry, ignoring the man's probing.

'Afraid?'

'Of revealing who you are in case there's a bigger price on your head than any other man here? Are you one of the great routier leaders? Gourney, Latimer? Perhaps you're Robert Briquet – he commanded a Breton company – or Hugh Calveley. Now there would be a prize.'

Henry's knowledge of the legendary mercenary captains made the man opposite him cautious. 'I rode with Sir Hugh.' He jerked his head to nowhere in particular. 'Fought with him at Auray not thirty miles from here. He's a commander among men is Calveley. Rode with him down to Spain after that. Made good money.'

'Then you fought against the Prince?'

'What? No, Sir Hugh wouldn't have any of that. He wouldn't put Englishmen against the Prince. We rode with Chandos. Killed Castilians and some heathen Moors.'

'If you rode with Sir Hugh then you rode with my father.'

The man's face creased, searching his memory. He was being tested.

'There were many men on the field at Auray. Too many to remember,' said the mercenary. Then, remembering what Henry had said earlier about his father hanging rapists: 'We left the field of battle and days later came across some prisoners held by a company of men who had fought at our side. Sir Hugh wanted them to join us. But they said no.' He paused, eyes resting on Henry. 'We heard later that their leader had hanged the prisoners at the crossroads. That man was Thomas Blackstone.' He leaned forward, gazing hard at Henry, who showed no reaction to anything the man had said. 'Who else would hang men for taking their pleasure where they find it? Blackstone is who. The King's Master of War. Is he your father?'

Henry ignored him, looking away to the high walls of a castle lying on the edge of a river. Men were scurrying up and down a lacework of timber scaffolding. Stonemasons shouted instructions to where they wanted their working platforms. The city gates were opening. 'Where is this place?'

The men followed his gaze. They could hear a raucous crowd as they drew nearer. Walter Mallin, the older man caring for his wounded comrade, called to Bezián. 'Arnald, is this Josselin? The Lord of Rohan's castle.'

'We must be further south than I thought,' said Bezián.

'It doesn't matter,' said Mallin. 'The crowd thirsts for our blood.' He turned to Henry. 'If you have a God, pray to him, lad. This is where we die.'

CHAPTER TWENTY-THREE

The horsemen led the cart through the gates. Garrison soldiers kept the people back as it trundled over the rutted track. News of the routiers being brought in had somehow reached the town, and the mob pressed hard against the soldiers. One burly character wearing a butcher's apron lunged through the ranks, hurling himself against the cart, hauling himself up, boning knife in hand.

Hugh Gifford pushed Henry aside, twisted and punched the man's face. His nose split and he tumbled back into the crowd.

'We get a chance, we need to fight our way out of here,' he said.

'Aye, better to die with a sword in our fist than strung up like a dog and gutted,' said Vachon. 'I will die first because I am French. They will show me no mercy.'

'That gives us all a better chance to fight then,' said the antagonistic mercenary.

'Fuck you,' said Vachon.

The cart pulled into a darkened archway. A man Henry took to be the garrison commander instructed his men to unlock the captives' chains. Then spears prodded them into a dungeon down a narrow cut-stone stairway. Mallin and Vachon helped carry their barely conscious comrade.

The stench of soiled straw and an overflowing latrine bucket assailed their senses. The humid dungeon's ceiling had a cowl of smoke from a burning torch held in a wall bracket. A turn in the narrow passage led into darkness.

A man called in a weak voice: 'Food, give me food.'

'Quiet, bastard!' the jailer shouted. 'Or I'll throw your shit bucket over you.'

He held the cell's iron gate open as soldiers herded Henry and the others down. Once inside the half-lit cell, they saw another prisoner hunched in the corner.

The jailer slammed closed the door and put a bucket of water with a ladle in reach through the bars. 'You can drink. Thirsty men with dry throats don't scream loud enough when they're gutted.' He laughed and turned away, disappearing into the darkness.

'Merciful Christ, you quarter me and I'll scream these walls down,' said Walter Mallin. 'Dry throat or not.'

Henry reached for the water ladle and took it to the dying man, dribbled water into his parched lips, then handed the ladle to Gifford who took his share and handed it to the next man. They drank thirstily. Henry eased open the dying man's blood-caked shirt. The maggots had eaten into the discoloured flesh.

'Well, lad, your idea looks to be working. Too late for him, though,' said Walter Mallin.

'Too late for all of us, you stupid bastard,' said the unfriendly mercenary.

Mallin nodded towards him. 'His name's John Terrel. The meanest among us.'

'You should learn to keep your mouth shut, old man,' Terrel snarled. 'A man's name is his own business.'

Gifford stepped between Terrel and the crouching man.

'This is no place to fight among ourselves,' said Gifford.

For a moment it looked as though Terrel would strike out, but the steadfast Gifford stared him down, and Terrel backed away to slouch against the wall.

The German nudged the toe of his boot against the prisoner who occupied the cell and had not moved. 'Who are you?'

'Me? My name is unimportant. I'm to die tomorrow. Before they hang and gut you.'

'You're an Englishman. A routier?' said Brun.

'Of course. Who isn't these days?' said the ragged-looking individual.

Gifford joined the German to question the man. 'Who else is down here?'

'One other. He's down the passage in another cage. Garnier. He'll die before me. He's French. They hate French skinners more than anyone. See them all as traitors.'

Vachon crossed himself.

'How were you captured?' said Gifford.

'We needed food so we raided a village. The peasants had left for safety behind a town's walls. They took their livestock and burned everything else. So we attacked the town. Damned nearly took it as well. Lost a dozen and more men. I was captured and sold to the local lord here.'

'Who was your captain?'

'Jean de Soissons.'

'The Claw?' said Arnald Bezián

The prisoner smiled. 'La Griffe. That's him.'

'Who is he?' said Henry.

'He's one of the most notorious skinners in Brittany,' said the Gascon.

'Aye, and has a price on his head with the French and the English,' said Terrel.

'He escaped from the attack?' said Henry.

'He did. The bastard abandoned ten of us when we were cornered. Saved himself,' the prisoner said. 'I'd put a knife in his throat myself if I could. Too late now. They hanged and quartered seven of my comrades these past two days. Then sewed the others into a sack and threw them in the river. I'm alive because it took them all the hours of daylight to enjoy their sport.'

Their gruesome fate silenced the men.

'If we are to die together, it would be better to know whom we die alongside,' said Henry.

The prisoner shrugged. 'I am Alfred Vaisey.'

'You know where he is, this la Griffe?' said Henry.

'I've a good idea for what good it'll do me now. I told these bastards where he was hiding to try and save my skin, but they were too scared to ride against him. They want our blood. Our screams are music to their ears.'

'How many garrison soldiers are there here?'

The prisoner shrugged. 'I don't know.'

Henry turned to the others. 'How many did we see?'

'Twenty perhaps,' said Brun.

'Another dozen on the walls with crossbows,' said Gifford.

'Walter?' said Henry. 'You've known towns like this – how many men would a local lord have behind its walls?'

'Forty, perhaps a handful more. If he had served the King, then he would have fought and lost men in battle. Aye, forty is about right. No more, I would say. Footsoldiers mostly, perhaps a dozen horsemen.'

Henry nodded and turned to the cell bars. He gazed out into the dim light from the spluttering torch. Through the darkness and up those steps lay their fate. He was not ready to die.

'If we stand together, we have a chance,' said Henry, turning back to the men.

'Every man for himself,' said Terrel.

'Listen to the lad,' the Gascon, Bezián, said. 'He's right. If we get to our weapons, we kill as many as we can and get over the walls.'

'You'll never get out of here alive,' said Henry. 'Those crossbowmen on the walls will cut us down even if we get past the soldiers in the square. We live if we use our brains.'

Walter Mallin cradled the dying man. 'Then we're dead men. Look about you, lad, we're fighting men. We follow our instincts.'

'If we give these people what they want, then we have a chance to live,' Henry told them.

'They've got that already,' said Brun. 'Us.'

'They want la Griffe more,' said Henry.

Gifford stared hard at the man he was supposed to protect. While the others did not yet comprehend what Henry suggested, the man-at-arms did. 'You're going to trade us for the Claw. How?'

'By convincing them we can,' said Henry.

'You're a fool,' said Terrel. 'But you have a way with words.'

'And if I find the way to bring in la Griffe, I will need men with me who will not desert once we are beyond these walls.'

The mercenaries looked at each other, uncertain whether the young man in their midst had lost his mind or might be clever enough to devise a plan.

Eckehart Brun nodded. 'All right. You save my neck and I'll ride with you. I give you my pledge.'

'Your word? You're a skinner!' Terrel sneered.

The big German faced him. 'My word is good. Yours is worth less than dog shit on my boot.'

Bezián stood next to Mallin. 'Him and me, we fought together for the King. I will give you my pledge.'

'Aye. Me too,' said Mallin.

Vachon nodded. 'Yes. You have a plan and it works, then we will ride with you.'

Hugh Gifford stared at Terrel. 'You'll die alone, then.'

The belligerent Terrel was cornered and he knew it. 'There

is no plan. There cannot be a plan.' He looked from one man to the other. 'You're damned fools. All right. You get us out of this and I'll serve you.'

'Terrel, you betray us or you run and we will hunt you down and kill you,' said Henry.

The threatened routier scowled and nodded. 'But will you convince them to let us hunt down la Griffe?'

Henry looked at his companion, Gifford. In that instant, the man-at-arms knew Henry did not have an answer.

CHAPTER TWENTY-FOUR

The next morning, Garnier, the unfortunate prisoner in the next cell, was dragged out by the guards. He fought and screamed, begging for mercy. One of the soldiers punched him in his stomach. He folded and they dragged him up the narrow staircase. Henry and the others heard the roar of the crowd as Garnier was taken outside, and they all fell into a fearful silence. Moments later, the first screams echoed through the stone walls. A banshee terrorizing the men awaiting death.

The gasps of the crowd told them that the man was being eviscerated. A final baleful howl of agony gripped them. A raptor's talon clawing deep into the innards.

Walter Mallin crossed himself and whispered a plea for help from the Lord Christ.

The surge of voices outside faltered, and then hushed quickly, followed by a roar of delight which told the condemned men that, following the disembowelling, the man's limbs had been severed and finally his head.

Footsteps scraped down the staircase. A dozen soldiers crammed into the space, their leader instructing the jailer to open the cell door. Spears were lowered to keep the routiers under control as Vachon was pulled forward, his hands manacled, and the chain fed through to the next man, Bezián.

'Better to die here than outside,' said Gifford.

'We have one chance out there,' said Henry. 'We must take it.'

Terrel backed into a corner. He cursed and spat his contempt. 'There's only twelve of them. We could take them.'

Henry was being manacled next to Gifford. 'And you wouldn't get past the door at the top of the stairs.'

Terrel resisted but got a split lip for his trouble and was soon chained like the others.

Walter Mallin was forced to carry his semi-conscious friend. Brun, the broad-shouldered German, turned and defied a spear to take the man's weight from the older mercenary. Once the men were chained together, they were prodded up the steps behind the guard commander. The light outside dazzled them after their gloomy cell. And as soon as Vachon stepped onto the outside steps the townspeople roared. One by one the men shuffled out and stood in a line along a low parapet before the crowd below. Directly to their front a pug-faced man who appeared to be in charge stood facing them; Henry took him to be the garrison captain. He wore a sword and tunic bearing a faded blazon on his chest. His left sleeve was pinned halfway up his missing arm. A priest stood by his side. Arrayed behind them were the town officials, men of some importance by the look of them. Probably merchants, Henry thought, given they were dressed in their finery.

The chained men stared across at a gibbet less than fifty paces away, a raised platform where a headless carcass was held by ropes and meat hooks. The man's stomach had been split open, his entrails still sizzling in a brazier below where his legs would have been. His head was on a pole, each of his limbs hanging from the gibbet.

Henry and the others knew the man had been alive when they disembowelled him, letting his innards fall like slop into the hot coals. Once cooled, they would be fed to the town's dogs.

The crowd roared, chanting for more gruesome deaths.

The garrison commander stepped forward. He raised his sword arm. The crowd obeyed and their voices fell to an inaudible murmur.

'You scum will die today. Your limbs will be hung on every crossroads leading to this place.'

'Is that where we'll find your missing arm?' said Terrel defiantly. He had nothing to lose.

The taunt earned him a blow from one of the soldiers. Terrel almost went onto his knees but, ignoring the pain, straightened up defiantly.

'Where is this place?' said Henry, taking a step forward, closer to the town's commander. 'A man has a right to know who it is that tortures and kills him.'

The question startled the commander. Condemned men usually begged for their lives, rather than asking where it was they were to die.

Hugh Gifford stared at the faded blazon on the captain's tunic. 'Those are Rohan's colours, I'm sure of it.'

The captain strode forward. His snarling face told Henry he was about to take a beating.

Henry stared directly into the approaching man's eyes. 'Tell me your name? When my father hears of it, he will visit his wrath on you and this place. My father is Sir Thomas Blackstone. I am his son, Henry.'

Henry might as well have struck the man himself. He stopped in his tracks. Henry's fellow prisoners looked round in disbelief. All except Gifford.

Henry nodded towards the man's blazon. 'You serve the House of Rohan. I withdraw my question. This must be Josselin. I am not your enemy. France and England are not at war. There is a truce between us. It is the routiers who are our common enemy.'

The priest placed a hand on the captain's shoulder and

lowered his voice so that only the captain could hear. Whatever was said, the captain's expression remained uncertain. The crowd, sensing there was an interruption to their spectacle, raised their voices again. The captain turned and bellowed at them to be quiet. The man's reputation must have been fearsome, for they obeyed immediately. He turned back to Henry.

'You travel with scum. They are the enemy.'

'I travel to join my father, who is with the Prince in Bordeaux. This man at my side is Hugh Gifford. He is a sworn man to Thomas Beauchamp, Earl of Warwick. He is my guide.'

Gifford exhaled a held breath, relieved that Henry had not mentioned he was also supposed to be his protector. That protector and protected were both chained and moments from death would have given the mob further cause for jeering amusement.

'And these other men were helping me in another matter,' said Henry.

Henry's story irritated the garrison commander. 'There is no other matter. They're skinners. They are the plague.'

Henry stepped forward as far as the chains permitted. He raised his voice and spoke over the captain's head to the crowd. 'Who among you remember the name Ronec le Bête? The man who burned and killed across Brittany?'

The captain turned to face the rising wave of anger from the townspeople. Cries of *killer, rapist, murderer*.

Henry waited until their passionate anger subsided enough for him to be heard. He raised his voice, his eyes scanning the distorted faces of the crowd, seeking to appease their hostility. 'Ronec le Bête. The Beast was hunted down and killed by my father, Sir Thomas Blackstone. He rid you of the terror. He defended the people of Brittany!'

Henry did not know whether these people would believe

that the English King's Master of War had defended them, but his father's legend was known across France and that was their only chance of not ending up on meat hooks. 'I am his son. I am Henry Blackstone and I came here to hunt another who has raided and killed across every village in Brittany. I came here to hunt down and deliver to you Jean de Soissons. La Griffe.'

A few voices cheered. Then others joined in. Soon the crowd was chanting: '*Kill la Griffe. Kill la Griffe.*'

The wild inaccuracy of his story had the men with him muttering curses of disbelief beneath their breath but Henry's desperate make-believe was their only chance. He shouted as loud as he could to the bloodthirsty townspeople: 'I will bring you la Griffe. These men know where he hides. You want blood? I will give you blood. I will give you la Griffe!'

The garrison commander stared at the agitated crowd. They had been given the torture and mutilation of one mercenary, had that been enough for the day? This young man, who stood head and shoulders over him, might just as well have thrown gold coins in their midst. Now they thirsted for more.

'You've rallied the crowd behind you,' said the one-armed captain. 'It won't be enough to save you.'

Henry shrugged and looked at the priest. '*Et vitam impendere vero.*'

He saw the priest's surprise that an apparently common man could speak Latin.

'He said what?' said the captain to the priest.

'He stakes his life on the truth,' said the priest.

The captain pointed at the English routier, Vaisey. 'He dies today. He rode with la Griffe.'

'No, my lord, he must live because he is the man who can take us to la Griffe,' said Henry.

Henry had flattered the garrison commander by using an

honorific he could never expect to earn. Titles and wealth came from valour in battle and ransoming other lords. Or from marriage, and what chance would a one-armed veteran of the wars have of marrying an heiress? But such an honour might also be awarded to those who rid a domain of a killer who inflicted terror.

'You're a smooth-tongued, clever bastard, Master Blackstone,' said the commander.

Henry nodded. 'So I am told.'

'You expect me to let you and these men go? Because you are Thomas Blackstone's son? If you *are* his son.'

The captain brushed dirt off Hugh Gifford's gambeson. The faded blazon of chevron and crosses revealed itself. 'Then you are Warwick's man,' he said. 'That much at least is true.'

'Until the day I die,' said Gifford.

'And you would die for this man?' he said, meaning Henry.

'I am commanded to do so if my life saves his.'

'Then you will stay as ransom to make sure he returns with what's promised.' He turned his attention to Henry. 'You will leave tomorrow. Be back here by first light three days from now with your prize or your friend will endure the blade and the scaffold.' He paused, looking at the wretched men and Blackstone's arrogant son. 'How will you capture la Griffe?'

'I will give him what he wants. This town and castle.'

CHAPTER TWENTY-FIVE

Henry and the six men had been travelling for the better part of the day. Henry had been taken to the captain's quarters where he convinced him of his plan and how he would return. A trap was set for when the notorious killer entered the castle. Henry knew the one-armed veteran would be ready. Henry also knew Gifford would die a gruesome death if he failed.

The horses supplied by the garrison were rounceys of poor quality, little use if they had to be spurred into a fight, but they served the purpose for Henry and the others to reach the camp of Jean de Soissons, the Claw, which Vaisey assured Blackstone lay beyond the forest. The dull sky flattened shadows in the trees as they rode along a single track through the woodland. The darkened interior offered easy concealment for anyone wishing to ambush travellers, even though the track was less frequented than any road. The dense forest served to keep everyone out apart from unwary, lost travellers, or men with a darker purpose.

The older fighter, Walter Mallin, was less concerned about an ambush from la Griffe's men than he was about his wounded comrade, Robert Helyer, left behind in the walled town with its bloodthirsty mob. The two men had stood shoulder to shoulder over the years. War and age had taken its toll on both of them and the thought of abandoning a friend and fighting comrade weighed heavily on Mallin. It was, at least, some consolation that Gifford had pledged to care for the wounded man.

They rode in column led by Henry Blackstone and the English mercenary, Vaisey. Behind Mallin was Vachon with Terrel, followed by the German and Bezián. Terrel had kept up a constant muttering about being vulnerable to ambush in the dense forest. Everyone ignored him until Brun told him to stitch his lips. A handful of men riding with no sign of wealth or supplies were unlikely to attract a routier renowned for pillaging, he told him. And that his whining was worse than a newborn denied the tit.

Terrel took objection, reined back his horse and heeled it around so that the German came alongside.

'I don't take orders from you,' he said, one hand resting on the knife at his belt.

Brun took no chances: he leaned forward and swung a muscled arm, sending Terrel sprawling. By the time Terrel rolled free of his nervous horse's hooves, sword in hand, Eckehart Brun was already standing ready, flanged mace in one hand, killing knife in the other.

'You slow-moving ox! Come on!' shouted Terrel, half crouched, ready to move quickly against the bigger man who remained still, feet planted firmly.

Henry turned and spurred his horse back to the belligerent Terrel and the man who faced him.

'You squabble like a crone, Terrel. Lower your sword!'

'Fuck you, boy!' snarled Terrel, waving his sword arm, spooking Henry's horse. 'I don't owe you for anything.'

Henry fought to bring his mount back under control.

'You gave your word,' said Brun.

'It means nothing when we ride to our deaths.'

Henry wheeled his horse, settled it, drew alongside Mallin and dismounted, the older man instinctively grasping its rein. Stepping between the two men, he gestured Brun to lower the mace and knife and then pointed at Terrel. 'Your mouth is a hog's arse. You shit on our chances of getting through here without raising the alarm. Put the blade down, Terrel, or I swear I will have Brun beat you senseless and we'll leave you for the wolves.'

Terrel's blood was up. Henry saw the shift in his stance and was already sidestepping when the sword's lunge came. He pivoted and punched Terrel below his ear. The wiry man dropped face first, sword falling free.

Brun and Mallin exchanged glances. Henry might be the youngest of them by far but he knew how to fight. Bezián leaned forward on his pommel.

'We should kill him now,' said the Gascon. 'If we stand together we have a chance. With a viper in the nest we can all die. I say kill him and be done with him.'

'Bezián is right,' said the German. 'Finish it now and we don't have to watch our backs.'

Henry picked up the fallen man's sword and knife. He looked up at the horsemen, who waited for his answer. He shook his head. 'We spare him and he is in our debt.'

'He's already in your debt, like us, for getting him this far,' said Mallin.

'Then we go on further,' said Henry. 'Together.' And watched as Terrel groggily rolled clear, staring at the unfriendly men looking down at him. Henry tossed his weapons next to him. 'This is the second time I've saved your life. Now is the time to decide with whom you stand.'

Terrel pressed the palm of his hand against the side of his head. His jaw hurt and the pain had buried itself behind his eye. Two hard blows from different men. He raised himself and picked up his weapons. Henry waited. If Terrel lunged again, this time he would kill him. The defeated man sheathed his blades. He nodded, spat blood and looked at each of the men who waited for an answer. He was no fool. They could have cut his throat when he lay helpless. Which is what he would have done. And, he guessed, so would the others. It was the lad who had saved him. As he had said. Again.

'I'll ride with you, Master Blackstone. You'll have no more trouble from me.'

'Then get mounted and let's find the man we came to snare,' said Henry, hauling himself into the saddle.

'No need,' said Vaisey.

Henry and the others saw the forest darkness waver as its shadows took form. Armed men nudged their mounts from the dense undergrowth.

CHAPTER TWENTY-SIX

The rough-hewn men surrounding Henry and the others saw that these men were no merchants carrying anything of value. They looked no different than themselves. Once Henry told them they sought la Griffe, the routiers – seventeen strong – escorted Henry and the others down a winding forest trail. The wind had shifted. Henry smelled burning flesh. He hoped they were not about to be delivered into a destroyed village. Men who slaughtered indiscriminately would have their blood up. Reason would not penetrate bloodlust and Henry needed to confront la Griffe without risking a swift blade to his throat.

He steeled himself and then realized his imagination had run away with him. They rode into a half-ruined hamlet built in the belly of a section of rising ground. Boulders the size of a tavern rose through the earth, and the forest clawing up the hillside made it difficult for a mounted attack: both made a natural defence for the camp. Whoever held this place commanded the area immediately below and there was no doubt in Henry's mind that, if it were ever besieged, the men who gathered here would have more than one way to escape through the forest.

The stiffening breeze lifted smoke from cooking fires in the clearing where a gutted boar turned on a spit. Reed and willow lean-tos angled against the old wood and stone structures. Henry's eye roved over the encampment. Perhaps, he thought, there was a time when men from another age lived here. A perfect defensive position chosen by someone who knew how to fight.

A handful of women attended to the fires and cooking pots. There were no children to be seen. This was a camp used by men who rode far and wide taking what they needed. Including the women, Henry guessed, seeing the pitiful and fearful looks on their faces as these strangers arrived. It was easy to imagine the life they led and their value to the routiers. Women could be passed around and traded.

Henry and the others dismounted, as did their escort. Several of them led the horses away while those remaining fanned out behind Henry as he faced lean, hardened men, some with grey shot through their hair and beard. One, taller and bulkier than the others, had a sword on his belt and a falchion in his hand, which he looked ready to wield if their guests proved to be unwelcome. His crinkled parchment skin, ingrained with dirt, matched his leather tunic, smooth from greasy hands being wiped on it; his hands had knuckles scarred white from heavy use. A fighter, then, who had to be the legendary Claw. He was much older than the rest of the group, as old as Mallin but without any sign that age had lessened his strength.

Behind the gathered men, and unseen as Henry had entered the hamlet, two men were fighting. The crowd of men glanced their way, then parted so that the contest could be witnessed. Henry and the others were surrounded and pushed forward towards the big man who appeared to be their leader; he grunted, a meaningless sound that could mean either they were next to fight or they should stay silent until the contest ended.

One of the contestants was a lad about the same age as Henry. Strong, broad-shouldered, capable and confident. His hair was tied back with a leather thong; he had a knife in one hand, a sword in the other. The man he fought was older and looked to be as battle-scarred as the others. The fight was fierce. On more than one occasion the older man's weight and strength looked to have the advantage, yet the youth was agile and quick. His opponent, Henry realized, was already bloodied. A wound to his arm, another to his leg. Neither debilitating. Both inflicted to torment.

Henry watched as the younger man ducked and swerved, his opponent's blade cutting through the air close to his throat. He pulled back, twisted, jabbed and dealt another light wound. Henry saw the youth's swordplay was more efficient than the fighter opposite him. His belt and sword looked to be of fine quality, perhaps taken as a prize from a man less skilled in killing.

At that moment the heavily built man, a cruel-looking leader of mercenaries, spoke. 'Enough,' he said without raising his voice.

It was a call to end the fight. The youth moved so rapidly Henry barely saw the lethal strike. Sword and knife slashed in a blur. It was unlikely the unfortunate victim saw the blow that finished him. As the man dropped into the blood-slick dirt, the men cheered.

'Vaisey,' said the fearsome older man, turning his attention away from the killing. 'You bring strangers into the heart of our camp. We thought you dead.'

'Captured, and then escaped with the help of him,' Vaisey answered with a nod towards Henry.

Eyes turned on him.

'We don't like strangers. And you've brought six more.'

'All fighting men. All near strung and gutted. Me too. The lad here saved us.'

The man's dark eyes stared hard at Henry. He stepped closer. 'You're no skinner,' he said. 'Any man here can see that.'

'You cannot always believe what you see,' said Henry. 'I have business with la Griffe.' Henry didn't wait for a response, but walked around him and faced the youth who was wiping the blood from his sword. 'You are Jean de Soissons, known as la Griffe.'

The lad stared back.

'And why would you think that?' he said.

Henry saw the glint of something in his eyes. Was it the spark of impending violence? He pointed to the youth's left hand. 'Your right hand wears a glove; your left is bent. Your fingers curl, twisted. No glove would fit over a claw hand. Who else could be la Griffe?'

The heavy-set man laid his falchion against Vaisey's neck. 'You betrayed his identity?'

'I swear I did not. If I had he would have gone straight to la Griffe.'

Henry's gaze remained steady on the young killer in front of him. 'He did not tell me. I wanted to see who would step forward and challenge us.' He glanced back at the man threatening Vaisey and then returned his gaze to the young swordsman. 'A smokescreen allows others to control events.'

The youth called to the falchion-wielding man: 'Leave Vaisey. Even if he described me to this person who has not yet declared himself, it is unimportant. What matters is why these men seek us out.'

'I am Henry Blackstone. I need men and your help.'

'There is a man who is legend across Brittany and France. You bear the same name.'

'With good reason.'

Jean de Soissons nodded. Blackstone's son was giving little away but had the courage to walk into what could have been certain death. And might still be.

'My help to do what?'

'Seize Josselin.'

The gathered men laughed. La Griffe shook his head and smiled, as if humouring a man who had lost his mind.

'That is a prize beyond even my grasp.'

'No, it is not. I can give you Josselin. I need to rescue a friend.'

'And you wish me to commit my fifty men against as many or more armed with crossbows? To storm a stronghold to rescue *your friend*?'

'Yes. And the chest of gold florins, leopards and nobles I carried for the English Prince in Aquitaine to pay men like you to fight against the Spanish.'

Daylight fled as quickly as the rolling clouds arrived. Bitterly cold rain splattered the compound. Fires were doused; the cooked food taken into the shelters. Henry sat with his six men opposite la Griffe and his henchman, whose name he learned was Pellan. The youthful killer la Griffe had a dozen men with him who, like Henry's companions, drank from clay beakers. The wine that he and Henry drank was served in silver goblets. Refined elegance in a dank stone-built hut. Cuts of roasted boar were offered on trenchers. The wind hissed and whistled through the cracks in the wall. Smoke swirled upwards through the roof's opening.

Henry studied his goblet. The inscription on its base was worn beyond recognition.

'They belonged to a merchant travelling from Rennes to Nantes. He got lost,' said la Griffe, using his clawed hand to grip his knife and spear meat into his mouth.

Henry realized that despite his twisted hand La Griffe had enough dexterity to pick up his knife. It was as if he had been deprived of a fully functioning hand but given one that seemed well suited to grip a knife or an axe's shaft. It was certainly not useless. And as strong as a vice.

He stared at Henry. 'Convince me.'

Mallin shot a brief, nervous glance at Bezián. Henry Blackstone had a quicksilver tongue but if it failed to convince la Griffe they would be fighting for their lives. Thankfully, the gloom hid his look of uncertainty.

'I was sent to England by my father to accompany my friend, Hugh Gifford, who serves the Earl of Warwick. Gifford was a messenger for the Prince. We were to return with arms and gold from the King to aid the Spanish campaign. Thirty archers from Cheshire and ten men-at-arms were with us as escort for the gold. We sailed for Bordeaux on the cog *Nicholas*. We foundered on the Breton coast. Only Gifford and I survived and with help from fishermen we salvaged the gold. Once ashore these fishermen turned on us and we killed those who attacked us and burned their village.'

La Griffe hunched forward, listening intently. Like a child being told a fairy tale, he hung on Henry's matter-of-fact words. Terrel saw the German and Bezián as engrossed as the mercenaries sitting opposite them. He caught Mallin's eye, who looked away and stuffed meat into his mouth. It hid his smile.

'And how were you taken into Josselin?'

'My father fought for John de Montfort during the war and secured Brittany for the King. Gifford and I were exhausted and I sought refuge, believing Josselin was held by the English.'

'Ha!' La Griffe blurted, flecks of food splattering the ground in front of him. 'Bretons have never let Josselin fall into English hands no matter who won the war. The House of Rohan will relinquish nothing to the English. You didn't know that?'

'I did not,' said Henry. He sighed. 'I failed my father and my Prince.'

'They're your father and Prince. Not mine! Where does the gold come into this?' said la Griffe, then swilled his mouth with wine.

Henry looked chastened. 'Gifford and I were to be imprisoned. These men with me, and your man Vaisey, were due to be executed. The captain—'

'Describe him!' demanded la Griffe.

'A one-armed man, features like a hog's arse. Skin pitted like old iron.'

'That's him.' La Griffe grinned. 'That's le Bourc. He lost that arm in the war. No wonder he held you. He hates the English. And us.' He peered at Henry, slitted eyes probing for flaws in the story. 'You and the gold.'

'You are one step ahead of me,' said Henry, to feed the youth's sense of self-importance.

The youth nodded. 'I am. And I will see you dead the moment I am convinced your story is a lie. The gold.'

'I have no reason to lie. I came seeking help.'

'The gold,' said la Griffe. 'I want to hear about the gold.'

'The gold,' said Henry, the tone of his voice softening as if relating the story of a lost one. 'This one-armed captain—'

'Le Bourc,' the youth insisted.

'Yes, he seized the chest and imprisoned me with these men.'

'If he had the gold why wouldn't he have killed you?' said Pellan, the henchman.

'Because he believes there is *more* gold.'

'There's more gold?' said la Griffe, shards of meat hanging from his teeth.

'No. There's no more gold.'

La Griffe looked confused.

'I told this... le Bourc... there was more gold buried on the shore where we were shipwrecked. He has taken half his garrison to secure it.'

'That leaves twenty men, a few more perhaps,' said Pellan. 'Not counting the servants.'

'He'll return from the coast the day after tomorrow, which means we can get into the castle, recover the gold and release my friend,' said Henry.

'But how did you escape?' the clawed youth asked.

'A drunken jailer grabbed and throttled. We made our way to the stables – there's a postern gate there. We thought they may have laid a trap for us. But the night watch was nowhere to be seen.' Henry sounded incredulous. 'No one challenged us. With le Bourc away no one is in command. It was too easy. And we can get over the walls. There are scaffolds up for stonemasons.'

La Griffe gazed into the middle distance, deep in thought. He lifted his claw-like hand to his mouth and worried a nail, cleaning the dirt behind it with his teeth.

'I don't like it,' said Pellan.

For a moment it seemed that Henry and the others did not exist as the youth considered the information. 'Gold, though. Even the one chest.' He suddenly snapped his attention to Henry. 'We take the gold. You take your man. That would be the trade.'

'That would be the trade,' Henry agreed.

CHAPTER TWENTY-SEVEN

The following day was spent travelling to the castle. Jean de Soissons rode alongside Henry until they were within sight of the walls. The bridge across the river would be in full view during daylight hours.

'We wait until dark,' said the Claw.

Henry turned in the saddle and looked at the band of routiers who followed. Road dirt and grime from sitting in smoke-filled shelters were ingrained into their hands and faces. They looked more ferocious than any man Henry had seen in the town's square. If these men scaled the walls and were let loose, would the one-armed captain have the kind of men capable of defeating them? Garrison soldiers had a bed and a blanket at night, they walked the walls with braziers burning at their watch positions, they had food. They were soft. Doubt crept into his heart. Convincing both the garrison commander and the leader of a band of vicious routiers had been almost effortless. Who else would have spun such a yarn? No court minstrel would have dreamt up such a lie. If la Griffe defeated the garrison troops, they would savage the town, tear apart the merchant houses, desecrate the chapel, rape and slaughter like the beasts they were. And then they would discover his lie. There was no gold. This might have been a terrible idea. A deadly mistake.

Pellan and his youthful leader withdrew to settle the men and prepare their attack. Henry's own men, as he now thought them to be, waited for his orders. He lowered his voice.

'An ambush awaits us. Le Bourc will show us no favours – his bowmen will shoot to kill everyone. Stay close to the walls. Make for the dungeon. Release our comrades.'

'And then?' said Terrel.

'Then we are in God's hands,' said Henry.

Henry stared long and hard at the walled town, remembering the layout of the town square last seen thronged with a mob whose bloodlust had led them to struggle against the soldiers as men died in agony. Henry's throat was dry and his heart thumped: a war drum in his ears. Was the one-armed le Bourc ready? Was he willing to sacrifice anyone caught on the parapets by the routiers? If the veteran was as tough and as experienced as Henry hoped, he would be lying in wait. Providing, that is, he had planned everything as he and Henry had agreed before he and the others were released to draw in the feared routier. It had been a conversation held in private. Private because Henry did not know if the men at his back were trustworthy.

A man's remains hung on a gibbet this side of the river at the mouth of the bridge, swaying in the night wind, a macabre dance of the dead. Henry expected la Griffe and his men to run across the bridge under cover of darkness and then skirt the walls on the river path until they reached the scaffolding. Rain threatened and the wind had increased. Both aided the assault. The night watch would hunch into their cloaks, stay close to their braziers and spend less time walking the walls.

La Griffe did not do as Henry expected. Their horses were tethered downwind in the forest, and the young killer crouched, beckoning Henry and pointing across the river at the nearest wood-framed skeleton of scaffolding clinging to the stone walls.

'First light is close. The men on the walls will be tired. Some asleep. You go across, we follow,' said la Griffe. 'You and your men first.'

'The river's flowing too fast – it'll take the men downstream. Those who can swim. The rest will drown.'

Pellan edged closer to his leader and dropped a coiled rope. La Griffe thrust one end at Henry. 'You swim, secure the rope; we follow.'

Pellan reached out and grabbed Henry's tunic. 'You and your men go over the walls first. You kill the sentry. You signal us.'

Henry grabbed the man's thick wrist and twisted it free, then snatched at the rope. 'Make sure you have the courage to follow,' he challenged the henchman.

The taunt made Pellan snatch at him again but la Griffe raised his clawed fist and stopped him. 'Master Blackstone knows what to do. We will play our part. There's wealth behind those walls.'

'Aye, and blood to spill,' said Pellan. He pointed a finger. 'And his will be the first to stain the ground if he has lied to us.'

Henry turned his back and joined the others, who were huddling away from la Griffe's men. Henry told them the plan.

'Damned water will be freezing,' said Terrel. 'A man loses his grip on the rope and he'll be gone. I'm no swimmer.'

'Nor me,' said Bezián.

The others murmured their agreement.

'Then don't lose your grip,' said Henry. 'Once we are across, they'll follow. We scale the walls first. That gives us a chance to stay close, as I told you. Get down to the dungeon. Guard the entrance. Our lives are as much at risk as la Griffe's.'

He looked from man to man, expecting complaint. There

was none. Without another word he crouched and ran to where la Griffe waited on the edge of the forest. Henry stripped down to his hose, wrapping his boots, shirt and tunic in a small parcel and then tying them securely with his sword belt. He hefted the rope. 'Make sure you secure this well. Men crossing a fast-flowing river will put strain on a line. Tie it badly and you and your men will drown. You will have no need of gold then.'

He didn't wait for an answer but played out the rope, reached the riverbank, crouched behind the reeds and tied the line off around his waist. The reeds provided good camouflage until he was waist deep. Gritting his teeth and holding his breath as the water clawed its icy fingers into him, he held his clothing above the surface as best he could and set off in a sidestroke through the eddies that tugged and turned him, forcing him to kick harder so that he would not be swept downstream. The river fought back. He almost lost his bundle of clothing, but he stretched his back muscles and raised his head higher, pulling hard with his free hand and kicking furiously. The trailing rope snagged. Something beneath the surface – he didn't know what: a waterlogged branch perhaps? – tugged hard at his waist and pulled him down. He swallowed water, but forced his head above the surface, thrusting his sword and bundle as high as he could, reaching for the sky. His efforts pulled him free of the undertow. Gasping for breath he reached the far shore, found his feet in the river mud and eased through the tall bulrushes.

Thirty yards beyond the reeds lay open ground on the far side of a riverside path leading to the walls and the scaffolding. Henry pulled his hair back from his face, gazed up at the walls and saw a sentry at the far end of the castle's walkway. The figure in its dark cloak would have been invisible were it not for the dull glow of a brazier. Henry untied the rope from his waist, pulled on the dry shirt, thankful for its warmth, and then the added comfort of his gambeson. He squatted on the dry bank and pulled on his boots, fastened his sword belt and with a last look towards the stationary guard, grabbed the end of the rope. He ran, crouching, towards the scaffold's base. Time was against them. Stonemasons and peasant labourers would start work as soon as dawn broke.

Henry secured the rope, yanked it hard and saw his men emerge from cover, each close to the next so that if one got into trouble his companion could help. They waded across fully clothed, having the advantage of the tied rope. As they emerged through the bulrushes Henry gathered them close together.

'I'll go onto the walls with Bezián.' Henry's father always put great store in Gascon fighters, and instinct made Henry make the same choice.

The Gascon nodded.

Henry continued: 'I go left, you to the right. We'll only be able to clear this front wall. We must hope our plan is in place and that le Bourc's men are ready. Don't kill the sentries. He might sacrifice men but we lay ourselves open to the mob's vengeance if we do.' Then he addressed the others. 'Once I give the signal, scale the walls and stay away from the open ground. Remember, if this plan works, la Griffe will walk into a trap. We don't want to be caught in it.'

They nodded their understanding.

Henry turned without another word, checked each sentry was at their station and ran for the base of the scaffold with Bezián at his heels. They clambered from one strut to the other until, muscles straining, they reached the parapet. Henry gazed down; the dark huddled men below had their faces turned towards him. Across the river there was no sign of la Griffe. For a sickening moment he thought he and his men had been abandoned. Then he saw shadows edging forward from the treeline and squatting, waiting for his signal.

Henry and Bezián crawled over the parapet, crouched, let their breathing settle and then, without another word, went left and right towards the unsuspecting sentries. Henry felt his heart thumping loud enough for the sentry to hear it and turn. The man remained unmoving, his hands extended towards what little warmth was left in the brazier. Henry's knife was in his hand; when he was an arm's length behind the unsuspecting sentry, he twisted his wrist and drove the knife's butt into the man's neck grabbing him with his free arm so that he did not fall into the brazier whose clatter would raise the alarm.

He crouched over the unconscious man, turned and saw Bezián drag his man down and lay his body next to the wall out of sight. The scale of the castle was such that the men on the furthest corner of the other walls were in darkness. Henry leaned over the parapet and gestured his men to join him. As soon as Henry's signal was seen by la Griffe the mercenaries ran for the riverbank and plunged single file through the bulrushes, took hold of the rope and dragged themselves across the river. By the time Terrel had hauled himself across the wall the first of the routiers had reached the scaffold's base. Henry led the men halfway along the walkway where Bezián waited at the top of the steps leading down into the square. Night lanterns still glowed dimly. The square was empty. The gibbet bore its gruesome bloodstained testimony to torture.

Henry led the way down the steps. Once at the base of the walls he signalled them to spread out, keeping clear of the open. Mallin and Vachon stayed close to the walls and made their way to the door leading down into the dungeons. Henry's chest tightened. His fist gripped his sword. Sweat trickled down his back and his throat dried. Death was close.

For a moment a thought startled him. How had his father and the men who fought with him ever overcome this fear? He took a deep breath. There was no answer to that. Perhaps no one ever managed to stop it. Imagination was dangerous. He forced the doubt from his mind and kept his eyes on the empty square. A scrape of boot on stone made him turn. Pellan was leading the routiers down the steps. They were soaked but undeterred; axe, mace and sword in hand, they gathered at the foot of the stairs. Pellan signalled them to flank the walls either side of him. He stared at the empty yard. 'Where's the night watch?'

'I told you. Half the garrison is chasing gold. The sentries on the wall are cold and tired. My men have secured the guardhouse,' he lied. 'The people are sleeping, safe in the knowledge that there is no threat.' He looked at the mercenaries. There were less than half their number. 'Where are la Griffe and the others?'

'He'll come when I call him. You think he's stupid enough to trust you? You think I am stupid enough to send my son in first?'

Henry's shock of learning that Pellan was the killer's father could not be disguised. Pellan grinned at seeing the effect of his words. Henry felt another enemy creep up on him. Panic. He calmed his thoughts. He had promised le Bourc to deliver the Claw and that plan had already failed. He had no other.

'Where is the gold?' said Pellan.

The routier's demand increased Henry's uncertainty. He nodded. And then pointed. His throat dried as fear gripped him. He took a deep breath and exhaled slowly. The arrangement he had with le Bourc was all he had now. 'Across the yard and in that door. Stairs lead to le Bourc's quarters. The chest is guarded. There will be a sentry at the door.'

'Only one?' said Pellan.

Henry's story became more desperate. 'Only one. Who would dare steal from the garrison commander? And who would escape with it?'

Pellan's lips curled. His face creased into a grin. 'Only us, Englishman.' He snatched at Henry's arm and before he could resist he was pushed forward. 'Go and see the way is clear,' he hissed.

Henry ran across the square and leaned his shoulder against the studded chestnut door. Its hinges creaked louder than he cared. He stopped. Looked behind him, saw Pellan and the mercenaries, backs against the wall. Henry eased past the half-open door into the chill of the stone hall and its staircase curving upwards. A staircase filled with armed men as one of le Bourc's soldiers raised a lantern and the one-armed man pressed a knife blade against Henry's neck.

'You have balls, I'll give you that. Most would have run for their lives,' said le Bourc.

'My man is here. I gave my word.'

Le Bourc grunted and lowered the knife. 'La Griffe is with you?'

Henry hoped the garrison commander could not see his throat bobbing as he swallowed his fear. He nodded. 'Can you not see him?' he whispered, allowing the door to open wide enough.

'No one here knows what he looks like. He is a devil ghost,' said le Bourc.

Henry was thankful for the dim light. His eyes closed; his breath eased. 'Big man, across the square. A wild beard shot through with grey. He wears mail. He is everything you would think la Griffe to be.'

Le Bourc squinted through the narrow slit. He nodded. 'Bring them across.' He faced Henry, his mouth close enough for him to smell the stench of rotting teeth. 'I have spared you so far, Master Blackstone, but when those bastards reach halfway all except the Claw will die. My men have been told the one you stand next to will be la Griffe. Be prepared. Save yourself. I can do nothing more for you.'

CHAPTER TWENTY-EIGHT

Henry was to deliver the Judas kiss.

It felt wrong, even though his own life and those of the men with him were at stake. Yet there had never been any alternative. It was survival.

'The way ahead is clear,' said Henry. 'We should move quickly before the garrison awakes.'

Pellan hesitated. Like a dog sniffing the air he looked up at the walls and then around the square. 'It doesn't feel right,' he said.

'Because half the garrison is away,' said Henry, reassuring him. 'But I don't want to get caught in the open when the castle wakes up. We need to get inside and take the gold. Your men can stand watch outside, but I'm not staying here.'

His urgency penetrated Pellan's doubt. He nodded, tucked his fighting axe into his belt and drew his sword. 'You'll go through the door first,' he said, eyes darting back and forth. 'One step ahead of me. No more.'

Henry nodded and strode across the open ground. Pellan's men followed their leader, half crouched, wary, turning this way and that. Henry's heart thudded, pounding in his ears as he reached the centre of the square. Suddenly doors slammed open to their front and side, disgorging the garrison troops, most armed with crossbows. They took a few paces, levelled their weapons and shot. Fifteen-inch-long, quarrel-headed, steel-tipped crossbow bolts made their own distinctive sound as they flew. A fluttering air wave ending in the dull, sickening impact as they tore into flesh.

Henry had gone down on one knee to avoid the lethal storm the moment the doors had slammed open. The surprise was complete. Men cried out in agony. Yelled curses when they saw they had nowhere to run. Half of Pellan's men fell where they stood. Others counter-attacked. More were cut down by the second wave of crossbowmen. The survivors' fighting instincts overtook their panic. They gathered themselves, back to back, fending off the swordsmen who ran to overwhelm them. Pellan and Henry were surrounded by several of his men. For vital moments Henry knew Pellan had not realized it was he who had betrayed them. The routier struck out, killed one of le Bourc's men, saw his own men being swamped, turned in that instant to Henry. Realization dawned.

Pellan, axe and sword in hand, jabbed at Henry, who parried but was too slow, his sword struck from his grip. Pellan hurled the axe but Henry rolled away, scrambling for his life. Wild with panic, half-raised knife in hand, he plunged the blade into Pellan's thigh, twisted it, pulled it free and struck again. The man's weight brought him down. The man's stench was in his nostrils. Without thinking Henry threw himself on the killer, who was strong enough to push him off. Pellan hauled himself upright as Henry got to his feet. The mercenaries were being cut down as the big man swivelled this way and that, lame, a wounded bull. Desperation surged through Henry. His sword was out of reach so he slid in the dirt and slashed hard with the knife, hamstringing him.

The cries of wounded men, the bellowing roar of attacker and defender: all faded in Henry's mind as he focused on the disabled fighter. Henry was trembling, fear and uncertainty clouding his mind. He had to kill Pellan before le Bourc learned he was not the routier la Griffe. A look of disbelief crossed Pellan's face as Henry threw his arms around the older man's chest, smothering his sword arm. His weight stopped the man's wounded leg from gaining enough purchase to squirm free.

'I'm saving us both from a vile death,' Henry said, the words unplanned, the truth spilling out, desperation driving the knife deep into Pellan's ear. The routier's jaw dropped, eyes rolling upward; his body shuddered with such force it threw Henry clear. He landed, his face a hand's breadth from the man's eyes, staring unseeing at his young killer.

Henry squirmed away from the dead man. He felt vomit claw at the back of his throat. What had just happened was a blur, but he knew he had been lucky. He had not killed the man with any skill but with a lucky slash that had crippled the man.

The sound of his knife grinding through bone and brain left him shaking.

Soldiers surrounded Henry, sword points at his chest and throat. A voice barked a command and the men stepped back. Henry wiped his mouth and cautiously got to his feet. Bodies lay scattered, blood soaking into the dirt as le Bourc came forward. The routiers had sold their lives at a cost. The captain looked at the dead man he thought was the mercenary leader. 'I wanted him alive,' he said.

'I was fighting for my life,' said Henry. 'He realized I had betrayed him. I had no choice.'

Le Bourc prodded the body with his bloody sword. 'We'll behead and quarter him. Let it be known la Griffe is dead. It's better than nothing.'

'And me, my lord,' said Henry. 'You gave your word. I deliver la Griffe and you would release me and the others.'

Le Bourc looked around. 'Aye, you can go, Master Blackstone.'

'We need horses. What we had were left across the river. Long gone by now. And food. We need supplies.'

'You have your lives. Count yourself fortunate. Be gone by the time the square is cleared of the dead. If you are still within these walls by then I'll put you all on the scaffold. No matter who your father is.'

Henry ran to the dungeon's entrance. It took him a moment to adjust to the near darkness. A figure moved on the stairs. Bezián peered, sword in hand, expecting trouble. He backed down when he saw who it was and led the way down to the dungeon. Hugh Gifford and the others waited.

'Master Blackstone,' said Gifford. 'I feared your mission was damned from the start.' He grinned. 'I should have known better.'

Mallin pointed to the crumpled body in the cell's corner. 'Helyer died of his wounds.'

'Then he is beyond help but we must help ourselves. The fight is over. Hugh, these men told you what happened?'

'Aye.'

'Le Bourc thinks Pellan is the Claw. We have to get out of here.'

'If the Claw still lives then he'll be waiting for you,' said Gifford.

'I know, but we have no time to think on it now. They are clearing away the dead and we must be gone before they finish.' Henry noticed Gifford had his sword buckled.

The man-at-arms grinned. 'The jailer fancied he'd trade it for wine.'

Henry looked at the men. 'Was he killed for it?'

'A sore head when he wakes up,' said Vachon.

'All right. You men are free to go your own way. Gifford and I will head for Bordeaux.'

Terrel was the unlikely spokesmen. 'Aye, well, we talked

about that, Master Blackstone. You have a lawyer's quicksilver wit, the lies of a tavern whore and the luck of the devil. Men like us need that at our backs. If you will allow it the six of us will travel with you.'

Henry looked at their earnest faces. Each held their gaze on him. 'Hugh?'

'Can't hurt to have men who'll obey orders when it's needed.'

'We will do that,' said Brun. 'We kept our word before. We give it again.'

They all nodded in agreement.

'Then we travel together,' said Henry. 'Fair warning to the devil.'

PART FIVE

THE KILLING FIELDS

CHAPTER TWENTY-NINE

Blackstone and his men rode north from Estella, expecting to meet the Prince's army advancing south from Pamplona. That would convince any suspicious minds in the camp that Blackstone had been sent out to reconnoitre the way towards the town of Logroño, still held by Don Pedro's loyal garrison. After fifteen miles there was still no sign of the army. Windswept rainstorms gathered on the mountaintops and hurled themselves into the valleys below where they expended their fury; then the clouds parted and sparkling rays shone down, a heavenly guide to earthbound fools.

Renfred and his men rode back after scouting the ground ahead. He reined in. 'Sir Thomas, there are stragglers several miles ahead. The Prince has changed his route.'

Blackstone looked at the German man-at-arms with disbelief. 'There is no other route. Through Estella onto Logroño.'

Renfred shook his head. 'No, Sir Thomas, they went north of Pamplona and then west. '

The men's bafflement made them fall silent until Meulon spoke. 'That's the worst of country. Renfred, you're sure that's what the stragglers said?'

'They are exhausted and struggling to keep up. The Prince has forced the pace. The men I spoke to said the army was marching for Vitoria and then to enter Castile and strike out for Burgos.' Renfred shrugged. 'There is no sign of them, Sir Thomas. They have gone.'

John Jacob looked back the way they had come. 'They couldn't have chosen a worse route. If we double back and head north-west through the mountain passes, we might intercept them.'

Blackstone turned and followed his squire's gaze. 'The rivers will be in spring flood. We would be lucky to find a ford and Trastámara will have raiding parties in the hills.'

They watched a black cloud of angry rain tumbling down the valley towards them.

'It'll be dark soon enough. Renfred, is there shelter anywhere on this road?'

'Yes. A mile down the road – an abandoned farmhouse.'

Renfred turned his horse, spurred its flanks. Blackstone and the men followed. If they could beat the storm a dry night in shelter would be welcome.

The abandoned farmhouse's barn had enough timbers on the roof to keep the worst of the rain at bay as the storm came in hard. Blackstone and his men hunched over a quickly made fire. The horses were kept saddled and hobbled at the far end of the barn, sharing the same space and what warmth there was as the men. Thunder rumbled across the mountains, the wind casting rain this way and that.

A trickle of water was swept through a crack and seeped into Blackstone's collar. He wiped a hand across his neck and pointed the stick he held at the crude model he had made of the terrain they would have to travel over. 'If the Prince has gone west from Pamplona, then he will soon be... here, which would be Salvatierra.'

Aicart pointed at the scratch in the dirt Blackstone had made. 'That valley, Sir Thomas, and these mountains, they will punish man and horse. Renfred, you know that route from when we were last here. How far must the army travel?'

The German leaned forward and touched where Blackstone had showed Salvatierra to be. 'To Salvatierra from Pamplona he has nearly fifty miles, maybe less. The pass at Arruaza is narrow: they will struggle with horses and mules, and knights with their armour on pack horses will curse the day. And if he goes on to Vitoria' – he placed another stone – 'then, another twenty miles between the two. In this weather and with the French commanding his troops, Trastámara can pick and choose when to harass the column.' He looked up from the model to Blackstone, who knew full well how poor a judgement the Prince had made. 'The Alavese Mountains, Sir Thomas. We were warned about those the last time we made our way into Castile.'

'Which is why we didn't take that route,' said Blackstone.

'He should have waited for us,' said Meulon. 'The Prince relied on us to bring him through the mountains.'

'Our Prince is not a patient man,' said Blackstone. 'And there are others at his side now who can influence his decisions. And with Bertrand du Guesclin and Marshal d'Audrehem leading the war for Trastámara they will block the passes and make cut-and-thrust attacks. They know better than to stand and fight.'

Ashford laughed. 'Aye, they learned that after Auray.'

'And Poitiers!' said John Jacob. He sighed. 'No, they won't face us on open ground. We'll leave enough blood on the road into Castile from their marauders.'

Blackstone tossed the stick into the flames. 'I cannot see any choice for the army other than to march to Vitoria. We must meet the Prince there. Then we bring him south. He cannot expose the men any further to a country that offers no cover from attack.'

Blackstone stood and went to the entrance where the rickety door rattled in the gusting wind. 'Get what sleep you can. We leave at first light. With luck this storm will blow itself out.' He stepped out into the night, pulling the door closed behind him. Rain swirled, clouds dashed across the night sky exposing crystal-clear stars, and the new moon glistened. The light exposed the black mountains in the distance; a track took his eye towards them. As it curved away the scarred ground yielded to the darkening mass of the next storm. A shiver ran up Blackstone's back. He was being watched. He spun around. Twenty yards behind him, coat glistening from the rain, the bastard horse glared at him, eyes glinting in the cold light, ears erect.

Blackstone had put him in the lean-to shelter at the end of the building to keep him away from the other horses. It must have heard or sensed him leave the barn, tugged free from its hitching post and now stood ready. Blackstone stepped towards it. Its misshapen head tilted and rose. It snorted. Its tail swished; a front hoof dragged dirt, then made no further move. Blackstone, wary of its vicious yellow teeth, laid a hand on the horse's forehead and ran his palm down its cheek. It seemed less belligerent than usual. A moment of calm, a lull in the storm. He stared into its eyes. The brute had been his constant companion. They both bore scars earned in battle.

'A hard road ahead,' said Blackstone, daring to let it snuffle his palm. 'You will carry me to war again.' Its nostrils flared. The horse let him turn it back towards the shelter as a gust of wind threw rain against them. 'But for how much longer will we fight?' he said, surprised at his own moment of reflection. 'How much longer?' he said again, his words swept away on the wind.

CHAPTER THIRTY

The route Blackstone and his men had travelled from Estella had been difficult, cutting through forests on meagre tracks that forced them to dismount and lead their horses. Darkness beckoned as Blackstone led the men into Vitoria. The bedraggled army was camped on the open plain. Blackstone looked down from the saddle; exhausted men stared back up at him as he rode through their ranks. He realized how these men had suffered. More worrying was that they appeared to be defeated even before they had engaged with the enemy.

Blackstone saw the Prince's pavilion and close to it that of King Pedro. He guided his horse towards them. 'John, William, Renfred, food for the men and fodder and water for the horses. I'll join you later. Find a place and keep everyone together. I can see no sign of Gilbert or the others.' Blackstone tethered his horse and strode towards the Prince's pavilion. The tent's fabric looked frayed, the pennons listless in the faltering wind. Sir John Chandos had seen Blackstone's approach and stepped out of the Prince's quarters. He raised a hand in warning and moved closer.

'Thomas, tread carefully,' he said, voice lowered. 'I advised he waited for you to lead the way. You know the ground. His brother...' He turned his head to check he was not being watched. 'His brother advised him to take this route in the belief they could outflank Trastámara.' He sighed. 'Thomas, it was one of the worst journeys I have experienced. The men are hungry; there is no wine, no bread. What supplies there are lag a day behind.'

Blackstone knew that if one of the most revered knights had not managed to convince the Prince then John of Gaunt must hold significant sway over Edward. He too, kept his voice low in case the wind carried his disparaging remarks. 'The Prince has never taken such a foolhardy decision like this before. Brother or not, what has happened to his instincts, his skill in out-thinking the enemy? Not this. Not putting an army across blade-sharp rocks and narrow passes. No cover. Nothing to take from the land.' He looked across the plain. 'These men are already defeated. Best that you and I share what thoughts we have and then convince him of the best plan to follow.'

Chandos nodded. He laid a hand on Blackstone's arm, saw the dried blood on his gambeson. 'You took the woman to safety?'

'We did. And there's news he won't want to hear. She told me who has joined Trastámara.'

Chandos was a man used to adversity, but the hint of more difficult times to come made his shoulders sag. 'Let's get to it, Thomas. Choose your words carefully, but do not spare him.' He led the way into the Prince's pavilion.

King Pedro lounged on one side of the pavilion. John of Gaunt sat closer to the Prince. Rain dripped through the layers of linen roof. Even royalty could not be as comfortable as they would wish. A buffeting wind flapped the pavilion's sides. Blackstone dipped his head to the Prince, deliberately ignoring the King.

'My lord, you did not wait for me to lead you through the mountains. You brought hardship on yourself.' It was the gentlest chiding he could give the man he served. It was not well received.

'And you are critical of your Prince,' said John of Gaunt.

Pedro leaned forward. 'He is insolent. If he were one of my knights, he would be whipped.'

Blackstone stared directly at the Spanish King. 'If I were one of your knights, I would likely be butchered.'

Blackstone's shockingly direct insult rendered Pedro silent.

John of Gaunt was on his feet. He pointed at Blackstone but directed his command to Sir John Chandos. 'Get this man away from here. His behaviour insults the King.'

The Prince raised a hand. 'Brother, his behaviour insults those who feel the insult. Sir Thomas speaks his mind...' He paused. '... as kindly as he can. Yes, Thomas, we took an arduous route that proved difficult, but it was the shortest route to take us closer to the Castilian border and now we and the army rest and then strike towards Burgos.'

'Lord, there is more hardship ahead. The ground is as harsh as you have experienced so far. Do you think Henry of Trastámara, Bertrand du Guesclin and Marshal d'Audrehem will wait on open ground to confront you? On our way here we saw riders scouring the hills. We stayed out of sight, but he will block your route into Castile. He'll control the heights. There's a mountain stronghold at Zaldiaran. It will be impossible to dislodge him. He'll hold the pass at Puebla. You will not be able to take the route you planned.' Blackstone watched the sobering effect his words had on the three powerful men. 'He has you where he wants you. The ground, the weather, an exhausted army. He will eat away at your strength with lightning raids as pestilence eats flesh.'

The pavilion fell silent except for the buffeting wind beating a sullen drumbeat on the walls. Blackstone told them what he had learned from Sancha Ferrandes, without mentioning her name or where she had been taken. Hearing of the crusading orders and Order of the Sash had the desired effect. The Sash was the equivalent of the Knights of the Garter: a kingdom's nobility brought together in a brotherhood of chivalry. The Prince remained silent. John of Gaunt had never faced a massed army like his older brother, blooded at Crécy, victor at Poitiers, a man who had led massive raids across France.

Pedro was the first to break the moment of reflection. 'We can break through the pass with persistent effort. Casualties will be high, but we will reach Burgos with enough strength.'

'You talk of sacrificing our men,' said the Prince. 'If we ask them to die in our name then they must trust our judgement.' He raised himself. 'The night is bitter. We shall retire and talk again with Sir Thomas and Sir John in the morning after prayers.' A servant came forward to wrap a warmer cloak around his shoulders.

Blackstone saw that when the Prince stood it was done slowly, as if he were in pain, or had no strength.

The Prince stepped to Blackstone. 'You serve us with diligence and love, Thomas, but there are times a prince must decide what road to take. That is his burden.'

'My Prince,' said Blackstone, his voice edged with concern. 'Where are Sir Gilbert and my men?'

'We sent five hundred men ahead with Sir William Felton. They will hold the ground so that we may join them without Trastámara and his men raiding us when we advance.' He turned away.

Blackstone's stomach knotted. Killbere and his men were under the command of a stubborn knight loath to seek advice from anyone. The Prince had put his trust in men set in their ways, unable to bend in the wind when necessary. He and Chandos bowed and turned back into the night. Once outside,

Blackstone squinted into the stinging wind. 'The Prince's instincts are dulled by whatever ails him, John. And Killbere with Felton leaves me uneasy.'

'There's nothing to be done until tomorrow.'

'Where is Hugh Calveley?'

Chandos pointed into the night. 'The far edge of the army.'

Blackstone gazed across the troops flung far and wide. 'John, we'll need him when we speak to the Prince in the morning. He fought against Pedro when we rescued him, and now he sides with the Prince so he should have known the ground would be hard-going.'

'War is a business, Thomas. He was paid by Trastámara back then; now he is paid by the Prince. I sold my sword and took my men south as well. You know that. But neither he nor I raised a blade in anger against you. We fought Pedro's men, not Englishmen sent to rescue him.'

Blackstone bore no ill will towards Chandos or Calveley. It was what fighting men did when their lord, prince or king had no further need of them in war. He had done so himself. And they had sold their skills before any command from the English King forbade them. 'I'll find him and make sure he joins us in the morning. Whatever we do we must blunt John of Gaunt's influence on the Prince. If ever there was a time he needed us, it's now.'

'Then seek him out. I'm camped close to John of Gaunt in the vanguard. Once you speak to Hugh, bring what men you have close to mine. That way we'll have a chance to keep John close to hand. We'll dog his footsteps and keep within earshot of him and the Prince. Pedro I don't give a damn about. He bears no influence.'

Wasp-stinging rain beat their faces as Blackstone turned to Chandos. 'I should have left Pedro in Castile instead of rescuing him.'

'It worries you, Thomas?'

'Aye. It does. Good men died, but even more will follow.'

'The Prince commanded you. There is nothing more to be said. Now, go and find Calveley.'

CHAPTER THIRTY-ONE

Blackstone made his way through the camp past huddled men in wet blankets, their fires struggling to compete with the gusting wind and rain. Some recognized him and tipped their heads respectfully. The further he walked the more he began to sense how remote the chances were of them succeeding in what lay ahead.

Sir Hugh Calveley's tent was not as grand as the Prince's but it bore the hallmark of a man who had received honours and wealth from Trastámara when he had fought for Pedro's adversary. 'Thomas! Come inside. The damned Spanish weather is worse than home.' His beard split into a grin. 'Wherever that might be.' The broad-shouldered Cheshire knight boomed with laughter.

Blackstone and the mercenary captain gripped each other's hand. 'Your men are scattered, Hugh. I didn't see many pickets.'

Calverley poured two beakers of wine. 'They need rest. No fool would venture out sword in hand on a night like this. Damned if they wouldn't trip over their own feet.'

'Still, best to be ready,' said Blackstone, knowing his comment would be taken as criticism. 'Trastámara's strength lies in rapid attacks.'

Calverley raised his beaker. 'Thomas, you forget I fought for him. *Cavalgada* is one thing during summer months when the ground is firm and the wind and rain does not blind lightly armed cavalrymen. I don't expect trouble.' He scowled. 'You came all the way here to tell me to post more sentries?'

'No, to bring you close to the Prince with me and Chandos. We must get the ear of the Prince.'

Calverley grunted and settled back onto his stool. 'Aye, well, John of Gaunt pulls his strings.'

'The Prince knows he made a mistake following his brother's advice. Between the three of us we can guide him.'

'You're the King's Master of War, Thomas; you're the one he should listen to, you and Chandos. I am a captain of men with his palm open for reward.'

'Even so. You and Chandos fought across Castile, as did I. We three know the ground. We cannot allow Gaunt to dictate or Pedro to hold sway. Three voices all as one. You, me and Chandos.'

Calverley drank and nodded his agreement. 'The order of march has me in the rear, Thomas, which is why I am stuck out here on the edge of the army. I want my men close to the Prince. Next after the Prince and Gaunt. I'm better suited in the vanguard.'

Blackstone swallowed the wine and stood to leave. 'Then bring your voice and your men tomorrow. Double your pickets, Hugh. If I were d'Audrehem, I would choose a night like this to raid.'

Calverley stayed seated. 'But that's you, Thomas. The rest of us need food, wine and sleep. Tomorrow, then.'

Blackstone nodded his farewell and went back into the night. By the time he had returned to his men the rain had stopped. The army slept fitfully. Braziers burned close to the Prince's pavilion, a lantern inside casting its warm glow. Close to John of Gaunt's pavilion he found John Jacob and the men, their backs against a rocky outcrop, a fire with boulders sheltering the flames. Horses were hobbled with feedbags on their heads.

A blackened iron pot squatted in the flames. William Ashford ladled out pottage and handed it to Blackstone, who sat on his bedroll laid out by his squire.

Ashford nodded. 'All the lads are fed, Sir Thomas. John and me have posted pickets. Safe enough here, I reckon, in the heart of the camp, but Renfred took a couple of his lads near to Pedro's tent, just in case the lady in question has a like-minded sister.'

Blackstone blew on the hot food.

'There's no bread, Sir Thomas,' said John Jacob. 'We cooked what we carried. Supplies are as scarce as dry weather.'

Neither Ashford nor the squire showed any sign of discomfort. Blackstone's men slept soundly.

'And we had enough wine between us to share,' John Jacob said with a grin, nodding towards the exhausted men.

'They deserve it and more,' said Blackstone. He recounted his conversations with the Prince, Chandos and Calveley. 'Tomorrow, we convince the Prince to change direction.'

'Then we lead the army again?' said Ashford.

Blackstone shook his head and finished the last mouthful of food. 'I don't want Sir Gilbert and the men separated from us. We'll join Felton and let the army follow.' He pulled the damp blanket over him. Casting an eye on the swirling clouds he saw the wind had veered. Blackstone rolled a shoulder to shift a stubborn stone and moments later fell asleep.

Blackstone lay wounded, face down in the mud. His left arm useless. Pain lay like a heavy rock on his chest. Breath came hard. Ghosts from battles past plagued his memory. Voices called. He answered. They were no longer there. The poison from when he escaped from Castile choked him. Persistent. A mailed fist around his heart. He forced his eyes open. He was on his back. Rolling clouds buffeting the sky. Swirling into black horses. Stampeding. Thundering above him.

Instinct drove him from the dream to his feet.

'To arms!' he bellowed, uncertain if the dream persisted or his sixth sense had warned him of impending danger.

His men were as quick to respond to his warning and for a moment crouched, weapons in hand, eyes scouring the dark forms of soldiers rising warily from their slumber. For a moment Blackstone thought he had given a false alarm but the sudden bellowing and screams from the far side of the war camp told him otherwise.

'Horsemen! They're attacking Calveley!' he shouted. His own men were with him and rousing others. He pushed through the weary and uncertain soldiers. Kicking those who were slow to roll out of their blankets. 'On your feet, damn you!'

Blackstone saw Sir John Chandos emerge from his tent armed and ready. Blackstone shouted. 'John! The Prince! Protect the Prince!' and then ran towards the sound of battle. *Jinetes*, the Castilian light cavalry, had swarmed into Hugh Calveley's badly guarded flank, pushing through deeper into the encamped and exhausted army.

Blackstone's men were at his shoulder, a broadhead-arrow phalanx with Blackstone at its sharpest point to break the line of horsemen. Roars of alarm carried on the wind behind him as the army woke to the fact they were under attack. Blackstone shouldered men aside in his effort to reach the enemy. And then the horsemen were less than thirty paces away. Stabbing and slashing, Blackstone's men broke the Castilian formation. Horsemen swirled this way and that. They wreaked havoc. Calveley's men died where they slept. Others were cut down as they tried to defend themselves from the shock assault. The baggage train was plundered. Vital arms and supplies lost to a daring enemy.

Blackstone regretted Will Longdon and Jack Halfpenny's absence. Their bowmen would have picked off the riders and saved helpless footsoldiers from javelin and sword. He plunged Wolf Sword into the armpit of a Spanish arm, raised – too late – in a strike against him. Horses buffeted men. Blackstone sidestepped a hulking mass of horseflesh, eyes rolling in terror, teeth bared, the bridle's bit pulled hard back into its mouth by a savage rider scything a bloodstained sword. Blackstone let Wolf Sword fall free from his grasp, held by the blood knot on his wrist, reached up and yanked the man's shield, hauling him from the saddle. In the mêlée, the man fell hard but rolled clear of his mount's lashing hooves, regained his balance and attacked. Blackstone was knocked to one side by the beast, giving the Spaniard time to lunge. John Jacob stepped between them. Dropping his shoulder, he bent from the waist and slashed upwards. The hardened steel severed the Spaniard's hand, causing him to falter. Jacob pivoted and thrust the sword blade beneath the man's chin strap.

Blackstone strode forward, John Jacob a step behind. The darkness aided the turmoil. Blackstone and John Jacob cut their way into the chaos of death, Jacob hamstringing horses, Blackstone killing their riders. The beautiful horses rolled and whinnied in agony. Men danced clear of flailing hooves; some were struck, bones breaking, and left lame and vulnerable, unable to defend themselves, ready to be slaughtered.

Blackstone grabbed a horse's bridle, throwing his weight down on the panicked animal, forcing it to fall to one side, trapping its rider. John Jacob leaned on his sword hilt, pushing the blade into the man's throat. William Ashford and Renfred worked together, as deadly as Blackstone and his squire. Renfred plunged a fallen javelin into a horse's ribs; it reared, then Ashford killed the unseated rider with his war hammer, piercing the man's helmet and skull. Blackstone's men, well practised in close-quarter killing, moved instinctively: one pair breaking to join another, four men effectively killing their enemy and then breaking off again. One man peeling aside to join another lone fighter. Then regrouping. Pressing forward. Smashing the enemy like a mailed fist.

A horseman raked his spurs, yanked his mount's reins and spun his horse against Blackstone. The weight knocked him down. Blackstone fell hard, the wind knocked out of him. A sudden stab of pain ricocheted through him. On the other side of the horse John Jacob fought the cavalryman but the experienced *jinete* parried his blows and stabbed his javelin repeatedly, his attack aided by the horse striking Jacob aside. Blackstone's squire went down. Iron-shod hooves lashed at him. Jacob rolled clear. A dazed Blackstone hauled himself painfully onto his knees, using Wolf Sword for support. The powerful beast struck him again. The Castilian rider raised his javelin against the easy target. A hulking shadow loomed from the scattered bodies on the ground. The last thing the *jinete* saw was the snarling face of a bearded giant. He did not see the knife that rammed into his skull between his eyes.

Meulon jumped clear. The rider fell from the saddle. The horse bolted. The throat-cutter hauled Blackstone to his feet. 'They're turning, Sir Thomas. They're retreating.'

John Jacob spat blood. 'Hard to kill these Spanish horsemen. Determined bastards.'

'Aye,' said Blackstone. 'And we invited them in. Our guard was down.'

The attack faltered. Blackstone saw the ragged groups of horsemen pulling back. John of Gaunt and Chandos had come in from the right flank, drawn up their men in battle formation. Unbreakable. They struck out, forging through the attackers, their men guarding the Prince, who was slower than Blackstone ever remembered seeing him, each sword blow taking effort. Don Pedro was no coward and he and his personal entourage followed John of Gaunt, but he was shielded from the fighting – most likely, Blackstone thought, on the Prince's orders. Pedro's safety was paramount if the crown was to be regained. As the defenders' numbers swelled, the army turned the tide of violence in their favour. And then the horsemen were gone. Their lightning raid a dispiriting success against the Prince and his captains.

Blackstone saw that his men had survived. Gulping air to ease their exhaustion, they leaned on their weapons, resting strained muscles. Most cut and bruised, some wounded, all defiant.

Don Pedro strode through the Prince's ranks and stabbed repeatedly at a dead horseman. The Prince admonished him: 'He is dead, my lord. He can cause you no harm.'

'They are traitors. They are Castilian. They turn against me. There can be no mercy even for their dead.'

Blackstone saw the Prince's thinly veiled disdain and turned back to where his horses were corralled.

The Prince called to him. 'Thomas?'

Blackstone stopped long enough to make sure the Prince heard his answer. The wind still buffeted men's ears and the screams of the wounded swirled across the camp.

'If they've attacked us, then they will have attacked William Felton and Sir Gilbert.'

Blackstone didn't wait for an answer. Killbere and his men were in mortal danger.

CHAPTER THIRTY-TWO

Sir William Felton and his four-hundred-strong reconnaissance force were encamped on a hill above the village of Aríñez. The wind had not brought the sound of battle from Vitoria four miles to the north-east. Men huddled in their blankets, their only security on the hillside the darkness that engulfed them. Killbere argued with the stubborn Felton that no fires be lit.

'The French and Castilians must know where we are,' Felton insisted. 'No force of any number attacks at night. Giving the men warmth and hot food is what will sustain them.'

'And I tell you that Thomas Blackstone and I have committed night raids and slaughtered men in their beds.'

'Men who attack at night are of low character.' Felton's words were harsh, showing no concern for the insult he directed at Blackstone and Killbere.

'Dishonour me and Sir Thomas and by God you'll know what violence is. I do not doubt your courage, Sir William, and nor do I doubt your stubborn reluctance to see things for what they are. I will let your insult pass this once but not again. Light your fires and be damned. If you insist on telling every French skinner and Castilian horseman where we lie, then I will withdraw my archers and men.'

'You are under my command,' Felton hissed.

'Aye, and I intend to live long enough to serve you as needs must. No fires, Sir William. I'll not have it.'

The two veteran knights faced each other. Neither looked to yield. And then Felton nodded and turned his back.

Killbere watched him a moment longer as the darkness enfolded him into the huddled masses. He and Blackstone had come up against Felton in the past. The old-fashioned insistence on following procedure he'd displayed when administrator of Poitou continued and served men ill in the field.

'Sir Gilbert?'

Killbere turned to Will Longdon, who approached from their own position on top of the hill near the treeline, a place chosen by the veteran knight as the best defensive position to hold despite Felton's knuckle-headed insistence that all would be well.

'Did he listen?' said the archer.

'Aye, as much as he preferred not to. We keep our picket lines, Will, damn him and his clerk's liking for neat columns in a ledger of accounts. Daylight will see us on the move again and forge ahead into Castile. That's his plan. What he doesn't understand is that we've been here before. These are not the gentle fields of Poitou. These valleys are treacherous and ideal for ambush from those who hold the heights around us. We keep what advantage we have on this damned hill and look after ourselves.'

The two veterans turned back up the hillside to their men's positions. Longdon and Killbere had known and fought alongside each other even before Thomas Blackstone had been brought into their ranks as a sixteen-year-old archer. Will had fifty archers and Blackstone's sixty men-at-arms made up their force. Blackstone and his men were few, always had been, and they travelled quickly and struck hard. Neither Longdon nor Killbere appreciated being under the command of a stickler for the rules of engagement like William Felton.

Longdon bent into the hill. His legs ached and he wheezed. 'Trouble is,' he said, halting to catch his breath, 'Henry of

Trastámara is fighting on his home ground and his brother Tello has a fearsome reputation as a cavalryman. You ally their fighting skills with those of du Guesclin and d'Audrehem and a dull-thinking knight like Sir William will be sorely tested. And us with him if he gets his way.'

Killbere snorted and spat, took a gulp of air and bent again into the ascent. 'Why do you think I sent Halfpenny and a couple of his lads into the village? If there's to be an assault on us they'll come through there first. And Jack's agile enough to get out and warn us.' He glanced at the breathless archer at his side. 'If I'd sent you we'd all be dead in our beds by the time you got word to us.'

Longdon groaned with the effort of the steep incline. 'Oh, long before that, Sir Gilbert. I'd have no breath to shout a warning. Damned if this hill has not grown in height.'

The village of Aríñez supported fewer than a hundred inhab- itants. Their stone houses, small and dark, with slit windows to keep out blistering summer heat and bitter winter cold, barely allowed any natural light to reach their interior. A tallow candle burned in one such house vacated by a villager who had taken his pigs to market. The room, bare except for a straw mattress and cot and cooking pot, accommodated Jack Halfpenny and two of his archers, Walter Root and Roger Fairfoot, young men agile enough to run like hares if the wolves of war gave pursuit. The candle flame was low, casting shadows barely noticeable through the narrow window. Its light allowed Fairfoot to concentrate on cutting slices from a smoked ham he'd found wrapped in sacking.

The two archers had been recruited in Bordeaux when Blackstone returned from Spain the last time. Good men had been lost rescuing Don Pedro, and these two, among a dozen more replacements, had been selected in a formidable test of their skills overseen by Will Longdon. Their loyalty, foremost, was to Jack Halfpenny, their ventenar, who had honoured them and chosen them to join Sir Thomas Blackstone, even though they were untested in battle.

Halfpenny let the two younger men sample the ham. 'That's enough, lads. We'll take the rest back for the others.'

Walter Root sprayed meat from his overstuffed mouth as he spoke. 'These Spanish know how to cure a ham.'

Halfpenny did not turn around but kept his focus on the flint- and stone-embedded road into the village. Any approaching iron-shod hooves would be audible as they struck the uneven surface. 'Aye, and the good thing is you cannot see the maggots in this light.'

He heard Root splutter and Fairfoot snigger.

'Quiet,' Halfpenny hissed. 'Douse the candle.'

Root obeyed and the two men crowded Halfpenny's shoulder as he stared into the night.

'You see something, Master Halfpenny?' whispered Fairfoot.

The seasoned archer didn't answer. His keen eyesight had noticed a slow, deliberate shifting of darkness. Something or someone at the approach to the village. The wind moaned as it found its way around the houses, but there was another sound, a soft rhythmic shuffling, muffled by the persistent wind, confounding his senses as he attempted to put an image to it in his mind's eye.

Being confined made it difficult to determine what had alerted him. He whispered: 'Outside. Stay low.'

Halfpenny eased open the door's leather-hinged planks. The opening led to the back of the house and the low stone dry wall of the empty pig pen. Halfpenny edged around the wall, one hand keeping a firm grip on his war bow. The others followed, shadowing Halfpenny's every move. He could hear their heavy breathing as they controlled their fear. He nudged his back into the wall and half turned.

'Stay here,' he whispered.

They nodded – no need to be told twice. Halfpenny belly-crawled into the open space between the wall and the next house, which gave him a less obstructed view of the road. He held his breath when he saw three horses abreast, their dark riders easing their mounts forward, their hooves wrapped in sacking as they led a column from the far end of the village. Once past the houses they would wheel, form up and charge the English position on the hill.

Halfpenny squirmed backwards until he reached the others. He touched Fairfoot's shoulder. 'Roger, you run hard and fast and warn Sir Gilbert and Lord Felton. Tell them hundreds of horsemen are about to attack. Hard, mind you, stop for nothing or anyone. Your life and everyone else's depend on it.' Halfpenny saw the young man's eyes widen. He nodded and turned into the night.

Halfpenny sighed. 'Now, Walter, we'll use the houses for cover and do what damage we can and then we run up the flank back to Sir Gilbert. Understand?'

The lad nodded, and without another word between them, Halfpenny and his archer skirted the house's shadows, getting as far ahead of the advancing cavalry as they could. Root followed his ventenar's example and stabbed half a dozen arrows into the dirt, then nocked an arrow shaft onto his war bow. They were fifty yards ahead of the leading horsemen that crested the rise in the road. The two archers shot into the dark shapes, uncaring whether they hit man or beast. Horses reared, whinnying; men fell from the saddle. Six arrows followed in rapid succession from each archer. The column broke. Riders spurred forward. Halfpenny and Root turned and ran, dodging between the houses. They stepped out into the open again and loosed two more arrows apiece. Horsemen were wheeling through the narrow confines between the houses, seeking those who ambushed them. Halfpenny turned, ran in another direction, all the while staying ahead of the confusion on the road.

'No!' Halfpenny called as Root turned the wrong way at the sound of a horse so close they could hear it snorting. Root faltered. The horse blocked his way. The young archer did not see the Spanish rider's javelin thrust forward, its point taking him below his throat, driving down into his heart and lungs.

Halfpenny drew and shot the rider; the man fell next to the dead archer. The horse panicked, the narrow gap between the houses giving it no means of escape. Halfpenny gripped his bow, ducked beneath the wild-eyed beast and clawed himself up into the saddle. He leaned back, tugged the reins, kicking wildly with his heels to back the horse away from the dead men and the confined space. He was clear. He yanked the reins to drive the beast towards the English lines. But he was cut off. Hundreds of French and Spanish horsemen were already storming up the hill.

CHAPTER THIRTY-THREE

Killbere waited, hands crossed on his sword's pommel, its blade point in the ground. He gazed down the hill into the night. Will Longdon's archers stood in a sawtooth formation, each bowman standing between a man-at-arms in extended line to either side of the veteran knight. Eighty yards below him Felton's men moved rapidly into battle formation, his archers split onto both flanks. Felton and his knights were the vanguard. The surge of panic had been released when a faint cry of '*Attack! Attack!*' reached their ears. Fairfoot's voice carried far enough on the wind to raise the alarm. And then fell silent beneath the rolling thunder of horsemen charging uphill, the ground shuddering, the power of horses pounding out their own drumbeats, drowning out Felton's drummers commanding his men where to fight.

'Jack hasn't returned,' said Longdon, in the knowledge that his trusted ventenar was probably dead.

Killbere nodded. 'He's done his duty. He's sent one of his lads to raise the alarm.'

The thud of horseflesh smashing into shields rolled uphill to Killbere. Felton's men were well trained and the stubborn man himself was no coward. They re-formed, struck back and held their line. A storm of arrows from Felton's archers flanking the main body fell onto the enemy, killing and maiming. But as one rank of Spanish and French fell, others charged through them. Killbere waited.

He turned to Will Longdon at his side. 'They will not let

their horses die needlessly, Will. The onslaught will come when they regroup and dismount. As soon as the line wavers and breaks, we go forward.'

'As good a place to die as any,' said Longdon.

Killbere spat towards the enemy. Felton's vanguard had been pushed back. Men were going down under javelin and lance. Horses were turning; French and Spanish soldiers were advancing on foot. 'Nowhere is a good place to die, you damned fool. Now let's be about our business and kill these bastards.'

Jack Halfpenny surged through the clustered horsemen that hurtled past him towards the battlefield. There were so many. He knew no one on that hill could survive such an assault. To ride back would be suicide, to ride to the Prince's camp and Blackstone was the hill's only salvation. The horse's blood was up. He tightened the rein with one hand and readied his bow to use its horned nock as a weapon. The horse bolted through the swirling mass of men with Jack low in the saddle. Despite the cold night air, sweat slaked Halfpenny's back. He was in the midst of Spanish *jinetes*. Perhaps they mistook him for one of d'Audrehem's mercenaries, or perhaps they were too surprised to see a lone horseman bolting through their ranks to react; whatever the reason, he was soon clear and galloping away towards Vitoria. Desperation made him grip the horse's heaving flanks. He squinted into the night. Clouds shifted. The wind punched him. Rain spat in his face. The night held him in contempt, but he didn't slow down. If he met more of Trastámara's men on the road he would die. There would be no chance for the archer's protector, the Silver Wheel Goddess he wore at his throat, to save him again. Next time she would ease his passing into death.

He stared ahead into the storm and felt his heart quicken. More horsemen appeared. They stopped, three abreast. He had nowhere to run.

Killbere and his men held the line. Sir William Felton had counter-attacked, forcing the French and Spanish back on their heels. Yard by yard the enemy resisted Felton's pressure, and then they regrouped and attacked in overwhelming numbers. Killbere, slashing and parrying, his shield battered and torn, tried to go to the aid of the man he scorned even while respecting his courage. But it was in vain. Felton went down, never to rise again. His own archers had long since emptied their arrow bags and fought among the men-at-arms, wielding their bastard swords and archer's knives.

Killbere saw Felton's men were being outflanked. 'Back, Will! Buy us time to reach the trees.'

Longdon's bowmen were thirty paces behind the men-at-arms. Longdon bent into his bow as he hauled back an arrow. His archers followed as one. Above the cacophony Killbere heard him shout: '*Loose!*' Arrows fell into the rear ranks of the attackers. Sudden death slowed the advance. Those on the front line fought on but lost the weight of men behind them as a second storm from Longdon's archers landed. The French and Spanish line fractured into smaller pockets of men. Killbere's men-at-arms and Felton's survivors had repulsed three attacks, but Killbere saw the hopelessness of their situation. Blood from a scalp wound blinded one eye, a blow that had creased his helm and put him on his knees. The man next to him had stepped forward, taking the killing blow, allowing the veteran knight to stagger to his feet and kill his assailant.

The ragged line of survivors stepped back a pace at a time, leaving bodies strewn across the hillside. Sir William Felton's force had been all but destroyed by the lightning raid. Further down the hill, knights surrendered and were taken for ransom. Killbere and the remaining men-at-arms reached the archers' line of defence. The treeline would be their redoubt. Their last stand.

The Spanish and French fighters were as exhausted as the defenders. The final incline slowed them further. They formed up again, their captains shouting for them to make one final deadly assault and claim the day. Men vomited from their effort; others laid back their heads and sucked in cold morning air to replenish their depleted lungs.

Killbere looked left and right. Half his men were missing, lying dead on the hill below like the hundreds of others. The bare trees behind them would be the only place that could give them a chance of survival when the attack came.

'Back to the trees, lads,' he called.

As the men were about to turn and obey Killbere saw the men below stare past them. They looked shocked; their line wavered. Killbere looked behind him. Jack Halfpenny and Blackstone with his captains had stormed the crest from the reverse of the hillside. Blackstone strode down to the sound of the men cheering, roused by his miraculous appearance. Pulses quickening, they yelled their defiance at the ragged line in front of them.

Blackstone and John Jacob, with Renfred, Aicart, Meulon, William Ashford and thirty more men drawn from John of Gaunt's contingent, took their place in the line. Still so few, but they were fresh fighting men, fearless and ready to kill.

Will Longdon and his archers each had one arrow remaining. He called out his command.

'Nock. Draw. Loose!'

Blackstone roared; his men bellowed in unison. The arrows tore into the men forty yards below. The survivors turned and ran. Their battle was lost. The English had won.

CHAPTER THIRTY-FOUR

Blackstone's arrival had saved Killbere and the survivors. Renfred had found the track up the rear of the hill but the final climb had been too steep for the horses, so the animals had been abandoned and the relief force had had to arrive on foot. They had been successful, but the cost had been high. Sir William Felton's courage in the fight overshadowed the fact that his defences had been poor.

When the survivors returned to the Prince's camp, barber surgeons attended to the wounded. Halfpenny sat hunched, head down, as Killbere allowed Will Longdon to stitch the cut on his scalp.

He growled. 'In the name of Jesus on the Cross, you are as clumsy as a one-armed man fastening his tunic.'

Will Longdon concentrated on the task at hand. 'Sir Gilbert, you have more scars than strands in my bow cord. If you tremble like a village whore at the sight of Meulon's cock then my hand becomes unsteady.'

Killbere gritted his teeth. He called to Halfpenny: 'Jack, you despair. No need, lad. You brought Sir Thomas to us.'

'I lost Walter Root, Sir Gilbert. I turned the wrong way and he was lost.'

'Men die at our shoulder, you know that. There's no blame to be had in a fight.'

'The lad was barely old enough to serve.'

'And yet you stayed and fought with him. God's tears, Jack, you sent Fairfoot to warn us. He raised the alarm and had the good sense to hide in a ditch when the attack came. He lived. You are in credit. You did what you were sent to do. And more. I'll not have you mewling here – go and see to your men. Those that live need to see the man who leads them. Go on. Away with you. And don't stoop like a whipped dog. You fought. You lived. That's all there is to it.'

Halfpenny stood and looked at the veteran knight and his centenar.

'Listen to Sir Gilbert,' said Longdon. 'See to your men. Wet bow cords or damaged fletchings are no good to us if another attack comes.'

'Aye, I'll check them,' said Halfpenny, and turned away to join his archers.

Longdon finished dealing with Killbere's wound. 'Jack will be all right,' he said, and then stepped back. 'Done.'

The veteran knight grunted. 'You bind a fletching with more skill than you attend to a wound barely worth looking at.'

'Aye, Sir Gilbert, but my arrows do not protest when I repair them. They fly straight and true in gratitude.'

Killbere stood and placed tentative fingers on the wound. 'Gratitude I give to God. You are sufficiently rewarded by me not putting my boot up your arse when you inflict more pain than the enemy.'

While his men's wounds were being attended to, Blackstone faced the Prince, his brother and John Chandos in the Prince's pavilion. Blackstone's anger was barely contained.

'You lead us to defeat, my Prince. Your commanders are ill prepared for the way Trastámara and his captains fight. We have become arrogant from years of success and they have learned their lessons well. The French have told them not to face us in battle so they are staging rapid strikes and our men die. We must take the initiative, my lords, or you will have no army left by the time you reach Burgos. If you must put that worthless king back on the throne then let us leave Spain with an army still capable of fighting. Disease, death and hunger await us in this place. It is cursed with his poison and our stupidity.'

'Thomas! For God's sake, remember where you are and whom you address,' said Sir John Chandos.

'John, I know full well.' He looked directly at the Prince. 'You're ailing, my lord. You have let your guard down. What men we have can still defeat Trastámara and his French and Breton mercenaries, but we must move now.'

John of Gaunt stepped forward, face flushed with anger, an accusatory finger pointing at Blackstone. 'Time and time again you insult your Prince. Time and again you are given the benefit of his good will—'

Blackstone cut him off as rapidly as Wolf Sword would cut through an enemy. Savage and determined, his raised voice halted John of Gaunt. 'Do not lecture me, my lord! I am the King's Master of War. I am loyal to King and Prince. You squander advice from me and Sir John, yet you have never fought in a campaign before. You are the Prince's brother. A prince who destroyed the French face to face. It is my Prince who must shoulder both success and failure. It is he and he alone who can lead us to victory. But he must grasp this army with a steel grip otherwise we are lost.'

For a moment it looked as though John of Gaunt was going to strike Blackstone. John Chandos stepped forward; Blackstone did not flinch.

The Prince stood, his anger sparking him into action. Voice raised: 'Enough!'

Blackstone's provocation had brought the Prince to his senses, dragging him from whatever ailment claimed him.

'Thomas speaks the truth and no delicacy of manners can hide it. We have lost our way in this campaign and we are to blame. We are deeply saddened by the loss of Sir William and his men. And we are grateful that Thomas arrived when he did to deny our enemy a rout. We did not believe Trastámara would dare to strike us the way he has. Rouse the army, Sir John, we prepare to move into Castile.'

Blackstone took a step forward. 'Highness, not yet. We cannot follow the road directly to Burgos. Trastámara holds the high ground at Zaldiaran three miles south of here. He will hold the pass at Puebla. And that stops you from reaching Burgos by that route.'

'How do you know this?' said John of Gaunt.

'We questioned one of their men who survived the attack. The rivers are in spring flood and he'll control the bridges. I know this country – my men scouted across it. We must get behind him, and then choose where to fight.'

Chandos looked at the Prince and nodded. Blackstone was the one man who knew the ground.

'Very well. What do you suggest?' said the Prince.

'We retreat, turn back.'

'Across the Sierra de Cantabria?' said Chandos. 'Those hills are rugged and hard on man and beast. Food is already short and the conditions will exhaust us further.'

'We know our way through,' said Blackstone. 'It is an easier route than the one that brought you here.' He glanced at John of Gaunt, no doubt responsible for urging the Prince to take the northern route. A grave decision which had had a heavy cost. 'They will shadow us along the next valley, but once we are through the mountains we will turn south-west to Logroño; the garrison there still favours Don

Pedro. We'll cross the bridge on the Ebro and then we are behind them.'

John of Gaunt was agitated. 'I say we stay on route. We can break through the pass.'

It was time for Blackstone to remain silent. He had offered the plan and now it was up to the Prince to accept it or not.

'Thomas, you have lost good men on our behalf. What is it you need?'

'Archers. I can recruit from the Cheshire men and I need men-at-arms. Half of mine are dead. Sir Gilbert and many others sustained wounds. There are good men who will serve.'

The Prince nodded. 'Choose them well, Thomas. You lead the army. We ride to Logroño.'

CHAPTER THIRTY-FIVE

The army's pace had quickened. Their sense of purpose had been heightened by the Prince's determination to take the fight to the enemy and with Blackstone now leading the way they could smell victory. Towns and villages along the way had opened their gates and come out to cheer the might of the English army and the renowned Prince of Wales and Aquitaine. Killbere offered his thoughts on the matter to Blackstone riding at his side.

'I'll wager Don Pedro takes their welcome to be a personal endorsement of his return to the Castilian throne. But if I were a peasant and saw this host, banners and pennons whipped by the wind and thousands of horses, knights and mounted archers, I'd cheer for the mad bastard. Wouldn't you?'

'Whether or not they're cheering for him, word travels fast. It will serve us well if Trastámara thinks Don Pedro is being welcomed back. It puts him under pressure to act decisively against us, and this time we will be ready,' Blackstone said.

Six days after breaking camp at Vitoria, Blackstone led the army over the great stone bridge across the River Ebro at Logroño. The army camped among the orchards and olive groves around the fortress town waiting for Renfred and his scouts to return with their report of where Trastámara was camped. Once the German captain had returned, Blackstone took him into the Prince's pavilion despite being unwashed and dishevelled from his reconnaissance.

Blackstone addressed the Prince, his brother, Chandos and

Don Pedro. 'Highness, my men have returned and Renfred has seen Trastámara's camp.' He nodded to Renfred, who dragged a stick across the dirt floor.

'We are here, the garrison and the river secure our rear, and Trastámara has shadowed us from the west as we thought he would. He holds the west bank of the River Najerilla here,' said Renfred.

'And the distance between us?' said Chandos.

'A dozen miles, no more, lord,' said the German captain.

'His army is camped there?' said John of Gaunt.

'Aye, my lord. It is a great host. We saw their blazons. Castilian, French and Breton. He brought his whole army south. He holds the road to Burgos.'

Blackstone nodded to Renfred, who bowed, and left the pavilion.

Blackstone scraped a line with the stick. 'It's open ground between us. There's a village here, and if we take the army there, we can attempt to draw him into battle.'

'Highness?' said John of Gaunt to the King. 'You know this place?'

Don Pedro looked at the crude scratchings on the ground. 'Navarrete. It would serve only as a place to camp. But if we have to cross the river he straddles then we'll be at a disadvantage.'

'He will not fight us on open ground, Thomas,' said the Prince. 'He will continue to raid us. We must find a way to draw him to us.'

'Not with the French and Bretons advising him,' said Chandos. 'They won't let him fight a pitched battle.'

Don Pedro had remained silent while his benefactors discussed the problem facing them. He stepped forward. 'I know this bastard King. How will he keep a firm hold on the crown if he does not fight? How does any king hold a country and its people if he does not fight? It is political, my lords. He is already weak because we have come in force to reclaim my throne. The people will not tolerate a weak king.' He addressed the Prince. 'We taunt him. We insult him. We challenge him. He knows he must ignore the French and Bretons if he is going to be seen as strong. His own Castilian advisers know this. The time is now.'

John of Gaunt turned to his brother. 'Insulting a king is best done by one who knows how.'

The three men looked at Blackstone.

Blackstone's men waited on their side of the narrow River Najerilla as Blackstone and Killbere splashed across the ford. Blazons curled and rippled from the pavilions. Shields were laid outside every tent. Blackstone recognized the colours of knights and lords, the renowned Orders of the Sash, Calatrava, Santiago and St John. It was a great host that outnumbered the Prince's army.

'A glorious sight, Thomas,' said Killbere. 'I can hear the trumpets and drums before they are even ordered to fight. It will be a wondrous day if we confront them on the field of battle.'

Blackstone looked uncertainly at the veteran knight, who shrugged and continued: 'They will slaughter us, for God's sake. How can we confront so many?'

'We've done it before,' said Blackstone.

'Aye, but God had abandoned our enemies back then, and now I fear He might turn His eyes from us. When was the last time we were shriven? A man should not die without his sins being confessed and absolved.'

'And you have more sins than most,' said Blackstone.

'I have my fair share.'

'The years I have spent at your side tell me otherwise,' said Blackstone. 'Look there, a monastery downriver. Perhaps they have a priest who would spend the next week listening to your confession. We could postpone the battle until he surrenders from exhaustion.'

Their horses reached the far shore.

'It would be wise to explore the place, Thomas. Who knows, they might even have nuns there.'

Blackstone spurred his horse forward. Their approach had been seen long before they crossed the shallows and the resting army rose to its feet, clearing a path for the English Prince's messenger. There were thirty and more pavilions laid out around that of Trastámara's, and great lords and legendary knights stepped into the open as Blackstone and Killbere drew up their mounts.

Blackstone recognized the blazons on the men who strode forward. Marshal Arnoul d'Audrehem had fought the Prince and Blackstone at Poitiers; the Breton Bertrand du Guesclin had been on the opposing side to Blackstone at Auray three years before. Other renowned names stood at their side. Mercenary captains gathered with them. At one time or another Blackstone had fought against them all.

Killbere sighed and said in barely a whisper, 'God's tears, Thomas. All the great and good are here. There are ransoms to be had. We could retire after this fight.'

'Sir Thomas,' said the French marshal.

'My lord. I have a message from my Prince.'

'Let's hear it then,' said a stocky man-at-arms.

'Petit Meschin,' said Blackstone, addressing the man. 'I thought I smelled a foul stench in the camp. How is it the presence of a skinner like you is tolerated by a king? Even a bastard king who has no place wearing a crown?'

The affront was enough to make the quick-tempered

mercenary reach for his sword but the French marshal raised a hand. 'There will be no violence here. Sir Thomas Blackstone is a herald of the Prince. And you, Sir Gilbert, I see you are still at his side.'

'Aye, my lord. His sharp tongue and sword have kept me alive these past years.'

'Then you should know that Castile is where you are likely to die. I would not wish it. You are both respected on the battlefield as worthy adversaries.'

'But unwelcome in the company of men of character,' said du Guesclin. 'You insult those who might otherwise be a companion in battle. There should be courtesy even between enemies.'

Blackstone leaned forward in the saddle to address him directly. 'You have chosen the losing side once too often. You know you cannot win against the Prince. Perhaps it is time to sell your sword to the English.'

Killbere groaned inwardly. Blackstone was here to insult the usurper King, not the men who held sway over him. Their antagonism could result in more lightning raids to thin out the Prince's army. At that moment the man who would rejoice at Blackstone's death and the defeat of the Prince of Wales stepped outside his pavilion. His slight beard covered the lower half of his face; his thin nose and small mouth reminded Killbere of a petulant child. Another man accompanied him.

'My brother Don Tello tells me you have brought a message from the first son of the English King,' said Henry of Trastámara.

The man at his side, who wore less regal clothing yet still bore the King's blazon, looked more like a common man-at-arms. It seemed obvious he was Don Tello, the man responsible for the lightning raids against the Prince's camp.

'I bear a message for the Count of Trastámara,' said Blackstone, 'or, as he is known, the usurper King of Castile.'

It was insult enough. Don Tello went to snatch at Blackstone's bridle but the bastard horse snapped its yellow teeth, forcing him to step back. Trastámara placed a restraining hand on his brother's arm. 'Do not rise to this common man's taunts, brother. He knows full well he addresses the King of Castile.' He stepped closer to Blackstone. 'You and the King's son defend a murderer. He is an unholy man.' By not referring to the Prince's rightful title, Trastámara traded insult for insult. 'And it is unthinkable that your King's son, who claims to be a pious knight, does so.'

Blackstone stared hard at Trastámara. He and his brother had succeeded in inflicting grievous loss on the Prince's army. If they could not be brought onto the battlefield, against the French King and his marshal's advice, then there would be no way of defeating him.

'Your father sired ten illegitimate children. You are but one of the litter. It is Don Pedro's God-given right to rule. You strike in the night at sleeping men like a cowardly dog afraid of a whipping. You are a puppet of the French King and these men he sent to control you. You have no right to be a king. A true king does not dance to another's tune. I know the French – I have fought them; I am their enemy – but you are nothing. You have no courage other than that given by these men. The Prince of Wales and Aquitaine is a warrior. He is the son of a warrior king. He despises cowardice.'

Trastámara's puffy cheeks flushed red. His voice trembled. His finger wavered as he pointed at Blackstone. 'You think to goad me into a battle, Sir Thomas. Well, I have already slaughtered hundreds of your men. I am ready to face you not because of your insults, but because I have seen how weak your army is.'

Blackstone saw the look of disbelief cross the French marshal's face. Arnoul d'Audrehem stepped forward, his voice barely able to disguise the plea it carried. 'Highness, we have the Prince and his army at our mercy. They fall in ever-increasing numbers. It is how we shall defeat them.'

Trastámara had not taken his eyes off Blackstone and the scar-faced knight had not turned his gaze away.

'Your French master says otherwise,' said Blackstone.

Trastámara snapped. 'We will take the field!' He pointed away to the side. 'We cross the river tomorrow. Tell my unholy brother he will die there. Tell your Prince he will be shamed and humiliated. And defeated. Tell him that.'

Trastámara turned back and strode to his pavilion. The look of triumph on Tello's face did not match the grim countenance of the French marshal or that of Bertrand du Guesclin.

Blackstone smiled. 'My lords,' he said. 'Take the sacrament before dawn because by nightfall many of you will be dead.'

He and Killbere spurred their horses away.

CHAPTER THIRTY-SIX

The Prince's army readied itself before first light. The main road ahead of their camp at Navarrete would lead them directly to the battlefield at Nájera. The lords and noble knights of the Prince's army gathered in his pavilion. John of Gaunt, Sir John Chandos, Don Pedro and his immediate entourage, among them the Count de Osona, a disgraced son of an Aragonese politician, one of many dissidents who had thrown in their lot with the murderous King. Behind the Prince and his brother stood the two marshals of the army, Steven Cusington and Guichard d'Angle; the Gascons Bertucat d'Albret and Jean de Grailly, the Captal de Buch – a long-time friend of Blackstone's; the Count d'Armagnac; the exiled King James of Majorca had his own Aragonese followers. The fighting men's armour glowed in the dull light of the lanterns, their blazons a proclamation of honour and courage. Mercenary commanders stood shoulder to shoulder at the entrance. The Prince's words would carry to them all and they would relate his commands to their captains and the thousands of men waiting.

The Prince, resplendent in his armour and showing no sign of the ailment that had plagued him, addressed them, his voice resonating with confidence and authority, spurred on by the expectation of battle and victory.

'The order of march will be led by our father's Master of War, Sir Thomas Blackstone. Our brother John will follow. My lords, we do not ride directly at our enemy. Sir Thomas has found a route that takes us through the hills past the village of Huércanos. It is shielded by a ridge and places us on Trastámara's left flank. He and his commanders will lose their battle formation when they turn to face us. We have spent the night in preparation and in prayer. We pray you safe and wish you good fortune. Look to your men.'

Blackstone led the army onto the broad treeless plain between the Prince's camp and Trastámara's chosen place of battle. After two miles he turned off the road and followed his German captain, Renfred, and his scouts who led the way uphill. The sullen rhythmic sound of an army on the move was all that could be heard. The jangle of bridles and the snorting of a horse here and there carried nowhere on the wind, cushioned as they were between the folding uplands. A winding steep ridge rose to the highest peak between the army and Trastámara's men. Several miles later Blackstone took them around a conical hill and through a broadening gap north of where Trastámara was waiting in battle formation. Blackstone halted the column and he and Renfred dismounted and crouched forward to gaze down on their enemy. Trastámara's army faced the road that led to Navarrete, still expecting the Prince to ride directly at them.

Blackstone and his captain ran back to the Prince.

'Highness, it is as we hoped. We are on their flank. Once we cross the crest of the hill we will be in full view barely four hundred yards from them but we keep the advantage of being on higher ground. If we move fast, within minutes we will be in range for our archers.'

'Who faces us?' said the Prince.

'Front ranks are horsemen, their main army behind them. They would have attacked us on the approach and scattered us before we took up position. Now they must wheel. Bertrand du Guesclin's blazon stands with the French marshal's in the vanguard. Trastámara's standard is with his Castilian lords and the crusading orders.'

'Thomas, you will hold centre ground in the vanguard. Sir John and our brother with you.'

The Prince dismounted, followed by the others; then he gave his orders to his marshals and the assembled captains for their line of march. He graced Sir John Chandos with the privilege of unfurling the great silk banner. He turned to Blackstone. 'Unfold your colours, Thomas. Let them see we are *Défiant à la Mort.*'

John Jacob raised Blackstone's banner. Killbere placed a finger on each nostril and snorted.

'Sir Gilbert,' said the Prince, 'you are fit to fight again? Your head wound?'

'Lord, I blow snot, not brains.'

The Prince took a step closer and lowered his voice. 'Gilbert, we value you. Younger men can take the vanguard.'

Killbere's restraint was admirable. Blackstone knew he must have chewed his tongue before answering. 'Sire, I have not yet reached my allotted three score years and ten. The French Marshal d'Audrehem has already passed his sixtieth year. Would you shame me, my Prince? Would you deny me battle? It takes a sharp axe to fell a mighty oak. It is not the vigour of a fighting man that counts, but his skill. Which, my lord, is why many a young woman prefers a man of mature years.'

The Prince did not disguise his pleasure at Killbere's answer. 'As always you remind your Prince of the value of stalwart men, Gilbert. We shall send warning to the tavern women of Burgos.'

'No need, highness. I told them I would return.'

The exchange between the veteran knight and the Prince lifted Edward's spirits. He laughed, facing his officers. 'We advance behind Sir Thomas Blackstone and Sir Gilbert. Let every man know his place, and stand his ground.'

Dawn lightened the sky. Banners unfurled; pennons of every hue were raised like a field of flowers.

Blackstone turned towards the crest of the hill.

The Prince of Wales and Aquitaine, with his Anglo-Gascon army, followed.

CHAPTER THIRTY-SEVEN

Fear knifed into Trastámara's orderly ranks.

Trumpets and drums reverberated across the battlefield. Cries of '*St George! St George!*' and '*Guînes and Prince Edward!*'

The startling appearance of the English on their left flank threw the frontline cavalry into confusion. Bertrand du Guesclin wheeled his horsemen as ten thousand footsoldiers packed tightly behind the horses jostled, uncertain of their orders as their captains bellowed for them to turn and face the surging English horde.

Du Guesclin was no stranger to the English fighting skills. He and Marshal d'Audrehem had pleaded with Trastámara and his brother Tello to rescind the pledge made to Blackstone. Raiding and killing was the only way to defeat the English, not by facing them on the battlefield, but his success at lightning attacks had made Trastámara overconfident. There was barely time to save the *jinetes*. Such light cavalry without heavy armour would not survive long against the English and Welsh bowmen that swarmed onto either flank of the Prince's army. And the Castilian heavy cavalry thought it demeaning to dismount and fight on foot. Du Guesclin had no choice but to charge the English vanguard and pray the footsoldiers were at his heels. If he could punch a gap in the English ranks they might still outflank them. He raised his shield and drew his sword. The men around him steadied their mounts, readied javelin and lance, and charged.

*

Blackstone and his men reached the place where the army would make its stand. Will Longdon and Jack Halfpenny had already instructed their bowmen to use broadhead arrows. John of Gaunt's archers on either flank would bring a hailstorm of bodkin-tipped arrows onto the riders but Longdon's arrows would severely wound or kill the horses.

Du Guesclin's initial charge faltered as the first fluttering storm of arrows fell. Riders who managed to stay in the saddle uninjured turned their mounts this way and that, trying to avoid the terrifying strikes. Horses barged each other; men fell beneath their hooves. But they came on. Courage was not lacking. Hatred for Don Pedro and his Anglo-Gascon allies drove them forward. Glory and honour beckoned. Men imbued with the chivalric code, the Knights of la Banda beneath their red and gold standard, gave others the courage to ignore their fear. But the charge, despite all its splendour of great lords with their tapestry of heraldic blazons, was doomed to fail.

Meulon's men rammed the foot of their spear shafts into the dirt. Two men gripped each angled shaft. Riders steered their horses away from the razor-sharp points, driving them in confusion towards Blackstone and his men-at-arms, each of whom fought with the man at their shoulder, stabbing and harrying the beasts, pulling down their riders, ramming sword points into helpless men. War hammers crushed bones. Killbere's mace crippled men who fell and were slaughtered. Men stank as bowels loosened, fear and death overtaking any control they had. Heaving, sweat-soaked bodies, unwashed for days, were rank. Men shrieked: pleas for clemency unheard above the cacophony of screams, whinnying horses, trumpets and drums. Men focused on killing. Most of those who plied their trade efficiently survived; others, despite their skill, were overwhelmed, trampled underfoot by iron-shod hooves or the fate-driven tip of a randomly hurled javelin.

The cavalry came again and again until their banners wavered and fell. Survivors fled the battlefield, giving way to the heaving mass of footsoldiers. The Prince's army stood firm. Ranks of men moving forward, stepping over the fallen, holding back the enemy. And it was the enemy being slaughtered as wave after wave crashed against an unyielding wall of shield and steel. Castilians fought their own in the English ranks: families torn apart by a rabid king and a bastard son denied the throne. Brother against brother.

'Where's Sir Gilbert?' Blackstone called out.

The furious fighting twisted men back and forth, bodies swirling, their backs facing the enemy, then turned again as hammer blows rained down, then falling, grappling for life, bodies one on top of the other.

There was no answer.

John Jacob held Blackstone's banner aloft. Blackstone saw the weight of Trastámara's army pressing onto his men and the others in the vanguard. Gaunt's men held, so too Chandos's.

'Now, John!' Blackstone cried.

Jacob twirled the flag in a circular motion. Men stepped back, yard by yard, shoulder to shoulder, slashing at those who dared to come after them, who thought Blackstone's vanguard was retreating. Blackstone saw John Jacob go down; his banner fell. It stayed down until someone heaved Blackstone's squire to his feet. The banner was raised again. The enemy's advance was slow but deliberate, yet it was they who fell beneath Blackstone's men's blades. Will Longdon and Jack Halfpenny's archers shot their arrows into the surging enemy until they had no more. It was then that Blackstone gave the order to stand firm, to retreat no further. 'Hold!' he yelled.

Men bent into their shields, heads tucked low, peering at a desperate enemy close enough to smell the stench of their sweat and breath. An enemy now embedded in the heart of the Prince's army.

Trumpets blared. The signal given. It was time for the Prince to go in for the kill.

The flanks either side of Blackstone closed in and encircled the heaving mass of footsoldiers caught in the trap. Blackstone's men pressed forward to where knights' pennons wavered. Blackstone saw one knight besieged by Gaunt's men-at-arms. He fought bravely. Blood stained his mail, his or another's Blackstone did not know, but Blackstone shouldered fighters aside to reach him.

The knight's shield bore the black-headed griffin holding a sword. It was Sancha Ferrandes's uncle.

Blackstone swung Wolf Sword rapidly with unrelenting blows, forcing the knight back on his heels. The man would not yield; instead, he found his footing, resumed the high guard and slashed with renewed energy against a man he knew to be a renowned fighter. The knight's sword slid down Wolf Sword's hardened steel, caught the cross guard, twisting it almost free from Blackstone's grasp. Had it not been for the blood knot he might have lost his sword. The fight eddied around them but the contest between Blackstone and Don Fernando Ferrandes of Castile remained a private duel – all other men avoided them. Don Fernando's standard bearer lay dead at his side, sprawled across the bodies of his fellow Castilians. The Spaniard feinted, catching Blackstone momentarily off balance. Blackstone swivelled on his heel, felt the glancing strike against his left arm, his mail saving him but the blade's bite cutting into flesh. He used the wound to his advantage: he lowered his guard, dropping his shoulder as if in pain, knees bent, shoulders hunched, offering the knight the chance of a killing blow. The high guard stroke came fast. Lethal and well aimed – at where Blackstone had been a moment before. He was now a pace to one side, his opponent thrown off balance with the force of his strike. Blackstone turned Wolf Sword and hammered its pommel down onto the base of the man's neck. He dropped. Still tough enough to try to roll clear from what he knew would follow – hardened steel plunged between his shoulder blades. Blackstone stepped on the man's sword, his weight rendering the Castilian helpless. The tip of his sword was now at the man's throat.

'Yield! There is no shame, Don Fernando.'

The man's free hand pushed up his visor. 'I yield.'

Blackstone and his captive remained silent, drawing cold morning air into their lungs. The Spaniard rose slowly to his feet, his sword laid at Blackstone's feet. They looked about them now that their close-quarter fight was over. The mêlée had gone beyond them, its urgency slowing. Knights were surrendering. Paroles would be given. Ransoms secured.

The fighting had forced Trastámara's footsoldiers further back in an ever-decreasing, enfolding manoeuvre. Blackstone and his captive were surrounded by the dead and dying. Exhausted men had sunk to their knees; others were half bent over their swords. John Jacob leaned against the banner's shaft, bloodied sword in hand, heaving for breath. Blackstone still could not see Killbere. Meulon was in the distance leading a final surge against the last resistance of a defeated enemy. Where were Will Longdon and Jack Halfpenny? They and their archers had fought on with bucklers and bastard swords once their arrows were finished. Blackstone feared for his captains. Other than Meulon they were not visible.

The Castilian knight's dignity remained intact despite his defeat. 'I am worth nothing. Don Pedro killed my family and seized our land. There can be no ransom.'

'You have land in France,' said Blackstone.

'My brother's. He's dead. And his family.'

'Not all of them,' said Blackstone.

CHAPTER THIRTY-EIGHT

The Anglo-Gascons chased Trastámara's army into the river that cut across one edge of the battlefield. The water ran red. Bodies clogged the narrow bend until the current shifted the carcasses downstream. It was a significant victory for the Prince and a devastating defeat for the Castilians and their mercenaries.

Peasants came from every nearby village. Crow-like, pecking away at the fallen, seizing what they could until soldiers scattered them with threats of violence as they themselves scavenged, only for the bedraggled peasants to settle and gather elsewhere and go among the dead again.

Blackstone saw Killbere sitting on a weathered fallen tree trunk, its bark as smooth as skin, slaked with blood. He had been fighting at Blackstone's side but as the horses had broken through their ranks, and the riders unsaddled, the killing had drawn him away. He had been struck down, but William Ashford and his men had shielded him until he regained his feet and began swinging his holy-water sprinkler – his spiked chained mace – again.

He poured wine from a skin, uncaring that it splattered his beard and chest. His helm was at his feet, his mace and sword resting at his side. He was splattered with gore. 'You're getting careless, Thomas,' he said, nodding at the mail on his arm, which oozed blood.

Blackstone touched it and felt the irritation of pain. 'A lucky strike is all.' He squatted on the log and took the wineskin. 'Where are the men? I have John Jacob looking for them.'

Killbere wiped a grubby hand over his face, sighed and spat. 'I don't know. We were scattered. William Ashford was with me and then he was not. I saw Meulon on the flank with his spearmen.'

'I saw him there as well,' said Blackstone, handing back the wine. 'But Will and Jack should have been among us.'

'Aye. They took their lads into the fray. I think they went after those trying to escape. There are belts and jewels to be had.' He went to pour more wine but stopped before it reached his lips. 'This wine will rot a man's guts. I'm in need of Gascon red.'

'And what is this?' said Blackstone.

He shook his head. 'Spanish. They probably use it to tan cow hides. It's sour.'

'Did you take anyone?'

'Me? No. I killed them before they could surrender.' He shrugged. 'I don't need ransom money. Besides, they don't always pay. Then I would have to spend years in court. God's tears, I'd rather die poor with a sword in my hand. You?'

'One knight.'

'Wealthy?'

'I don't know. It's the Ferrandes woman's uncle.'

Killbere stared at him. And then, after a minute, shook his head. 'I despair for you, Thomas. I'll wager you saw him on the field of battle and thought: Ah, there's a blazon I recognize. I think I shall rescue him, hold him for ransom, and then the Ferrandes woman will show her gratitude and take me to her bed. For God's sake, man.' He bent down and pulled free a soiled silk scarf tucked into the breastplate of a dead cavalryman at his feet. He wrapped it around Blackstone's wound.

Blackstone drank and for the first time tasted the sourness. He winced. 'Not too damned tight: you'll render my arm useless.'

'Better it should render your brain or balls useless, whichever it is that stirs you to such foolishness.' He wiped his bloodied fingers on Blackstone's hose.

'He's her kin,' said Blackstone. 'There was no need for him to die. It serves no purpose – a loved one being killed.'

'Except keeping him alive does.'

'She has nothing; now she has something gifted back to her. A life is valuable, Gilbert.'

Killbere stood, blew snot, and laid his chained mace over his shoulder. 'Aye, well, tell that to them,' he said, gesturing towards the expanse of fallen bodies that lay before them and the scavengers picking over them.

Many valued captives had surrendered at the point of exhaustion, and their lives were not forfeited like those of their lesser-valued comrades, who were slain as they begged for mercy. Chivalry was reserved for the lords and knightly classes alone. Trastámara's captains, French, Castilian and Aragonese, were captured and held for ransom.

The Prince and Don Pedro took over Trastámara's pavilions. They were sufficiently lavish for the heir to the throne of England. During the battle the Prince had fought off a counter-offensive by Trastámara's brother, Tello, and the fight had invigorated him. As heralds went among the dead searching for Trastámara's body, the Prince and Don Pedro watched the prisoners being paraded before them.

Blackstone stood in line waiting to present his captive, Don Fernando Ferrandes of Castile, to the Prince. The two battle-worn men had Sancha Ferrandes in common.

'My niece is headstrong, Sir Thomas, like her father. I am grateful you saved her life but regret she failed in avenging our family.'

'I was sworn to protect Don Pedro,' Blackstone answered.

'And in doing so you prolong the misery he will inflict on his people.'

Blackstone shuffled forward as the line drew closer to the Prince, looking to where Don Pedro stood at the Prince's side, accompanied by several of his noblemen. Blackstone knew it was even more demeaning for the vanquished men to see who gloated at their defeat.

'Don Fernando, if I had not saved your niece she would have either been cut down by Pedro's guards or executed by my Prince, and it is he you should thank for sending her to a place of safety away from the man she wished to kill.'

'And for that I am indebted. But we are still in danger from Don Pedro. He will find us both soon enough. There are those who would betray us for favour with him.'

'Don't worry, you'll soon be with her and then you can escape to her lands in France.' He shot the Castilian a quick look. 'They are hers? By right? You do not control her property?'

'She is a woman with her own wealth. It is modest enough, but she has her independence.'

They moved closer to the Prince, who spoke to some of the captives. Men from noble families were often known to each other.

Don Fernando rubbed a hand over his face, etched with dirt and dried sweat. 'There is more to her than first appears, Sir Thomas. Before Don Pedro slaughtered our family she was close to an arranged marriage with one of the Frenchmen who serves the Duke of Anjou. He'll fight for Trastámara.'

'Betrothed?' said Blackstone, surprised at the feelings that lurched in his chest.

'They were chaperoned, of course, and it seemed to both families that it was a good match. These things take time, but... yes, they appeared to accept the arrangement. But I am uncertain of her true feelings for the man. He pursued her and my brother saw it as a good match. He is a knight and if he has escaped the battle then he will seek her out.'

Blackstone fell silent. If Sancha Ferrandes loved another man, and he her, then why should Blackstone care? he told himself. And the answer was sharper than he dared admit. He cared more than he should. Blackstone could not suppress the desire to find out more.

'And who is this knight?'

'Gautier de Fleur.'

'His blazon?'

'Azure field with two black chevrons. A good family but poor.'

'Then if they are both of the same mind they have an assured future,' Blackstone said by way of finalizing the matter.

Don Fernando's face creased in doubt. 'If he finds where she is he will come for her and take her back to Trastámara for her own safety. And if it is her wish to be with him then I cannot stop her even though I have my doubts about him.'

'Why?

'He wants her land.'

'That's often why men marry,' said Blackstone. 'Fighting a war can be expensive and land gives a man wealth.'

'Of course. And what man would not wish to have a wife with a dowry? No, that is not my main concern.'

Blackstone and Don Fernando had moved closer to the Prince.

'Then what is?'

'If she does not wish to go with this man will I be able to stop him?' He paused, and flexed his hand as if it caused him discomfort. 'He's young. He's strong. He may be from a poor family but he is respected.' The Castilian looked rueful. 'Sir

Thomas, let us pray she has genuine feelings for him, then we can all live out our lives in peace because he would have the better of me. I would die if I tried to stop him.'

Blackstone saw the man next to him in his true colours. Honourable and without men to fight at his side. There was nothing Blackstone could do about it. If the woman wanted to go with one of Trastámara's knights then at least she would be protected from Don Pedro. If she did not wish to go? Then that was no longer Blackstone's concern. Or so he told himself.

He heard the Prince ransom the Breton mercenary commander Bertrand du Guesclin for 100,000 Castilian *doblas*, near enough £20,000, a significant sum that would make a modest contribution to the Prince's costs of the war. Marshal Arnoul d'Audrehem was next in line and bowed in front of the Prince. He had still not paid his full ransom from when he was taken at Poitiers years before.

'You have broken your parole,' the Prince accused him. 'You forfeited your honour.'

The old Marshal of the French Army showed due respect to the Prince but refuted the accusation. 'I did not fight against you, highness, I fought against his cause,' he said, pointing at Pedro. 'He used your army, but it is he who is a man without honour.'

The Prince offered no further rebuke. The battle was won. He nodded for the veteran fighter to move on. Don Pedro, who stood next to him, would regain his crown soon enough and the Prince knew there would be savage retribution if he did not place himself between the King and the vanquished.

'The Castilians must be put to death,' Don Pedro insisted when he saw how many Spanish lords had been captured.

The Prince met Don Pedro's sudden outburst with a calm but firm response. 'No, my lord, they belong to their captors.

They are to be ransomed. And by their honour the captors are obliged to protect their prisoners,' the Prince insisted.

'I will pay for every single Castilian knight and lord taken on the field. I will decide their fate, not you. This is a matter of Castilian honour.'

The Prince half turned so that none of the men being paraded heard him. 'My lord, you must first pay the money you owe me for my army and this victory.'

Don Pedro glowered. 'You will not dictate the terms of my authority.'

'My lord, I will dictate whether you are to be escorted onward to Burgos and your coronation or abandoned here and left to the anger of those who escaped us. They still number in their thousands.'

Don Pedro dipped his head. 'I will leave you to your victory. I am tired after the fighting.'

The Prince's voice lowered. 'Tired, my lord? I saw no blood on your blade.'

The insult was enough to hasten Don Pedro's departure. They were close to the line of prisoners when the Count de Osona said something to him. What happened next was so unexpected that no one, not even Blackstone who was standing with his prisoner, could have stopped Don Pedro's sudden thrust with his knife, its blade plunging into Don Fernando Ferrandes's throat.

His body fell into Blackstone's arms as the shocked knights around them stumbled clear. Swords were drawn; Osona and the others with him shielded Pedro, who turned to face the Prince holding his knife blade aloft.

'Now do you see the blood on my blade?' he called.

Blackstone had cradled his prisoner for the few moments it took for him to know the man was beyond help. He rolled clear, onto his feet, his archer's knife already in his hand.

'No! Thomas,' the Prince bellowed.

Guards ran between Don Pedro's men and Blackstone. Two other knights abandoned their own prisoners and grabbed Blackstone's arms, barely restraining him.

'Thomas, do not defy the Prince,' urged one, his hands bloodied from Blackstone's wound, a wound the Master of War was ignoring in his effort to reach the murderous king.

The Prince was on his feet. The two marshals, Cusington and Guichard d'Angle, reached the men protecting Don Pedro.

'Lower your swords!' Cusington demanded. 'You dishonour the Prince.'

Guichard d'Angle stepped close to the Count de Osona. 'Sheath your blade or as God is my witness we will have you killed where you stand.'

'You would kill a king?' the Count sneered.

'Those who instigated this foul deed,' said Guichard d'Angle.

It was a standoff.

Don Pedro wiped his blade and pushed it back into its scabbard. 'Enough, my friends, we will find more traitors to kill in the days to come.'

His men lowered their weapons and stepped back.

'There was more than one bastard king on the battlefield today,' said Blackstone. 'Whenever the day of your death comes, I pray I will be there to watch you squirm in your own blood. And your pack of curs will not be there to save you.'

Don Pedro did not hold Blackstone's gaze. He and those with him turned away.

CHAPTER THIRTY-NINE

A heated argument took place in private between the Prince and Don Pedro. To dishonour any knight who had offered his protection to a captive was against the chivalric code. Reparation would normally be made to any knight whose prisoner was injured or killed in a malicious, unprovoked attack. But Don Pedro refused to make any reparation to Blackstone and there was no way to force the King to do so. Once Don Pedro had left the Prince's pavilion Blackstone was summoned.

'We will recompense you, Thomas,' the Prince told Blackstone.

'Highness, I did not capture Ferrandes for ransom, but to secure his safety and reunite him with his niece.'

The Prince nodded. He looked exhausted. He sat, cloak pulled closely around him. Blackstone wondered if it was the energy expended during the battle or the argument with the volatile Don Pedro that had drained him. Whatever ailed him was taking its toll.

'Thomas, with God's help our losses were few. The heralds have gone among the dead. All told, they say five thousand men lie out there. It is a terrible glory.'

'But Trastámara is not among them, is he?' said Blackstone. Had the bastard King been among the dead, the knowledge would have cheered the Prince.

'He is not. He has run for France and the protection of the French King. And we know the French will accommodate him. They will find new men to fight at his side. Go after him, Thomas. If he can be caught then return him to his brother at Burgos.'

'He'll be butchered,' said Blackstone. 'Better I kill him.'

'If you find him then his life is in your hands. There is another matter. The woman. Once Don Pedro reclaims the crown at Burgos he will send out men far and wide in search of her. We thought her safe from his anger but not now. He will kill her as he killed Don Fernando. Living witnesses to his murders are valuable to his enemies. What he did here was to show his strength to his followers.'

'Then you will return to Bordeaux, lord?'

'No, we stay at Burgos with the army until after he is crowned and we secure his payment for the cost of this war. We have nothing left in the Treasury. Our purse is empty, Thomas.' The Prince smiled, the rueful tone in his voice needing no further explanation. 'He gave his pledge.'

Blackstone was still bloodied from the fight. His own wound needed attention, as did those of his men. No one had escaped injury. 'Then I'll go back into Navarre and the convent at Estella. My men need their wounds attended to and from there we'll go after Trastámara.'

'We have sent a messenger to Gaston Phoebus, Count of Foix, seeking permission for you to cross his lands. He will accommodate us and yes, before you ask, Thomas, we are aware that he will also pay lip service to the French. It is the price we pay for his neutrality, but you will pass unhindered. Chandos will also take his men across the border but will travel through Aquitaine. Agree on a rendezvous. Trastámara will have routiers with him, paid for by the French. He will seek sanctuary somewhere, most likely with the Duke of Anjou. You and Chandos have a better chance of finding him together.'

'And if he cannot be found in the months ahead?'

'Then return to Bordeaux with Sir John. Our army will be depleted once we release the routiers from our service. They will be first in line wanting to be paid.'

Blackstone recognized the Prince's burden. Chasing after Trastámara was a ruse to get Blackstone away from Don Pedro. 'Sir John needs no help from me, highness. Better I take the woman to safety and return here to serve you.'

The Prince sighed. 'Thomas, you are oil to the flames. You know full well why we send you. Do as we ask.'

It was a gesture of respect for the Master of War that the Prince issued a request rather than a command.

'All right. But if you stay close to Don Pedro to enforce payment, you know it will take time – perhaps into the summer. You'll have few supplies, and the summer heat brings insects and disease.'

'Were it not for the sacrifice you and your men have already made, and were it unnecessary to have an ally on the border of Aquitaine, we might even have considered denying Don Pedro's divine right to rule and begging God's forgiveness for doing so. The bastard half-brother might prove a less cruel king.'

'Better you and the world had been spared their stain on the earth and that they died at birth,' said Blackstone. 'They are from the same mongrel litter.'

Blackstone led the way back to the Convent of Santo Domingo de Estella. One by one Blackstone's men had emerged from where the chaos of the battlefield had swept them. Will Longdon and Jack Halfpenny with their surviving archers had seized what plunder they could from the dead. Longdon had suffered a blow to his face: his lip was split, a front tooth half broken. A small price to pay. William Ashford and Aicart had fought with the Gascons and been caught up in the turmoil only to find themselves on the heels of the retreating enemy who fought a desperate rearguard action until the Prince's cavalry, held in reserve, swept down and gave chase into nearby villages. The enemy was rooted out of houses and killed. Blackstone had lost nine archers, mostly from the replacement Cheshire men that Halfpenny commanded. The Welsh bowmen under Will Longdon had broken ranks in search of plunder once their arrow bags were empty and three of them died for their greed.

Peasants had been paid to bury the dead except for those fallen Castilian knights from renowned families whose bodies were washed and dressed, then wrapped in linen and returned to their families for burial. The same respect had been accorded to Don Fernando. His body was carried on a litter to the convent.

Blackstone's German captain Renfred had scouted ahead with his men. There was no sign of routiers or Castilians who had fled the battlefield, groups of men who might still lie in ambush. It was late in the day when Blackstone rode up to the convent walls and strode inside to meet the abbess. The woman's expression betrayed her shock at the dishevelled and wounded knight who stood before her. The abbess edged around her desk. The dirt-streaked face that stared down at her was gaunt with tiredness and did not invite questioning.

'Is she still here?' he asked.

The abbess nodded. 'She serves this house of God with diligence and humility. She is a good woman.'

'Take me to her.'

'You will cause no harm to the woman. There will be no assault on her virtue. This is a house of God.'

Blackstone turned and tugged free the small leather pouch

at his neck that bore the abbess's inscription that would have released Sancha Ferrandes of Castile into the custody of whomever he sent. He tossed it to her. '*Res est sacra miser.* A person in distress is a sacred object.'

Blackstone followed the abbess to the laundry at the rear of the building: a space half inside, half out, so that the steam from the cauldrons of hot water could escape the room's confines. Laywomen and novitiates used stout poles to turn the clothing in the tubs. The women had their backs to the abbess and Blackstone. She pointed.

'There, near the far wall.'

Blackstone saw Sancha toiling in the steam's heat. She wore sandals, a simple linen chemise with a draped wimple. Her sleeves were pulled back as she stirred clothing or bedding being washed in the boiling water. For a woman born into a noble family it was humble work, reflecting her determination and willingness to comply with the convent's discipline.

'Some time back, I brought a Jew here from Pamplona. His name was Halif ben Josef. He was a surgeon. I returned him to his vineyard,' Blackstone told the abbess.

She looked puzzled, but only for a moment. She had not known the old Jew but his return had been spoken of. 'Yes. I remember him. He was murdered. And the people who worked for him.'

'I killed the man responsible.' Blackstone let the information sink in. The old nun showed no sign of fear but Blackstone knew what he said reinforced his standing. No promise or threat he made would be misconstrued.

She nodded. 'Then you did this town a service,' she said. 'I had no dealings with him. Jews and Christians, we live in harmony here, but we keep ourselves to ourselves.'

'You live in harmony because King Pedro willed it so. He borrowed money from the Jews and gave them his protection. So, there are traders and moneylenders still in Estella. My men have trophies to sell. I need you to send word and find men who will pay for them.'

'I will not have this house turned into a place of moneylenders.'

'My men will go to them.'

'Very well. What else do you need?'

'My men need rest. Their wounds need attention.' Blackstone took the old nun's gnarled hands and spilled three gold *doblas* into her leather-skinned palm. 'Give them the best treatment. And I need food for them and fodder for my horses.'

'That will be difficult. We must ask local farmers. They will not give up what remains of their winter fodder without demanding a high price.' She hesitated. 'Unless you intend to take it by force?'

'No one suffers harm from my men, providing they do not turn against us.' Knowing she saw a chance to make more profit for the convent he gave her two more coins. 'See to it.'

'I will. Is there anything else?'

'There's a priest in the town?'

'Of course.'

'Send for him tomorrow. We have a man to bury.'

She nodded. 'You're wounded,' she said, seeing his blood-encrusted mail.

'It can wait. See to my men.' He turned his back on her and strode towards Sancha Ferrandes.

She called after him: 'And I still do not know your name.'

Blackstone did not answer, nor did he look back.

CHAPTER FORTY

Blackstone led Sancha Ferrandes back to her cell. It was no different from when he had brought her to the convent. The clothes she had worn when she first arrived were folded neatly on the stool. She stood by the bed, looking up at the scar-faced knight who had rescued her, standing in the doorway.

'The battle is over?'

'Yes. Trastámara was defeated.'

She nodded. 'I expected that once the English Prince sheltered Don Pedro.' She looked up, a brief flicker of hope in her eyes.

Blackstone understood. 'Don Pedro lives. He took little part in the battle. But his bastard brother escaped.'

'Then he might return.'

'Not until he raises another army. We killed thousands.'

She repeated the abbess's observation: 'And you are wounded.'

'Like my men. We'll rest here for a few days.' He glanced behind him and nodded. 'John, bring it.'

She heard the scuff of boots along the passage and then John Jacob appeared in the doorway. The squire handed Blackstone a bundle tied in a blanket and then went back the way he came. Blackstone laid the blanket on her bed, untied the bindings and spread out Don Fernando's sword, scabbard and belt.

He saw her flinch.

'You killed him?'

'No. I saved him, but Don Pedro murdered him. Your uncle was my prisoner. I was going to bring him to you.' He watched as she tentatively touched the bejewelled belt. 'I'm sorry.'

'He was the last of my family.'

'I brought his body here to be buried.'

She showed little sign of distress, but nodded, her voice subdued. Her small hands took his dirt-encrusted hand and brought it to her lips. 'Thank you, my lord.' She stepped back. 'I will have the Mother Abbess take his body into a chapel. Then I will bathe it ready for burial, and afterwards, if you permit me, I will attend to your wounds myself.'

He nodded his agreement. She had not asked about the young knight who pursued her affections and her domain. Would she not wish to know if he survived? Blackstone wondered. Did she fear that knowing he had died would be too much to bear? Or did she not care for the ambitious knight's attentions towards her? There was no way for Blackstone to know the answer, except that not telling Blackstone about him might well be an attempt to shield the man's life. Blackstone had checked with the heralds before he left Nájera. There was no sign of the man's blazon on the battlefield. So, if he had fought in the battle, he had survived and escaped.

Blackstone went among his men with his captains. A handful of lanterns cast their warm glow across them as they arranged their bedrolls, stripped and bathed, while others prepared food. Groups of men gathered around their fires, the convent walls sheltering them from the brisk north wind. Meulon and Will Longdon's men had corralled the horses and kept Blackstone's horse far enough away from the others to stave off any chance of injury from the belligerent beast.

'Personally, I have a liking for nuns,' said Killbere. The

veteran knight stood next to a bucket of water and cloth on a bench, and was bent double as Will Longdon helped him peel off his mail.

John Jacob assisted Blackstone to remove his own mail and then handed him his gambeson.

'I gave my word that the nuns here would be safe.' Blackstone shrugged on the padded tunic. 'Any woman here, be they novice or otherwise. The captains know this, Gilbert. Don't make me put you in chains,' he said, with humour in his voice.

Killbere nodded his gratitude to Longdon as his body was released from the mail. 'Thank you, Will.'

'Like peeling a damned orange, Sir Gilbert.'

Killbere pulled free his sweat-soaked shirt. 'Thomas, it is not I who stalks beauty like a predatory creature in the forest. My greatest failing is that women have an irresistible attraction to me. Especially nuns. Did I ever tell you about the time—'

'Many times, Gilbert,' said Blackstone.

'Merciful God, Sir Gilbert, I remember the nun you bedded—'

'Not just bedded, Will,' he interrupted. 'It was not only passion I felt, but also love. I nearly married her.'

'Aye, I remember. She was gargoyle ugly,' said the archer.

'Beauty is in the beholder's eye,' said Killbere with a shrug. 'She had a dowry, Will, and that makes any woman a creature of beauty. Her family had committed her to the care of nuns because of her insatiable desire for rutting. I nearly succumbed from exhaustion. It was a difficult decision to leave her. Marry and take her out of the convent and live barely a couple of years more in comfort, or find my fortune elsewhere and live a longer life.'

'I am grateful you chose the path you did, Gilbert,' said

Blackstone, 'but while we are here, do whatever is necessary so the nuns can resist being drawn to you.'

Killbere grinned and shrugged, swabbing his arms and chest with the wrung-out cloth. 'I will turn my face to the wall, Thomas.'

'And spare us all,' Longdon muttered to himself as he went back to his archers.

Satisfied that his men were provisioned and that those who needed care for their wounds were being attended to, Blackstone dismissed John Jacob and entered the cloisters. Here and there, indeterminable shadows flitted past the columns. Scuffed footfalls and whispers. There was no threat: it was the devout going to their prayers. Imploring the Almighty that the violent men who now rested under their roof and against their walls sought only shelter and care for their injured.

Blackstone was twenty paces from the infirmary when one of the shadows stepped from behind a column. In the dim light, he saw it was the abbess. She blocked his way. Blackstone stopped and waited. The old woman made no further approach towards him, her hands tucked into the sleeves of her habit.

'I have learned that you are Thomas Blackstone,' she said.

'I am.'

'I misjudged you, Sir Thomas.' She came a few steps closer. 'I thought you a barbarian. Now I am told the Jews in the town revere your name for what you did for one of their own, the man you told me about, the physician Halif ben Josef. Their leaders wish to greet you here tomorrow.'

'Very well, but now I need to attend to my wounds and get some food and sleep.'

As he went to step around her, she raised a hand. 'I will not have them inside the convent.'

'I'm sure they will be happy to meet me in the stables or elsewhere.'

She nodded. 'I'm pleased you understand.'

'And you should understand, Mother Abbess, that if I so chose, I would meet them wherever I want. I'm a guest here, a paying guest, and my men were cared for by the old physician. They bear no ill will towards his people.'

'Your men want only money from what they stole off the dead. Moneylenders and thieves go hand in hand.'

'Moneylenders have no choice other than to pursue that trade. And my men are not thieves. They take what is rightly theirs after spilling their own blood. Do not preach to me or to them or you will find out how much we dislike contempt being shown towards those who have earned our gratitude.'

He brushed past her. She grabbed his arm. 'I have God's protection. I am not afraid of you.'

They were close enough for lantern light to show their faces. Blackstone stared hard at her. His voice barely audible, but laden with intent: 'You should be.'

Sancha was waiting in the infirmary. With the help of four novitiates, she had prepared the Castilian knight's body for burial and was ready now to treat Blackstone's wounds. Bandages and ointments were laid out on a table. Tallow candles reflected light off the arched ceiling. She arranged two lanterns closer to where he perched on the edge of the table, told him to strip off his gambeson and shirt and then examined his injuries. The cut made across his mail had split the skin and muscle on his arm. The blood was now congealed. Bruises and welts from blows struck in the battle disfigured his back, chest and arms. A knife or sword point had pierced the mail in his side. The wound seeped blood when she peeled away the linen. Blackstone had pushed a clump of cloth beneath his shirt during the ride to her. It was sticky with gore.

She remained silent, soaked a cloth in the bucket of heated water and bathed him. There was an astringent smell from the water and, as she slowly wiped away the congealed blood, the cuts stung. It took several attempts to clean the wounds.

'Your arm and side should be stitched,' she said, finally raising her face to his.

He shook his head. 'I've had worse. Clean them, put herbs or whatever you have into the wounds and bind them.'

She nodded obediently. Choosing a clean piece of linen, she bathed his back, neck and uninjured arm, washing free the grime embedded in his skin.

His eyes closed as each stroke of her comforting hands soothed his aching muscles. His mind flew back, arrow fast, to another time when he lay so badly wounded he was not expected to live. Taken from the battlefield at Crécy as a sixteen-year-old archer he was cared for in Castle Harcourt, tended to by the young woman he had rescued before the battle. Christiana. The girl who would become his wife. The wife and mother who was murdered.

Blackstone opened his eyes and banished the past. This young woman who bathed him now was as tender as the memory. Once the wound oozed blood again; she dabbed it dry with clean linen and pressed ointment into the cut, bound it, and stepped back. Washing him and sealing the wound had been a slow process. Bloodied cloths floated in the bucket of water. She wiped her hands. Until now she had not looked up from the task at hand.

'I can do nothing more,' she said.

He stood and placed his hands on her arms. 'Thank you,'

he said. He kissed her forehead. Lingered a moment too long. Betraying his feelings.

She lowered her gaze, feeling something more than his gratitude. His desire. 'I cannot,' she said. 'I beg you not to force me.'

Blackstone lifted her chin. 'I promised you my protection. That no harm would come to you,' he said gently. 'Nothing has changed.'

She nodded and fussed with his shirt. A distraction. It needed more than a wash. 'This should be burned. It's rank with sweat and bloodstained. Do you have another?'

'Yes.' He pulled on his gambeson.

'What is to become of me now Henry Trastámara has been defeated?'

'When I captured Don Fernando, I was going to bring him here so that he might escort you to your lands in France. Once my men and horses are rested, I'll take you there.'

Blackstone gathered his bloodied shirt and walked back along the cloisters. Memories had been stirred. Moonlight cast shadows from the columns, accompanying him like ghosts from his past. This time the scuffed footfalls and whispers were not the devout going to prayer. They were the echoes of loss and regret from lost loved ones and fallen comrades. And the taunting reminder that what he desired could not be his.

CHAPTER FORTY-ONE

The priest looked fearful. Keeping his distance from the dozen men who stood at the freshly dug grave, he hesitated. They looked like brigands. One of them, a grizzled fighter, face etched with lines and eyes that pierced him even from that distance, pointed and called out.

'Get your arse over here, priest,' Killbere shouted, 'or I'll drag you here myself.'

Blackstone gave Killbere a look that needed no words. But he added some anyway. 'Gilbert, you not only scare the priest but the dead man's spirit.'

'Thomas, these priests are quick enough to hold their hand open when it comes to taking money from the poor. It would be better if they shuffled with more enthusiasm when they are being paid to administer their calling. And the dead man's spirit is already languishing in heaven.' He shrugged. 'Or not.'

The priest turned to flee what appeared to be the likelihood of him ending up in the ground along with the corpse.

'*Estimado señor!*' a young woman's voice called out.

The priest saw a woman dressed in black, her face behind a veil, clutching a rosary and a small book of prayer, who came out of the convent accompanied by the abbess. Sancha stood next to the ruffians as the abbess went quickly to him. She spoke rapidly, assuring him all would be well and that he would be paid. Well paid.

The priest looked from her to the woman and the men. One of them, the tallest with a scarred face, beckoned him.

Gripping the holy book to his chest, the priest crossed himself and accompanied the abbess to the graveside.

'Priest,' said Blackstone, 'the man whose body lies here was a knight of Castile. He was slain in a cruel act. He was this woman's uncle. You will perform the burial rites and then you will hold a month of prayers in your church for the redemption of his soul. Is that understood?'

The priest nodded. His voice trembled. 'It is customary to hold a vigil of prayer before a committal.'

'A vigil was held last night. It will have to do,' said Blackstone. 'We all live in preparation of death. It comes as no surprise to us.'

Blackstone's captains nodded respectfully behind him.

The priest looked uncertainly at their stern faces. 'This… this is a humble funeral for a man of exalted status,' he said, a note of supplication in his voice as he gained confidence. 'Is there… no one else to attend? A knight of Castile should have a coffin, not be wrapped in linen like a common man.'

'We know what he should have, Padre,' said Sancha, 'but he was a man of humility. He would be gratified to know he is to be buried in sacred ground and not left to rot on a battlefield, scavenged by crows. Will you honour him?'

The priest looked again at the assembled men. One of them, short and stocky, grinned back. He had a broken tooth that made his smile appear more like a snarl.

'Very well,' said the priest. 'Will there be hymns? Will you sing to raise his soul to heaven?'

The stony-faced men answered his question with silence.

'Will all of you… any of you… be attending mass afterwards? It is customary.'

'Customs are set aside today,' said Blackstone. 'You will accompany the woman who grieves for her uncle to the convent where you'll hold mass for her, the abbess and nuns.'

Blackstone and three of his men bent and lifted the ropes beneath Don Fernando Ferrandes's body and lowered him into the grave.

The priest licked his lips. Everything about the burial lacked tradition. The sooner he complied, the safer – and richer – he would be.

Once the ceremony was over, the priest did as Blackstone commanded and led Sancha and the abbess inside the convent to hear mass.

Blackstone waited until they were inside and the doors firmly closed. Neither the priest nor the abbess had seen the group of men standing below the sloping ground. Blackstone raised his arm for them to come forward.

Killbere and the captains watched them make their slow progress towards them.

'At least they had the good sense to keep well away from a Christian burial,' said Will Longdon as he and Meulon shovelled the last of the dirt pile onto the grave.

'Aye, if word got back to the town that they arrived just as the priest committed Don Fernando's soul there would be killings tonight,' said Meulon and used the shovel's blade to knock in a simple wooden cross.

Six elders from the Jewish community stood at a respectful distance from the convent, their robes flapping in the chill north breeze. They bowed their heads as Blackstone and Killbere approached with the men.

One of them stepped forward. 'My lord, Sir Thomas, are we far enough away from the convent not to cause offence?'

'You are,' said Blackstone. 'And because you stand with me, no one will dare be offended.'

The older man dipped his head. He did not show any sign

of subservience. Lifting his head to face Blackstone squarely, he addressed the renowned English knight as one would address an equal.

'We are honoured to meet you. I am Abraam Abroz. I speak for our people here in Estella. We greet you.'

'And I you,' said Blackstone. 'This man is Sir Gilbert Killbere. Together with our men, we brought your old friend Halif ben Josef home last year. We mourned his loss, but we gave him justice.'

'Sir Thomas, we are grateful. And now we understand you have returned Don Pedro to his rightful place.'

'He is soon to be enthroned at Burgos by our Prince,' said Killbere.

The six men looked approvingly at each other. Smiles broke out. 'We rejoice,' said the Jewish leader. 'His half-brother did not protect us as did Don Pedro.'

'You and Muslims alike,' Blackstone said.

The old Jew spread his hands and smiled. 'No one is perfect, Sir Thomas,' he said without malice.

'You rejoice, but Don Pedro used you for raising money. He'll do the same again,' Killbere said.

The older man shrugged. 'Nothing changes for us, but at least we feel only the sharpness of his demands, not the point of a sword.'

Blackstone looked back to where his men were camped. 'My men have taken spoils from the battlefield. They have finely tooled belts encrusted with precious stones; weapons of value; bejewelled scabbards and rings. They need to exchange them for gold *doblas* or florins. Nothing less. No letters of credit.'

'We will do what we can to oblige.'

'You will treat them fairly. I respected Halif ben Josef, and I returned him here. That will count in my men's favour when you offer them a fair price.'

'It will,' said Abraam Abroz.

Blackstone turned to indicate his companions. 'These are my captains, only they and one other of their choosing will come into the town. Every captain will know what each of their men has for sale.'

The Jewish leader pointed towards the town. 'There is a covered place where the women wash clothes. Send your men and we will set up tables and inspect what they have.' One of the other men said something Blackstone did not understand. The older man nodded. 'My friend raises a concern, Sir Thomas. There are some Christians in the town who might resent us trading with you. We do not wish to incite violence against ourselves.'

'You tell anyone who raises their voice or their hand against you that you have the blessing of King Pedro of Castile and León and the protection of the English King's Master of War. Any man harms or causes your people injury or death while we are here will hang. I give you my word.'

Smiles broke out among the delegation. Abraam Abroz stepped forward and extended his hand. 'Will you shake the hand of a Jew, Sir Thomas? In friendship and trust?'

Blackstone gripped the man's hand.

The elder dipped his head. He sighed. 'If only you could stay here; our lives would be the better for it. Our safety would be guaranteed.'

'Every man's life is precarious, my friend. One man cannot stand in the way of Fate. I have tried and failed. It takes us where we are meant to be.'

As Blackstone and Killbere walked back towards their men, who had watched the exchange from a distance, Killbere put a hand on Blackstone's arm. 'Thomas, we cannot linger here much longer. Another day, perhaps two, but the men will become restless and they'll look for drink and women.'

'Which is why I'm not sending them into town. There must be no trouble here. Whoever accompanies their captain will act as witness to the fairness of the trade. When it comes to men's plunder, Gilbert, there must be no misunderstanding as to its value.'

'Then they will wait until we are clear of this place. Pamplona has a fine brothel and cheap wine and the King of Navarre will no doubt be hiding somewhere safe. Do you agree?'

'Tell them that's where they can spend their money,' Blackstone said.

'And Thomas, the woman. What's to become of her?'

'You're worried that she has a hold on me?'

'I worry you are thinking with your balls and not your head.'

'Or my heart?'

Killbere sighed. 'You still harbour feelings for her – her courage in trying to kill the King captivated you. Thomas, this woman is not Christiana.'

'Gilbert, this woman does not possess me.'

'But you desire her.'

'What man wouldn't?'

'Then what happens if she takes you to her bed?'

Blackstone smiled. 'For all I know she might cut my throat.' He looked back to where the Jewish delegates were making their way back to the town. 'She's not important, Gilbert. Don't fear for me or what might happen between us. Let's get the men their payment and then we leave this place.'

'And go where?'

'Back across the mountains to France, then north-east and

follow the River Ariège beyond Foix. That's where her lands are.'

'We take her? Thomas, that's a two-week ride and takes us into the heart of French-held territory.'

'The Prince wants us to find Trastámara and any of the lords who escaped with him.'

'Then why slow ourselves down by dragging the woman along if she has no grip on your vitals?'

'Because I promised her.'

'And for that we ride into the French King's nest of vipers?'

'She serves a purpose, Gilbert.'

'It escapes me.'

'She's bait.'

PART SIX

PURSUIT AND CAPTURE

CHAPTER FORTY-TWO

Duchy of Anjou
North-west France

When Henry Blackstone and the men with him escaped from Josselin after Henry fought Pellan, they had no choice but to run hard and fast in case they were pursued by the castle commander's men. Without horses or supplies they could only survive for as long as their legs and lungs held out. Worse still was the knowledge that the killer la Griffe had held back men from assaulting the castle, leaving instead his father Pellan to go inside and then give them the all-clear. That had not happened, which meant the Claw must know he had been betrayed by Henry Blackstone.

Henry knew la Griffe was on the other side of the river and would shadow them. At the first opportunity, be it ford or bridge, the murderous routier would be across and then Henry and his men would suffer a gruesome death.

Hugh Gifford, the man-at-arms instructed by the King to protect the younger Blackstone, kept a steady pace behind his charge. His duty had flung him into conflict and killing far away from the Oxford spires where Henry was still supposed to be studying. It had been a calm life, interrupted by the occasional tavern brawl.

'This is a death trap,' he gasped, legs tiring, breath coming hard. 'They'll be on us, Master Henry. I can see their horses in the meadows over there.'

'Save your breath,' said Henry.

The men behind were tiring. 'Need to stop,' cried Walter Mallin, the oldest among the men who had made Henry their leader. He snatched at a sapling on the riverbank and bent double, chest heaving.

Henry stopped and looked back. 'We run until we drop,' he said. 'Our lives are in our own hands.'

'Aye, easy for you to say, young Master Henry. I'm done.' He spat a globule of phlegm. 'Go on then. Leave me be. I'll take my chances.'

Henry went past the others, who stood heaving for breath. 'Walter, you're an old goat. You can keep the pace until I find a means of putting distance between us and those who will come after us.'

Mallin shook his head. 'My old legs won't carry me.'

'You did not abandon your friend Robert Helyer.'

'Aye, well, he succumbed back in the prison cells. Nothing more I could do for him.'

'Then we will not abandon you,' said Henry. He turned to the broad-shouldered German, Eckehart Brun. 'Can you help him? We share the load among us. You first.'

Brun nodded, wrapped his arm around the older man's waist, gripping his belt and supporting him. 'Run, Master Henry. You go ahead. Find a way out for us. We will follow.'

Henry slapped Hugh Gifford's shoulder. 'Faster, Hugh. We need horses.'

Henry loped away.

'We need God's angels,' Gifford answered, following the fitter, younger man along the riverbank.

The breadth of the river kept the horsemen on the opposite bank out of crossbow range, but at the next bend in the river it narrowed. The riders on the other side dismounted, and a sudden shock of violence tore into the trees around Henry and Gifford. They threw themselves down.

'They'll shoot again,' said Gifford. 'Get past the bend in the river!'

Running hard, they fled deeper into the trees, hoping to put as much distance as they could between themselves and the crossbowmen. They heard la Griffe shout.

'You will not escape! I will follow you as long as it takes!'

Lethal bolts swarmed into the trees, some deflected by branches that whipped Henry and Gifford's faces. Henry crouched behind a tree trunk, Gifford at his shoulder. Both heaving for breath.

'We're dead if we stay here,' said Henry.

Gifford heard the tinge of fear in the young man's voice. Facing a swarm of crossbow bolts was every fighting man's nightmare. They crippled and killed. A fourteen-inch quarrel with an iron-tipped bodkin point would tear through sinew and muscle. And Gifford knew Henry Blackstone had never stood shoulder to shoulder with men on the battlefield.

'Stay still, Master Henry. Movement draws the eye. We let them watch and wait. They'll soon move further downstream and seek another narrow place to ambush us.'

Gifford felt Henry's breathing settle. The lad had courage and nerve enough. And experience would teach him more about staying alive when others were trying to kill them.

Peering through the trees and saplings and then beyond the bulrushes, they realized the killer and his men had lost sight of them. The mercenaries were looking across the river, but the Claw ordered them back to their mounts.

'They'll shadow the river for as long as it takes,' said Gifford, easing himself up, still with a watchful eye across the river.

'Then we need an advantage,' said Henry.

'Even if we find horses, Master Henry, sooner or later they'll find a crossing and then we're hares before the hounds.'

Henry pushed through the undergrowth to the riverbank. He stood for a moment, looking up- and downstream. 'We won't find horses. Not enough for all of us. And even if we did, we would ride through domains that might still be contested between the English and French. We need to get as far downstream as we can.'

'Aye, well, you and me might be able to swim, but I'll wager those men coming up behind us won't. Most will drown quicker than a fish chokes out of water.'

Henry turned to him and smiled. 'Hugh, we cannot ride, we cannot swim and we cannot fly.' He pointed downriver. 'But we can float.'

A narrow, shallow-draught fishing boat with a single mast and sail tacked against the river's breeze, its slim sail catching what wind there was thanks to an experienced hand on the tiller.

'He won't come near the bank when he sees us,' said Gifford.

'Every man wants payment.'

'Huh. With what? Le Bourc stripped us of every sou we had.'

Henry reached inside his tunic and tugged free a leather purse. He weighed it in his hand.

'How did you keep that?'

'I took it from Pellan when I killed him. I hid it because I didn't know whether I could trust the others.'

'And me?'

'You, I trust, but I couldn't risk showing it in case any of them saw me.'

'Then how do you bring the fisherman shore?'

Henry grinned. 'I reel him in.'

'And what do I do?'

'Land him.'

Henry pushed through the bulrushes, waiting until the small boat tacked towards him. The sail hid the fisherman from view but as he came closer the sail luffed before catching the breeze again. Henry raised a hand.

'My friend. Can you help us? We are pilgrims chased by routiers.'

The boat wallowed as the air spilled from the sail, the man's panic clear to see. The boat was almost midstream, but the current pushed it closer to Henry, who threw coins into his boat. This added more confusion for the fisherman as he abandoned the tiller to snatch at the coins, fish-scale silver, enough to keep a man and his family fed for a year.

'We will pay you. More than I have just given. Help us. We will cause you no harm.'

The fisherman gathered his wits, turned the bow into the breeze and stayed midstream.

'You are armed men. I cannot risk it. My lord, I am fearful. I cannot.'

The man stood at his tiller to get a clear view of Henry, who was waist-deep in the river.

Henry tossed a few more coins. 'We are in fear of our lives. La Griffe pursues us.'

'La Griffe?' The mention of the name provoked horror on the man's face. 'No, no. I cannot.'

'You would leave us to die?'

'So that I might live.'

'Very well,' said Henry. 'I do not hold that against you.'

'Thank you, lord.'

Henry shrugged, smiled and waved. The man raised a hand and then fell headlong over the side as Gifford rocked the boat on the far side. Gifford had swum from downstream out of the man's view. Now, he clambered aboard and lowered the sail so the current would bring the boat into shore.

'He's drowning,' Henry called, pointing at the floundering fisherman. It was not unusual for men who made their living on the water to be unable to swim.

'Do I leave him?'

'No! Help him.'

He heard a curse but Gifford steadied the boat and reached over the side. He was strong enough to haul the man half aboard.

'We mean you no harm,' Gifford told the choking fisherman.

By the time the boat came alongside the bank the fisherman was sitting huddled in misery. Henry clambered aboard, placed one hand on the frail-looking man's shoulder and then with the other spilled more silver coins into the fisherman's palm. 'Not only will you live, my friend, you and your family will live well.'

The fisherman clasped the coins tightly.

'Now,' said Henry, 'we need to be taken as far downstream as possible.'

The man stared at him. He nodded. His eyes widened. 'Who are they?'

Henry saw Brun and the Gascon, Bezián, helping Walter Mallin through the trees, accompanied by the others. 'They're my friends.'

CHAPTER FORTY-THREE

His name, the fisherman told Henry, was Yagu. His wife had borne him seven children. Three died in their first two years; the others repaired nets with the women. His catch was usually salmon, pike and zander. In summer when fishing was not allowed he worked on the coastal salt marshes harvesting salt. It was a hard life.

Terrel gripped the side of the boat as Yagu swept it slowly back and forth across the river. The small sail was meant to power one man not the eight crammed aboard.

'He talks a lot for a man who was about to shit his breeches,' said Terrel.

'The more he talks the less fearful he becomes and the more he does what he does best,' said Henry.

Yagu the fisherman continued telling Henry and the others about the vagaries of life on the river, but by the time the sun had arced across the sky, lurking behind grey clouds, his meandering monologue faltered. The men in the boat were asleep, rocked by the creak of wood and breeze-stretched sail, a cradle rocking gently, moving silently through the open landscape.

Henry had stayed awake until he too succumbed.

Gifford jabbed him awake three hours later. The boat was no longer moving. It had nudged into some reed beds. Henry looked to where Yagu sat at the tiller. The sail was down and the fisherman sat watching the men as if gazing at his catch. The night sky showed black clouds scudding across the horizon, the wind ruffling moonlit water.

'Where are we?' said Henry.

'I can go no further,' said Yagu.

'Why? The river is broad; there's a breeze. Take us further.'

'I cannot, lord.'

Henry got to his feet, balanced against the rocking boat and faced the stoic fisherman. 'I have paid you well,' he said.

'Lord, you have been generous, but I am not allowed to fish any further along this river. I must turn for home. We are close to the Duke of Anjou's lands.'

Gifford groaned. 'And he sides with the French. He's no friend of the Prince.'

The fisherman pointed to nowhere in particular, meaning the countryside that lay beyond the reed bed. 'I berthed here so we will not be seen. There are soldiers protecting the villages and if any of the fishermen along the river see my boat they will send for them.'

'We can defend you,' said Gifford as the others awakened at the sound of voices.

'Yes, but when you leave my boat I'll be too far downstream. They'll will put a blockade across the river because they know I must return. Then my boat will be destroyed and I'll be killed.'

Eckehart Brun nearly capsized the boat when he stood, stiff muscles making him unsteady. Raymond Vachon, the French mercenary, cursed as the others told him to be careful.

'Keep your voices down,' Gifford told them. 'Sound travels across water.'

Henry looked at the men, the river, the sky and then at Yagu. 'Then we'll leave you here,' he said.

Mallin wiped a sleeve across a running nose. 'If we walk from here, Master Henry, we're bound to come across Anjou's men or la Griffe's skinners. Why don't we just take the boat?'

Looking at the men's faces, even in the shadows, Henry saw they thought the proposal had merit.

'Because I gave him my word that no harm would come to him and this boat is his livelihood.'

'Aye, but you paid him well,' said Terrel. 'We can leave him here. He can make his way home. He has enough to build another boat.'

'I gave my word,' said Henry again.

'He's a peasant,' said Vaisey the mercenary. 'Damned if we should put ourselves at risk when we don't have to.'

'You'll do as Master Henry says or you'll be floating face down on this river,' said Gifford.

'Six of us and two of you,' Vaisey said.

'I saved your life,' said Henry. 'Is this how you repay me?'

'I gave you la Griffe. The next time he finds me I'm skinned alive.'

'That's the risk we all take.'

'No!' Vaisey shouted. The boat rocked: the men clung to the sides; Brun had to squat down to avoid falling into the river. 'I don't see it that way. We have a boat, we kill the fisherman or he'll raise the alarm, and then we go further south on the river. We get to Poitou. The English will welcome you because of your father and we will go our separate ways.' Vaisey appealed to the others. 'You see this, don't you? See how we can be hunted down on foot? I say we take the boat,' he said, pointing at the fisherman, 'and the money.'

Henry saw the men looked undecided.

'Get off the boat,' said Henry. 'You don't travel with us.'

'He'll find la Griffe and betray us,' said Bezián. 'Better we keep the boat and stay together.'

'No. He goes,' said Henry.

'You're throwing us between the devil and certain death at

the hands of Anjou's men if they find us,' said Vachon. 'We are all condemned whoever finds us.'

'You can go with Vaisey if you wish,' said Henry. 'Any man here who no longer wishes to follow me can go now.'

The boat rocked again as Vaisey drew his sword and took a step towards Henry. Gifford turned and Vachon's knife was at his neck.

'No, Master Henry, it is you who must walk,' said Vachon.

Vaisey grinned, moonlight distorting his features. Eckehart Brun reached out, grabbed Vaisey's crotch and squeezed. Vaisey choked, doubled over and the German's knife pierced his throat. It happened so quickly Vachon had no time to react. As Vaisey's body tumbled into the water, Gifford's knife pierced the Frenchman's neck. His jaw fell slack, eyes rolling back; blood seeped from his mouth; his body shuddered. Gifford heaved his body away from Henry, who had recoiled from the stabbing. The Frenchman was pushed over the side to join Vaisey's body bobbing in the tide.

Henry knew he had not been quick enough to defend himself against Vachon. He nodded his thanks to Gifford, who turned away to face the men, knife still in hand. The killings had given Brun control of the bow of the boat and Gifford the stern.

'There's a choice to be made,' said Gifford. 'You decided to follow Master Henry. Now is the time to change your mind.'

'I made my choice,' said Brun. 'Master Henry saved all of us. We were men of honour once. He has given us the chance to be that again.'

Terrel looked at him. 'Honour is for mighty lords, kings and princes. We are common men, you stupid German lump of gristle. We live by our wits not with bloody honour. Merciful Christ, it is their so-called honour that casts men like us into war fighting for their kind. We loot and we rape and we take what we can to survive.' He spat over the side and shook his head. 'Honour,' he said dismissively. 'I followed Henry Blackstone because of what I said before.' He pointed at Mallin. 'In future keep your ideas to yourself. Two men are dead because of your feeble mind. Maybe we should put you in the river as well.' He looked at Gifford. 'Aye, we'll follow, but I wouldn't count on any of us being at your side when either the Claw or the French come at us. It's every man for himself then.'

'So be it,' said Henry. He climbed over the side into the reed bed. The others followed.

The fisherman had not moved, petrified with fear at the sudden violence. Henry leaned on the boat. 'Go home to your family. You have done us a service. It will not be rewarded with violence.' He pushed the boat into the stream.

'May God protect you, Master Henry,' said Yagu the fisherman and steered his boat into mid-river.

'Amen to that,' said Gifford.

As the men pushed through the reeds towards dry land Gifford placed a hand on Henry's arm and spoke quietly. 'The next time you challenge men like these, have your knife in your hand. These are lessons that must be learned, Master Henry. It's not only your life at stake.'

Henry's guardian pressed on to the riverbank as Blackstone's son looked back to the moonlit river. One man sailed home to his family. Two others floated downstream.

Gifford needn't have been concerned. The lesson had already been learned.

CHAPTER FORTY-FOUR

La Griffe and his men watched the breeze ruffle the running tide on the empty moonlit river. The men they pursued had been swept by the wind far from their reach. The trees beyond the bulrushes on the opposite bank were dense enough to obscure any movement, even if they had managed to keep up with the fisherman's boat that carried la Griffe's prey. They had followed as far as they could. Forest and bog along the riverside had slowed them until Jean de Soissons knew they could go no further.

'Jean, we could go around the woodland,' said one of his men. 'A day extra and we'll be back at the river.'

'Or push our way through the trees,' said another.

'And lose horses in the bog?' said his companion. 'Easy enough to snap a leg in there. And I've seen horse and rider go down in a mire and never be found.'

La Griffe shook his head. 'We are already too far from home and even if we force the pace they will be too far down the road. This is Louis of Anjou's domain. If any of his patrols found us we would hang from those trees. No, this is as far as we go.'

'And let the bastard get away with what he did? He betrayed Pellan. Your father hangs butchered outside the walls, a fate planned for you,' said the man at his side.

La Griffe showed no sign of anger at being reminded. His men looked from one to the other, waiting to hear what plan their leader would offer.

'Are we to let them go, Jean?' said one.

La Griffe nodded. 'We let them go.'

Disbelief creased the men's faces. No man, woman or child who had ever caused the Claw displeasure, no matter how slight, had lived. And usually died badly, giving his men the sport they lusted for.

But then he gifted them the chance of killing. 'For now,' he added.

Broad grins and laughter broke their mood.

'And how do we get to them later?' one asked.

La Griffe nudged his horse. 'Two, three days' fast travel. How many of you dare ride with me to Paris?'

It was not only disbelief this time that gawped back at him, but fear.

He faced them. 'There is a prize to be had and we will be well paid for delivering it.'

'In Paris? The King?' said the man closest to him.

'Yes.'

'They would flay us alive as soon as we got to the city gates.'

'You think city officials who spend their lives behind those walls know what we do? Who we are? No, they won't cause us any harm. Once they hear I can deliver the son of the man most feared in France, we will have the King's blessing to track him down and deliver him. The difficulty is getting past the King's advisers. If we convince them, then our reward will be more than we can gain in a lifetime of scouring the land.'

It took a while for the men's uncertainty to be put aside.

'I'll ride with you, Jean,' said one.

And then so did the others.

CHAPTER FORTY-FIVE

Henry and the men followed a single track that skirted the riverbanks, concealed mostly by the tall bulrushes. Each time the path broke cover Gifford bent low and studied the far bank. There was still no weir, ford or bridge that would allow anyone on the other side to cross rapidly and butcher them. And for the past few hours of daylight, there had been no sign of la Griffe or his riders on the far bank.

'We need food,' said Mallin. 'And horses. Or a cart. We cannot walk to Bordeaux.'

'Bordeaux? You befuddled old bastard, we'll be lucky to get through today without being caught by the French,' said Terrel.

'At least it won't be the Claw who gets to us,' said Bezián. 'He'll still have twenty men with him. We need a French patrol from a local lord. Then we could seize their mounts.'

'Seize their mounts?' Terrel scoffed. 'Sweet Jesus on the Cross. You and Walter have been drinking too much river water. No wonder the old bastard's mind is addled. And you, Bezián, a man expects more from a Gascon weaned on your good red wine. No, what we need is a simple miracle. The clouds to part and the Almighty's hand to lift us up and set us down gently in Bordeaux. That's all we need. Anything else is a child's fairy tale.'

'My brain might be slower than I would like, but I swear I can remember roasted rabbit. I taste it on my tongue,' said Mallin.

Henry and Gifford were a dozen paces forward of the straggling men.

'They bicker like washerwomen,' said Gifford.

'A busy tongue stops them thinking too hard about how desperate our situation is. How far do you think we came by boat?'

'Hard to say. How fast was the current? Daylight hours and into the night. I can only guess.'

'A hundred miles? Perhaps more?'

'Aye, thirty or forty leagues would be my thoughts on it.'

'Then we might be close to a border with Poitou and if we can—' Henry stopped mid-sentence, went down on one knee and signalled the stragglers to follow suit. Gifford asked no questions. He knelt at Henry's side. The others fell silent and scurried to him at the crouch, huddling together, eager not to be seen or heard.

'That roast rabbit you tasted, Walter. It was not in your imagination. Smell that.'

The breeze had veered away from the river and rustled through a copse of alders fifty yards inland; their trunks were thin compared to the dense forest that lay beyond, but their budding leaves, some opening, helped to obscure anyone camped as the wind rustled the spindly branches. Water-thirsty trees were rooted closer to the meandering stream that branched from the river eighty yards ahead.

The men peered into the copse, seeking movement. There was no smoke, so whoever was in the trees had lit a fire a while ago and fed it dry sticks. Perhaps whoever was there did not wish to be seen. Poachers maybe?

Henry looked at the bulrushes. They swayed. And then dipped. The changing wind might soon put Henry and the men upwind, and then they might be heard. Or if they were hunters in the trees, they would smell the men's rank sweat.

'We should go past them,' whispered Mallin.

'And risk alerting them?' said Bezián, as quietly as the older man.

Teller said, 'There could be two men or twenty in there. I say go on.'

'And lose the advantage?' said Brun.

Henry didn't know what to do. He chewed his lip. Gifford's face close to his ear.

'Well, Master Henry?'

There was enough moonlight even from behind the drifting clouds for Gifford to see Henry's uncertainty.

Henry made sure the others couldn't hear him. 'What would you think we should do?'

'We should have stayed in England.' He relented. 'You lead these men. They're experienced fighters. Now they look to you. No man wants to stumble into an unequal fight. What would your father have you do?'

'He's not here,' said Henry.

Was that a note of irritation? Gifford wondered. 'He's always here,' said the man-at-arms.

Henry nodded. Hugh Gifford was his guardian, but he was making him think for himself, and any son of the King's Master of War carried his father's spirit. Or burden.

'Know your enemy,' said Henry. 'That's what he would have me do.'

'Then?'

Henry turned and looked at the faces turned his way. 'I'll go and see who's waiting in those trees.'

'And if you don't return?' said Terrel.

'Every man for himself. Isn't that what you said?'

Terrel grimaced. 'You get caught by whoever's in there and you'll squeal like a pig being castrated if they torture you. Then we're as good as dead.'

'You hear me scream, you can run. I'm not asking for help. If I'm silent, then be here when I get back and make your decision then.'

The others nodded.

Henry unbuckled his scabbard and gave it to Gifford. 'I don't want this snaring any low branches.'

Gifford pointed. 'See that patch of shrub? It's sitting in a boar wallow. Get into it. They won't smell you and they won't be tempted to look for you if they're alerted.'

Henry gave him a questioning look.

Gifford nodded. 'It'll stink of pig piss and shit. It's the best cover you'll have and you'll get close to where they're camped if this wind shifts again.'

Henry remained silent. He glanced at the men, all of whom stared at him, wide-eyed to see him clearly, moonlight ringing the whites of their eyes. Without another word, he ran crouched towards the foul-smelling mire.

'We should get off the track,' said Gifford quietly. 'We'll edge closer and lie low in the grass. If whoever's in there gives chase, we can give him a chance.'

'If a dozen men come after him, what chance for us?' Terrel hissed.

'The lad has courage,' Bezián said. 'He deserves help.'

'Aye – not by risking my skin, though.'

'Then you stay here and we will go without you,' Brun said.

Gifford checked the others. They nodded and followed him into the low shrub and grass on the other side of the track.

Terrel grimaced. 'Fools. It's every man for himself,' he murmured. He watched as they disappeared into the undergrowth. Wind made the trees creak, and as clouds glided past the moon, its light exposed a witch's claw of a branch that dipped low. Terrel crossed himself. The night had taken shape. What creatures might lurk in the darkness? The path behind him and to his front might well be an animal's hunting track. Were there wild boar close by? No, surely they would be deep in the forest. Still, he reasoned, better to be safe. Cursing himself, he bent double and stepped quickly to where the others lay out of sight of the trees. Seeing Bezián, he lay next to the Gascon man-at-arms. A good fighter was worth having at your shoulder.

Bezián's expression questioned him.

Terrel shrugged. 'You're right. The lad might need our help,' he whispered.

'Then your skin is no more valuable than ours,' came the hushed reply.

Henry crept towards the wallow. The thorny branches of a wicked-looking bush spread protective branches across its black mud. Boars might like to have their tough hide scratched, but the thorns would tear Henry's clothing like a bodkin point piercing mail. And once he had gagged on the wallow's stench, he knew it took a different fighting man than him to immerse himself in it for the sake of getting close to a potential enemy.

The scent of cooked meat carried on the breeze. He was still downwind but could not understand why there was no sign of firelight. He edged forward. He heard the indistinct sound of men's voices, their low register telling him he was close. Darkness loomed in the trees. Henry tentatively reached out a hand. His palm touched black rock. A massive slab of boulder loomed five yards high and wide. The men and their fire must be concealed on the other side. The boulder tilted forward allowing Henry to get a handhold; his boots found purchase, and hand over hand he edged up. A boot slipped on silken moss; he clawed his fingers and gripped the rough-hewn rockface, found a better foothold and edged closer to the top.

Peering over, he looked down into a small clearing where three men squatted around the fire, its heat more from embers than flames. A rabbit turned on a spit as one man skinned a second. They had pottage on the fire cooking alongside the meat. Henry's mouth watered. The men were relaxed as they shared a wineskin. He tried to check if they wore a blazon on their tunics, but the shadows meant he couldn't see any emblem. A movement caught his eye. Beyond the edge of the clearing a black horse shifted its weight, the gleam of its coat caught for a shimmering moment by reflected firelight. Henry stared hard into the trees but could not see the other two horses that would belong to the men below.

At least, he thought, these were not la Griffe's men. There was scant hope, though, that they were not the Duke d'Anjou's, and if they discovered he was an Englishman, he would be seen as the enemy. Louis of Anjou was the French King's brother. Henry stretched wider to support his weight. His fingers touched wet moss; his weight went onto his right hand, the slip making him unsteady, throwing him off balance. His fingers clawed at the rock face, but his toeholds were gone. He slithered down and thumped into the ground, the wind knocked out of him. Pain seared through him. Blackness darker than the night embraced him.

He coughed, eyes open. How long had he been unconscious? Moments or longer? It made no difference: he awoke with the men standing over him, one with a sword tip at his throat.

'You a spy, lad?' said the man.

The pain in Henry's back pierced his lungs. He wheezed air, shook his head.

'He isn't carrying a sword,' said one man to the others. 'He's no fighting man.'

The third bent down and grabbed Henry's tunic, hauling him to his feet. He pushed him against the rock face, a grubby fist, slick with rabbit blood, tight under his chin. The swordsman had barely backed away. Give the wrong answer now and Henry would be dead.

'I was hungry,' he said, 'and afraid. I wanted to see who it was that had a fire and food. I've travelled a long way.'

The swordsman looked at the others. He nodded. 'Bring him to the light.'

They pushed him around the boulder to where their fire glow revealed more of his features. The three were suspicious. The swordsman lowered his blade, but it would take only a flick of his wrist to plunge it into the intruder. The other two men drew their swords and stepped away from the fire, merging into the darkness to check their perimeter.

'Who are you?'

'Henry de Sainteny.'

'Uh-huh. And you're alone?'

'Yes.'

'And how is it you are here? You say you travelled far?'

'I sailed on the cog *Nicholas* from England, but we were shipwrecked off the Breton coast. I swam ashore and then I was attacked by fishermen. After running from them, I found a boatman who would take me to Paris.'

'Paris?' the man grunted. 'You're a long way from Paris.'

'He robbed me.' Henry patted his belt. 'Took my purse. If I had not gone over the side and swum for my life I think he would have gutted me like a fish.'

'Aye, well, that might still be your fate.'

The two men came back into the firelight. 'No sign of anyone out there. The horses are quiet.'

The swordsman sheathed his blade. 'Watch him.' He stepped around the rock face and bellowed into the darkness. 'We have your man! Henry de Sainteny! Show yourselves or we cut his throat!'

CHAPTER FORTY-SIX

Hugh Gifford grimaced. 'Damn,' he said to himself.

Terrel and Bezián belly-crawled closer. 'The lad's got himself caught!' Terrel hissed. 'Who knows how many are in those trees? Time we made our own fortune. He's done for.'

Whispering brought their faces closer. Gifford smelled the man's breath. 'Whoever has him doesn't know who he is. The lad's given them his mother's name.'

'I don't give a rat's fart if he gave them the Pope's name. He's a dead man,' Terrel said.

'No, Gifford is right,' said Bezián. 'They're bluffing. If they knew he was Blackstone's son, then they might kill him, or take him for ransom. Being no one of importance was quick thinking on his part. He poses no threat to them.'

Terrel looked from one to the other. 'So what? He'll be dead by now.' He squirmed back, keeping flat on the ground. 'I'm not waiting. They'll come looking.'

A meaty hand caught hold of his leg. Pain burned into his calf muscle. Terrel winced and looked behind him. Eckehart Brun's eyes glared at him.

'You run now and you might alert whoever has him. Use your head. Be silent. We stay together.'

Terrel sucked his teeth in pain as the grip tightened. He nodded fiercely. 'All right, all right. Mother of God, you'll cripple me.'

Bezián pointed towards the place Henry had been taken. 'First light?' he asked Gifford.

Gifford nodded. 'We'll split up. We must stay downwind of the horses. This breeze coming up the river can veer and then they'll get our scent.'

'I'm good with horses,' said Mallin.

Terrel twisted his head to look at the older man. 'Mallin, you fall over your own feet in a fight.'

'Perhaps so. I've been in plenty of fights and it's true I'm not as agile as I used to be. But I am good with horses. They like me. I can keep them quiet.'

Terrel shook his head. 'All we need is an organ grinder and a dancing bear and then we can entertain whoever is out there.' He looked at Gifford. 'All right, how do we know the lad isn't already dead?'

'Because he would have shouted a warning. He'd have put up a fight. No, they're holding him. We'll get him back.'

Terrel grunted. 'Or his corpse.' He pointed at Gifford. 'And don't expect me to be there when you tell his father we let his son die and did nothing. Not me.'

'You do what you have to do when I tell you to do it,' Gifford said. The threat was plain to hear. 'We might have only one chance to save him.'

Terrel fell silent. Mallin edged away, back towards the river. Bezián's expression asked the question.

'I need something for those horses,' the old soldier whispered back.

Henry was bound to a tree close enough to share the fire's warmth with the three men. They left his hands free so that he could eat the slices the men cut from the rabbit on the spit and put onto a battered pewter plate for him, together with a spoonful of pottage. Henry savoured every mouthful, taking time to make the meagre meal last longer. As the men ate and listened to him, he gave his explanation of being in Anjou as part of a drawn-out story of his life as a Frenchman whose grandfather was killed by the English when they invaded before he was born. As he related that one true event, he could not help but feel a pulse beat in his neck, knowing that it had been his own father who had done the killing when he landed in France as a sixteen-year-old archer. The tragic coincidence of a young archer killing an old man who turned out to be his own wife's father had been revealed to him years before and had caused misery to his mother; the truth forcing itself between her and his father. Beyond that truth he expanded his lie and told a laboured saga of being granted a scholarship to study law in England by a French nobleman who sided with the English, but now he wished to return to his homeland and study law at the great university of Paris. The lie grew more deliberately boring in the telling. By the time the food was finished and the wineskin passed around a few times, the storytelling had become too much for his captors.

'You must be studying law. Only a lawyer could drone on longer than a summer bee. I have never heard anyone talk for so long about something of no interest to those listening,' said one of the men. 'We need sleep and you have dulled our minds enough to give it to us.'

The men spread their blankets and then the swordsman bound Henry's hands. 'We ride for Paris. There's no spare horse so we'll set you on the road tomorrow, but we cannot risk awaking to find you have stolen our purse and a horse.'

'I wouldn't do that,' said Henry. 'Not after your kindness.'

'Aye, well, so you say. But we've travelled far and sleep heavily,' said another.

'How far have you come?'

'It's been a long and arduous ride from Spain.'

Spain?' said Henry. 'The war down there?'

'That's right. We fought the English and their allies, Bretons and Gascons mostly, alongside King Henry of Trastámara's Castilians. And now we're travelling home to see our families before riding on to Paris.'

The swordsman settled the blanket over his legs and tossed another handful of wood on the fire. 'Summoned by the court to relate the story of the battle and praise the King's brother, our Lord Louis,' he said, a note of derision in his voice.

'Better they left that kind of thing to commanders and lords. All we want now is to settle by a fireside with our children by our side,' said one of the others. 'They're the audience a man needs, not a crowd of peacock courtiers.'

The third man curled himself into his blanket and cursed. 'Aye, and much good they were. Arrogant bastards, the Castilians. Their light cavalry were fast and fierce, but they did not heed the warnings we gave them. Don't fight the English on horseback, we told them, but they refused to dismount. Sweet merciful Christ, those bastard English archers tore them to shreds.'

Henry remembered the English man-at-arms in the Oxford tavern where Henry learned of his father's imprisonment. He feigned ignorance. 'Did the English King win?'

'Not Edward,' said the swordsman, 'no, his son, the Prince. Him and his commanders. Sneaked up on our flank.' He put dry branches on the fire and watched the sparks crackle. They held his gaze, a mirror to his memory. 'We lost many a good man. They held their centre, retreated, stood firm, drew in du Guesclin, and he's a fine commander, but he had no choice, and when he led the light cavalry against the English centre, their flanks...' He scratched two enfolding curved lines in the dirt. '... they rushed forward and closed in around them like a vulture's wings. It was a damned slaughter.'

'And gave chase and cut us down,' said the swordsman's companion.

Henry's throat tightened from his pounding heart. Had his father been at the battle? 'It... it sounds frightening to someone like me,' he said, playing his chosen role, 'but it must have been a glorious sight to see the banners and pennons of all the great knights and noblemen.'

The men fell silent and then the swordsman, who seemed to be their spokesman, said, 'It is, lad. It fills a man's heart and gives him courage. There were men on the field of battle who are legends. Never mind the Spanish orders in all their glory fighting with us, we were against the finest the English Prince could bring to battle.' He fell silent.

Henry detected a sense of loss: not the loss of a battle but of something more – a regret perhaps that men like these might never see such a sight again. As if to confirm Henry's suspicion, one of the others eased onto his elbow and pointed a finger in Henry's direction.

'You will never know the fear such a host instils in a man's heart, or the pride of being there. To say I was there and faced the English Prince and his brother, their commanders, Chandos, Calveley, the King of Majorca... aye, it was a host to behold.'

The men fell silent again. 'We could have won,' said the swordsman.

'If the bastards had dismounted and fought like we told them.'

The third man sighed and pulled the blanket tighter beneath his neck. 'Aye, and if the battle line had not been held by Thomas Blackstone.'

Henry barely swallowed the gasp that spilled from his chest. 'Was... was he not killed holding the line then? Is that not the most dangerous place to be on a battlefield?' he asked with apparent naivety.

'It is. But who knows if he survived? We threw everything we had against him.' The man-at-arms paused, shook his head. 'I don't see how any man standing where he did could survive such an onslaught. We saw his banner fall.'

All Henry could hear was the rush of blood in his ears. He had to turn his face away, tears stinging his eyes. It seemed likely his father had escaped imprisonment only to fall fighting for the Prince.

CHAPTER FORTY-SEVEN

Walter Mallin had located the plants he wanted. In summer their flowers would be pin cushions of white; now their colour and energy had retreated to their roots, leaving grey withered heads. After several minutes of effort digging with his knife, he pulled out a handful of roots and cut them free of their stems.

Gifford and the others were ready to move at first light, but Mallin needed time to make his way to the horses. He had cut and crushed the bulbous roots into the palm of his hand and, taking his time, edged through the trees. The wind shifted and the old soldier caught the horses' smell. He stopped and peered into the half-light spearing through the trees from the moon that came and went behind the clouds. He waited for the darkness again and let the dull light and the smell of the horses guide him closer. He was grateful not to be involved in the attempt to release Henry Blackstone. None of them knew how many men might be in the camp, and Mallin was aware he was better suited to standing his ground in a fight rather than attacking. He held his breath when he felt the breeze move from his face to the side of his neck. The wind had shifted again. He was still ten paces from the first horse; its companions were tethered a few feet beyond it. As he drew closer to the stationary shadows, he realized there were likely to be no more than three men who held Blackstone's son. He saw the shadow move. Its head raised. Had it smelled or heard his approach? How long before that grey dullness of first light infiltrated the camp? The horse gave a gentle snort. Mallin dared to edge to one side, wanting the breeze to carry the scent of what he held forward in his palm towards the horses' nostrils. He moved closer. The first horse showed no sign of fear or panic and the closer he stepped, arm outstretched, the more confident he became the horses would remain calm.

His right hand hovered close to its muzzle, his free hand soothing its face, his breath and gentle assurances blown closer to its nostrils together with the aroma of the crushed roots it inhaled. His eyes grew accustomed to the shapes of the trees and he saw the two other horses pick up the scent. He stepped between them, letting them snuffle his hand. There was nothing more he could do other than stand quietly with the horses and wait for the killing to start.

Gifford stepped around the boulder that loomed in the first hint of light. A wisp of smoke from the smouldering fire stung his eyes. He saw Henry slumped, bound to a tree, and three men curled tightly in their blankets, deep in sleep, one uttering a muffled snore. Gifford saw his three companions, swords drawn, move into the clearing from where they had skirted the area. He made out Terrel's grin. Clearly the man thought that this was going to be an easy kill. Gifford cursed himself. Only three men. Had he been too cautious during the night by waiting? His own voice of experience told him otherwise. First light was when men hunched in their blankets against a chill in the air that was not felt at any other time. He saw the wineskin and knew the men had used it to help their ragged sleep on uncomfortable ground. The remains of a meal were visible too.

Henry Blackstone's head was slumped on his chest, but

something woke him. There had been no sound, no whisper of a blade being drawn from a scabbard or heavy footfall on rough ground. It was something deep within him. A sixth sense for danger. His head snapped back. He saw Gifford, Terrel, Brun and Bezián closing in on the three sleeping men. Terrel raised his word to plunge it into the man nearest him.

'No!' Henry shouted.

His cry caught Gifford and the others by surprise. They faltered, took a step backwards. It all happened quickly. The sleeping Frenchmen rolled clear of their blankets, reaching for their weapons.

'Don't kill them!' Henry shouted.

The moment of confusion lasted a heartbeat. Gifford had his sword at one man's throat, Brun knocked Terrel's sword arm aside as he and Bezián laid their blades against the startled men.

'Don't fight these men,' Henry told the Frenchmen who were on their knees, not yet able to rise and defend themselves. 'Terrel, cut me free.'

The belligerent Terrel pointed his sword. 'They were dead men. You can't have a soft heart when it comes to killing.' His blade released Henry from his bonds.

Henry rubbed the stiffness from his leg and used the tree to help him stand. 'These men caused me no harm. They gave me food. They were going to release me. There is no need to injure them.'

The man-at-arms Henry had mentally named the swordsman dipped his head. 'Young Master de Sainteny, we are in your debt.'

'Who are you?' said Gifford.

'Look like skinners to me,' said Terrel.

'Are you routiers?' Gifford demanded.

'I am Bernard de Lagny. This man here is Hugo Muset and

the other Nicholas de Mitry. We are not routiers, we are men who fought for our Lord Louis d'Anjou.'

Henry gestured the men to stand. 'Throw clear your knives and take off your boots.'

The men obeyed.

Henry kicked their knives away. 'They fought in Spain and are on their way home.'

'Against the Prince?' said Bezián.

'Yes, we fought the English Prince and his knights. We were defeated,' said de Mitry.

Terrel scoffed. 'Had your arses well and truly kicked, eh? Goddamned French, we should have slaughtered more of you when we had the chance.'

'That's enough,' said Henry. 'These men served loyally. Let us not disrespect that. A soldier needs a safe passage home to his family. We will not stand in their way, but, my friend'—he faced de Lagny—'it will be a long walk. All right, on your feet.'

'Three horses and five men. How far will you get?' said the swordsman.

'Six men,' said Gifford. 'One of us calmed your horses. And we will get far enough.'

'Then you are not a student of the law as you told us,' said de Mitry, turning to Henry.

'I was, but I will not be studying in Paris.'

Eckehart Brun had gathered the men's weapons and boots and piled them away from where the men stood.

Terrel tugged free the men's purses. 'I'll wager our young Master Henry spun you a tale though.'

De Lagny nodded. 'And told it well.'

Henry held out his hand for the small leather pouches. Terrel looked as though he would refuse, but he caught Gifford's glare and handed them over. Henry weighed each one and then handed one back to de Lagny.

'You return what is ours to take?' Terrel spat.

'I give back enough for them to buy what they need on their long way home. A rabbit does not always oblige a hunter and his snare.' He tossed the two remaining pouches to Gifford. 'We also need food.'

Mallin led the three horses from beyond the camp.

'Do you know of a man called Jean de Soissons?' Henry asked the Frenchmen.

'La Griffe?' said de Mitry.

'Aye, that's him,' said Gifford.

'He pursues us,' Henry told them. 'You should beware. He has come south from Brittany.'

'He wouldn't dare strike through Angevin territory,' said de Lagny.

'There's no telling,' Henry said. 'And if he captures you, selling information about us to him will not save your lives. He'll kill you.'

Muset spat. 'We give nothing to scum like him. You go your way and leave us to go ours.'

'Then we have given you fair warning. When we go, retrieve your boots and weapons and steer clear of main highways. He has twenty men with him.'

'We will,' said de Lagny. 'We know our way.'

'You told me you thought the English had suffered the loss of their Master of War,' said Henry.

'So it seemed,' said Muset. 'Aye, his banner fell, the line gave and then re-formed. We thought him dead.'

Gifford looked at Henry. 'Have you told them of your interest in this matter?'

'There is no need. If my father survived, he will be in Bordeaux with the Prince,' Henry answered.

De Lagny faced Henry. 'I'm no fool, de Sainteny. If you express concern for the King's Master of War and, in the same breath, you seek your father, then you're his blood.'

'Yes. I'm his son.'

'Then you can be sure of one thing. If la Griffe doesn't kill you he'll sell you to our King.'

'We are not at war with France,' said Gifford. 'There would be no reason for the French King to want anything to do with Sir Thomas's son.'

'Of course there would! Thomas Blackstone has caused the realm untold damage, and he has evaded the King and his father before him for years. As for la Griffe, you could be the prize that gives him back his father's lands and scrubs clean his own reputation.'

Henry's heart beat faster. He had made an enemy more powerful than he had imagined. 'I killed his father,' he said without bravado.

De Lagny's look of surprise matched those of his companions. 'You spared us, young Master Blackstone, and we're in your debt. So I'll tell you that you have been in the shadow of death from that moment.'

Muset grinned. 'The pestilence would kill a man quicker than what la Griffe will do to you.'

De Lagny took Henry's comments more seriously. 'Even your men here, they cannot save you. You do not know what you have brought upon yourself. Do you think for one moment that our King would turn down the chance to trade you for your father? That he would soil his own hands and risk war? What would be done would be carried out by others. And who better than a banished son of a disgraced, impoverished knight?'

'La Griffe?'

'Yes. A family of low birth, but his father was knighted by the old King, given lands and income only to be cast out because of the son's brutality. Banished. Why else do they raid and inflict terror in Brittany? There they are far enough away from the King's reach. If you don't yet know the story of Jean de Soissons, then you are running like a rabbit in the night from a vicious creature who has eyes that see in the dark.'

'Better that we make haste before he catches me then,' said Henry, forcing a smile.

'Dead or alive. It would serve him just as well,' de Lagny said.

'So show us the way to Bordeaux.'

CHAPTER FORTY-EIGHT

The French King's Palace
Hôtel Saint-Pol
Paris

French history had been forged for hundreds of years by kings and princes, diplomats and soldiers who had travelled over the Grand Pont across the River Seine past the moneylenders' stalls and into the royal residence, the Palais de la Cité. Paris, the most cultured and vibrant city in Europe, surged with commerce. Raised voices echoed through the half-timbered houses, their cantilevered floors stealing light from the narrow streets below. The Seine was at last free of ice but it felt as though winter had crept back along the river. It made man and beast shiver. Steam seeped from whipped oxen hauling overladen carts. The pungent stench from human waste in the streets and butchers' and fishmongers' stalls created a miasma of foul air that the sickly King blamed for his ill health.

His palace on the Île de Cité had been abandoned and given to civil servants and their administrative offices. Over several years he had built onto and renovated the Hôtel Saint-Pol and its ancillary buildings beyond the city on the right bank of the River Seine. The cleaner air of its gardens and cherry orchards and its position sheltered from the intrusive cacophony of the heaving crowds improved the King's health, or so he was convinced, and better suited his contemplative life. A life Simon Bucy, the French King's special adviser, recognized as being created by the Almighty to defeat the English and reclaim France. Charles V was no warrior. He could not even ride a horse. He would never lead an army into battle like his late father. No, Bucy accepted, this snivelling, sickly, pious King, who attended to prayer the moment he rose, had surprised everyone with his sewer rat cunning.

Bucy looked out from the carriage that bore him to the King's new residence. He was pre-occupied with news of the English King's Master of War, Thomas Blackstone. Bucy had come into possession of information that, if true, could finally bring about the downfall of the scourge of France. God knew the French kings had tried for years to kill Blackstone. Bucy, the old lawyer who had served the previous and now the new King, was wise enough to know that entrapping the scar-faced Englishman was as unlikely as Charles invading England. But like a fisherman casting a broad net and gathering it in slowly, his catch could soon be beached.

He was escorted into the royal council room. Even here, the King's desire for opulence was evident. A chamber where affairs of state were conducted might be expected to be more austere. Not this one. Bucy looked out onto one of the gardens. Exotic creatures from around the known world were housed in the great menagerie. Caged lions snarled as their keeper pushed a haunch of venison through the bars. Birds screeched from the aviary. None of it seemed real compared to the ongoing struggle French peasants endured in the countryside. Routiers still raided and crops still failed and there were always outbreaks of pestilence. Bucy sighed. He was feeling his age. Two more winters and he would reach four score years. And the young King, bless him, always allowed his respected adviser to sit in his presence, even placing his loyal servant's stool close to the fire in a further gesture of compassion.

Bucy waited away from the enticing warmth. Better to be offered the seat. He was no fool. Such a gesture made the King feel magnanimous. It was better to embrace the man's vanity and make use of it when necessary. He heard voices behind the closed door. A servant dressed in royal livery stepped forward and opened it. The twenty-nine-year-old King came in with his usual sycophantic retinue. There were other valued advisers, but they would wait in the great hall where the King presided over matters of state at the council. Bucy was always glad their meetings were private. The great hall teemed with ambassadors and courtiers and what he shared with the King was for his ears alone. More importantly, the King trusted him above those who grovelled for a kind word or gesture. Charles swept into the room, the gaggle behind him quickly stopped by the doors closing. The elderly man bent down as far as he could. Dear God, thought Bucy, he's still sniffling. The King blew his nose into an embroidered handkerchief and dropped it. A servant darted forward and retrieved it.

'Simon, no need,' he said with a gesture for Bucy to raise himself. 'By now you could have retired to your estates after so many years of loyal service to our father and to us. Your presence and wisdom give us comfort.'

Only since he had backed the man who sat before him against the failing old King, thought Bucy. It had been a wise choice. Loyalty was grace and favour and survival.

The monarch sat on the padded stool with bow-shaped arms at one end of the fireplace and gestured for Bucy to take the stool at the far side.

'Simon, what news do you bring that might interest your King?'

'There is nothing yet confirmed, highness, but I have information that might allow us to draw in Thomas Blackstone.'

Surprise made Charles V pause. He looked into the flames, extending his hands towards their warmth. 'So many times we have tried and failed, Simon. Not only our father, but we also have laid traps over the years and still he survives. We are told he was poisoned when he brought Pedro to safety. Even that did not kill him.'

'True, sire, and now he once again brings success for his Prince in Castile.'

Bucy was aware of the bead of moisture on the end of the King's long nose. It was always a challenge not to gaze at what seemed to be a permanent drip and keep his attention on the matter at hand. His memory was still sharp, his skill at holding the King's attention never wavered, but he sometimes missed small pertinent facts if he did not concentrate.

'Highness, the business at hand concerns a man and his son who were banished from here some while ago, and began to inflict violence on the countryside as lethal as any plague. The man's son has appeared at the Porte Saint-Martin, asking to speak with anyone in court close to you.'

'Then he does not know how many people we have here. He holds rank?'

'No longer, sire. He is a crude character. Perhaps you will remember the name? He is Jean, son of Pellan de Soissons, whose lands your father confiscated when he banished them both. Prior to that, the father, Pellan, had fought for France, but when his son took to violence so extreme, and so cruel, and could not be stopped...' Bucy spread his hands. 'Your father had no choice.'

'Pellan de Soissons? I remember. Did our father not condemn father and son to death should they venture closer than fifty leagues from here? And he was at the city gate? Did you hang him?'

'Not yet. He is in the prison.'

'Why?'

'I wished to confirm his story before approaching you. He and his father were a scourge on the people of Brittany. Now, the son tells me his father is dead, and he wishes to beg your forgiveness in return for delivering...' Bucy paused to emphasize important information. 'Thomas Blackstone's son.'

The King's rheumy eyes focused sharply on his old adviser. 'This given without torture?'

'Given freely. In exchange for a pardon from you and a purse of gold. And permission to offer his services to find Blackstone's son.'

'A liar, no doubt, and a desperate man seeking easy money. Flog him and then hang him.'

The King had clearly dismissed Bucy's information as worthless, so before Charles considered leaving the fire's warmth, Bucy grasped his rod of office and stood, steadying himself. Looking down on the King gave him an air of authority. 'I think he is telling the truth. If you remember, sire, you asked for any fighters whom your brother, Louis, had recruited and who survived the battle at Nájera to be brought here so that you might know of the circumstances of the defeat.'

'What has this to do with the man at the gate? Are the two matters connected?'

'There are times, highness, when the Good Lord sends information favouring those who love Him more deeply than others do. Your piety ensures that God blesses France and our mission to one day defeat the English and take back all that has been stolen.'

Charles appreciated his adviser's earnestness. And flattery.

He nodded. 'Very well, Simon, sit down. Your mind is stronger than your legs. Let us think upon it.'

'The information is sound,' said de Bucy. 'Blackstone's son is currently using his mother's name, de Sainteny. He was protected in England, but when his father went into Castile, he absconded from his studies.'

Bucy had now piqued the King's interest. 'I know the name from when I was Dauphin but I cannot recollect where I heard it. But I remember when Blackstone came to our father's court all those years ago he had a young boy with him.' He paused. 'And does this...?'

'Jean de Soissons.'

'Yes, does he say where the boy is now?'

'No longer a boy, highness. By now a grown man.' He smiled. 'The years fly by. But de Soissons can identify Blackstone's son. And as for seeking him out, that is why he has come to us. Henry is apparently heading for where his father is, and we know from our spies in the Count of Foix's court that the English Prince sent a messenger to him seeking permission for Blackstone to cross his domain once he came across the Pyrenees.'

'But beyond that, we have nothing more on where Blackstone is going. The information is still too vague. These men-at-arms who returned from Nájera. How are they con-nected to this matter?'

'They came near death at young Blackstone's hand.'

'Here? In France?'

'Anjou. On their way here.'

Bucy could see the King was confused by the fragmented information, which would frustrate him and make him dismiss everything Bucy was working towards.

'Fate favours us, sire. I had sent a messenger and a clerk to these fighters' homes to ensure they could still attend the court, and when the clerk questioned them, they spoke of their meeting with Henry Blackstone.' Bucy hunched forward, his voice tight with eagerness. 'Henry Blackstone was being pursued by Jean de Soissons!' he hissed triumphantly.

The King cast him a thoughtful look but remained silent. That was a good sign as far as Bucy was concerned. Bucy had not merely been flattering Charles; it was true that the King was a pious man, that he began each day with his devotions on bended knee in his private chapel, humble before the Almighty. Perhaps it was that which gave him a calm mind and the ability to think clearly: a trait his late father had not always possessed. Silence meant the King was thinking.

'And these men explained this to you?'

'Sire, the story is that a ship from England sank, the cog *Nicholas*. That much I have discovered is true. These men say Blackstone's son survived. That he is trying to reach Bordeaux.'

Charles sighed; Bucy was unsure why – was it exasperation at being drawn into Thomas Blackstone's life again?

'Simon, we are at peace with England. But we will soon be at war.'

Bucy's eyes widened. As close as he was to the King the subject of another war with England had never been discussed.

The King nodded to reassure the old man. 'If Blackstone's son were found it might be of benefit. We received word that the Italian priest who represents the Bardi bank has once again travelled back across our borders after visiting the English King.'

This was news to Bucy, but he was quick to realize that it must mean the English King's finances were as dire as his son's.

'And he has not committed to the Prince's war chest in Aquitaine for the Castilian campaign,' said the King. 'Is it possible the Italian banks no longer wish to support a king who cannot repay his debts?' He dabbed his nose before continuing. 'The Prince is unwell. He has no money to pay his men. Pedro will never pay what is owed. Already there are defections.'

'From his allies?'

'Yes. The Prince plans to raise taxes to pay for the campaign. Some of those who supported him have approached us to swear allegiance to France instead. If we held Blackstone's son and traded his release for Blackstone's parole not to fight when war comes, then the King of England and Prince Edward would lose the one man whose skill could give them victory...'

The King's gaze settled on the flames. 'Very well. Release this Jean de Soissons and use him to flush out the boy. Offer him a substantial reward and a pardon if he brings Blackstone's son to us. Give him enough to raise routiers so that he has men at his back. But, Simon, we must not involve our brother Louis in this matter – we need him to regroup Trastámara's army, yet we must also have witnesses to any confrontation between de Soissons and Blackstone's son.'

'Then we should ask the Count of Foix,' Bucy replied. 'He is neutral in the matter between England and Trastámara.'

'He allowed Edward and John of Gaunt to gather his men in his domain.'

De Bucy shrugged. 'Sire, he is caught between two great kings. Your brother gathered an army on behalf of Trastámara and yet we are not fighting the English directly. It is a matter of careful positioning for any noble lord. Yes, he allowed the English and Gascon army to pass through his domains, but as a result he will now be more obliged to do as you ask of him. It is a question of balance, sire. He will have advisers who can see that de Soissons does as you command.'

The King considered Bucy's advice. 'Soissons will not be

granted the return of his lands if he does not comply with our mandate. Send him to Gaston Phoebus at Foix. On pain of death, no harm must come to Blackstone's son. Make that clear to de Soissons. *No harm.*'

'Sire,' said Bucy, bowing his head.

'Our brother Louis is in Languedoc with Trastámara. Arrange for us to speak to those men who fought at Nájera. If war comes, we must communicate again with our brother. Perhaps these men will be of use in that matter.'

The young King stood quickly and in a compassionate gesture extended a helping hand to the slower-moving Bucy. For once, words failed the old lawyer. He kissed the hand covered by the gown's long sleeves. 'Highness... I... thank you.'

'If the sea gave up Blackstone's son alive, it might signal the tide has turned in our favour. We close in on the English King and the Prince and finally have the means to stop Thomas Blackstone.'

CHAPTER FORTY-NINE

Bernard de Lagny and his companions, Hugo Muset and Nicholas de Mitry, spent four days with their families. They had little money left between them to give to their wives after Henry Blackstone had relieved them of their purses, but a small payment had been promised by the court when they appeared to give testimony about the battle.

Another two days' journey saw them in the heaving streets of the old capital. The night before their summons to the King, they crossed the river and slept in a dimly lit, dirty and overpriced room near the palace, which, thankfully, was set far enough away from the old city to avoid its stench. Humble fighting men were seldom invited to speak to their King, and that was why they had stayed in rooms some distance from the temptation of whores and rowdy taverns.

They awoke early, scratched their bites from the infested beds and stepped out into the murky early morning light. Avoiding human excrement that lay in the doorway, they pushed their way through the narrow muddy streets, elbowing aside porters and workmen, avoiding the open gutter flowing with human waste down its middle. Shopkeepers opening their shutters kept a wary eye on them. Hard-bitten fighting men had a swagger and sense of purpose about them. Eager to arrive on time at the Hôtel Saint-Pol for their audience with the King, and without the street odour that clung to clothing, they bellowed at and threatened those ahead who clogged the street with mules laden with baskets of wood and charcoal.

A quick glance back from any of the street vendors froze the curse and insult on their lips, making them heave their beasts aside for the three men-at-arms. The nearest bathhouse helped wash the street stench from them while an urchin wiped the detritus from their boots and they despatched another to the local washerwoman who had washed the sweat and grime from their spare shirts the night before.

At the Hôtel Saint-Pol they were ushered through the outer courtyards, guided along corridors, passed from one servant to another, each more senior than the other by the look of their livery and their demeanour. They were finally brought into a lavishly decorated reception room: high ceilings, ornate plasterwork, large windows filling the room with light. Their heels clattered on the marble floor. Told to wait, they wiped their palms dry of sweat. An old man came into the room. The three men bowed, following the servants' example.

'I am the King's adviser,' said Simon de Bucy. He gestured with his staff of office. 'Through those doors, your King will receive you. You will walk twenty paces. You will stop. You will bow. Your heads will stay lowered until I tell you to raise them. Understand?'

'My lord,' said de Lagny.

'You are Louis, the Duke of Anjou's men?'

'We are, my lord,' de Lagny said.

De Bucy saw that the man who answered was the most confident and appeared to speak for the three men-at-arms who stood nervously in front of him. He continued, 'Your lord, the King's brother, sent his own men as well as routiers and Castilian cavalry to wage war against Don Pedro of Castile. Your defeat at Nájera is to be related with no ill reference to the King's brother, to the Marshal d'Audrehem or the Breton captain du Guesclin.'

'My lord,' said Nicholas de Mitry, 'the defeat lies in the

hands of Henry of Trastámara. He went against the advice even of the King. The Spaniard was told to dismount and fight. The English challenged him to fight in a place not of his choosing – not where du Guesclin had set our battle lines. Trastámara rose to the bait. That is why the battle was lost.'

'And who made that challenge?' said de Bucy, hoping that the answer would be the man who was the bane of French Kings.'

'Their Master of War,' said de Lagny.

De Bucy's voice softened. 'And all of that, from the beginning, you will relate to the King. And then if I see the King tire, I will ask you about Thomas Blackstone's son.'

The three men looked uncertainly at each other. The shorter, more muscled man of the three dipped his head. 'We had but a brief meeting with him on the road,' said Hugo Muset. 'We know nothing of the lad.'

'You know enough,' said de Bucy. 'And you will follow my prompt.' He tapped the end of his rod on the floor. Servants on the other side of the two imposing doors opened them to reveal a vast hall. The King of France sat on a velvet-draped dais, eighty yards from where de Lagny and the others stood. A hundred or more courtiers, dressed in their finery, gathered behind the King, eager to see the three survivors and hear their story.

The three men hesitated.

De Bucy whispered: 'Twenty paces!'

Bernard de Lagny made a faltering start. The King's expression showed no sign of impatience, but remained politely attentive. And then the man-at-arms found his voice. He brought his companions into the telling of how the men had gathered under the great commanders and made lightning raids on the English camps. The more they relived the experience, the more animated they became, and in turn the images conjured of galloping horses and cries of battle stirred the courtiers. The three men bounced their account back and forth between them like seasoned actors.

Emboldened by the rapt attention of their captive audience they emphasized the success of the night attacks on the Prince's men at Vitoria and that of Sir William Felton on the hill at Ariñez. Both attacks had taken the English and Gascons by surprise. But honour where honour is due, de Lagny told the King. Sir William fought hard and the English repelled attack after attack. He died bravely and thereafter the Spanish had named the place *Inglesmendi* – the hill of the English.

The courtiers murmured in excitement at the fighting men's retelling, and exclaimed as the soldiers embellished the tale with examples of their own personal courage, only to be silenced when the King raised his hand.

The men-at-arms faltered. Had they overplayed their part? Extolled too vigorously the virtues of their commanders? Or their role in the fighting?

The King made a small gesture towards Simon de Bucy. The adviser nodded to the King's chamberlain, who tapped his staff sharply. It was a signal for the gossiping courtiers to leave. What the King had to discuss next was not for them to hear.

The King waited for them to shuffle from the room, herded by the chamberlain. Once the great doors echoed closed, de Bucy ushered the three men closer to the King.

Hesitatingly, they approached. Once they got within ten yards, de Bucy told them to stop.

'And what of the King's Master of War's son, Henry Blackstone?' said the King.

Hugo Muset and Nicholas de Mitry looked to de Lagny

to relate that part of their encounter. From what the King's adviser had told them, this appeared to be a crucial part of their journey home from the battlefield, but none of the three knew why.

De Lagny explained how they had captured the young Blackstone, thinking at first he was a thief.

'And then, highness, we lowered our guard, thinking he was alone, but he had men with him and they had remained hidden.'

'Fighting men?'

'Yes, lord, four of them. They were rough-hewn men who we took to be routiers. But Master Blackstone stopped them from killing us.' De Lagny needed no dramatic pause to accentuate the moment. 'A sword was at my throat. I was a breath away from death.'

The King looked puzzled.

'Why would young Blackstone save you?'

De Lagny was as mystified as the King of France. 'I don't know, sire. I sensed he did not believe in murder. And he told those with him that a loyal soldier deserved a safe passage home to his family. Before we learned his real name, he was concerned to discover whether Thomas Blackstone had fallen on the battlefield. He was searching for his father. I bear that lad no ill will, sire. We are in his debt.'

De Bucy saw the King absorbing the brief narrative describing Henry Blackstone's character, the youth's image forming in his mind's eye. And no doubt he was seeing the value such an honourable son would have to his father.

'What else?' said the King after a few moments' reflection.

'Nothing, sire. I hoped I had gone some way to repaying the debt I owed for my life in warning him about la Griffe, who was hunting him.'

The King looked at de Bucy. 'La Griffe?'

De Bucy's expression told the King he was just as confused by the name.

The King's tone of voice caused the man-at-arms to look at them both in surprise. 'La Griffe, sire,' said de Lagny. 'He is a renowned killer. Henry Blackstone killed his father and la Griffe is tracking him down.'

'What is la Griffe's real name?' said de Bucy.

'Jean de Soissons.'

The King snapped his head back as if de Lagny had raised a hand to strike him.

De Bucy ushered the three men away. 'All right, enough.'

Confused, the men hastily bowed and stepped back.

'No!' the King said.

Now it was de Bucy's turn to be uncertain.

'Simon, let these men stay. We have more to ask.'

De Bucy moved aside so that the King might address the men directly.

'There are issues of state that do not concern you,' said the King, 'but this much you should know. Jean de Soissons approached my advisers. He described how he knew where to find the Master of War's son. He has been commissioned to raise men to seek him out, and to bring him to us here, in Paris, so that he might be held captive. Such an act would ensure Thomas Blackstone's parole not to fight against us.'

De Lagny shook his head. 'No, sire. No, that will not happen. The man's swordsmanship is renowned in Brittany. Henry Blackstone would have no chance against him if he's caught. Jean de Soissons will kill him. He would betray you. And if he has men to ride with him, then ...' De Lagny looked at the stricken de Bucy and then back to the King. 'Forgive me, sire, but you have given him the force he needs to wreak havoc wherever he rides. He will be emboldened. As God is my witness, highness, la Griffe is a monster. If he dares to return to Paris, he will do so with Blackstone's son cut into pieces in a sack.'

Simon de Bucy's hand gripped his staff of office more tightly to stop its tremor. A miscalculation had been made and he was its architect.

The King stood; the men bowed. He walked a few paces left, and then walked back again, stopping in front of the men. An impatient gesture to de Bucy indicated they should straighten up.

'I will not have the young man's blood on my hands. His death was never our intention. And so we are indebted to you, Master de Lagny, and your companions, for allowing us to rectify a grave error. News that we have armed a killer to hunt down and kill Blackstone's son will unleash fury from the English and from their Master of War, and the time is not yet right for us to meet them in battle. You serve our brother, Louis. Now we ask you to extend that service and do your King's bidding.'

'Yes, sire,' the three men said in unison.

'Ride south. You will be given strong horses and money for supplies. Our brother is in Languedoc with Henry of Trastámara. We do not wish you to seek him out, but rather reach the Count of Foix. You will ride hard and fast and warn him of what this... la Griffe intends, should he find Blackstone's son.'

'And are we to raise his men, highness? To attack la Griffe?'

'That will not be possible. The Count is neutral. He cannot be drawn in. We have sent de Soissons to him so that he will provide a witness to ensure, when Henry Blackstone is found, that he would yield and be de Soissons's prisoner.'

'Sire, I and my companions will give our lives to serve you, but if you now intend to stop la Griffe and we must fight him, he will kill us. There is no doubt of that. And then your plan will fail, Master Blackstone will be dead and the English will destroy everything that lies in their path to exact their revenge.'

The King sighed. 'Then reach Gaston Phoebus, Count of Foix, before la Griffe does. The fate of France lies in your hands.'

PART SEVEN

SHADOW OF DEATH

CHAPTER FIFTY

Blackstone led the way back across the mountains with John Jacob and Killbere by his side when the pass allowed it. Sancha de Ferrandes rode alone several horses behind them, with Ashford and Meulon following. When snow swirled on the high narrow passes she dismounted like the men and refused Meulon's offer to take her horse's reins and lead it along the narrow track. She held her cloak's hood tightly with one hand and gripped the horse's bridle with the other, guiding the nervous beast and keeping herself between the horse and the rock face. If it reared at the sudden gusts from the banshee wind and lost its footing, it would either fall into the precipice or crush her against the rock wall. She shared the same dangers as the men.

By the time they descended into Saint-Jean-Pied-de-Port and the less violent weather, her hand was blistered from gripping the wet bridle, but when they camped that night she once again refused any help from Ashford, who had stayed close to her over the mountains.

'She keeps herself to herself,' he told Blackstone when asked how she was coping with the journey.

'Better that way, William,' said Blackstone, ladling food from the blackened pot.

Ashford sighed. 'She's a woman with backbone, but we risked our life taking her to the convent. You'd think she'd be more grateful – but her manner is cold.'

Blackstone laid a hand on his captain's shoulder. 'She does it to protect herself.'

'We pose no threat, Sir Thomas. But she doesn't show any gratitude. We've treated her well – some common courtesy in return wouldn't hurt her.'

'William, she's on Trastámara's side. She knows we saved her but she's distancing herself from us in case we are caught by our enemy and killed.' He turned away with the bowl of food. 'She's sparing herself pain.'

Will Longdon had made Sancha de Ferrandes a fire. She offered no thanks to the veteran archer and he sought none. If Blackstone wanted the woman safe then it was the centenar's task to be certain she had the basics of warmth and food, so he went back to his own campfire to bring her a bowl of pottage. This time she was courteous enough to nod her thanks. Longdon saw Blackstone approaching.

'Sir Thomas brings you food from his own cooking pot. If you would prefer to eat from it then I'll take back my own.'

She looked up at him. 'Is his food any better prepared than your own?'

'We all eat the same, my lady.'

'Then your offering is more than acceptable.'

Blackstone stood next to her fire. 'I see my centenar has already served you. And lit your fire. It seems you have my men at your service.'

'They showed kindness. I did not ask for it.'

Her cool response had a bite of antagonism.

Longdon realized he might soon be in the middle of an argument. He spoke quickly. 'I mentioned to the Lady Ferrandes that my cooking was likely to have a more refined flavour than yours, Sir Thomas,' he said with a broken-toothed grin.

'Will, I fear you're right, John Jacob has not yet found the means of turning the simplest food into a palatable dish.' His look told Longdon it was time for him to return to his men. Blackstone waited until he was out of earshot. 'You treat my men with indifference but your safety depends on their goodwill. Not mine alone. Theirs. They have already put themselves in danger for you. They ask for nothing but to receive a lady's grace. It warms them. They won't admit it because they fear it makes them appear weak but they see little tenderness in their lives.'

'And are you weakened by my gratitude, Sir Thomas?'

'You have no hold on me.'

'That's not what I felt when I bathed your wounds.'

'I was heartened by your humility. Your pride was scourged after being saved from a death sentence.'

Blackstone saw that for a second she appeared to soften. Her quicksilver moods seemed to pass like a shadow across the moon: one moment she was a feisty knife-wielding assassin; the next a humble woman, tender and caring. She looked up at him. Which of the two women he had experienced gazed at him now? he wondered.

He sat next to her and eased a blanket over her shoulders. Despite her thick cloak she shivered in the night wind that scurried across the ground, biting like hungry rats.

'Your uncle told me of your betrothal. Had there not been another man then I would not have suppressed my desire. What you sensed when you bathed my wounds was a memory of love and tenderness. It was a welcome memory. I yielded to it.'

'The man my father wished me to marry might be fighting. He might even be dead. In battle, bodies are hurled from their mounts, crushed into the mud, blazons scattered. Your Prince's heralds might not have recorded his death.' Anguish creased her face. 'If he is dead ... which I pray he is not... then... then

I would hope that you might look more kindly on me.' She hesitated. 'More than I had first wished.'

It was her first admission of attraction to him. For a brief moment Blackstone embraced the warmth it offered.

'Yet you hold back. Every time we are close you keep distance between us,' he said. 'If it's because you still suffer from your loss then I understand – I've been on that journey. I tread its path every day like a flagellant walking barefoot to Compostela for his sins.'

She turned her face away from him. 'I want no more such pain in my life. You and your men have done me a great service. And now you risk your lives returning me to lands my family own in France. What can I offer? There can only be regret, Sir Thomas. Perhaps for both of us. How will any of you survive so deep into your enemy's territory?'

'So you shield your emotions because you fear for me and my men?'

'I will be caught between the English King's Master of War, who saved me, and Trastámara, who would avenge me and my family. You have so few men. Trastámara has Louis, Duke of Anjou, riding with him. Do you think the French King will allow you to better his brother again?' She looked at the bowl of food in her lap and stirred it with the wooden spoon as if divining the future. 'I have no desire to lower my guard, Sir Thomas. I have no wish for my heart to suffer a thousand cuts when I watch you and your men die because of me.'

Blackstone pushed a few more sticks onto the embers and stood ready to leave. 'You should unburden your heart, my lady. You place too much importance on yourself. When a fight comes our way my men will not die for you, they will die for each other.'

CHAPTER FIFTY-ONE

Like an undulating sea, the rolling swells of the Pyrenean foothills bellied out onto the valley below. Blackstone had skirted any sign of villages in the sparsely populated area. They were in French-held territory now, beyond Aquitaine's border as they edged north-east towards the River Ariège. There had been no contact with the French- and Breton-led routiers and the Spanish army who had fled from the battlefield through Aragon and back into Languedoc.

Blackstone's German captain, Renfred, and his scouts appeared over the crest of the next hill.

'He's using his spurs,' said Killbere as he saw the fast-approaching horseman.

'And if Renfred's in a hurry, then there's trouble ahead,' said John Jacob.

'You can be sure he's not hurrying back for Will's cooking,' said Meulon.

Longdon stood in his stirrups to look past Meulon's bulk. 'And if you looked past your stomach, you'd see a wisp of smoke beyond those hills. There'll be Frenchmen and skinners there, I'll wager.'

'I don't see it,' said Killbere.

The veteran archer's keen eyesight did not let him down. 'It's there. Gone now on the wind. I saw it,' said Longdon.

Blackstone kept his gaze on one spot beyond Renfred. 'Will's right. There's a smudge on the skyline. The wind's beating it down beyond the rise.' He turned in the saddle.

'Will, if Renfred is being chased then we shall fight here.'

Renfred and his men pulled up. Their horses' flanks were flecked white, nostrils flared.

'Sir Thomas, there's a French camp over that hill. They have bedded down and they're blocking our route.'

'How many?' said Killbere.

'Three hundred or more. They have supplies: food, tents. It looks as though some of those who escaped Nájera had this as one of their supply caches.'

'Did you see Trastámara's colours?'

Renfred shook his head. 'They're French lords. Men-at-arms who still have their weapons. And from what I could see, there are plenty of skinners among them.'

'Can we go around them?' said Blackstone.

Renfred turned in the saddle and pointed in the general direction of unseen landmarks. 'A river bars our way over there. Broken ground on the other flank. We cannot go around, Sir Thomas. Whatever route we take they will see us and we will be defenceless. They must have come through a pass beyond us otherwise we would have seen their tracks.'

Killbere scratched his beard. 'Three to one,' he said. 'We've had worse odds.'

Blackstone twisted left and right, checking the landscape. 'Aye, but even if we draw them to us we'll take casualties.' He glanced back to where Sancha Ferrandes rode. He lowered his voice. 'And we need to get her to her estate because once the French know she's returned, then someone will come for her and that will lead us to Trastámara.'

He nudged the bastard horse forward so that only Renfred could hear him. 'Did you see a French blazon of a double chevron against blue on any tent or pavilion?'

Renfred thought about it and then shook his head.

'All right,' said Blackstone and turned to Killbere. 'Gilbert, form the men up just in case they catch our scent.'

Killbere turned his horse without further question. Low, urgent commands were given to the captains. John Jacob waited.

Blackstone nodded for his squire to join him and then turned to Renfred. 'Show me.'

After hobbling their horses, the three lay flat and peered over the rim of the hill. Stretched out before them on the narrow plain below was a French and Spanish camp, men who had escaped the slaughter at Nájera. To Blackstone's eye it looked as though this was a place where they had hidden a supply of food and tents. Had they thought they might lose the battle and given themselves a place to retreat to? He studied the men, who were preparing themselves for the night. More fires were being lit – there was more smoke now than that seen by the keen-eyed Will Longdon – and he could detect no sense of alarm that they might be pursued beyond the mountains. No picket line was evident. Voices were not lowered; snatches of conversations carried on the wind. These were men grateful to have survived. Of the three hundred men down there – if Renfred's estimate was accurate – most had small bivouac shelters, grouped for a dozen fighters at a time. Each group with their own fire. Clusters of men who would not react as quickly as they might have done had they been encamped in formation ready for any surprise attack.

Their horses were corralled in a natural concave gap in the hillside on the right flank of the men, with cut branches acting as a barrier to stop them escaping.

'It wouldn't take much to scatter the horses,' said John Jacob. 'We're downwind.'

'Especially if even one man worked his way around the back of them,' Renfred added.

Blackstone's eyes swept back and forth across the huddled men. 'Those knights in the centre. Their pavilions weren't carried back here from the battle. These Frenchmen and their skinners set up this place as their escape route. They'll be waiting to join up with the Duke and Trastámara.'

The distant river glistened in the fading light, its breadth and depth a natural defence against attack. Nature had also provided protection on the opposite flank where the horses were corralled. Rocky, uneven sloping ground, rising to the jagged, cloud-enshrouded peaks.

'Sir Thomas,' said John Jacob, 'we could turn back and find a shallow crossing. Probably no more than twenty miles.'

Blackstone looked at him. His squire would not suggest being so cautious without good reason.

'Go back?' said Blackstone.

John Jacob shrugged. 'If we try and ride hard through them we'll get halfway. If that. The Lady Sancha will call out. She'll bring them down on us like a swarm of crows pecking the dead.'

Blackstone didn't reply, but he knew his squire's concerns were valid.

'Or we charge through them in the dark,' said Renfred. 'Our men are rested, Sir Thomas. I could take my scouts and create a diversion.'

Blackstone kept watching the camp below. 'No, if we fight them here we'll take too many casualties.'

'Then how do we get past them?' said John Jacob.

Blackstone smiled, turned and edged down from the rim. 'We walk through them.'

'Even with the lady?'

'Even with her,' said Blackstone.

★

Blackstone rode back and had his captains pass the word that when the moon rose high the men would ride three abreast, the hoods of their cloaks raised, their blazons concealed by carrying their shield beneath their cloak. If challenged their answer was to be that they were from Nájera and riding to meet the Duke d'Anjou.

Sancha Ferrandes waited with Meulon as her escort. 'My lady,' said Blackstone, 'I must impose an indignity upon you. There are routiers ahead encamped with French lords and Spanish survivors. There are too many for us to fight here so we intend to ride through their camp in the dark.'

The Castilian noblewoman was no fool. 'And you're fearful I will cry out because they are Trastámara's allies.'

'You could not be blamed for doing so.'

'Then you would wish to gag me?'

Blackstone said nothing.

'And if I give you my word that I would remain silent?'

'It would be too much to ask, my lady. To be so close to those who fought to put Trastámara on the throne and you knowing that with one cry you could bring them to your rescue.'

'But I am no captive, Sir Thomas. You do me a service by taking me to my domain in France. I would not betray that.' She paused. 'I swear I would not.'

Killbere, who was close by, groaned. 'You're putting our lives at risk, Thomas. Trusting a woman to keep her mouth shut is like asking the Pope to give up his mistress. An impossible request.'

'I trust her,' said Blackstone.

'Thank you,' she said.

Blackstone gathered his reins and glanced from Sancha to

Killbere. 'Besides, if she dared to cry out Meulon would cut her throat in an instant,' he said.

Blackstone nudged the bastard horse alongside William Ashford.

'Sir Thomas, you would have Meulon do such a thing?' he said quietly.

'The threat was enough, William. You and Renfred choose two men apiece. Bring them to me before midnight. Looking at those clouds beyond the mountains I'll wager we'll lose the moonlight soon after.'

He posted two men on the ridge overlooking the camp. His captains went among their men, readying them for the slow, dangerous ride between their enemy's ranks. They knew that if Blackstone's plan failed, they could be overwhelmed from both flanks.

The night wind moaned through the lofty peaks but kept Blackstone's column downwind of the camp. Hours later the lookouts returned.

'They're bedded down, Sir Thomas,' one of the men reported. 'Still no sign of pickets.'

'Go to your captains, rejoin your men.' He looked back at the formation of horsemen, three abreast, cloaked and hooded. He thought that if he were in that camp, lying next to a meagre fire, half awake and saw the column pass through, he would think of these dark riders as harbingers of death.

As they would be if the alarm was raised.

Blackstone heeled his horse forward at the walk.

Saddles creaked; bridles jangled softly. Horses snorted, heads raised, ears alert as they rode into the enemy camp, picking up the stench of stale sweat, latrine pits and suppurating wounds that mingled with the acrid wisps of smoke from dying fires. Riders steadied their mounts. An overeager horse, battle-scarred and used to plunging into the fray, was the last thing any of Blackstone's men wanted if it broke ranks.

Blackstone led the way, feeling the bastard horse's muscles quivering beneath him. He tightened his reins, murmured low curses to the beast whose ears pricked back momentarily at the sound of his low threats.

As they progressed through the centre of the camp, some of those on the ground stirred. Occasionally one of them raised himself and stared at the unhurried procession. Yet those who awoke appeared to assume that the dark riders posed no threat. A slow-moving column of hunched men were likely to be escapees from the battlefield crossing the mountains.

The pace was agonizingly slow. Every yard forward felt like a mile. Blackstone's men looked neither left nor right, their hoods keeping their eyes focused ahead of their horse's ears. They were almost through when one routier, the worse for drink, staggered alongside Meulon's horse, his fist gripping the stirrup strap, rambling incoherently about the Spanish battle. The clouds suddenly retreated and moonlight exposed the camp and the slobbering wretch, who now seemed to be asking for wine. When Meulon refused to answer the fighter reached up to snatch at Meulon's hood, his horse shied and the others nearby wavered. In her efforts to control her skittish horse, Sancha's hood fell free. The light was enough for the drunk to see her beauty.

He bellowed. 'A whore! They have women with them! Whores!'

The swift arc of Meulon's knife cut his throat. The mercenary clutched his neck and staggered back with a look of bewilderment. By the time he was on his knees, blood seeping through his fingers, others had raised themselves. His cries of alarm were enough to get the fighting men closest to him on their feet, sword and axe in hand.

There were barely 150 yards before the camp's end. Blackstone spurred his horse, pressed with his left leg, kicked with his right and turned the belligerent beast back along the line. 'Ride! Gilbert! Get her clear!'

Killbere knew there was no time to argue. The men would be free of the camp and the awakening mercenaries once they breasted the hill ahead.

Blackstone cantered back along the line, Wolf Sword in hand, John Jacob at his back. Groggy men stumbled forward; the war horse barged them aside as Blackstone's blade slashed others. Those who avoided his deadly strikes fell under John Jacob's sword. Blackstone reached the rear of the column. By then Killbere and his men were galloping clear. He cast a glance to where they had entered the camp. Men were running for their mounts. He prayed the task he had given to Renfred and William Ashford did not cost them their lives.

He wheeled the bastard horse, saw the surge of the corralled horses break free and stampede into the camp. Hundreds of mounts pounded into men and tents. Renfred and Ashford with their chosen men rode hard towards Blackstone. Herd instinct took over most of the free-running horses as they galloped after the escaping column. The camp was in disarray. Men were trampled, fires kicked into the night sky, embers and sparks whisked away on the wind. Cooking pots and men's equipment scattered. Blackstone and John Jacob wheeled their horses. Killbere had led the column to safety over the next ridge. The gamble had paid off. There would be no pursuit.

CHAPTER FIFTY-TWO

Days later Blackstone led the men along a valley, following the curve of the River Ariège. Renfred was ahead of the main body on the high ground, his men scouting for any sign of French or routier forces. Blackstone followed them north into a gorge beneath sheer limestone cliffs, their slopes covered in pine forests. A shallow ford allowed them to cross the river without difficulty. As they followed a meandering tributary, it brought back Blackstone's memory of the limestone cliffs and wooded hills of the place where he and his young wife had started their life together. Wherever he and the men were now, it was a place that offered an abundance of water and good grazing and triggered his melancholic recollection. The gently flowing water and whisper of breeze through the branches created an air of tranquillity far removed from any conflict. Slabs of rocks jutted into the shallows from the low bank, suggesting a place where children might play safely in the water and then stretch out to dry on the sun-warmed rocks. Blackstone slammed closed the lid of the chest that had unexpectedly revealed his sadness.

'How much further?' he asked Sancha, who rode at his side.

He noticed her expression had changed. It was no longer creased with sullen uncertainty, but softened by what must have been a sense of homecoming. She looked radiant. Her smile was one of genuine happiness.

'Almost there,' she said. 'The last time I was here, I was only a girl. My father brought us.' She unconsciously reached out and touched his arm. 'Thank you, Sir Thomas.' Her eyes were moist. Then her smile broke through again and she impetuously spurred her horse forward.

Blackstone's bastard horse snapped its teeth at the horse daring to sidle past his head, but Blackstone held it on a tight rein.

Killbere, who rode behind, cursed. 'God's tears, Thomas. There could be a hundred Frenchmen over that hill. It'd be like hitting a hornet's nest with a stick.'

Blackstone shrugged. 'Let her be, Gilbert. Renfred would have warned us if there's anyone other than villagers.'

'Villagers? Do you see any smoke from huts? Do you hear dogs barking? I'll wager she's brought us to a derelict place that hasn't had a lord of a manor for twenty years.' Killbere snorted snot from his nostrils and spat. 'Harking back to the past does no one any damned good and damns a soul to misery. Damned if it doesn't.' And the look he gave Blackstone needed little more explanation.

Blackstone dug his heels into the bastard horse. He crested the grassy hill and in the distance saw an ancient château built of rough stone, likely to have been standing for the better part of a hundred years. The main dwelling was small, and would have once been nothing more than a fortified house before surrounding walls were built encasing a yard. There were scattered dwellings, some fenced sheep and a few cows, and a line of stables running inside the length of the enclosing walls. Broad-plank double gates set in the stone walls were shut, and the walls were low, easy to scale with ladders. A church bell clanged a warning, the sound dulled from being poorly cast. Figures scurried inside the walls. Men mostly, from what Blackstone could see. They were not running to hide but to man the wall's walkway. There was no sign of weapons other than axes, pitchforks and scythes. Determined peasants prepared to defend their homes.

Sancha had slowed at the bell's ringing and the sudden appearance of the people. She pulled up her horse when Blackstone called for her to halt. He grabbed her rein to stop her horse from bolting as the men on the walls roared their defiance. A rain of stones flung through the air, whistling with lethal speed from slingshots. The missiles fell short.

'Stay back!' he ordered her as John Jacob raced to Blackstone's side. Sancha's horse was close to bolting. If it went forward, the next storm of bone-crushing stones could kill her. Blackstone heeled the bastard horse to stop her mount from lunging forward. 'Hold her!' he shouted as John Jacob's mount blocked the terrified horse. Blackstone's squire grabbed her reins. It took only moments for the two men to stop the frightened animal panicking and in that time Killbere and the men had galloped down and positioned themselves behind Blackstone.

'Thomas? What is this?' said Killbere. 'Not the welcome she'd have expected.'

'Stay here. I'll find out.'

'You're going to talk to these belligerent bastards? They're French peasants spoiling for a fight.'

'Gilbert, if you were a French peasant and saw horsemen crest the hill, wouldn't you want to defend yourself?'

'If I were a French peasant, I'd have cut my throat long before now,' said Killbere. 'I'll wait here. If you get stoned to death, you've only yourself to blame.' He grinned. 'Then I'll kill them all in revenge, so for the sake of the peasants, stay out of range.'

Blackstone edged the bastard horse forward. He raised an arm and then pulled up. 'This domain belongs to the Lady Sancha Ferrandes of Castile. It is hers by right. If you contest her right, then we will retrieve it for her.'

The men on the walls looked uncertain. Then heads bobbed and voices called to someone behind them. No one answered

Blackstone, but neither did they attack him. A white-haired man appeared, obviously the one who had been summoned. He shielded his eyes against the light.

He called out; the strength of his voice belied his aged appearance. 'Who are you?' he demanded.

'Who I am is of no importance. I have escorted the lady from danger to what should be a place of safety and you people nearly killed her.'

'The lady is here?' said the old man.

One of those on the wall next to him pointed beyond Blackstone.

'Bring her closer,' he said.

'And risk her life?'

'I give my word no harm will come to her.'

'Then you come out and I give my word no harm will come to you,' Blackstone answered.

There appeared to be an argument between the old man and others on the wall and then the white-haired man ducked out of sight. It didn't take long for one of the gates to open. The old man was a priest. His black cassock trailed behind him as he limped forward, leaning on a gnarled staff. A rosary and a crucifix hung from the rope around his waist. He walked twenty yards and stopped.

'Well? I am here!' he bellowed. 'If you are cowardly routier scum who wish to inflict more harm on us than you have already, then I shall be your first victim.'

His courage impressed Blackstone. That, and his belligerence. Blackstone gestured for John Jacob to escort Sancha closer. When there were thirty yards between her and the priest, Blackstone gestured them to rein in their horses. He glanced at the walls. There was still danger, but the men on the walls were concentrating on their priest and the woman who had approached him. It would have been easy to take the walls and force through the gate had that been Blackstone's intention.

The old priest remained defiant as he peered at Sancha. 'Is this a trick? Who are you?' he called.

Before John Jacob could stop her, Sancha dismounted. The squire grabbed the reins to stop her skittish horse from running free as she strode towards the priest. Blackstone gestured to his squire to stay where he was. The priest took a step back in a moment of uncertainty about what her action meant.

'Mon Père Éraste, it is I, Sancha Ferrandes of Castile.'

The priest frowned. He shook his head. 'It is not you.'

Sancha tugged free a small bronze pendant cross from around her neck. It was plain, with no inlaid precious stone or enamel. Not the religious jewellery a noblewoman would likely wear. A simple gift such as an impoverished priest might offer.

'You gave me this so that I would be humble before God.'

The priest stared at it. 'You were a child.'

She took his hand gently and kissed it. 'I was seven and you were old even then.'

He nodded. 'So, it *is* you. Always the cheeky one. Now, you have come to visit after all these years.' He kept hold of her hand, glancing at Blackstone and the rough-looking men behind him. 'With unsavoury-looking characters.'

'Who have given me protection.'

'Unsavoury,' he said again for emphasis, with a churlish grimace. He made a rapid sign of the cross towards Blackstone and the men behind him. He lowered his voice. 'Even men like these need to be blessed at least once in their lives. Now! Where is your father, your mother; where is the rest of your family?'

CHAPTER FIFTY-THREE

After Père Éraste heard the tragic news of Sancha's family, he grasped both her hands and whispered a prayer for their souls. He ordered the gates opened and ushered the last surviving member of the Ferrandes family into the great yard, followed by Blackstone and his men. As the old man guided Sancha through the gathered villeins he proclaimed her rightful place among them. The villagers gathered as close as they dared, bowed and clasped their hands together as if giving thanks to God that she had brought fighting men to defend them, even though their fearful expressions at the sight of Blackstone's men contradicted their gratitude.

Blackstone's captains billeted the men in the stables while he accompanied the priest and Sancha Ferrandes into the stone-built house at the far end of what could only be called a walled village – but barely that, Blackstone thought, as the crumbling walls and time-beaten house all looked in need of repair.

The entrance was through double doors at the top of fifteen stone steps. The priest took a heavy iron key from his cassock, used both hands to try and turn the lock. He failed. Blackstone stepped forward and twisted the key, then stepped back, allowing him the dignity of being the first to welcome Sancha Ferrandes back to her home. The old man instructed two of the villagers to heave open the heavy chestnut doors. Blackstone stayed at the entrance as Sancha walked into a house full of memories.

'Nothing has been touched for many years,' said Père Éraste. 'Your father returned several years ago but since then no one has come. At times I thought we had been abandoned but I prayed that one day your family would return.'

Sancha was gazing at the room, her eyes sweeping across the old moth-eaten tapestry that hung on the wall. Cobwebs stretched from every corner. She turned and thanked him, her manner subdued, her eyes moist.

It was apparent to both the old priest and Blackstone that she didn't care about the condition of the room. Sancha Ferrandes of Castile had been reunited with her own domain in France.

'I will have women light the fire and attend to you,' said the priest.

Blackstone walked back to the square with the old man.

'How many people live here?' he asked.

The priest coughed and wheezed, shook his head and coughed again. 'Here? None. No one lives here. Only me. I attend my daily prayer in the chapel.' He pointed to the small bell tower above a nondescript building. 'And when local people need sanctuary I am here for them, as would Lady Sancha's father have been. This place has long needed a strong man efficient with a sword.' His glance revealed he thought that the man beside him might be such a saviour.

Blackstone ignored it and gestured to the livestock, the sacks of grain, the women and children, the stored woodpiles. 'I don't understand.'

'These people arrived yesterday for safety. We lit no fires last night. We stayed behind the walls hoping the murdering scum who attacked their village had gone.'

'Their village was attacked? How far away?'

'A day, day and a half ride. We are usually safe here. Soldiers who fight the wars and return to rape the land usually ride along the Rhône Valley to the east. But there are other brigands,' the old priest said matter-of-factly.

'You use this as a place of sanctuary?'

'Of course. These are free men and woman. But they serve Ferrandes of Castile. They pay what they owe. The Lady Sancha's father insisted the grain stores must be refilled once the locals had taken what they needed. His command was always followed. It meant this was not only a safe place for the villagers around here but also a source of food during a bad winter. He was a wise man.'

Blackstone placed a restraining hand on the priest's arm. 'You have lived here all these years since her father last visited. You bring people here for sanctuary against raiding brigands. Yet a determined child and a three-legged dog could scale these walls. You have made no improvements.'

The old man sighed. 'I know. They give shelter when the north wind brings snow, and over the years when farmers brought their grain we constructed walkways behind the wall as lookouts. And these people, they do not lack courage, which is why we tried to stop you.'

'Any brigand would happily use this place as a camp.'

The priest nodded. 'True.'

'But you have survived.'

'As you see, sir knight.' He smiled. 'The Lord bestows His blessing on us in unusual ways. Terror comes in many forms.' He peered across the square. 'Today we were lucky. Had you been determined men intent on harm we would all be dead by now.' He called to someone across the yard. 'Marcel! Yes! You! Come! Bring the flag!'

Blackstone watched as a boy, no older than ten years, dodged through the dozen or so sheep that grazed on winter fodder spilled in the yard. He carried a pole with a furled flag. He was breathless when he reached Blackstone and the priest.

'What are you?' demanded the priest.

'I am slow, Père Éraste.'

'You are. And your fear overtook you when the horsemen appeared.'

'It did,' said the boy. 'And I beg forgiveness for failing you.'

'Today you are forgiven,' said the priest. 'Now unfurl the flag for this knight to see.'

The boy unfurled a black banner.

'The pestilence,' said Blackstone.

'When horsemen came close we raised the flag. No man would risk entering an infected place.' He nodded to the boy to roll up the cloth. 'Today, well... we were slow.' He gave the boy a benevolent smile and gestured him away.

Blackstone strode to the wooden steps leading to the parapet. The old priest shuffled along with him. By the time they reached the top the priest needed to catch his breath as Blackstone took in the view from the meagre defensive position.

In the far corner at the back of the wall, away from where Blackstone had approached, a deep scar ran at an angle for three hundred yards into low scrub and regrown saplings from where the edge of the forest had been cut down over the years. A convenient place to cut firewood. The gulley was more than a ditch; it looked as though it had once been thought of as a moat or a defensive trench. It was broad enough for two horsemen to ride side by side and deep enough for them not to be seen from the open plain to the front of the domain.

'What is that?' he asked when the priest caught up with him.

'It was dug years before the Ferrandes family owned this land. Whatever came out of the ground built these walls.'

Blackstone studied the dig. 'More than that, priest. Whoever first built this place used it as an escape route into the forest.' He pointed to the back wall and a single solid door. 'That stonework is different.' He looked down into the teeming yard. 'These villagers, how long will they stay here?'

'Until we feel certain the brigands have moved on.'

'And how many men attacked them?'

The priest shrugged. 'When those who work the fields see smoke on the horizon they run.' He nodded towards the people gathered in the square. 'Some say it was no more than twenty men, others that it was a hundred. Fear distorts everything.'

Blackstone turned back towards the steps. 'Until we find out more, this place needs to be organized and better prepared. Your black flag might one day fail you. The walls need reinforcing. Livestock and feed separated and animals penned. We will stay here for a week or so and then return these people to their homes. You will feed us and the men here will share duties on the wall with mine. The women can attend to cooking and washing our clothes.'

'Some of these women sleep with an axe at their side. They stand shoulder to shoulder with their men.'

'Good. Then they can do their turn on the walls and their men can do our washing.'

CHAPTER FIFTY-FOUR

Henry Blackstone and the men took it in turns to ride or run alongside the three mounts taken from Bernard de Lagny and his companions. Each man in the saddle kept the horse at a steady pace while the other gripped the stirrup strap. They continued like this until the men could run no more. Walter Mallin suffered the most. His age was against him. He barely managed to run a quarter of the time. Terrel, true to character, refused to give up any time on his mount to accommodate the older man. Brun was too big and heavy to lope along at a horse's pace, so he too had to switch more often. It came down to Bezián, Gifford and Henry to surrender their riding time. Despite their interrupted passage, they made good progress towards Bordeaux. Or so they hoped. The intermittent storms and ongoing cloud cover made being certain of their sense of direction impossible.

By the third day their nerves were ragged. Their stomachs growled. There had been no sound of a distant church bell or smell of woodsmoke on the breeze telling them a village was nearby: a place where food could be bought. Henry had trapped a lone rabbit the day before, but the morsel did not sustain the six men for long. Thirst was the more demanding need, and it was their mounts that led them to water. A stream meandering through a clearing allowed man and horse to drink. They flopped back in the wet grass, letting the horses graze.

'Master Henry, we're losing the sun behind the clouds too

often to know which way to go,' said Eckehart Brun. 'We might be running around in circles.'

Henry raised himself and looked at the trees they had left behind them. His father had taught him the lore of the land when he was a boy. Some of the trees were misshapen, bent by the wind. Lichen grew on one side rather than the other, but whether the lichen clung to the trees' southern orientation or if the prevailing wind that bent the trunks was mostly from the east or the north he didn't know. Nature could play its own tricks. But Henry knew it was important for the men's confidence that they believed they were going in the right direction. John Terrel lay on his back, staring at the sky, emitting a long, monotonous stream of complaint, full of defeat and misery, as unrelenting as the gurgling stream.

'The sun has passed overhead. We can see that even with the clouds, so we've made good progress since first light,' Henry assured them. 'The wind blows from the north,' he added, pointing at the forest, 'which is why those old trees are bent.' He smiled. 'There's nothing to worry about. We'll soon find a trader's route going south and there'll be villages to feed us along the way.' His eyes swept the forest. Shadows moved. The light changed deep amidst the trees.

Sixty yards from where the men rested, a rider walked his horse forward out of the forest. Henry's smile faded. Whoever the rider might be, he wore half-armour, mail and surcoat. His shield, scuffed and dented from battle, was slung from his saddle. His helmet's raised visor revealed a dark bearded face. The man was sturdy. Broad-chested. Astride his mud-splattered, caparisoned horse, he loomed large. Large, fearsome and apparently fearless. He remained unmoving in the saddle. His sword sheathed in its scabbard. The horse dipped its head, fighting the bit. It stared at the other horses, which had turned to face it. Horse and rider looked to challenge anyone or anything in their path.

And then it became apparent why the lone horseman appeared so unconcerned about facing six armed strangers. Men-at-arms emerged from the forest. More riders than trees it seemed. All bore the same blazon as the knight who held the middle ground between Henry and the treeline. They reined in behind their leader. Sixty or seventy men. Possibly more. Their jangling bridles and snorting horses alerted the lazing men at the stream. Gifford was the first to scramble to his feet and stand at Henry's shoulder. The others were a breath behind him. Terrel fell silent except for a whispered curse.

'There has been killing and looting of villages,' said the horseman. 'This land is under my jurisdiction. I hang routiers or, if the river is deep enough, sew them into sacks and drown them.' He nodded beyond the men. 'The river lies half a mile beyond the stream. You can choose.'

Henry stepped away from the men. 'My lord, we are travellers, not routiers.'

The bearded horseman shrugged. 'Travellers or routiers. You are thieves. And I treat thieves the same as skinners. Three horses with good saddles but by the look of you there's not a sou between any of you.'

'We have money,' Henry said. 'We took those horses from some men who captured me.'

'And why would they wish to capture you and then release you?'

'I stumbled on their camp. I thought *they* might have been skinners.'

'And were they?'

Henry hesitated, seeing the trap being laid out before him. Admit they were not and confirm he was a thief. Or say they were and extend the lie into unchartered territory. 'They were not.'

'But they let you take their horses. If there were three of them and six of you, then they must be dead and you will suffer the same fate.'

'My men—'

'*Your* men?' the horseman interrupted.

'My *companions* rescued me.'

'And you killed the men who were not routiers and took their horses. And their money.'

'We did not kill them and I took a third only.'

'Generous of you. Do you know the names of these men?'

Gifford spoke quietly. 'Master Henry, he's toying with us. He could have had us killed without the questioning. If he's a local lord, whose side is he on? Be careful what you say next. Even your name might be our death warrant.'

Henry knew if he lied and said he did not know the men's names, perhaps this knight and his men did. Had they come across them on their journey to Paris and been told of the robbery? And even if they had not met them on the road and admitted their names, this fearsome man might be on the side of the French King, as were de Lagny and his friends.

He took a step closer to the war horse. Its head was as scarred as his father's horse. The bearded knight's breadth of chest and muscular arms showed him, as witnessed by the men behind him, a war leader. Their mud-splattered caparisons showed darker stains. Dried blood.

'My lord,' said Henry. 'If you have come from a recent battle, then it would benefit me to know whose side you favour because our lives are in your hands. It might be better to lie and deny all knowledge of the men's names in case they are compatriots of yours – or make up names to reassure you and save ourselves. But I will tell you the truth – and I give my word – we did not kill them. They had returned from fighting the English Prince and the Spanish King Pedro. I honoured their courage and wished them safe journey to their families. And then we took their horses.'

'Your lives are forfeit anyway, you insolent bastard. You dare to question me?'

'I say we run for it,' said Terrel under his breath. 'Split and run. Every man for himself.'

Henry squared his shoulders. It was now or never. 'They were three Frenchmen. Bernard de Lagny, Hugo Muset and Nicholas de Mitry. They told us of their defeat. And I... I thought it a cruel murder to kill brave men on their way home to their families, even though they are my enemy.'

For a moment the bearded man studied Henry and the others. 'Then you are Englishmen?'

'We are. Except for one who is Gascon.'

'English, Gascon, French. It makes no difference. Routiers gather together like flies over shit. Brigands die at my hand. You deny you are such, so why are you here?'

'I don't even know where here is, lord.'

'Poitou.'

'Then we are in the English Prince's domain.' Hope flared and died quickly. If this hulking man was like de Lagny and his companions, Frenchmen returning from war, it made no difference if they were on the Prince's land. 'I seek my father who fought with the Prince. I am trying to reach Bordeaux. If the Prince is there, then so too will be my father.' Henry took a deep breath. 'Sir Thomas Blackstone, the King's Master of War.'

Henry heard Gifford groan.

The horseman's chin tilted. His hands tightened the reins. The truth was out. The silence was broken only by the horse's snorting and the cry of rooks in the trees. Gifford thought it was now or never that the horsemen would seize them. His hand edged towards his sword's hilt. The others saw it and did the same.

'The Prince is not in Bordeaux. He waits at Burgos. I am Guichard d'Angle, Marshal of Aquitaine. And if Thomas Blackstone is your father, I know where he is.'

CHAPTER FIFTY-FIVE

For a few moments after Guichard d'Angle had confirmed that Henry's father had survived and returned to France, north of Foix, Henry Blackstone felt a renewed sense of hope. Uncertainty soon devoured it. The marshal told him how hordes of disbanded soldiers, no longer needed by the Prince, had come together and formed new companies of routiers. They had crossed the Pyrenees and once they had reached Saint-Jean-Pied-de-Port had torn across the countryside in search of supplies. They had already struck east across Quercy and into Rouergue, heading north for the rich pickings and wealth of Burgundy before next winter set in. It was the old pattern repeating itself. Men who had been paid for war and then released from their contract needed to live by other means. The marshal warned Henry that riding to find his father meant he was bound to encounter such men, or French men-at-arms protecting towns and villages.

'I have spare mounts for your men. Stay in Aquitaine and you will reach Bordeaux. The Prince will return at some stage and no doubt your father will join him. Be patient,' Guichard d'Angle urged the young man.

But Henry ignored the marshal's warning. Impatient to reach his father, once again he had given the men a choice. They could leave and fend for themselves or accompany him.

'The angels are on your shoulder,' said Terrel. 'Damned if they're not. I'm with you, Master Henry. Eh, lads?'

Bezián shrugged. 'We have had three narrow escapes. If the angels favour him, then we live another day.'

'Aye, but when the Almighty runs short of angels to do His work, Fortune's Wheel turns,' said Mallin. 'We've a better chance to live if we stay in Aquitaine. If we strike south-east, we either run into routiers or, like the marshal said, the French defending their domains. And if we are in the middle...' He grimaced. There was no need for further explanation.

The six men stared Fate in the face.

'What Walter says is true,' said Eckehart Brun. 'There aren't many of us.'

'But there're pickings to be had!' Terrel urged. 'If skinners are riding north then we'll be ahead of them. We need have no fear of them. Nor will dumb French bastards standing in their way bother us.' Terrel was loath to miss the chance of any looting. 'We've got this far and we can't help ourselves in Aquitaine. Merciful Christ, if we did then the old bastard marshal would hunt us down. No, I say we go with the lad, and take what we need.'

'There'll be none of that,' said Gifford. 'We cause no harm unless we are forced to defend ourselves.'

Terrel bared his teeth and pushed his face closer to Gifford's. 'You get paid to do your duty. Us here'—he gestured to the others—'we've had to take what we can when we can.'

Gifford headbutted him and before Terrel hit the ground his sword was at the routier's throat. 'You skinners never change. Master Henry should have handed you over to the marshal and let him hang you.'

Henry touched Gifford's arm. 'Leave him. He can go his own way.'

Gifford stepped back. Terrel wiped his bloodied nose and

got to his feet. 'You and Gifford have not had to forage to live.' He pointed towards nowhere in particular. 'You go out there into a wild land, riven by war, unwanted by any lord, prince or king because there's no money left in his war chest, then you either die of hunger or you take what you need.'

'Or pay for it,' said Henry.

'With what? You expect us to buy our way to your father? We've at least ten days of hard riding. What do we have? Enough to get us along the road for two, three days? Do you see a farmer selling his wares? We will have no choice but to do what we must.'

'I will pay for any food we need. There will still be hamlets and villages untouched by marauding skinners. I bear my father's name. I will not dishonour it.'

Walter Mallin scuffed the dirt. 'Damned if we haven't all lived like runts of a litter. We had no guardian like you, Master Henry. No one paid our way. So don't condemn men for doing the best they can.'

Henry saw the mood changing. Gifford was a retained man-at-arms while he had been sent to Oxford, his life cushioned by the King's largesse, payment for his father once again having saved the Prince.

'You're right. I am now privileged. But it wasn't always so. I condemn no one. Do what you will and go where you wish, but if you follow me, nothing changes. There will be no looting. No rape. I'll kill the first man who does.'

Henry turned away from the men. Gifford watched his back until he was safely away from anyone making a sudden lunge with a blade.

'Master Henry told me how he killed Pellan. He rammed his knife into his ear. Pierced his brain with one thrust. He did that to save you. Don't forget that. You owe him your lives.'

Henry and his guardian rode away, leaving behind the men who had so far shared their journey.

After half a day's ride Gifford guided Henry off the track. They waited, concealed, as hoofbeats came closer. Once the four horsemen had passed he called out. 'Your heads are up your arses. Did you not see our tracks veer off the track? Skinners would have you dead already.'

The horsemen reined in. Bezián turned in the saddle. 'We decided that we would follow Master Henry and, God willing, if we reach Sir Thomas Blackstone then we ask to join him.'

'And you, Terrel?'

The chastened fighter nodded. 'Aye. Me too. It's agreed.'

There was enough distance between where Gifford was and the others for them not to hear what he said if he lowered his voice. He turned to Henry: 'Master Henry, we're taking a big risk in having Terrel along.'

'He seems more subdued.'

'No, he is play-acting. He is a scavenging dog who will bite the hand that feeds him.'

Henry nodded. 'Then let's make sure we always wear our gauntlets.'

CHAPTER FIFTY-SIX

For eight days their journey was uneventful. They eked out the supplies given them by Guichard d'Angle for six of those days and then went hungry. A man's misery can be counted in days of hunger but spring berries and Henry's boyhood skill, taught by his father, at making a fish trap in a local stream kept them fed.

By now they suspected they must have left the relative safety of Aquitaine a couple of days before. They had already seen signs of churned earth where more than twenty riders had crossed the countryside. It was not long before their suspicions seemed to be proved correct. The scent of smouldering wood filtered through the forest, too potent to be the smell of a campfire. They were on a narrow track that offered little by way of a view ahead.

'There's no sign of horsemen having gone ahead of us,' said Bezián.

'It's in the forest somewhere,' said Brun.

'Could be charcoal makers,' said Henry.

Gifford shook his head. 'There'd be evidence of cut timber. I say we turn and go slowly through the trees. If we stay on the road we risk turning a corner and finding we've walked into skinners who've come from a different direction.'

The men murmured their agreement, drew their swords and followed Gifford as he nudged his horse through undergrowth and low-hanging branches. Two hundred yards later the acrid smell revealed its source. Gifford halted the men. They were still ten yards back in the trees away from a woodland clearing that held a hamlet of ten houses. None remained standing. Only the charred outline and smouldering wood indicated where every hut had been located. These were the homes of forest dwellers who had cleared a space in the woods, cut back undergrowth, grubbed the soil, planted what crops they could and lived a bare existence. And those lives had ended a day before by the look of the curled smoke.

A dead dog lay in the middle of the clearing. What must have been a pen holding a few pigs was smashed, the animals taken. The entrance to the hamlet was on the far side of the clearing, one way in and out, and even from where they watched, Gifford and the others could see the hoofmarks where a band of horsemen had entered and left. They were long gone.

Henry and the others followed Gifford into the clearing. Men lay sprawled, killed as they tried to defend their homes and families. An axe, a scythe, a billhook, a length of timber. None of them any use against brutal and efficient swordsmen. Charred bodies lay in the first hut. Flesh blackened, limbs curled from the heat. Children slumped dead in the clearing, seven at first glance, each telling their own tale of terror having failed to reach home and the protection of a parent. The women lay in the narrow spaces between each neighbour's house, dwellings huddled for warmth against winter storms, close enough to be almost touching. They were mostly on their backs, clothing pulled up over their heads, their private parts exposed, legs splayed. Knife thrusts into their hearts and throats.

Henry dismounted, sheathed his sword and went to the first woman. He tugged down her clothing to cover her, lurched back at the accusing eyes and gaping mouth and the slit across her throat. The horror reached down into that place below his heart, the void which holds all the sickening and frightening memories that loom large when triggered. A haunting recollection of being nine years old on a river barge heading for safety in Avignon with his mother and young sister under John Jacob's protection. Of the silent struggle as his mother was raped by one of the soldiers accompanying them. Of trying to save her – and failing. It was John Jacob who had cut the rapist's throat and heaved his body overboard.

He looked back at the men, who had dismounted. They went among the bodies, checking whether, against all odds, there might be a survivor. There was not. Brun and Walter Mallin followed Henry's example. Terrel heaved a dead dog aside. Stepping over a fallen villager he whooped with joy as he cornered a panicked chicken. He swooped, quickly wrung its neck and brandished his trophy.

'We eat tonight, lads.'

'Merciful Christ, you are a savage,' said Henry.

Terrel shrugged and grinned. 'You'll not be wanting any when I roast it then? You can let your belly stick to your ribs like these peasant bastards here. Death was a release for them. I'll wager they lived off netted birds and a meagre crop. They'd have kept a pig for salting and traded the rest. They're peasants. It's what they expect – to die like sheep.'

Gifford stepped over one of the bodies. 'A man must eat when the chance is given him,' he told Henry.

Brun dragged two of the slain villagers into the clearing. 'Master Henry, do you wish us to bury the dead?'

Gifford placed a hand on Henry's arm before he answered. 'We would waste our strength by staying here and burying them. Wolves and wild boar will come from the forest soon enough. They'll eat what's left of them.' He shrugged. 'We all live off the dead.'

Henry shook his head. 'Not the children, Hugh. We bury them. Cover their graves with rocks.'

Brun nodded to Bezián, who scoured the clearing for any surviving tools. He found a broad-bladed hoe and began scraping and digging. Walter Mallin used a plank of wood to scoop the dirt to one side as Gifford and Henry went among the hamlet and gathered the dead children.

'Eckehart,' said Henry. 'One grave for them all. That will suffice.'

The four men looked to where Terrel squatted on a chopping log plucking the chicken.

They had camped further back in the forest away from the devastation. Mallin had found some stored turnips, Bezián a blackened cooking pot that had the scraps of food remaining in the bottom. Gifford had scoured the burnt-out ruins and discovered a dried goat's cheese. Brun had added chives and wild garlic to the mix; that and the cooked chicken made a nourishing meal which raised the spirits.

Gifford had insisted that a watch system be put in place. They had taken a risk cooking the meal, no matter how long it had been since the village had been attacked. By morning no threat was forthcoming and Gifford led them beyond the village and across an open meadow, avoiding the well-travelled road. Once they reached the forest he called a halt.

'We are on dangerous ground now,' he said. 'Those tracks beyond the village go both north and south. I don't know how many men we risk facing but we need to plan how far and how fast we can ride.'

Bezián pointed across the meadow towards where the ground had been churned the most. 'North will be men returning from war and scavenging, south will be either French reinforcements for the King's brother while he regroups, or men riding for a French lord trying to protect the villagers.'

'Why would the French send men to the Duke? The war is won,' said Henry.

'The marshal did not say Trastámara was captured or killed. This year, or next, if he's alive, then the French will support him again.'

Terrel scrubbed a hand over his beard. 'We're going south so we could ride into these men head on. Or if we come across those who fought with the Prince, they've no reason to cause us harm. And Master Henry's name alone would give us protection. But did you look at the tracks that went into that village back there? They came from the north. So, just who is killing French villagers? It won't be their own kind.'

'Brigands,' said Brun.

'You're not as stupid as you look,' said Terrel. 'There are skinners out here who side with no one, that's as plain as the scabs on Mallin's arse. We need to go across country and avoid roads but I'm the first to admit I have no idea where we are or how we're supposed to get to wherever Sir Thomas is.'

The men looked from one to the other. None of them knew where they were.

'We use open ground and forest tracks, then,' said Gifford. He glanced at the sky, the sun's position obvious despite the cloud cover. 'We keep our mouths shut and our ears and eyes open. We're downwind so if luck's on our side then we'll have some warning.'

'Not for whoever's riding behind Mallin,' said Terrel. 'His silent farts are enough to make the devil choke.'

For the next two days, Gifford led the men at a steady pace south-east. Merging in and out of forests and waiting patiently as each man scanned the open ground that lay before them before riding hard across it to the shelter of distant trees. Their confidence was bolstered by the lack of any sign of men travelling north. If men-at-arms had left the Prince's army in Spain and gathered in force to strike into Burgundy, they had already passed or taken a different route.

'No good heading for those cliffs,' said Gifford. 'If there's a settlement anywhere it'll be in the valley or beyond the forests.'

The landscape ahead was no longer softened by rolling plains interrupted by low forested hills; the horizon became more rugged, with distant limestone cliffs and tall pine forests now mingled with denser oak. There was no obvious route open to them. What tracks they had crossed on their journey since leaving the destroyed village had shown no sign of horsemen. Now that they had emerged from the forest they saw it fringed the open ground, running for miles in a long sweeping curve.

'We cannot risk travelling this far south across ground like that,' said Brun. 'If the French have patrols we'll be as plain as—'

'The scabs on Mallin's arse,' said Bezián, which at least made everyone except Walter Mallin laugh. Even Henry grinned at the crude reference.

The older man nodded and wiped a sleeve across his dripping nose. 'Aye, make fun of an old soldier. If I've scabs on my backside it's because I've spent a lifetime in the damned saddle.' He shrugged and turned his horse. 'Take my advice. We go the long way round, stay close to the treeline.'

The others nudged their horses to follow him.

'It's better to make less haste than take more risks,' said Bezián.

No sooner had Bezián muttered agreement than Mallin reined in and pointed. By turning their mounts they now faced low distant hills swathed in undergrowth on the lower slopes with more dense foliage as the trees clustered into yet another woodland. A breeze rustled across the open ground, dulled by the rising ground and undergrowth. The breeze veered and from within the forest a swirl of smoke plumed through the top branches.

'Skinners,' said Terrel.

The smoke was a long way off but a hawk's piercing cry carried.

Brun and the others searched the sky. There was no sight of any raptor.

Once again the high-pitched cry pierced the air.

'Dammit, that's no bird of prey,' said Gifford.

CHAPTER FIFTY-SEVEN

Terrel kicked his recalcitrant horse from where he was wedged between the German and Bezián. There was little room for manoeuvre.

'Move, you damned fool. Get out of the way!'

Brun snatched at Terrel's reins and held back his horse. Terrel's knife slashed the air, but Bezián gripped his arm from the other side and as Terrel turned to curse harder and louder Brun's fist struck him in the chest. Terrel fell hard. He lay winded. The others danced their skittish mounts around him, calming them.

'Making a run for it would do you no good, you stupid bastard,' said Gifford. 'Strike out across that open ground and you'll be seen. Whoever's causing that hurt could see you and have men on you before you reached the other side.'

'If we approach from here we can at least get close enough to see if we can do anything,' said Henry.

The others looked as aghast as Terrel, who, wincing, was trying to get to his feet. He staggered upright. 'Sweet Jesus, you have a death wish. I swear it. You would ride to where a place is being burned, and a man tortured, knowing what we know, having seen what we have seen?'

Henry's bravado was dented by everyone staring at him, but he insisted, 'I would. Yes. This time, we might save innocents.'

The men made no reply, but their sullen silence was enough to tell him they had no desire to ride into trouble.

Terrel, a hand on his lower back, bent to pick up his fallen knife. He held it, looked apologetically at Brun and shrugged. 'Instinct. No harm done, eh?'

Brun tossed him his reins.

Henry urged them to follow him. 'I believe we are close to where my father will be. If you seek to be accepted by him then what we do on our journey will count in your favour.'

They didn't look convinced.

'So be it,' said Henry, and turned his horse towards the distant plume of smoke.

Hugh Gifford followed without question.

By the time Henry and Gifford had travelled half a mile the others were trailing behind them. Gifford raised an arm to halt them going any further. Tortured cries suddenly pierced the woodland. They were close. No more than three hundred yards. The men tensed.

'We go on foot from here. If there are too many of them for us to kill, then we make our way back.' He looked at each man. They nodded.

An animal track meandered conveniently through the trees, allowing them to get closer without forcing their way through the undergrowth. Gifford led the way. The track eventually curved away from where the treeline thinned out. Any animal hunting at night would wish to avoid contact with a settlement. It meant they had to ease carefully through the trees. Outcrops of boulders blocked their way ahead. Gifford and the men hunched behind them. They were now so close they could see flames leaping into the sky. Henry tried to edge around, but Gifford grabbed his shoulder and shook his head. He nodded for Henry to follow him to where some tumbledown boulders meant the men could remain hidden but have a clearer view of what was happening.

This settlement was more established than the previous burnt-out village. Here, the houses, twenty or more at first glance, were built of stone with sod roofs. The flames were coming from a stacked bonfire: long, firm branches laid into a conical shape. Already fifteen feet high, more and more saplings and branches were being added by five men. It must have been burning for hours because the heat from the fire's core reached Henry and the others who hunched out of sight fifty yards away. One of the five threw a log into the heart of the blaze. Henry recoiled and gripped Gifford's shoulder. As the log struck some uprights collapsed into the heat. A man, or what remained of him, had been tied to the poles. He was dead now but it was likely it had been his cry they had heard.

From where they hid, the size of the fire blocked much of their view. Mallin crawled closer to Henry and Gifford, tapped them on the shoulder and pointed beyond the fire and the few houses visible to a gap in the trees on the far side. There were saddled horses tethered there. Five were visible.

'Them beasts are too good for the likes of skinners,' said Mallin. 'There must be French men-at-arms around somewhere. Perhaps that poor bastard in the fire was one of them.'

Gifford nodded. 'We need to see more.' He glanced back at the others, who remained hunched behind the rocks.

Henry pointed behind them. The undergrowth was dense enough to get them back into the forest without being seen. Gifford nodded, gestured to the rest and ran, bent double. Once they regained the safety of the trees Gifford led them around the village perimeter. He squatted when they had a clearer view of what was happening. Two routiers dragged a man from a hut in front of where Henry's men crouched. His hands were bound. A rope around his neck. He had been stripped of his gambeson and his linen shirt was bloodstained.

He struggled but they struck him on the side of his head. His legs nearly gave way but the rope yanked hard and he was dragged out of sight around the hut.

The man cried out, begging for his life. His cries were quickly strangled into silence. The two routiers returned and squatted on logs, passing a wineskin between them. A third joined them and emptied a wicker basket of assorted knives, sword belts and purses.

'Dig out the stones from those belts and scabbards. These bastards carried precious little money,' he said, weighing a purse in his hand.

'We've counted five so far, and now with these three are there only eight of them?' whispered Henry.

Gifford shrugged.

Bezián moved closer. 'Where are the villagers? There's no sign of anyone. This is a ghost settlement.'

'Perhaps they got away if French men-at-arms bought them time to escape.'

'That fire has been burning for at least a day. These skinners have made themselves at home,' said Bezián. '

'There must be more of them we can't see,' said Henry.

'What do we do now?' said Brun.

'Backtrack and get out of here,' said Terrel. 'There's no one to save. If these are French men-at-arms being killed, that saves us doing it.'

'Let's move further along,' said Henry. 'We might see how many men are in the clearing.'

Gifford looked behind him at the men. 'Wait. Where's Mallin?'

Walter Mallin had been at the back as they had crept around the perimeter. Now he was nowhere in sight.

'Merciful Christ,' said Terrel. 'The old bastard has made off.'

'He was behind you,' said Bezián. 'How could you not see he was no longer with us?'

'What? I have eyes in the back of my skull?' hissed Terrel.

Henry raised a hand to stop the argument becoming more agitated and voices being raised. Their uncertainty about what to do next was answered by Mallin appearing from ahead of where the men huddled.

His blackened teeth broke into a grin. 'Saw a track. Smelled their horses. There're only ten skinners in the village.' He pointed back to where he'd come from. 'There's an old tree back there. Can't see it from here. They strung up that man they dragged out of the hut. There're two others hanging with him.'

'We saw five French horses tethered on the other side.'

'No, there are six,' said Mallin. 'One's out of sight.'

Then there must be two more men held in that hut,' said Henry.

'Bastards still outnumber us,' said Terrel. He pointed an accusatory finger at Mallin. 'You're a danger to us, you are. That's the second time your big mouth has got us into trouble.'

'I'm telling Master Henry here what I saw is all.'

'Aye and he'll be damned keen to try and kill these skinners.'

Henry shrugged. 'Well, there are far fewer here than what we saw from the tracks back at the village.'

Teller curled a fist in constrained frustration. 'You want to save Frenchmen?'

'I want to save anyone facing a vile death at the hands of these bastards. They'll carry on raiding and killing. There'll be other villages and there's no saying any men-at-arms will be there to help.'

A fourth man joined the routiers who were digging out any precious stones embedded in the looted scabbards and knife handles from the defeated French men-at-arms. One of the men handed him the wineskin.

'I say we wait till night, use the fire glow to move in and kill them while they sleep. They'll have enough wine in their guts by then,' said Gifford.

Terrel shook his head, and lowered his eyes. 'Shit, shit, shit,' he said quietly.

Bezián nodded his agreement. 'We go in from different directions. They'll be sleeping close together.'

'And Master Henry stays out of it,' said Gifford, and before Henry could argue, turned to him. 'You get into that hut and release the other two Frenchmen. We might need their help.'

Brun grabbed Henry's shoulder. 'Look, Master Henry.'

'Bastard,' whispered Mallin.

'This is worse than we thought,' said a hushed Terrel.

Gifford didn't understand.

'That man drinking,' said Henry. 'He was one of la Griffe's men. We went into their camp before we got you out of that dungeon.'

'The Claw is here?' said Gifford. 'Impossible.'

CHAPTER FIFTY-EIGHT

Henry and the others retreated to the safety of the forest. How one of Jean de Soissons's men could be so far south could not be explained. But the fact had to be accepted. What appeared to be obvious was that the Claw was not among these men who had burned a man at the stake and hanged three others. The only way they could determine if la Griffe was anywhere near this area was to keep the man they had identified alive.

Hours after nightfall, guided by the fire's glow, Henry and the others slipped into the shadows. Six of la Griffe's men huddled around a smaller fire where a cooking pot was cradled in the embers. What Gifford and Henry's men did not know was where the other four were sleeping.

Terrel and Bezián approached from one side of the village houses, Brun and Mallin on the other. Like the silent killers they now were, the four men cast long shadows in the night. Hugh Gifford lit a reed torch and, with Henry behind him, crept through the narrow passages between the houses on the far side of the village. The man-at-arms would stand ready while Henry went inside to release the prisoners when they reached the hut where they hoped the Frenchmen were being held. Edging forward, they stood at the entrance.

Terrel and the others had the more dangerous task of ensuring that la Griffe's man was not one of those sleeping. If they hesitated for too long in identifying their intended victims and they awoke, then the alarm would be raised. They closed in on the sleeping men, guttural snores telling them the skinners were heavy with drink. Bezián glanced across to where Gifford stood outside the hut, who handed the torch to Henry and then raised a hand. Let the killing begin.

Bezián and the others used their boots to nudge the men's faces and see them more clearly. Some grunted, two stirred, and then Bezián and the others plunged their swords in. One man, less drunk than the others, curled upwards in agony as Mallin's sword pierced his chest. Eyes wide, mouth gaping, his hands clutched at the blade, inflicting further wounds. There was enough air in his lungs to cry out. Mallin kicked him in the face and heaved back his blade.

'Master Henry!' Gifford hissed. 'Hurry now, if you will.'

Henry swept the spluttering torch across the room. Two men, stripped down to their hose and shirts, barefoot, bloodied and beaten, lay on the ground, hands tied behind their back, ankles bound. One raised his head as best he could, eyes wide with fear at the sight of a stranger bearing a knife.

'Don't cry out. I'm a friend,' Henry urged him.

He knelt and cut through the rope binding the man's wrists, then did the same with his fellow prisoner, who remained unconscious. The Frenchman, stiff from being held and weak from hunger and punishment, tried to undo the ankle ropes.

'Thank you,' he said, his voice croaking from a dry mouth.

Henry saw he could not manage the bonds, leaned across and sawed them through. The Frenchman leaned back against the wall and painfully stretched out his limbs as Henry cut free his companion. He rolled the man onto his back.

'He's wounded,' the Frenchman told him. 'Is he alive?'

Henry put away his knife and felt the man's face. He nodded. 'Can you walk?'

'I don't know. I think my ribs are broken.'

A bellow of rage from outside the hut snatched their attention.

Gifford ran into the clearing as four routiers ran from another house and attacked Bezián and the men. Mallin was the nearest to them when he turned to face their assault. As he twisted, he fell. A blade scythed through the air, barely missing him. Mallin rolled away. The man was off balance. Terrel took two strides and blocked the man's rapid recovery. He parried a sword strike, grabbed the man's belt, pulled him in, kneed him between the legs, headbutted him, and as the stunned routier stumbled over Mallin, Terrel lunged forward and down and drove his sword into the man's throat.

As Terrel fought and killed like a backstreet fighter, the others defended themselves from the routiers' assault. Bezián and Brun were no less hardened men, but three against two would soon prove decisive. Gifford came at them from the side. One turned when he heard Gifford's approach. It was la Griffe's man. Sword in one hand, knife in the other, he strode forward to attack.

'This is him!' Gifford yelled.

La Griffe's man hesitated, not knowing why he was being singled out.

Terrel rejoined the fight, plunging his sword into the back of one attacker fighting Bezián. Mallin clawed himself upright. Gifford blocked a sword strike from la Griffe's man, who then slashed with his knife at the stocky man-at-arms. Gifford backtracked, avoiding the sweeping cut. Bezián and Brun fought the remaining routier viciously, ramming their sword points into him front and back, and when finally he went down, Brun pulled free his blade and broke his neck with a last brutal kick.

La Griffe's man was surrounded. Eyes darting back and forth, memory struck home. 'I know you men!' He stared past Gifford as Henry emerged from the hut helping the Frenchman. 'Blackstone,' he muttered. Incomprehension creased his face.

'Yield,' said Henry.

La Griffe's man, a cornered beast, shuffled in a tight circle. 'I'll kill more than one of you before I go down,' he threatened.

'You'll die slowly,' said Henry. 'We'll hamstring you, then cut you apart piece by piece. Burn what's left of you while your heart still beats. Yield and we'll give you a clean death. I give you my word. Rope or sword. Your choice.'

'Fuck you, boy!' he said, and lunged at Terrel.

Gifford was quicker. He rammed his sword into the back of his leg, then slashed the hamstrings. La Griffe's man fell hard. Helpless now, he dropped his weapons. Agony creased his face.

'Drag him into the light,' Gifford told Mallin and Terrel. 'Brun, Bezián, help Master Henry.'

Henry handed the Frenchman over to the Gascon's strength. 'Brun, there's another man inside.' He stepped to the hut with the torch.

The tall German bent low through the door, checked the man was still alive, and then folded him into his arms.

Back outside, the two rescued Frenchmen were laid by the warmth of the cooking fire. Henry eased wine into the conscious man's lips. He spluttered, nodded his thanks and looked up at Henry. 'You're English.'

Henry nodded. 'I ride with three others and a German and a Gascon.'

The unconscious man responded to the fire's warmth. He groaned.

'Bezián, can we find hot food for these men?'

The Gascon nodded and went in search of what was needed.

'Brun,' said Henry. 'Stay with them while I speak to la Griffe's man.' He pointed at the man regaining consciousness. 'Try to get wine into him.' Henry called to where Mallin stood with Gifford and Terrel guarding the wounded routier. 'Walter, these men will have bedrolls on the saddles. Bring them. They need more warmth than this meagre fire.' He looked down at the Frenchman he had dragged from the hut. 'We'll attend to your companion's wounds. With food and warmth, you'll soon be strong enough to continue your journey.'

'We are your enemy.'

'Today, routiers are our common enemy.'

The Frenchman nodded. 'We saw signs of these bastards when we rode south. This was a friendly village. There was a mendicant monk among them. They offered us food and shelter. We held those men off and gave them all a chance to escape.'

'Then you serve a local lord?' said Henry.

The man hesitated. He shook his head. 'You will not look so kindly on us when I tell you that we were on our way to join the fight in Spain against the English.'

'You were already too late. The English Prince won the war.'

Henry left them in Brun's care and strode across to Gifford and Terrel, who stood over la Griffe's man. The bonfire that had burned so brightly was smaller now but still gave enough light for Henry to study the man more closely.

'How is it you are here?'

'We broke away from la Griffe ten days ago.'

'How many men are with him?'

'Fifty.'

'La Griffe's domain is Brittany. None of you would survive

travelling this far south in such small numbers. There are French lords who would have your heads on poles without even asking your name.'

The wounded man was propped against a rock, one hand gripping his leg. He grinned. 'No French lord would go against their King.'

Terrel stepped on his wounded leg, making him flinch. 'Lying bastard.'

'Enough, Terrel. He'll tell us what he knows.'

'The French King does not consort with the likes of you,' Gifford said.

'He does when we promise to bring him Thomas Blackstone's son alive.'

Henry, Gifford and Terrel could not hide their surprise.

La Griffe's man coughed and spat. He sighed. 'I'd rather choke to death than have my throat cut. I'll not die by a blade if there's drink to be had. I'll need wine and plenty of it if you are to put a rope around my neck.'

'You'll have as much as you want,' said Henry, recovering from the shock of what he had been told. 'But I want to know everything.'

The routier nodded his agreement.

And told Henry the full story.

The wounded killer was given enough wine to dull his fear and then hanged by Brun and Terrel hauling on the rope. It was a slow, choking death that Henry did not watch. His men cut down the Frenchmen's comrades and buried them. Then they strung up the dead routiers with a sign for the monk to read on their return that it had been Englishmen who had killed them.

The seriousness of the French King's ploy to capture him

alive and gain his father's parole not to fight left Henry with a difficult choice. Stay on course to locate his father and risk la Griffe finding him, or abandon his intended course of action. The French King's plan to deliver Henry to Paris using the disgraced mercenary was shrewd. Bezián and the others related to Gifford how they had witnessed the Claw's expertise as a swordsman: Henry would have no choice but to yield. They did not share the French monarch's scheme with the rescued Frenchmen, who would soon go their own way. The less they knew, the better.

Terrel said, 'If we let them ride south to join Trastámara, there'll be a chance, a good one I'll wager, that they'll come across la Griffe and tell him how a young Englishman and a handful of men rescued them. The bastard will backtrack and find us. He knows you're looking for your father. How many young Englishmen are there likely to be around here? Let's kill the Frenchies now and leave the way ahead clear.'

'We don't kill these men,' said Henry. 'The Claw is already south of us. If he is obliged to go to the Count of Foix, then he's already looking for my father. It won't be difficult for him to find where he is. The King's Master of War does not go unnoticed. Someone, somewhere, will have seen his blazon.'

'And we need to find him before la Griffe does,' said Bezián. 'You'll be safe under his protection. No skinner is going to challenge your father.'

'For Christ's sake,' said Gifford. 'What if it's Master Henry the Claw challenges? Then he has to face him. If he refuses, he loses respect and his honour. He'll be branded a coward, and that reputation will taint Sir Thomas. I say we make our way to Bordeaux. Get back into Aquitaine. Avoid la Griffe.' He put a hand on Henry's shoulder. 'Avoid the risk of a challenge, Master Henry; that way you save your father because once the French have you, he will give his parole not to fight.'

Henry's sullen expression and silence prompted Walter Mallin to try and offer him some comfort. 'When we know we cannot defeat an enemy, there is no shame in avoiding the fight. I've seen good men die needlessly in battle because of such foolishness. And a man's pride can heal, Master Henry. Grow old and leave regret at the kitchen door.'

Gifford agreed. 'We can turn west and return to Aquitaine. Sooner or later your father will go back to Bordeaux.'

The men nodded and murmured their agreement. 'There are French towns who swore loyalty to our King,' said Gifford.

'Providing they don't see us as skinners,' said Brun.

'Which is what we were,' said Bezián. He looked at the others. 'It's true, we have lived as badly as any other.'

'But no longer,' said Henry.

'Easy for you to say, Master Henry,' Terrel said. 'But now we are not seeking to join your father, we go back to the old problem of needing food and money.'

'Can we sell our swords to a town?' asked Henry. 'Offer them defence against brigands?'

'If they don't string us up first,' said Mallin. 'Let's not forget there are towns who sell skinners to local lords. They might only pretend to hire us to get us inside their gates – then we are dead men. Who can we trust?'

Henry's distress was plain to see. 'To have come all this way. To have done what we have and to turn away now when we must be so close to finding my father.' He shook his head. 'I say we wait another two days to give the Frenchmen a chance to recover from their injuries. Then we carry on as planned. And if I have to fight la Griffe, then I will. My father would not have me turn my back. I know it.'

CHAPTER FIFTY-NINE

The men roped the dead Frenchmen's horses so that they could be led once they left the village. They were good mounts and worth more than the rounceys that the Claw's men had been riding. Those could run loose; their herd instinct would make them follow the men. Despite Henry's belief that they were far enough south to find his father, there was always the chance that they would need to seek safety if they came across marauding brigands, and horses could be bartered in any town or village for sanctuary and supplies.

For the next two days the skies were clear. The rolling hills and forests cushioned broad open meadows. Distant mountain peaks, still covered in snow, drew the eye as Henry and Gifford led the men across the open plain. Spring flowers had already appeared in the sweet grass and the horses grazed when the men made camp. If time had permitted them to stay longer, then the horses would have soon regained weight lost over winter.

'Wait,' said Gifford, pulling up his horse.

The men rode up alongside the man-at-arms, who stood in his stirrups, a hand shielding his eyes from the bright sky, the sun still low enough in the sky to cause a man to squint into its glare.

'You see something?' said Terrel.

'I'm not sure. Henry, do you see any movement ahead? Far back. Beyond the low bushes and tall grass.'

All the men followed Gifford's example and stared into the distance.

'There's a long shadow across the end of these fields,' said Bezián. 'Trees lie beyond. Could be a trick of the light.' He lowered his gaze and turned to the others. 'I think it's the treeline we're seeing.'

'Aye, most likely,' said Terrel.

'Then let's get across and into that forest. Feels too exposed out here.'

They spurred their horses on, but within 150 yards pulled up short again.

'Merciful Christ help us,' said Walter Mallin, crossing himself.

What Henry and the others had thought to be the wavering shadows of a forest now became a phalanx of horsemen several hundred yards in front of them, and what must have been a spearhead formation now became the wings of a raptor. The approaching horsemen's flanks spread out into a half-moon designed to envelop and kill. There was no escape.

A litany of curses spewed from Terrel's lips.

Henry and his men drew their swords. There could be no surrender. The horsemen showed no sign of wanting to talk.

'The Claw?' said Gifford.

'Can't see him clearly,' said Henry.

'Skinners, anyway. They fly no lord's banner,' said Brun.

'Form a line,' said Bezián. 'We must at least stand together. It'll be like a boar hunt if they split us up. We'll be cut down one by one.'

The men formed up on either side of Henry and Gifford. The two Frenchmen joined them. Henry nodded his thanks.

'Routiers are our common enemy,' said the man Henry had saved, repeating his words.

The ground rumbled from the pounding hoofbeats.

Henry's mouth dried. He had never experienced a frontal charge. He gripped his sword hilt and took another turn around the reins to calm his trembling hands. The death trap was closing in. Then, for some reason, the assault slowed and finally stopped a hundred yards from where the line waited, each rider fighting to control his nervous horse. Henry blinked and stared hard. The man who led the charge rode a massive horse with an oversized head. Its dappled hide was covered in burnt cinders from when it was conceived in hell. So the legend went.

'Father?' he called.

The men snapped their heads towards him.

'That's Sir Thomas?' said Gifford.

Henry's face broke into a smile. 'No one else rides that horse,' he said, sheathing his sword and spurring his mount forward.

Blackstone waited as his son's horse trotted across the ground between them.

'God's tears, Thomas, he's as tall and broad as you,' said Killbere.

'And more damned wilful,' said Blackstone.

'And as resourceful, Sir Thomas: give the lad credit. He absconds from Oxford and here he is,' said John Jacob.'

'I'll box his ears for disobeying me.' Blackstone's tone was as stern as his countenance but the sight of his son riding towards him, the low sun catching his features, made his heart beat faster.

Killbere laughed. 'You might have a fight on your hands, Thomas.' He snorted with pleasure at the thought of the coming reunion. 'I'll be damned. Wait until Will and Jack see him again.'

'Master Henry!' Meulon cried from the flank as Henry got closer. The big man's joy was plain to hear. Henry raised a hand in greeting, his pleasure at seeing old friends unmistakable. 'Meulon!'

Henry drew his horse up far enough away from the bastard horse for it not to lunge and snap with its yellow teeth. 'Father, I cannot believe I have found you.'

'Nor I,' said Blackstone without smiling. He glanced at Killbere, whose look suggested Blackstone had to let his own happiness overcome the annoyance that his son had abandoned his studies. 'But I'm pleased you are safe.'

'Thank you, Father,' said Henry, realizing that this was not the place for either of them to express their feelings. Not in front of the men. But Henry couldn't stop smiling. 'Sir Gilbert, you are well?'

'I am invigorated by seeing you, lad. You caused us all great concern by absconding from Oxford.'

'I had a good reason and there's much to tell. John Jacob, still at my father's side, I see.'

'Where else?' said Blackstone's squire.

Henry shook his head in disbelief at seeing the men who had been part of the Blackstone's family for so many years. 'I am so happy to see you all. Where are Will and Jack and the others?'

'A day's ride back. We hold a small domain,' said Killbere.

Killbere and John Jacob beamed their pleasure at seeing him, but his father remained solemn, and Henry began to feel nervous. His awkwardness was broken when he saw a hundred peasants emerging from the trees in the background with tethered goats, a cart of caged pigs and a cow on the end of a rope; the men and women carried bundles on their backs and children in their arms.

'Are you escorting these villagers?'

'Henry, who are these men with you?' said Blackstone, ignoring his son's question.

'Oh, they are good men who have been at my side since Brittany.'

'Brittany?' said Killbere.

'I've a story to tell, Sir Gilbert,' Henry answered, but his enthusiasm was tinged with uncertainty at his father's glare. 'The man-at-arms there'—he turned, pointing—'is Hugh Gifford. He is Warwick's man and my guardian.'

'These others look to be skinners,' said Blackstone.

'No, Father, they have been true to me and helped saved my life. Two Englishmen, a Gascon and a German. Good men. Rough, yes, but with me these past weeks.'

'Then we'll hear of your adventures when we camp tonight. Until then, we return these villagers to their homes.'

'But we left an abandoned village yesterday, Father. We killed the routiers who had ravaged it. I'd not be surprised if it were the same place. It's where we rescued these two Frenchmen who lost comrades, buying time for the villagers to escape the skinners. They are riding south to join Trastámara.' He hesitated. 'I gave them my word they would have safe passage as long as they rode with us.'

'You did, did you?' said Blackstone. 'So, now you have hardened men and our enemy at your side.'

'They are honourable men.'

'What lord do they serve?'

'I don't know, Father. The one at the end is Louis de Roche. The man next to him is Gautier de Fleur.'

The moment Henry mentioned the name, Killbere and Blackstone's chins tilted up in recognition. The young knight facing them was the man long awaited by Sancha Ferrandes. Who stood between Blackstone and her.

Killbere gritted his teeth and turned aside to Blackstone. 'Maybe we should kill him now.'

CHAPTER SIXTY

Before Blackstone denied Killbere his wish, some villagers recognized the two Frenchmen and called out a greeting. They turned and passed the word, a murmur of gratitude rippling through their followers.

'He's a popular man,' said Blackstone.

'He and his men placed themselves between the villagers and the skinners,' said Henry.

The village elders and the mendicant monk pressed through Blackstone's men and knelt before the two survivors. Gautier de Fleur urged them to stand and return to their friends. He told them it was Henry Blackstone and his men who had killed the routiers, and that they would see the evidence once they returned home.

Killbere sighed quietly and muttered softly enough so that Henry did not hear him: 'We can't kill the bastard now.'

Meulon ordered the villagers back to their places in the caravan that trailed Blackstone's men. Blackstone turned to his son.

'Henry, you and I will speak tonight. I am thankful you are alive. I did not think I would see you again. However, today we have a duty to return these people to their village. Join your men and ride on our flank.'

'Yes, Father.'

Henry tugged the reins and rode back to Gifford as the bastard horse walked on without needing a command.

'Life has just become more complicated,' said Killbere.

'If we send the Frenchman on his way, we cannot follow him to Trastámara,' said John Jacob bringing his horse alongside Blackstone.

'You think he'll be heading for Trastámara once he sees the Ferrandes woman?' said Killbere.

'He may not decide to take her with him,' said Blackstone's squire.

'And the Pope neither drinks nor fornicates,' said Killbere.

'Gilbert, put him and his companion under parole,' said Blackstone. 'They have no reason to stay. They'll be gone in the night. I'll decide what to do with him when we get back.'

Killbere gathered his reins. 'Him and the woman, Thomas?'

As he watched Killbere ride towards the two Frenchmen, Blackstone knew the veteran knight's question would soon need an answer.

When Blackstone drew a halt, it was already dusk. He had pushed the villagers hard, demanding they keep up a relentless pace. He had left his archers and William Ashford with the Gascon captain Aicart to defend Sancha's domain. If marauding routiers came across the low-walled château, it would be Longdon and Halfpenny's archers backed up by the two captains' men who would have to hold it. And now the fickle bitch Fate had placed Gautier de Fleur in their midst, there was that additional problem to consider.

Henry and Meulon approached as John Jacob prepared the fire and food for Blackstone and Killbere.

'Father, you sent for me.'

'Is there anything else, Sir Thomas?' said Meulon.

Blackstone shook his head. 'See to the men.'

Meulon nodded, putting a hand on Henry's shoulder and giving him a friendly smile as he left.

'Do you remember the last time we spoke before you rode to Avignon?' said Blackstone.

Henry's puzzled expression told the gathered men he did not. 'It was a long time ago, Father.'

'It was. But you are a scholar. Your memory should retain the instructions I gave you. When we are alone, you may address me as your father, but when we speak in front of the men there must be no sense of privilege or favour and so you will address me correctly.'

Henry's face flushed. He nodded, gulping his embarrassment. 'My lord, I apologize.'

'Good. Then sit and tell us everything that has happened since you absconded from your studies at Oxford.'

Henry squatted by the fire, took his mind back to the time in the Bear Inn when he had heard the man Flemyng brag about his fictitious time serving with Blackstone's men and the discovery that his father had been imprisoned. He told a story unembellished by all the emotions that drove him on, simply narrating the facts, day by day, almost, of the journey. By the time he had finished, John Jacob's food was ready. What Henry had omitted from his tale was being pursued by Jean de Soissons, la Griffe.

'Damned if that is not an adventure that should be written,' said Killbere. 'Well told and to the point. Any herald of worth would have stirred our emotions with tales of clashing swords and charging horses.' He reached over and patted Henry's knee. 'Related like a true lawyer,' he said, his tone leaving Henry uncertain whether it was meant as a compliment or a pointed comment about where his skills truly lay.

'I admire your determination,' said Blackstone. 'I commend you, Henry. You saw the challenge through.'

Henry could not stop his smile of happiness.

'But it was misguided,' Blackstone went on. 'If I was

imprisoned, what did you hope to achieve? Could you have released me? Would you have begged the Prince to intervene? Demeaned our name? Your mother gave you the joy of books. Of reading and education. Had you perished on your journey, you would have squandered her inheritance.'

'I have your inheritance as well!' Henry snapped. 'I would have found Sir Gilbert and John, knowing they would be close at hand and that I could have joined them. To take my place at your side. I am not a good scholar. Sitting behind a desk and sharpening quills and smudging my fingers with ink does not suit me. I practise every day with a skilled swordsman. Hugh Gifford was more than a guardian; he taught me far more than I ever learned before.' He took a breath and calmed his frustration. 'I can fight. I too have my honour.'

The three men had listened patiently. Blackstone offered no further rebuke.

'Then we will explore more of what your future might hold over the coming days,' Blackstone said, his tone conciliatory. 'Do not despair at being questioned so directly, Henry. Men must stand up for what they believe. And you have done so. That is more than many could do.'

Blackstone's words were a soothing balm to Henry's injured pride. 'Then, am I to stay with the men who rode with me?'

'You chose them,' said Blackstone.

'They chose me.'

'Then there must be something in you they trust and a leader of men should attend to them first before he sees to his own needs.'

'We have little food with us. The village was scraped clean by the skinners.'

'All right, speak to Meulon.'

Henry hesitated. There was obviously more he wanted to say, but the three men were ignoring him. John Jacob attended the fire, Killbere was tugging off his boots, then his father gave a questioning look, raising his attention from where he sharpened his archer's knife.

Henry nodded and turned away.

Killbere stretched his bare feet towards the fire. 'Bit harsh, Thomas, even though you smoothed his ruffled feathers at the end. He was a fifteen-year-old boy when he took his wounds at Avignon and was given sanctuary in England. Now look at him. He's damned near your size. He carries himself well. He has the making of a good captain. Shall we not bring him into the fold at last?'

'We've had this conversation before.'

'And every time the subject was raised, we acknowledged he was still too young. Now he is not.'

Blackstone pushed his knife back into its scabbard. 'John? What do you think? You were his guardian.'

'Only when he was still a child, Sir Thomas.'

'But your opinion now?'

John Jacob ladled out the pottage; he handed the first clay bowl to Blackstone, and the next to Killbere, who spooned the food into his mouth, gulped and huffed at its heat, fanned his tongue but persevered with eating.

'He's strong and carries himself well, like Sir Gilbert says. He has a sharp mind and a generous heart. He looks for respect. He wishes to prove himself. What youth doesn't? He undertook a dangerous quest with great courage. There is much to commend in his actions. Who among us has not committed to a course of action without knowing what the outcome would be?' John Jacob paused.

'But?' said Blackstone.

'I believe your instincts are correct. His future lies not with the likes of us. We are blunt instruments to serve those who rule. When laws in the future are written, there will be more negotiation and less killing. Such is my hope, at least. And Henry has seen and experienced death. He lost his beloved mother and sister and he has killed in defence of others and himself.' John Jacob sighed. 'In truth, I would hate to see the lad harmed,' he said. 'I hope you will convince him to return to his studies.'

Blackstone nodded his thanks for his trusted squire's counsel. 'Gilbert?'

Killbere shrugged. Ran a finger around the empty bowl and sucked the last of the juice from it. 'John's a better philosopher than cook, but I will indulge in another bowl.' He stretched forward to the pot's ladle. 'Do as you said. Give it a few more days. See what we find out. The men who ride with him are rougher than a bear's tongue.' He slopped food into the bowl. 'When the opportunity arises, the man we must speak to is Hugh Gifford.'

Firelight speckled the meadow. The villagers, safe in the knowledge that Blackstone was guiding them home, gathered in small groups around the fires. They had been given permission by Blackstone to light them against the night's chill. If there were any marauding routiers moving north, they would steer clear of a meadow pinpricked with a hundred and more campfires. Henry had stayed with Gifford and the others after arranging food from Meulon. The big man was generous with his supplies, telling him to eat as well as he could because once they returned to the town Will Longdon guarded, their stomachs would be punished by the archer's cooking.

Blackstone and John Jacob edged their way through the firelight, calling Meulon to join them to check the pickets on the camp's perimeter. Henry watched them merge into the shadows and turned back to where Killbere sat massaging his bare feet.

'I need new boots, Henry, but I have yet to kill a man whose size is the same as mine.'

'Can I talk to you, Sir Gilbert?' said Henry, keeping a wary eye out for his father's return.

'You've eaten? You and your men?'

Henry nodded.

'You have always been able to talk to me, and John Jacob, and Will and Jack and Meulon. There's not a man among us who would not listen to you.'

Henry's discomfort was obvious.

'That he does not favour you does not mean he has no love for you,' Killbere said, knowing full well Henry wanted to talk about his father.

'And yet he never shows it. I have seen him weep at the loss of his men. Where is that love for me?'

Killbere scratched and picked something from between his toes. 'I'll tell you something about what war demands of a man's heart. It does not allow a man who commands others to show favour, despite their love. Courage comes in many forms. The Prince of Wales stood in the vanguard at Crécy and when it looked as though he was to be overwhelmed, his father, the King, showed him no favour either. And he was a lad the same age as was Thomas. I took your father to war when he was a boy of sixteen. He and his brother were orphans, and it was Thomas who cared for his deaf-mute brother and who saved them both from the rope with his wit. His brother could not keep his cock under control, and that was a problem. But those two were the best archers I had ever seen and even Will Longdon, who by then could not be bettered, knew your father was a master bowman.'

'He never speaks of his brother. I know nothing about his young life.'

'Your father would throw himself unarmed at a pack of wolves if a loved one was in danger. At Crécy, his brother went down under a swarm of men. Thomas ran from the ranks to save him. He failed, but his attempt put him between the Prince and a Bohemian knight. A damned fine knight at that. You've seen the mark of the running wolf on your father's blade, hardened steel from the makers in Passau: they were master sword makers who learned their skills from the Saracens. Well, when Thomas killed the man wielding it he did so with the last ounce of strength he had. And he saved the Prince's life. It took a long time for your father to recover from his wounds. He was within a breath of dying. As he lay close to death at Castle Harcourt, a young woman nursed him. And she became your mother. Thomas Blackstone has suffered great loss in his life and he holds you so close to his heart that he fears for you.' Killbere rubbed the last of the dirt from between his toes. 'Where your father excels at war, you should excel at your studies. It is the lawmakers who will decide men's futures.' He tugged his boots back on. 'No one questions your courage, Henry, and wherever you go, the name Blackstone will be your shield. Bear it with honour.'

Henry bowed his head and when he lifted it to face Killbere, his anguish was plain to see. 'Better you hear this from me than from one of the others,' he said. 'There's something I have not yet told you.'

CHAPTER SIXTY-ONE

Killbere waited until the next day before relating everything to Blackstone. A night's sleep might ease Blackstone's anger.

'Merciful God,' Blackstone sighed when he heard the full tale. 'Not only does the disobedient son of a tender-hearted mother bring an unwanted Frenchman into our midst to cause more anguish than I'd wish, but he kills a master swordsman's father and is now being hunted. A hunt proposed to the French King by a killer who wishes to reclaim his honour and his lands by exacting revenge on my son. And it is sanctioned by the King to stop me from raising my sword and my men against him. My son brings this trouble to us, Gilbert. *He* does this to us.'

'Thomas, take a breath,' said Killbere. 'We know his actions have consequences. We will deal with this matter if the time comes.'

'Gilbert, a man who has so much to gain does not rest until he has achieved what he set out to do. The hunt will never end. You are too calm about this. Henry must be sent back home.'

'And where is home? For any of us? It is where we are with whom we ride. That is home, Thomas. Henry has the English King's Master of War as his father. He is an Englishman by birthright. But he's French born, with a French mother. So where is *his* home? France or England? He spent most of his life here. As you have spent half of yours.'

'Italy. I'll send him to Father Torellini in Florence. He banks our money. There is enough to give Henry a good life and he can continue his studies.'

Killbere glanced over his shoulder to where John Jacob rode half a length back. It was a look and a gesture that asked what he should say next.

John Jacob shrugged.

Killbere nodded. 'Well, I've always liked Italy. There is warmth to be found there with their climate and women if the season is right. Why don't we all go to Italy? We can find a cause to serve there. Torellini would welcome us. Thomas, I think that's a good idea.'

'Dammit, Gilbert, are you forgetting who it is we serve and at whose pleasure we do so? We are sworn men. I'll not have my son's behaviour come between us and our duty. We are commissioned to find Trastámara.'

The bastard horse needed little encouragement to break away from Killbere and John Jacob.

'Best let him solve this problem on his own, John,' Killbere said as the squire went to ride after him.

Blackstone rode over to Henry and his men on the flank. His demeanour left Henry in no doubt that his father had been told of the man who hunted him and the bounty placed on him by the French King. Blackstone reined in the bastard horse and glared angrily. Henry's men shifted nervously in their saddles.

'Master Gifford!' Blackstone called.

'Sir Thomas?'

'With me.'

Without another word, Blackstone turned and rode away from the line of men. Gifford spurred his horse to follow.

'We are in the shit pit, I know it,' said Terrel.

'Sir Thomas is going to question all of us. He has to, to make sure everything that has been said is true,' said Walter Mallin.

'And the truth is what?' Terrel grimaced. 'That we are skinners who met young Master Henry when we were all captured? Is that what you told him?' he demanded, turning to Henry.

'I made no mention of what you were or what you might have done before we were thrown together in that dungeon,' Henry said. 'I told my father everything from that time onward. Nothing more.'

'I knew this was a mistake,' said Terrel. 'I knew it. Felt it in my piss. We should have gone off on our own. We have walked into a damned man trap being here with Blackstone's son.'

Bezián spat in disgust. 'You turn tail quicker than a slithering viper. You were the one who favoured Master Henry.'

'Aye, and it was his quick thinking that saved us from being gutted and hung on a hook,' said Brun. 'You would do well to remember that you owe loyalty to the man who saved your life.'

'And you think Blackstone is going to welcome us now? When he knows his boy is being hunted by la Griffe? That's what this is about – why else would he be so angry? Isn't that so, Master Henry? Does he know? Have you told him?'

Henry edged his horse around so he could face Terrel. 'You will show respect. He is Sir Thomas to the likes of us. Yes, he knows about la Griffe. He'll question Gifford as to what has happened and where the information came from. And if he questions any of you, tell him the truth. Tell him all he needs to know. There's no need to talk of your journey before we came together. If he presses you then each man can tell his own story that suits him.'

Gautier de Fleur and his companion remained silent at the men's heated voices. Finally, his companion, Louis de Roche, still cradling his injured arm, called out to Henry.

'Master Henry, Gautier and I didn't know that la Griffe was pursuing you.'

'And what would you have done? Turned back to Paris?' sneered Terrel.

'No, we would have advised Master Henry to let us lead him to safety. We would have found sanctuary for him, for you all. If la Griffe believes you will be with Sir Thomas, then you will soon be found. It is not too late, Master Henry, for us to repay our debt to you.'

'We will be back at the village before the end of the day,' said Gautier de Fleur. 'Then we can guide you through the forests – there are French lords who will offer shelter. Men we trust. I give you my word.'

'Until they or you sell us to your King,' said Terrel.

De Fleur leaned on his pommel and addressed Terrel. 'We know how to repay the debt of life. A man's word must not be questioned. If it is, then it must be met with a challenge.'

'You bastards. We saved your necks and now you challenge me?'

'We are on parole. We gave our word not to fight. When I am free from my promise, then, yes, if you question the pledge I give, there must be a challenge.'

Brun, whose horse was next to Terrel's, snatched and held Terrel's wrist as he went for his sword hilt. The Frenchmen did not see the sudden threat averted, but Henry did.

'There will be no contest between us,' said Henry. 'What must be faced will be met by me alone.'

He nudged his horse forward to rejoin his father's men, shepherding the villagers who would be home before nightfall. Then he would return with his father and await the arrival of the Claw. For if there was one thing as certain as his father's anger, it was that la Griffe would find him.

Hugh Gifford slowed and then pulled up his mount when Blackstone halted the bastard horse. Gifford knew they were far enough ahead of the main body of men and the villagers, and Henry's position on the flank, for whatever was asked and answered not to be heard by anyone else.

'Name the men with my son. And what you know about them.'

Gifford told him what little he knew of the men – which was only their names. They had never shared their stories, even when they shared a dungeon or were travelling south together.

'You are Warwick's man?' said Blackstone.

'I am, Sir Thomas.'

'How long in service watching over my son?'

'Two years and a few months now.'

'The previous man?'

'A man called Tate. He fell ill and died and I was his replacement.'

'Not a welcome task for a man-at-arms.'

'Thomas Beauchamp, Earl of Warwick, is my lord. He in turn serves the King and when the King decrees your son is to be protected, there are great forces of state to be obeyed. I was honoured, Sir Thomas.

'How was he? My son. At Oxford, as a student. Good? Or was he indifferent?'

'All I heard about your son was praise for his ability,' Gifford said, but failed to sound as positive as he had wished. And he saw that Thomas Blackstone watched and listened to answers with a keen eye and ear. Time to speak plainly.

'Master Henry is well educated. The learning comes easily to him. As if it takes no effort.'

'Then he makes only the least effort necessary.'

'That is one way of seeing it, Sir Thomas. The other is to be impressed at his ability. He absorbs knowledge like a barber surgeon's sponge absorbs blood – it's something to behold. I cannot tell you how clever your son is, but he has a quick mind and tongue and he can think himself and others out of a dangerous situation. He saved my life.'

'By killing the father of the man hunting him.'

'An agreement was struck with the captain of Josselin to deliver la Griffe. I was held as ransom should he not return or fail. It was only after he lured the skinners behind the castle wall that he knew La Griffe had laid his own trap and sent his father in first.'

'And the death of this man?'

'His name was Pellan and I did not witness Master Henry killing him.'

'And the Claw? You saw him fight?'

'No. I was imprisoned.'

'So we do not know how my son would fare against a man burning with vengeance?'

'I trained with him whenever time permitted.'

'When he was not studying?'

Gifford knew he was being drawn into a bear trap of truth. He had no desire to expose more of Henry's way of life as he drank, fought and whored his way around Oxford. Gifford's breath faltered for such a brief moment that he did not think Blackstone had noticed.

Blackstone saw the hesitation. 'A gifted scholar who does not need to expend more than the bare minimum of effort on his studies had time for the taverns then?'

Gifford's silence was as much confirmation as Blackstone

needed. 'A story unfolds, Master Gifford. A boy who has a quick tongue and a sharp mind that instils confidence. He spends more time in taverns and bedding whores than sharpening a quill, and his guardian tries to keep up his fighting skills.'

'He has courage and honour and will fight for the right cause. The lad has that.'

'Confidence and courage. As good a combination as shield and sword.' Blackstone thought on it for a moment. 'So he believes he can talk his way out of trouble, and has the courage to do what he believes to be right. But all of this, Master Gifford, tells me that when he faces someone like this la Griffe, then confidence will not equate to ability; and the moment that knowledge is apparent in a fight, death quickly follows.'

Blackstone let the picture he now had of his son settle in his thoughts.

'As I said, Sir Thomas, I did not witness the Claw's skill. The others did.'

Blackstone turned the bastard horse back towards the men. 'Then we must find out if he has a weakness and use that against him.'

CHAPTER SIXTY-TWO

When they reached the outskirts of their hamlet, the villagers swarmed through Blackstone's ranks. Voices raised, they cheered and shouted to each other as they ran for their homes. Animals were penned up, cooking fires lit, smoke soon curled through the roof holes. Children gathered in front of the hanged men and hurled stones at their rotting, crow-pecked bodies.

Blackstone encamped beyond the village, his men readying their own cooking fires.

'John, come with me and Sir Gilbert; we need to find out what we can from these men who ride with my son.'

The three men strode across to where Henry and the others huddled around a campfire, warming their hands in the chill evening air. Terrel was already sampling the pottage from the blackened pot over the flames. There would be a heavy dew that night; the temperature would drop beneath the cloudless sky; blankets would become wet and men's bones would ache. A belly full of hot food was the most comfort they could expect. Henry and his companions got to their feet when Blackstone approached. The two Frenchmen were not part of the group and watched from their own campfire a few yards away.

'My lord,' said Henry.

Terrel was still chewing, but swallowed quickly when Killbere glowered at him. There was no doubt the two men who accompanied the King's Master of War were hardened survivors whose mere presence commanded respect. Especially when they stood this close. Terrel glanced nervously at Bezián and Brun, who seemed as wary as he did. Gifford stood a pace behind Henry's shoulder and showed no sign of concern. Walter Mallin shifted his stance slightly and scratched his arse.

'I offer no man a place without them being questioned,' said Blackstone. 'My captains choose their own. I hang rapists and those who disobey me or my captains. You are worthless to me if you cannot stand in line and face the enemy. You are worthless to me if you turn and run. I drive men hard. I am not a man who forgives easily. I am a man of vengeance. The road to hell is paved with the men I have killed. And if you believe me to be a harsh taskmaster, then you have not yet crossed swords with Sir Gilbert Killbere, who stands at my side.'

Henry stood next to Hugh Gifford. His father's challenge would make the men before him think twice before joining him. There were easier ways to live that also offered a better chance of survival.

As Blackstone moved along the line of men, they removed their coifs as a mark of respect.

'We share the spoils of war. You take from the dead. We do not take from those less fortunate. I offer you the chance to stand with us because you have travelled with my son.' Blackstone looked along the line of men. 'He has spoken well of you all.' Blackstone's gaze settled on Terrel. 'He has made no complaint against any one of you.'

Henry looked at Gifford, who remained stony-faced. For Blackstone to end his speech facing the one man whose trustworthiness was in doubt meant that Gifford must have told Blackstone his opinion of every man who had shared their journey.

Blackstone remained in front of Terrel, who could not hold

his penetrating gaze. Terrel's eyes flicked left and right before settling back on Blackstone, his nervousness obvious. He shuffled his feet.

'You are John Terrel.'

'I am, lord.'

'What were you before you took to the sword?'

'I was a gravedigger, Sir Thomas.'

'And a thief?'

'A thief, my lord?'

'We plunder the dead. Those we kill. Is there a difference?'

'I took a pair of boots once from a dead merchant before I filled in his grave.'

Blackstone gave no sign of acceptance or disapproval. 'We need gravediggers. We can find you work that suits your skills.'

He moved to Brun, who was the only man of the same height but who lowered his eyes respectfully, and then returned Blackstone's gaze.

'And you are Eckehart Brun?'

The German nodded. 'I was a village blacksmith. The pestilence came. Few survived. I sold my strength to those who paid for it, Sir Thomas. Not every man I served was honourable. But I have never slain a woman or a child. Innocent men, yes. I admit. But not them.'

'No fighting man is innocent of wrongdoing, Brun. But there is a line some of us do not cross. I can use a blacksmith.'

Blackstone stepped along to Walter Mallin. 'You look too old to stand against a cavalry charge,' he said to the older man.

'I am, lord. Far too old. I can hold my ground long enough to save a better fighting man at my side. That's about all I am worth. But I know horses, Sir Thomas. It's our smell. We are alike. Damp and weather-worn. It calms them. I was a farrier before I took to the road.'

'You can still shoe a horse?'

'I can.'

'Then I can make use of you. Not every man needs to stand in the front ranks. Our horses need care.'

'Then I shall strive to serve them,' said Mallin, dipping his head.

Blackstone faced the Gascon man-at-arms. 'Bezián. Arnald Bezián. Some of the Gascons who serve me have heard the name before. This Bezián murdered a priest years ago. Strung him up in a town square against his lord's command and butchered him like a pig. He was then forced to run from his lord's wrath. And is still wanted for the killing.'

'I have heard that, Sir Thomas,' said Bezián. 'In truth the priest was a pig but deserved to die a worse death, strung upside down so that his cock and balls could be severed and rammed down his throat before he bled to death. He raped a widow whose husband had fought for the English King. The priest took advantage of her because her lord did not protect her. Then he did the same to her nine-year-old child, and she turned to her dead husband's brother for help.'

'You appear to know this story well, Bezián.'

'It is a well-known tale, Sir Thomas.'

Blackstone nodded his acceptance and addressed them all. 'Your choice is to stay or go. Raise a hand if you wish to ride under my banner.'

Each of the men showed their willingness.

'All right. Master Gifford was imprisoned when my son rode with you into la Griffe's camp. Who among you witnessed this man's fighting skills?'

Brun stepped forward to speak for the men. 'We all witnessed it, Sir Thomas.'

'Then I'll ask each of you to tell me what you saw. His strikes, his stance, his ability.'

Terrel's unconscious snort of derision caught everyone's attention. He grimaced, realizing his error, and adopted a more conciliatory tone. 'It was a sight to behold, lord. His blade cut the daylight faster than anything I have seen.'

The men murmured their agreement.

'His sword arm is tireless,' said Bezián.

'And his claw wields knife or mace. If his sword is parried then his claw strikes rapidly with a vice-like grip that cannot be broken,' added Brun.

'He's young and very fast, lord,' said Henry, unable to hide his concern at what he had witnessed in la Griffe's camp.

'You tell us little more than we can imagine for ourselves,' said Killbere.

John Jacob looked at each man. 'Master Henry's life depends on us finding this man's strengths and weaknesses. We have all seen men slash and kill in battle. What else does this man do that makes him so lethal?'

The men fell silent, searching their memories. All except one.

'He dances,' Walter Mallin said simply.

All eyes turned to him.

'Aye, that's right. He's like a girl at a goose fair. He skips and shuffles his feet, this way and that. Light, as if he weighs nothing at all, as if he floats. That's how he kills so effectively. One moment he is there, the next he is not.'

'There's a pattern to his strikes?' said Blackstone.

Mallin shrugged. 'I'm no swordmaster, Sir Thomas. He moves his blade differently than any other I have witnessed. It swirls and twists so rapidly. He does not start from the high guard; he has the agility and skill to put his blade wherever he wishes. So it seems to me at least.'

Killbere turned to Blackstone. 'He has the best eye among these scab-arsed whoresons.'

Blackstone nodded. 'Who among you is closest in height to the Claw?'

They looked among themselves.

'Not me,' said Terrel, eager to discount himself.

'I am,' said Bezián. 'La Griffe is a head shorter than Master Henry. But he is lighter in build than me.'

'Henry, you will fight this man,' Blackstone said, pointing to Bezián.

'Now, lord?' said Henry, uncertain.

'You would rather eat than be ready? This creature who hunts you, he could appear at any moment. It's a bright enough moon for him to ride across those hills. We need to see how you fight now that Master Gifford has spent patient hours with a tavern brawler as a student. Aye, don't look so despairing at your guardian. He did not tell me anything I could not already see for myself.'

Henry's angry glance at his father and the two men with him earned him no flicker of understanding. The stony-faced men were now his strictest critics.

'None of us have shields,' said Henry, and knew it sounded like a lame excuse the moment he said it. It raised an eyebrow from John Jacob and a despairing look from Killbere.

'Mother of Christ, boy, are you afraid to spar with only your skill as a shield? Get to it, dammit,' said Killbere.

Bezián stepped forward, buckled his sword belt, drew his sword and stood ready. Henry paused, his heartbeat racing with humiliation. But then his mind and pulse settled, his focus sharpened. He started from the high guard as did the Gascon. Bezián was quick. He closed the space between them, expecting Henry to be forced back, throwing him onto his heels, unbalancing his upper body. But Henry sidestepped, caught the downward strike, the Gascon's blade running down his own until Henry twisted the crossguard, deflecting the blow and then slammed into Bezián with his shoulder. The Gascon was an old hand at close-quarter fighting. He let the blow half turn him and used his free hand to punch his fist down into Henry's neck. Had the contest been a real fight and there been a knife in his hand, Henry would have been dead.

Gifford could contain himself no longer. 'Feel his blade! Remember what I taught you! Forget the man. Feel and see his blade!'

The man-at-arms's comment earned an approving glance from Blackstone to John Jacob and Killbere that went unnoticed by the men who watched Henry quickly recover, turn, strike again with a thrusting lunge that would have pierced Bezián's side had he not sidestepped.

'Damn you, boy!' swore the Gascon, realizing how close he had come to being wounded.

Henry was no longer in his right mind. He advanced rapidly, forcing Bezián back in a surprising assault of power and intensity. Being shorter than Henry, Bezián hunched, forcing Henry onto his toes as he struck downwards. Bezián blocked the attack by gripping the far end of his blade and then swung its pommel, punching Henry on the side of his head. He went sprawling and as he thudded into the ground, Bezián took two paces, ready to put the sword point at Henry's throat. He had not bargained for the savage kick that took his ankles from under him. Henry straddled his chest, his knees deadening Bezián's arms. It would take a simple forward movement for the blade to cut Bezián's throat.

Blackstone grabbed Henry's collar and hauled him off, throwing him aside in case the blood mist had not cleared from his eyes.

'Bezián, you have my thanks for your restraint.'

Henry clambered to his feet. 'I had him under my blade!'

'He could have mortally wounded you half a dozen times,' said Blackstone. He turned to Gifford. 'Your pupil has skill. You taught him well. You cannot be blamed for the anger that overcomes him. When we get back, you will train with him until I see improvement. I will guide you, Master Gifford. Between us, we might keep my son alive.' He faced Henry. 'The fire inside you burns intensely, Henry. It's good to have. But you are not yet ready for a master swordsman like this la Griffe. Understand?'

Henry nodded, thankful his father had not humiliated him any further than was necessary. That soon changed.

'So why did you not use your instinct and intelligence?'

Henry did not understand.

'You say you witnessed the Claw fight one of his men?'

'I did.'

'And you heard Mallin tell us plainly that he does not start from the high guard. Yet you took that stance. You let Bezián dictate the terms of the contest. Are your ears stuffed with feathers from burying your face in pillows while bedding Oxford whores?'

'No, lord,' said Henry, chastised.

'Then you would do well to listen to what is being said and what your ale-soaked memory has witnessed.'

Blackstone turned away. Killbere nodded sagely. John Jacob gave Henry a rueful smile.

Henry watched as they walked away, then faced Bezián. He extended his hand. The Gascon accepted. Gifford clapped him on the shoulder.

'It's no different from sharpening a blade. You need honing is all. We'll sharpen you up. You're out of practice.'

The others spoke up in support, until Terrel intervened.

'They're lying, Master Henry. They want to be in favour with Sir Thomas. They don't care what happens to you. None of us do. We fight for who pays the most and Sir Thomas's success means more plunder for the likes of us.'

Gifford grabbed Terrel's collar, pushing his face close. 'Perhaps we should offer you up to la Griffe first, so he can tire himself out before facing Master Henry.'

Terrel yanked himself free. 'If we had any sense we would turn and run now. Go with the Frenchies.'

'You change direction more than the damned wind,' said Mallin.

'Better to run and live another day. If we don't, the Claw will have him cut fine enough for a cooking pot.' He looked at Henry while pointing back at the other men. 'They know that... and so do you.'

Bezián levelled his sword at Terrel. 'You should choose. Can we trust you now that we have been accepted by Sir Thomas?'

Terrel looked at them, all silently accusing him. 'Aye, I'll stay with those I know and be grateful to ride behind Sir Thomas, but you should face the truth. The Claw won't be coming alone.'

CHAPTER SIXTY-THREE

Blackstone led the men back into Sancha Ferrandes's domain. William Ashford and the Gascon captain, Aicart, had kept the men busy, rebuilding the walls and fixing leaking roofs. Will Longdon and Jack Halfpenny's men had shared the work and sentry duties on the parapet. The camp was organized now that the villagers had left and the men had been billeted by their captains.

'I know this place,' said Gautier de Fleur. 'You've seized it?'

'It was deserted except for an old priest and the villagers who took sanctuary here,' said Blackstone, not giving anything away about Sancha's presence.

'Can I speak to the priest? I must ask him something.'

'Later,' said Blackstone. 'Attend to your companion. He needs rest and food. My men will see to your horses.' Blackstone drew up the bastard horse and dismounted. He called out to Henry. 'Do you think you can still manage my horse? To stable and feed him?'

Henry beamed and jumped down from his mount. 'I'm the only one who ever could. Apart from you.'

'I've never had much joy with the belligerent beast. Only when he permits it.'

Henry stepped slowly around the animal and reached out his hand. Yellow teeth snapped and the bastard horse tossed up its misshapen head, but Henry stood his ground and spoke in hushed, soothing tones, letting his open palm get ever closer to the flared nostrils. He waited. The horse eyed him, ears pricked forward, snuffled his scent and waited. Henry turned his back and walked slowly to where he could see the stables. The horse did not move. Shook its mane. And then walked docilely after the boy he remembered.

Killbere laughed. 'That damned horse has a memory longer than a split man's guts.'

'Get the men fed and rested before my son's misfortune comes knocking at the gates.'

'Where will you be?' Killbere nodded. 'No need. I can guess.'

Blackstone glanced to where de Fleur was helping his friend down from his horse. 'Keep the Frenchmen out of sight until I see which way the wind blows with her,' he said.

Blackstone had barely reached the top of Sancha's steps when the door swung open. Her pleasure at seeing him was obvious, but she restrained herself from reaching out.

'I saw you lead the men in,' she said. 'I was worried. It felt that you were gone too long.' She ushered him inside. A servant was laying down fresh-cut reeds on the floor; the fire's heat filled the room. A bench and table had been decorated with sprigs of rosemary and spring flowers, barely opened, picked early in the season as a gesture to welcome him back.

'Villagers walk slowly.'

'Please,' she said, taking his hand, guiding him to sit by the fire on the bench. 'You must be hungry. The kitchen has food ready.'

'I'll eat with the men.' He glanced around the room. She had found some thickly woven material and draped it across the window lintels, and a tapestry now covered the draughty door. Was this gesture of comfort made on his behalf? he wondered. He guessed the items had been in a chest from the time when her Castilian family stayed here.

'I am grateful for you taking those people back to their village. They remembered my father, but the older ones still think of me as a child, even though I am now responsible for them.' She gave him a glass of wine. Her hand lingered a moment longer than was necessary as he took the glass from her.

She sat next to him.

'You have found old treasures, then? The door tapestry, the windows, this glass. Are you sure your father didn't hide a cache of *doblas*?'

There was an almost indiscernible flare in her eyes. Blackstone had inadvertently hit on the truth. She covered it well.

'I am confident that I can support this place and allow the people freed by my father to go about their lives. They will pay what they have agreed. They have done so even in his absence.'

'You need men here to protect you. And for the villages that your family depends on for food and loyalty. You know that. Twenty men, or more if they could be found and paid for.'

'I would be pleased if you would consider staying here,' she said. The words came more rapidly than she expected and caused her to cast him a glance of uncertainty. Colour spread into her neck and face. Embarrassed, she turned away. She sipped her wine, barely wetting her lips.

Blackstone's wife's death had crushed his heart and since then he had not experienced feelings such as those which came over him now. He reined them in. Emotions were as unpredictable as the bastard horse. His desire for Sancha Ferrandes had not left him, but the way ahead had become more complicated. Her nearness to him was unsettling. He stood up and placed the half-finished wine on the bench. 'Your family was at war with Don Pedro and I was tasked to save him. I would gladly see him dead, but cannot because I'm sworn to the Prince. And so here we are. On opposite sides. And neither of us would want to live with that conflict.'

'Don Pedro will die one day,' she said. 'Trastámara will win. It can be no other way. The French King will always want an ally across the Pyrenees. Your Prince will never strike again – you know that, Thomas. In your heart, you know it. The Prince cannot afford to keep waging war so far from home. And if we both accept that, then there is a chance'—she faltered momentarily—'that you could be here.'

'*Here* is French territory. If I claim it for my King, would you side with the English? Would you switch your loyalty away from my enemy?'

She looked helpless. 'I know a good man has come into my life.'

That moment almost broke his resolve. 'God help me, Sancha. I swear if Fate had brought us together at another time or place, then we would be together.'

He offered no further explanation, went to the door, and beckoned someone. He stood to one side when Gautier de Fleur appeared in the doorway. He looked confused as Sancha Ferrandes stood, trembling, hand to mouth, made a half-step towards him and then stopped herself. Waiting in disbelief. De Fleur looked at Blackstone, who said nothing. The Frenchman took a few tentative steps. Then he too faltered and halted.

'My lady,' he whispered.

Sancha Ferrandes pressed her lips to her steepled fingers. Tears filled her eyes.

Blackstone closed the door behind him, looked at Killbere,

who was leaning against the wall. Blackstone went past him down the steps.

'We've work to do,' he said.

Killbere nodded and followed Blackstone. Another chapter had closed on his friend's life.

CHAPTER SIXTY-FOUR

Over the next few days Blackstone's men continued to reinforce any weakness in the château's walls. There was no telling how many mercenaries had been brought together by la Griffe.

Killbere and John Jacob squatted with Blackstone and his captains. Scratch marks in the dirt marked out a diagram of the walls where the men should be stationed if a concerted attack was made.

'We must decide who will take Henry's men under their command,' said Blackstone.

Aicart raised a hand. 'I'll take Bezián. Be good to keep the Gascons together, Sir Thomas. And he already has a reputation, so that will sit well with my men.'

'Brun could ride with me,' said Renfred, 'but he's too big to travel far at pace.'

'No, I'll take him,' said Meulon. 'He'll make a good spearman. I'd trust him to stand his ground. The heavier men are best suited at a shield wall.'

'None are any good to me,' said Will Longdon. 'Not an archer among them.'

'That leaves Walter Mallin and Terrel,' said Blackstone. 'Mallin is best kept with the pack horses. It will suit him and the beasts.'

He looked at Renfred. 'Terrel?'

Renfred shook his head. 'He won't fit in with my men. Not him.'

No one else offered to absorb Terrel into their command.

'William?'

Ashford grimaced. 'I beg you not to push him onto me, Sir Thomas. We have men of low character among us, but they are loyal and they fight hard for you. Terrel is the arse end of a latrine pit. I'll wager he'll be on the end of a rope before too long.'

Blackstone sighed and looked at Killbere.

'If he rides with me, he rides with you,' the veteran knight said. 'John Jacob and I have forged good men around you in the vanguard. Terrel will be a weakness we don't need. Kick him out.'

'He stayed loyal to Henry,' said John Jacob. 'Perhaps we could keep him with Walter Mallin and the horses.'

'And he'll welcome not being in a fight,' said Aicart. 'I've heard from Bezián how Terrel would rather run than fight.'

'Then it's settled,' Blackstone said.

Killbere grunted. 'If the Claw comes with more than a hundred men, he might choose to ignore Henry and attack us instead. He has the French King's support and a sack of coin to pay roaming skinners. He might see himself become a favoured name at court if he rids the King of a scourge that makes France bleed.'

Renfred dragged a finger in the dirt, an arc across what represented the ground outside the château. 'I could take my scouts and spread out here, Sir Thomas, a few miles south; then we will know when they're coming.'

'You'll be too thin on the ground,' said John Jacob.

Renfred shook his head, and then addressed his fellow captains. 'Each of my men will know where his companion is. If la Griffe is coming from the south, as we think he must, then we can be forewarned. If he comes in strength, then we can either harass him while I send back word or we can rejoin you all here.'

'He comes from the Count of Foix,' said Killbere. 'It's possible he'll travel the same route as ourselves.'

'Renfred, take your men and do as you suggest. Don't engage him. You and your men are my eyes and ears, and I don't wish to be struck blind and deaf.'

The German captain got to his feet and strode towards his scouts. Words of good luck followed him.

'We don't know how many days it will take before he reaches us,' said Meulon.

'But if this whoreson comes ready to fight Henry... what if the lad's skills can't be raised in time?' said Will Longdon. 'I've seen him with Gifford... he's, er...' The veteran archer shrugged. 'Impressive. Yes, I think he's improving.'

'Your lies are worse than your damned cooking and both can poison a man in different ways,' said Killbere. 'The lad needs me and Thomas to kick his arse and make him see what he's up against.'

'Leave Henry to me,' Blackstone told them. He paused. 'How is the wounded Frenchman?'

'De Roche is stronger,' said Aicart. 'He can use his arm better and his ribs are bound. De Fleur looks after him well. Are you going to ask him and de Roche to side with us against la Griffe?'

'No. I want them gone.'

'The moment they are free of us, their parole ends,' said John Jacob.

'We're supposed to use the Frenchie to find Trastámara,' said Longdon.

'And he could meet the bastard who's coming to kill Henry and tell him how few we are here,' added Killbere. 'And if that scum knows we harbour the woman, then it's more fuel to his determination to attack us.'

'De Fleur and his companion won't ride to Trastámara. Not now. They'll seek refuge in a French stronghold.'

'You can't know that,' said Killbere.

'I'm sending Sancha Ferrandes with them.' Blackstone looked at each of his men. 'I would have used her as bait to see if de Fleur led us to Trastámara if all he wanted was her dowry and her land. But his feelings for the woman are genuine. He won't risk her life needlessly. Whatever happens, he'll want to protect her. No, we let them go, rid ourselves of the responsibility, and when everything is settled, we ride on. We'll join up with Chandos and harass any reinforcements riding south.'

'What do Ferrandes and de Fleur say?' said Killbere.

Blackstone stood. 'I'm about to tell them. Gilbert, go through our plan of counter-attack in case we are overwhelmed. Aicart, send one of your men to de Fleur. Take him to her quarters.' The Gascon captain stood to leave. 'And, Aicart, fetch the priest as well.'

A serving woman ushered Blackstone into Sancha's quarters. Her mistress dismissed her and waited by the fire. Blackstone kept his distance from the woman he had desired. Still did – although he would not accept what he felt. He had raised a mental shield against the thought.

'I have not had an opportunity to thank you for bringing Gautier to me.'

'Your thanks should be given to my son, Henry. It was he who saved him.'

'Gautier and Louis de Roche both told me what happened. I shall attempt to speak to your son, but he has been practising with his tutor for so many hours I did not wish to distract him.'

'Are you to marry?'

The blunt question caught her by surprise, but the reasoning behind it was clear enough. 'Yes.'

'Get it done, then,' said Blackstone in a no-nonsense manner. 'You and the Frenchman are leaving.'

Before she could answer there was a knock at the door. Blackstone opened it. One of Aicart's men stood on the threshold. 'I have him, Sir Thomas.'

He stepped aside. De Fleur entered, looked from Sancha to Blackstone and then went to her and put himself in front of the Englishman whose scarred face seemed to offer more of a threat than a greeting.

'I remain in your debt, Sir Thomas, but if there is going to be conflict between us, I ask you to attend to it privately, not here.'

'I have no intention of causing you harm.'

'Sir Thomas wishes us to leave,' Sancha said, instinctively clutching de Fleur's arm. A gesture that did not go unnoticed by Blackstone. Another confirmation of where her emotions lay.

'It's not a wish, it's a command. He knows as well as I do that routiers, led by a killer, are on their way. They will come in force given that your King has paid them,' Blackstone said, stabbing an accusatory finger at de Fleur. 'And being a Frenchman won't save you or her if they overwhelm us.'

'Louis and I can fight at your side.'

'For pity's sake. See the truth for what it is.' He glanced at Sancha. 'I have.'

Sancha Ferrandes thought she saw a look of regret in Blackstone's eyes.

De Fleur appealed to Blackstone. 'Those with la Griffe will see that this place is defended. Once you leave, then I can find men of my own. De Roche and I can recruit among those abandoned by the war.'

Blackstone barely hid his frustration. 'You will have no time. When the business with la Griffe is done, you will be alone. A belligerent priest waving a black flag will only spare you for a short while. Get her out, de Fleur. You can make a life together. Will you be able to find sanctuary?'

De Fleur nodded.

'Then do as I say. Use that time to find good men. Pay them well. And then come back when the Spanish fight is settled because Trastámara will not accept defeat.' His tone softened. 'War is coming. The French King bides his time, but it waits like a gathering storm. You and I might soon be on opposite sides.'

'I'll not fight against you, Sir Thomas. I give you my word.'

'But there'll be others in my place, so use the time to ready yourselves. You have a fine woman, with great courage, for a wife.'

'But we are not yet married.'

Blackstone opened the door. The priest stood uncertainly in the entrance. Blackstone beckoned him inside.

'Then don't waste time.'

CHAPTER SIXTY-FIVE

Blackstone and the men rested. If there was to be a fight, it would come to them. Horses were attended to; sword, axe and knife blades were honed. Will Longdon and Jack Halfpenny's archers checked every arrow in their bags. Bowstrings were waxed and fletchings checked. By midday Louis de Roche had thanked Henry and then Blackstone and tethered the pack horse with supplies. He waited for his newly married companion.

When Sancha Ferrandes of Castile came down the steps from her quarters, she wore a common man's coif over a tight-fitting black cloth covering her tied-back hair. She had dressed in plain clothing except for a dark blue embroidered surcoat bearing her family's blazon of a black griffin bearing a sword. Her belt bore the sheathed knife she had used to try to kill the Spanish King, which Blackstone had returned to her for her own protection. Horses were ready for her and Gautier de Fleur. The Frenchman tied saddlebags to his horse.

The old priest bowed. She took his gnarled hand and kissed it. 'Père Éraste, will you not reconsider and come with us?'

'My lady, you know I cannot. Your father built my chapel. He graced it with the altar cross and reliquary. I am their guardian, and besides, I must ensure everything is as it should be for when you return.'

'And that will not be long: I give you my word.' She gathered her dress, stepped onto the mounting block and sat astride her mount. 'And make sure you raise the flag of pestilence when Sir Thomas leaves,' she said, offering the old man some comfort with her smile.

He blessed her with the sign of the cross.

Nudging her horse forward, she approached Blackstone, Henry and Killbere, who waited at the gate.

'You see how she leads the way, Thomas? Ahead of her husband?' said Killbere. 'I'll wager no man will get her to know her place.'

'He might have sense enough not to curb her spirit,' Blackstone answered. 'But it was he who tied the bags onto his saddle. So who do you think carries the money?'

Killbere sighed. 'Ah, true enough. But that might simply make him a beast of burden, not lord of the manor?' He grinned at Blackstone. 'You might not think so now, my friend, but one day you will count this Frenchman's arrival as a blessing in disguise.'

She pulled up her horse. 'Master Henry, I offer you my thanks for your courage in saving Gautier de Fleur and Louis de Roche. I have asked Père Éraste to offer prayers for your safety in your trial of combat. We owe much to you and your father.'

Henry dipped his head. 'My lady, I had brave men with me.'

'But they followed your example, Master Henry.'

Blackstone stepped to one side to let the horse pass.

'Sir Thomas, I am the sole survivor of the Ferrandes family of Castile. I will not let my family name die. It is because of you that I and my name live on. One day, I will avenge my family's death. Until that time comes, I will remember you in my prayers.'

She leaned down and extended her hand. Blackstone held it for a moment. Everything that could have been between them was felt in those few seconds.

'And in my heart. God bless you, Thomas,' she said softly.

Sancha heeled her horse forward into a quick canter, followed by de Fleur and de Roche, both men grasping Henry's hand before they followed her lead.

'Get back to your practice,' Blackstone told Henry. 'You helped save a village and a damned Frenchman. Now you need to learn how to save yourself.'

Henry turned and strode briskly to where Gifford waited patiently to begin another strenuous training session.

'And so she'll be safe and sound now. While we face an unknown horde of bastards,' said Killbere, turning his back on the retreating woman and her new husband.

Blackstone let his gaze stay a moment longer. And then he joined Killbere. He didn't look back.

'He's willing enough,' said Killbere as they walked through the compound, looking to where Henry was being put through his paces.

'I spoke further with Bezián. He said no one saw Henry kill la Griffe's father. They were in the dungeon ready to defend or release Gifford and another man.'

'Who else was there?'

'A wounded man Walter Mallin had tried to help. He had died by the time they got Gifford out.'

'So there is no witness to what happened with Henry and the man he killed? This whoreson they call the Claw has no actual proof Henry killed his father.'

'It makes no difference. Henry led him into a trap. Whether he was alive or dead when they butchered him and hung him at the castle gates, the act was Henry's doing.'

'Did Bezián say anything else?'

Blackstone shook his head. 'No one has seen Henry fight. Only Gifford when they were attacked by the fishermen.' He shrugged. 'Bezián said he did not think Henry killed any of the skinners in the village. He freed de Fleur and de Roche.'

Killbere grimaced, pressed a finger against his nostril, and blew the contents into the dirt. 'Well then,' he said. 'He's not exactly been busy with a sword since he left England.'

They stopped thirty yards from where Gifford and Henry were practising. The man-at-arms was a solid fighter and worked Henry hard.

Blackstone watched a moment longer. He sighed. 'Bezián said Henry was quick-witted and merciful.'

Killbere grunted. 'God's tears, Thomas, we all know that. Good virtues to have if you're not facing a killer ready to cleave you from neck to groin.'

Blackstone nodded. 'Stay and watch. See if there's any improvement. I'll check the men.'

Killbere watched him walk away, saw the stoop of his shoulders from the burden of what lay ahead for his son. The veteran knight turned his attention back to Gifford and Henry. He squinted as Gifford forced Henry back, his heel catching a pail of water that spilled across the dirt. The soft light playing tricks on his vision made it easy to imagine it was a gush of Henry's blood that seeped into the dirt.

CHAPTER SIXTY-SIX

An hour later Blackstone came back. He looked across the courtyard to where Henry and Hugh Gifford still practised, both men saturated with sweat.

'Gilbert?'

Killbere was where he had left him. He was eating an apple. He spat out pips as he gnawed the core, then tossed the remains into the dirt. 'Perhaps,' said the veteran knight.

'Perhaps?' Blackstone queried, turning his attention away from his son.

Killbere shrugged. 'Fate might be kind. He might get lucky. The Claw might take a wound, slip, and then Henry can finish him.'

Blackstone sighed and shook his head. 'By all accounts, Jean de Soissons is a master swordsman. Taught by his father. He used to win tourneys. It was the beast inside him that destroyed what his family had.'

'Like I said. Luck plays its part. Besides, fighting in a tourney isn't fighting for your life. If it was his brutality that cast him out of favour, then he's a butcher. He kills innocents. He kills his own men by way of practice. You forget, Henry killed a man when he was a boy and again in Florence when he was still a youth. Look at him. He's as broad and tall as you and a damned sight better looking. He has his mother's beauty.'

'Gilbert, for God's sake! Is that all he has to beat la Griffe? An inflamed heart broken by assassins killing those he loved and had sworn to defend. How old was he in Florence when I lay wounded in Bordeaux and he killed the man sent to kill him? And he was hurt in that fight. And Fate will not favour him because he has his mother's gentle heart and features. It's likely to be those which get him killed.'

'Well, like Hugh Gifford said, he killed men in that fishing village.'

'Fishermen, Gilbert! Fishermen! There is no comparison.'

'Well, he somehow finished off la Griffe's father, whether or not there was a witness. All I'm saying is he has killed and can kill again. He has not recoiled from the act. I'm trying to give him the benefit of the doubt. What more is there to say? The lad has stamina, I'll give him that. You can see with your own eyes.' He pressed his back against the wall and folded his arms as they both watched Gifford and Henry. Slow, methodical strike positions.

'Merciful God,' sighed Blackstone. 'I taught him those master strokes years ago. I see no finesse. Do you? Do you see a man who has thrown himself at developing his fighting skills?'

Killbere kept his eye on Henry, who momentarily got the better of Hugh Gifford, but then took an unnecessary step to the side and lost his balance. Killbere sighed and spat out another pip lodged in a tooth.

'Thomas, we should have Will put an arrow through the Frenchman when he rides up to the gate. End it there.'

'We cannot. No, we cannot in honour do that,' said Blackstone.

'Christ, Thomas, we kill easily enough. If a man needs to be killed, it doesn't matter how it's done. We have to look after our own and Henry is to your heart as Wolf Sword is to your fist. The blood knot binds you both.'

'He won't turn his back on this, Gilbert. He has the

ambition to win the fight but not the skill.' He paused. 'Or the temperament.'

'Does la Griffe have battle experience?'

'Does Henry? Gilbert, I'm sending my son to his death.'

'You don't know that. He has the heart of a warrior. He's young. He's fast. You've sparred with him.'

'And he's not yet skilled enough to face a challenge one to one. Dammit, even I'd fall short against the fast-moving Frenchman.'

Killbere grunted. 'You're getting old, no doubt about it.'

Blackstone winced. 'God's tears, you call me old? You stand your ground in battle because your lungs wheeze and your knees creak too much for you to move at speed.'

'Which is why I'm still alive. Why run into battle? Let the enemy come to you. I pile the bodies in front of me and the bastards have to clamber over the dead to reach me.'

Blackstone nodded. 'Well, that won't work with the Claw. I must talk to Henry.'

Killbere reached for his arm as he stepped away. 'Thomas, are you going to tell the lad he can't win and defeat him before he tries, or put strength into him and give him hope?'

'Either way, he is condemned. Hope vanishes when a man betters you in a few strokes.'

'We should ride on. Turn our back on this matter. There's no honour to be had here. None of us will think badly of Henry if we are not here when the skinner turns up. He will feel it an insult to his pride, but it's just a flesh wound. He can. bear it.'

Blackstone nodded. 'I'll try. I'll offer him a way out. But would either of us turn our back?'

He strode across the yard. His men were idly watching from

the stables, some pretending to groom or clean hooves, others shaking out the horse blankets, but all of them were watching the boy now grown to a man as he practised. Will Longdon and Jack Halfpenny waxed their bowstrings; Meulon sharpened his knife on a whetstone. The men who rode with Henry had told the story of their journey. Blackstone's men had listened. Pictured in their mind's eye the lethal killer. Now they turned their attention to Henry's efforts. From what had been said they all knew, as did Killbere, that Henry Blackstone was not good enough to fight Jean de Soissons and survive. And would he yield if given the opportunity?

'I've watched him grow from a child. Remember when he killed a man trying to protect his mother and sister from the Jacques?' said Will Longdon.

'Aye,' said Meulon. 'How old was he then? Ten? Eleven?'

'Damned if I know, but he fought for them and from what John Jacob says, he reckons young Henry still blames himself for not saving them from that bastard assassin.' Longdon spat in disgust at the memory.

'We could wait on the road and deal with the Frenchie,' said Halfpenny. 'Me and Fairfoot could put a shaft each into him, split up, and be back here before they knew what had struck them.'

'Sir Thomas would cast us out no matter how good our intention,' said Meulon.

'No, Jack, we have to leave this in Thomas's hands, but I hope they fetch the priest and have the lad shriven,' said Longdon.'

When Blackstone was twenty paces from his son, Hugh Gifford stepped back from his lesson, lowered his sword and tilted his chin respectfully.

'My lord,' he said, his breath coming hard from exertion.

'Master Gifford, a moment with my son.'

Once again, Henry's guardian dipped his head and then walked away out of earshot. Blackstone's son rested his sword, leaning on the pommel and stared at his father. He dragged a sleeve across the sweat streaking his face, dripping from his chin. 'You come here to warn me not to fight,' he said. 'Don't bother, Father, you cannot stop this now. It has gone too far.'

'You think I've come to stop you?'

'Well, haven't you? You don't believe I'm able to defend myself.'

'Defence is not enough. There should be only one thought in your head and that is to kill the man who challenges you – fast, and violently and without hesitation.'

Henry grimaced. A vein pulsed in his neck. Anger rising. 'You have never wanted me to live by the sword and now you urge me to kill as viciously as the man I face.'

'This is not about living,' Blackstone growled, releasing his urge to impress on his son the severity of what lay ahead. 'This is about being prepared to die if you don't find that savagery inside you.'

Henry's affront was plain to see. 'Again, you insult me. I can fight!'

The two were still three yards apart, as if the distance between them were sacred ground. 'You fight well. Hugh Gifford's guardianship these past years has seen to it. There is still room for improvement, every fighting man knows that, unless he is arrogant enough to believe otherwise. And arrogance kills those who own it.'

'I know my weaknesses in a fight. I'll be ready.'

'I embrace you, Henry. You are my son but your mother's blood runs deeper in your veins than does mine,' said Blackstone. 'I remember your words when she and your sister Agnes were slain. Do you remember what you said?'

The memory was a shared agony.

Henry shook his head.

'You faced me and said, "I cannot kill like you. I have no wish to do so." You said you wished to do what your mother always wanted for you. To study and become a learned man, and forsake this way of life.'

'As you said, Father, I was only a child. Now I am not,' Henry answered, subdued by the images from that time.

'You have a gift that I do not,' said Blackstone. 'You have an ability to read and understand so much of what you are taught. You are a scholar and that is her doing. She shared her love of poetry and literature with you and instilled a gentleness in your heart.' Blackstone stepped forward and gripped his son's arm. 'But you do not have my gift.' He watched as the reality sank in. 'I beg you with the love I have in my heart for you. Do not do this.'

Henry raised his eyes. They were misty with tears. 'I have wanted nothing more in my whole life but to stand at your side, yet you pushed me away. I understand why, Father.' His voice trailed to a whisper. 'My mother has blessed me with the hunger for knowledge and it comes easily to me and that ability cannot be taken away.' He stepped back, wiped a hand across his eyes, and faced him squarely. 'But I cannot do what you ask. I have to fight him.'

Blackstone nodded. It was the answer he had expected. Determined to appear more positive, he smiled, his voice lifting. 'All right. As you wish. You will fight in my colours and your enemy will know my blazon was gifted by the Prince and was won honourably. And you will carry my shield and Wolf Sword. There's no better blade and its blood knot will hold it fast in your grip. '

'Father, I...' The change in his father's demeanour momentarily confused Henry as relief and gratitude swept over him.

'It's as it should be, my boy. Does what I've said meet with your approval?'

'Yes, Father. Thank you.'

'Good. And when the fight is done, you will go to Italy and continue your law studies. And you will go using your mother's name. You are to return as Henry de Sainteny.'

'I am your son. Father, I beg you. I would be hiding like a child behind my mother's skirts. Let me bear your name. I cannot deny my heritage.'

'After the fight, every master swordsman will seek out and challenge the man who killed the Claw.'

'Then I can beat him?' said Henry, suddenly hopeful of his father's belief in him.

'Killbere and I will tell you what can be done to ensure you know how to kill this bastard. Understand?'

'Yes, Father. Thank you.'

Blackstone saw his son's gratitude was still tinged with uncertainty. No matter what praise or encouragement Blackstone heaped on him, Henry Blackstone still harboured doubt. And fear.

'Henry, once the fight is done and you have killed him, then you cannot live under such a burden; you will spend a lifetime being challenged if you keep my name. Will you use your mother's?'

In his mind's eye, Henry saw the future unfold beyond the contest. A time ahead that beckoned. 'If that is to be our agreement, then yes.'

'There can be no other. Say it.'

Henry looked uncertain, but his father's insistence was etched on his features. It was an agreement Henry Blackstone knew he had to accept. To have his father's blessing and the chance to prove himself to him was a price worth paying.

'Yes, Father, when the fight is done I will go to Italy as Henry de Sainteny and continue my studies in law.'

For a moment it looked as though father and son would embrace. A moment of awkwardness followed. Henry shuffled his feet and turned to leave.

'Son,' said Blackstone.

Henry turned. His father hugged him, pulling him tightly to his chest. 'Know that I always carry you in my heart.' He held his son at arm's length. 'And remember, no matter what happens to us in this life, never look back. The past is over. It does not exist. Only its ghosts linger. And some will always share our journey. Now, go and rest. Wash and spend time in prayer.'

Blackstone strode away from his son. Hugh Gifford had kept his distance. 'Master Gifford.'

'Sir Thomas?'

'You are sworn to protect my son. By the King's command.'

'I am.'

'Then you will do as I ask.'

CHAPTER SIXTY-SEVEN

A hundred and twenty horsemen darkened the horizon as riders eased their mounts into an extended line. They gathered far enough beyond the low walls of the château to be out of the bowmen's range.

Killbere squinted through the gap in the town's gates. 'Enough of them to cause trouble,' he said. 'If we let them.'

Despite the chill, Blackstone wore only his shirt. The wound on his side had seeped blood, staining his shirt. Killbere said nothing about it. He scratched his beard. 'We can get behind them. Will and the lads, here and there.' He pointed beyond the gates to one side. 'Shoot into them while we go out that gate at the back, Thomas. Do it now. Get it over and done with rather than wait.'

Blackstone stared out at the ragged line of horsemen. 'That would not end the matter between de Soissons and Henry. Have you done what I asked?'

'Aye, but I still think we should strike while there's daylight.'

Blackstone placed a hand on Killbere's shoulder. 'Gilbert, what happens this night will haunt me for the rest of my life.' He paused. 'You know that.'

The tinge of sadness in Killbere's voice was unmistakable. 'I do.'

'Then stay with what we planned.' He turned to his squire. 'John, fetch Henry. Make sure he's dressed as I instructed. They must see that he bears my colours.' He beckoned Will Longdon. 'Will, we shan't let them see our strength here. Keep

411

half your archers on the wall either side of the gate. It will be enough to hold them back for now.'

Longdon ran back to where his archers and Jack Halfpenny waited. Blackstone turned for the gate and called out to the man who sat at a grinding wheel sharpening his sword. 'Bullard, if there's fighting to be had, your wounded leg will keep you out of it.'

Sparks flew as the blade was honed. 'Sir Thomas, Meulon has promised to lift me onto my horse. Nothing wrong with my sword arm once I'm in the saddle.'

'No, Bullard, I want you to be at the gate when Sir Gilbert needs it opened. You and Walter Mallin must attend to it and watch for anyone trying to storm the back walls. Can you manage that?'

The man-at-arms, crestfallen at his bad fortune, nodded. 'As you wish, Sir Thomas. I'll be ready.'

Blackstone pointed. 'Spare me your crutch while you sharpen your blade. I have a long walk out there.'

Bullard looked quizzical but then handed over the roughly hewn crutch. Blackstone settled it under his armpit. John Jacob was approaching with Henry and Gifford. Henry expressed his concern when he saw his father testing his weight on the support.

'It's nothing,' said John Jacob. 'The wound weeps and your father has no wish to reopen it further.'

They joined Blackstone and Killbere.

'Don't forget, Henry, glare at this whoreson as if he's already dead,' said Blackstone. 'Now, let's go and face this cruel bastard and taunt his soul.'

The horsemen waited patiently as their leader, Jean de Soissons, prompted his mount forward and faced the men standing on the low walls. There were a few archers on the ramparts either side of the wooden gates, but he knew that if he killed Henry Blackstone, those bowmen would send a storm of lethal yard-long arrows into his men, even at the distance at which he'd kept them. The archers would use wind, strength and skill to reach them. Such was their prowess even at three hundred yards and more. And then the English King's Master of War and his horsemen would charge through the gates and unleash their fury. There was no doubt in his mind that he would kill Blackstone's son. He would make his excuses to the King. Swear perhaps that it was Blackstone's son who had challenged him. What la Griffe needed was for the scar-faced Englishman to pledge on his honour that no retaliation would take place. And that was why he had done as the French King had instructed and brought a vital witness. He nodded to the three men who accompanied him to come forward.

The first, an older man, wore the colours of Gaston Phoebus, the Count de Foix. His clothing signified he was a man of importance in the Count's household. It had been his master's territory where the Prince of Wales had gathered his army before going into Castile. The Count de Foix was a neutral player in the ongoing antagonism between the Spanish claimants to the throne and the French support for one side and the English for the other. And it suited the Count to accommodate both sides of the conflict.

The other two men held back. This meeting was not their concern.

La Griffe and his companion pulled up their horses halfway between the gathered routiers at their backs and the château's walls. The hefty wooden gates creaked open. Five men emerged.

'Who is that?' la Griffe asked.

Gaston Phoebus's man stared at Blackstone, who walked

slowly, leaning heavily on a crutch. For a moment he could not be certain. He had never seen the English King's Master of War so weakened. 'That is Sir Thomas Blackstone. Sir Gilbert Killbere is at his side, as is Blackstone's squire, John Jacob.' Two other men held back twenty paces behind Blackstone; one a short stocky man he did not recognize, who flanked the tall, muscular youth next to him. 'I do not know the other men.'

'I do,' said la Griffe, unable to keep the satisfaction from his voice. 'That is Henry Blackstone. Perhaps the man with him is his nursemaid?' He grinned.

La Griffe looked carefully at the renowned fighter, Thomas Blackstone. He was obviously recovering from wounds. He was dressed in only a shirt, armed with nothing more than his archer's knife at his belt. Still, injured or not, Thomas Blackstone could as soon turn into a ravening wolf and hurl himself upon him and, before he could cry out, his throat would be slit. These thoughts flashed through his mind, a warning to tread carefully.

De Soissons saw that Henry Blackstone wore a plain woven surcoat of a rich sanguine hue. Sewn onto its left breast was his father's blazon, a black image of a sword held in a gauntleted fist below the curved-down crossguard. For now, the killer decided he would resist the urge to hurl insults at his opponent. The bitterness he felt towards Blackstone's son was an alchemist's brew that could explode at any moment but there would be no discourtesy given. No, this would require a soft approach. His companion dismounted as Blackstone drew near.

'Sir Thomas,' said la Griffe. 'I am Jean de Soissons. This matter with your son needs to be settled. I bring a witness so that there can be no doubt that the contest is fought and won without interference from others.' He glanced up at the archers. 'The man beside me serves the Count of Foix. He will carry word of the outcome from this challenge.'

The older man bowed his head respectfully. 'Sir Thomas, my Lord Gaston Phoebus sends his warmest regards. You are remembered with much respect for what you did for the Count in the past.'

Blackstone stood a yard away and acknowledged the older man.

'I remember you, Master Alphonse. You are the Count's steward.'

The man smiled. To be remembered by a fighting man of Thomas Blackstone's reputation was an honour.

Jean de Soissons looked uncertain. He did not know of Blackstone's association with the Count.

The steward saw la Griffe's look of uncertainty. 'Sir Thomas and his men were my lord's guests some years ago.'

Jean de Soissons scowled. 'There's to be no favouritism here. You serve as witness. Nothing more.'

'Understood,' said Master Alphonse. He addressed Blackstone. 'Sir Thomas, shall we decide on a place?'

'Here,' said Blackstone. 'No armour.'

So, it was to be a contest of speed and agility, la Griffe reasoned. That played into his hands. If the young Blackstone thought he could outpace him with a sword in his hand, then he would soon be maimed and killed.

'And where?'

'Before these walls. Three hours after compline. Prayers must be said. The sacrament must be given. If a man is to die, his soul must be prepared.'

Master Alphonse looked uncertain. He glanced up at Jean de Soissons, who looked equally perplexed. 'Fight in darkness? Two hours before midnight?' said La Griffe.

Blackstone stared up at him. 'We have braziers and torches

prepared. It will demarcate the contest ground. You and my son fight on foot.'

'Madness,' said la Griffe. 'Dawn. We fight at dawn so there can be no betrayal. No assassin lurking beyond the firelight.'

'I have other places to be tomorrow,' said Blackstone. 'Are you afraid to die at night? Do Satan's imps lurk in the shadows to snatch your soul? If you are afraid, go back to your master. You made a devil's pact with the King of France. Are these the men he gave you?' he said, meaning the line of horsemen.

'Men who joined me along the way. Of like persuasion. All of them have been promised payment to see me returned safely.'

'You have this one opportunity to skulk back to Brittany. Tail between your legs. You cannot beat my son. I have trained him myself. He wears my colours.'

'A blazon is no amulet against death.'

'This is your last chance. My men will let you ride back. I will not give the order to pursue you. Master Alphonse can bear witness.'

For a moment la Griffe was uncertain. The wounded Englishman was not trying to buy him off. Showed no sign of protecting his son. Was Blackstone so confident his son could outfight him?

The steward remained silent, but kept his attention on de Soissons. If the Claw declined to fight, that would end his reputation as a skilled swordsman. And what else? He saw the doubt on the man's scowling face twist into a vicious expression. Blackstone had baited him. Even de Soissons's horse sensed its rider's tension. It fought the bit. La Griffe tightened the reins, never once unlocking his gaze from Blackstone. And then he looked beyond the three men who stood below him and called to Henry Blackstone. 'Are you willing? Will you fight in darkness?'

Henry was struggling to keep his courage intact. Bravado had long abandoned him and even the determination to uphold his honour was wavering. The reality of the fight was now stark and frightening. Yet he took a deep breath and answered firmly.

'Day or night, Jean de Soissons, I am happy to fight you.'

'And if you need a priest, I'll send him to you,' said Blackstone to la Griffe. He held the younger man's eyes again. 'No man should die unshriven.'

'I need no priest. Ring the compline bell, and when your son's knees blister from fearful prayer, send him to me.' He wheeled the horse and spurred it back to his men.

Master Alphonse nodded to Blackstone, tried to raise a foot into the stirrup, but his age challenged him. John Jacob quickly stepped forward and cupped his hands as a mounting step. 'I am grateful,' he said. 'My heart aches for you, Sir Thomas, and for your son. I wish my lord had not set an old man like me such an onerous task.' He gathered the reins. After a brief glance towards Henry Blackstone, he lowered his voice. 'I will pray that when your son is disarmed, he is not badly wounded and will yield willingly.' The steward shifted his eyes slightly. 'Look behind me, Sir Thomas, to the three men who serve as my guard.'

Blackstone looked into the distance. He could make out three horsemen who stood away from the main body of men.

'Those men brought word from Paris. A warning. From the King himself. The mission was to capture your son alive. However, these men knew the truth, and so now does the King. La Griffe always fights to kill. That will be an end to it. The contest won. The vengeance achieved. Do not expect honour to override his anger. Honour is not a word he recognizes.

You should know the King did not wish this. This was not the agreement. That is why he sent them to my master: so that you might be warned. When a contest is close fought, who will be able to swear whether your son yielded?' He shook his head. 'I and these men are here to witness that there is no interference in the fight from others and that your son's surrender is honoured.'

'My thanks.'

Throughout the exchange Blackstone had kept an eye on la Griffe. The gates were still open. A challenge could be used as a cover for an attack, no matter what had been agreed between the skinner and the King of France. 'Where will you be so you can bear witness? I wouldn't trust la Griffe's men when my son defeats him. They might cause you harm and blame me. Come inside the walls. You'll be safe with us.'

Master Alphonse pointed beyond the extended line of horsemen. 'I stay separate from these men. Those three men-at-arms served the King's brother. If there is any hint of danger after the contest they will do what they can to defend me and take word to my master. If de Soissons kills me, he will be hunted across France. I am grateful for your concern. God bless you and your son, Sir Thomas. I will pray for him.'

Blackstone and the others watched as the steward turned his horse and trotted to where the three men-at-arms waited.

Henry stared hard into the distance. 'Hugh, do you see those three men? Are they familiar?'

Gifford squinted. 'I can't see their faces clear enough at this distance. Do you recognize them?

'I'm not sure,' said Henry.

Blackstone hobbled back towards the gates. 'We have the braziers and torches prepared?' he asked his squire.

'Aye, Sir Thomas. Fuelled and ready. Ramparts as well,' said John Jacob, 'so that they will see our archers.'

'And I've posted extra men on the dark side of the walls in case these bastards have scaling ladders with them,' said Killbere. 'Creatures of the night embrace their own inner demons. A fight in the open is a damned good distraction to let a hundred men come up behind us.'

'And us behind them,' said Blackstone.

They turned back for the gates.

'Have every horse saddled and ready,' Blackstone told them.

He drew closer to Henry and Hugh Gifford. 'All right. We will prepare you. It'll be dark soon.' He put his arm over his son's shoulder. 'I'll sit with you a while before the priest comes.'

Henry Blackstone stepped into his father's embrace. The others held back and let father and son make their way to the château.

And their destiny.

CHAPTER SIXTY-EIGHT

The compline bell had rung and the priest's candle marking the hours had burned down. The priest had been escorted back to his quarters after prayers had been recited. John Jacob ensured that Blackstone's weapons were ready to be handed to his son for the fight. Blades had been honed and tested and Gifford made sure Henry ate sparingly but well. The pottage was enriched with red Gascon wine; bread and cheese had been served him and Will Longdon had brought apples from the stable's winter storage. Blackstone sat with his son as Gifford laid out a fresh linen shirt next to his surcoat, belt, scabbard and sword.

Blackstone handed him his open-faced helm.

'That's too big for him, Sir Thomas,' said Gifford. 'One strike against it and he'll be bareheaded.'

Blackstone went to the door. 'I'll ask John Jacob for his lid. That'll protect you better. There's always time in a fight to raise the visor and get air on your face. You just have to remember to close it again. Understood?'

'Yes, Father.'

Blackstone stepped outside where the men waited.

John Jacob was waiting, a querulous look on his face. Blackstone nodded that all was as expected as his squire handed him his own helm. Blackstone went back into the room where his nervous son waited. Closing the door, he handed the helm to Gifford.

'Try it first, Master Gifford. See if it's better for him.'

The man-at-arms tugged on the helm. The padded interior was a better fit. He pulled it off and nodded at Blackstone.

'I think it needs some more padding, Sir Thomas, but we can fix that.' Acting like a squire, he stood over Henry and lowered it onto his head, fixing the strap beneath his chin.

'See how this feels, Master Henry.'

Henry fussed it. He pushed the visor up and down a few times. He nodded to Gifford, who undid the strap. Henry pulled the helm free, a hand quickly smoothing his ruffled hair. A nervous gesture that did not go unnoticed.

'Yes,' he mumbled. 'Perhaps a bit more padding. I don't know. Can we tighten the strap?'

'I'll have it ready for you,' said Gifford.

The lad's head was down, his shoulders slumped. Already defeated, Gifford thought as he put the helm on the cot next to where Wolf Sword rested in its scabbard alongside Blackstone's knife, fighting axe and shield. Gifford and Blackstone exchanged glances.

Blackstone picked up the axe. Its short, curved blade had a stout pick at the rear of its head.

'When the time comes, you strike with the blade and hook with the pick. Pull your man off balance. It's sharp and will pierce his mail. And remember, he'll do the same to you.'

Henry nodded, but he was barely paying attention. He was naked from the waist up ready to be dressed, a blanket across his shoulders for warmth. The fire radiated heat into the room, but he shivered and could barely swallow the food. His stomach tightened at the thought of the impending fight, but he followed his father's insistence that he ate slowly. Hot food put strength in a man's arm.

'Give him more wine,' Blackstone told Gifford.

'No more,' Henry said.

'Do as I say. You'll sweat it out. Gascon red feeds the heart. And it will calm the fear.'

Henry did not have the bluff humour of the fighting men he'd known since childhood: he couldn't raise a jest to bat aside the anxiety that tightened his throat. His hand quivered. The beaker hovered near his lips.

'Drink it all,' said Blackstone. 'Every man who has ever stood at my side in battle would fill his belly with wine or brandy. It warms the bones and adds vigour to your efforts.'

Once again, Henry did his father's bidding.

Blackstone sat quietly, watching the boy he still thought of as being more his mother's son than his own. Her tenderness and learning resided in his heart and mind. But Blackstone acknowledged he had had courage enough to fight and defend himself in the past, and from what Hugh Gifford had told him, was brave and clever enough to outwit a garrison commander and a mercenary killer. But that was not the kind of courage needed tonight. The shadow of death waited in the darkness. This fight required a viciousness Henry Blackstone did not own. The rapid onset of violence that he'd need came from a seasoned sword arm and an instinct bred over years of battle. The one thing Henry Blackstone did not possess was a rage to kill.

'Listen to me, Henry. Wolf Sword can cleave a man from shoulder to hip. Put strength behind the blade. Use your back muscles and drive the blade down with the strength in your arm.'

'You have told me a thousand times, Father.'

'And I will tell you a thousand and one times more.' He studied his son for a moment, glanced at Gifford and then: 'All right. That's enough food and drink. Time to ready yourself.'

Henry tried to stand and faltered. Gifford grabbed his arm, but he snatched it away. 'Hugh, I'm not a child.'

'The stool leg gave way, Master Henry,' his guardian lied to cover his response.

Henry regretted snapping at the man who had stayed loyal since they fled Oxford. He nodded. 'Forgive me, Hugh.' He pointed to the shirt on the cot. 'Let's be done with this matter.'

Hugh Gifford pulled the clean linen shirt over Henry's head. Henry fussed at its folds, tugging each sleeve, rolling his shoulders, not wanting any wrinkle of the material to offer discomfort once the mail was pulled on. Gifford hefted the mail over Henry's shoulders. Henry became flustered, stretching his arms into the long sleeves, shaking his head as if clearing his thoughts, cursing as his hand refused to push through far enough to the cuff.

Blackstone watched as Gifford heaved the mail across the boy's shoulders.

'Remember, Henry,' he said, watching his son's struggles, 'swing from the shoulder, arm straight, keep your sword rigid. Be sensitive to its feel and the blows you make. If you do not, you will soon tire. If you flex your arm, the mail will bunch and pinch at your elbow.'

Henry was nodding repeatedly, but confusion was setting in. 'I can't move like this, Father.'

'You've never worn it before because you've never had to. You're unaccustomed to it.'

Henry's distress and discomfort were plain to see.

'Before Hugh finishes preparing you, use the latrine bucket. Rid your bladder of the wine.'

Henry turned, encumbered by the restrictive weight of the mail. He faltered, staggered a moment, and then his knees gave way. He blearily twisted his head back to gaze, questioning, at his father, and then he slumped.

Blackstone was on his feet, any sign of limping injury gone, the pretence of comforting his son put aside.

'I hope I didn't give him too much of that potion, Sir Thomas,' said Gifford. 'I could have killed the lad.'

'If you have, blame Will Longdon. He's the one who knows how much to give a man and render him senseless when he pulls an arrowhead from a man's leg. Throw a blanket over him and put more wood on the fire. Stay with him and pour away what's left of the wine.'

Blackstone reached for his weapons and stepped out into the night where John Jacob and his captains waited.

'He'll not forgive you,' said Killbere.

'But he'll be alive,' Blackstone answered. John Jacob helped him dress quickly, second nature after the years of battle. He strapped on his belt and scabbard, tucked in his fighting axe and hefted his shield. He pulled on Jacob's helm and looked at the waiting men. They were unaccustomed to staying behind walls. They wanted to take the fight to their enemy. 'Is everything ready?'

Killbere grinned. The men nodded.

'Then light the fires,' said Blackstone.

CHAPTER SIXTY-NINE

Beyond the walls, men dipped burning torches into the iron braziers' oil-soaked wood. Each brazier ten feet from the next in a circle sixty feet wide flared into life. Along the château's ramparts, torches ignited between each of Will Longdon and Jack Halfpenny's few archers chosen to be seen manning the walls.

The gates swung open.

La Griffe stood in front of his men, peering beyond the flames to the empty gateway. Other than the torches on the wall and the crackling braziers, the place was in darkness. He peered harder. Out of the unlit château yard, a man strode forward. He wore a surcoat over mail, with only greaves for his legs, pauldron and vambrace to protect his arms.

Jean de Soissons tested his claw hand. Once the shaft of an axe or a knife hilt was pressed into it, the claw held the weapon like a vice. He turned to his men.

'I didn't think he would have the courage to fight.'

He pulled on his helm; one of his men tightened its straps. La Griffe strode forward into the ring of fire and joined the man he thought to be Henry Blackstone. No sooner had he entered the circle than the man unexpectedly ran at him, slamming his shield against his. La Griffe staggered back, found his balance and braced his arm against the next attack he knew must come, but Blackstone's strength had spun him into a half-turn. De Soissons barely twisted aside in time before Blackstone's sword arced through the air and cut across his shield. Had he not moved quickly enough, he would have lost his arm. The top corner of his shield was cut through. Blackstone rammed him again and turned on his heel, pivoting his strength, trapping La Griffe's sword arm, pressing him back against a brazier. The searing heat compelling him to half turn again and retreat from the rapid assault designed to stop him moving quickly, as his fighting style dictated.

Blackstone took a half-dozen strides towards the inner circle, shadowing the man as he collected his wits, regained his poise and came forward with renewed determination. La Griffe's rapid sword strokes were those of a master swordsman who knew how to disarm and kill a man. His feet shuffled quickly, finding equilibrium, moving again, never allowing his stability to be compromised. It was skilful, instinctive fighting, adapting every lesson taught, every contest fought. Unpredictable.

Instead of moving backwards, Blackstone stood his ground, feet firmly planted apart, hunched to absorb the sword strikes and allow his shield to take the full force of the attack.

La Griffe grunted with effort, a wave crashing against an immovable rock. He sidestepped, danced to one side and then the other. His feet moved rapidly, but at every strike he made, Blackstone protected himself until his shield could take no more punishment. He had drawn la Griffe into delivering a killing blow and saw the high guard attack before de Soissons brought his arm down, his shoulder half turning. Blackstone sidestepped. It had been a feint by La Griffe. The Frenchman shifted lightly on his feet, changing the blade's angle. Blackstone twisted away just in time as the blow aimed for his neck clanged against his helm. The force of the blow shuddered through Blackstone's neck and shoulders. He staggered. At the end of its arc the tip of La Griffe's blade caught Blackstone's shoulder, numbing the muscles and sharp enough to cut into his mail. His sword arm became momentarily lame.

The strike had taken la Griffe a yard past Blackstone, who shook free his shield and hurled it at him as he turned to face him. Blackstone's left hand tugged his axe from his belt. Wolf Sword hung loose from its blood knot as Blackstone clenched his fingers, squeezing blood and feeling back into his hand as he took the fight to the younger and more agile man. The Frenchman swiped aside the thrown shield as he was pushed back again, but he knew his opponent was wounded. Firelight glowed on Blackstone's mail and the red reflection was more than the tint of colour from the flames. Blood seeped down from the shoulder wound to a useless arm and a trailing sword.

La Griffe's men cheered when they saw what looked to be the Englishman's imminent defeat and death. Their attention was held by the *danse macabre* taking place in the circle of fire; they failed to notice that every second archer on the wall had slipped away out of sight.

Blackstone angled his attack, smashing repeated blows with his axe against his opponent's shield. La Griffe held his ground, edging his body round so he could bring his sword to bear on Blackstone's useless arm. An arm that still dragged a sword by its blood knot and, even if Blackstone's strength returned, could not be raised high enough to deliver a blow. There was little time for de Soissons to strike back. Blackstone's axe hacked into the shield's rim, splintering what remained of its rigidity after that first sword strike.

La Griffe knew that if he did not abandon the shield and take up his own battleaxe the force of Blackstone's attack would drive down his guard. He needed to spin away and sweep up with his sword blade to cut away Blackstone's leg that kept him braced in the attack. Throwing his shield arm wide, deflecting the axe strikes, he turned on his heel, bringing the weight of his body to scythe his sword low to cut Blackstone's leg.

He was too late. The lame arm he thought still trailed uselessly now gripped the sword's hilt and drove its pommel upwards – a punch that caught his chin guard. It snapped back his head, throwing him off balance. He flailed, feet scrabbling for purchase. He fell into a brazier. Sparks flew.

The sound of his men's cries of alarm swept across the night.

The brazier saved de Soissons from the downward plunge of Blackstone's blade as the iron basket tumbled between the squirming man and his attacker. La Griffe shook himself free, cast aside his battered shield, crouched and gripped his axe. As Blackstone came forward, La Griffe spun like a top, slashing his sword low in another attempt to sever Blackstone's leg. Blackstone rammed Wolf Sword into the dirt. The Frenchman's blade shuddered its full force against it.

Blackstone pulled his blade free. Both men swung their axes. Shaft met shaft. Blackstone headbutted his opponent. Helm against helm. He twisted his axe hand, reversed its blade and swung the pick into his opponent's mail behind his shoulder and yanked with all his strength, twisting his body, using his weight to pull his opponent down. The Frenchman went onto his toes, flailed for balance but fell heavily. He rolled; his feet caught Blackstone's legs. Blackstone lost the grip on his axe as he went down. La Griffe couldn't roll away quickly enough. Blackstone's weight fell on him. La Griffe struck the back of Blackstone's helm with his axe but it was a futile attempt to cause serious injury. Both men's lungs heaved, faces sluiced with sweat trapped in the enclosed helms. The narrow slits afforded limited vision and even less air despite the pepperpot visor protecting their lower face.

Searing pain pierced Blackstone's shoulder where the earlier sword strike had cut into his mail. La Griffe had reached for his dagger and aimed for Blackstone's neck but his hands were slippery with blood and the blade glanced off the helm and penetrated Blackstone's already wounded shoulder. Then, stabbing and slashing wildly, the blade bit into Blackstone's thigh. He jabbed again and again, piercing Blackstone's mail, driving the narrow, sharpened point into Blackstone's flesh. Ignoring the pain Blackstone struggled yet failed to bring Wolf Sword to bear: the blood knot held firm, stopping him from angling the blade and ramming it into the Frenchman's armpit. He grabbed Wolf Sword's blade with his left hand and pressed the hilt's crossguard down into the slit of the Frenchman's helm. La Griffe bucked and kicked, but Blackstone's weight was too much. He raised his shoulders and forced the crossguard down into the killer's eye.

The Frenchman screamed. Blackstone kept pressing until the guard could penetrate no more. He heard and smelled la Griffe vomit into his helm. Blackstone rolled clear. The Frenchman's strength was such that he got onto one shoulder to raise himself. He fumbled with the helm's straps, desperate to pull it free, but his fingers were encumbered by his gauntlets and his clawed hand.

Blackstone cut free de Soissons's straps and yanked off the Frenchman's helm. Vomit clung to his beard. His blood-strewn face and empty eye socket were ghastly in the flickering light. His remaining eye stared at the man who had bested him. He knew he would not live long. Blackstone stood over him as la Griffe flopped back. Moaning in pain, his body quivered and shook. Blackstone's boot pressed onto his throat. La Griffe's death throes took less than a minute. Blackstone remained where he stood, leaning his weight on Wolf Sword to rest his wounded leg. Firelight bathed victor and vanquished. The braziers, sentinels to the killer's death.

Blackstone turned for the château's gates as they swung open to receive him.

Jean de Soissons's men spurred their horses. At the very least, they would trample to death the man who had killed their leader and then surge inside the walls and kill the few men he had with him. There would be reward enough for his death from the French King.

The ground shook from their horses' charge. Blackstone turned and faced, unflinching, the line of horsemen three hundred yards away.

CHAPTER SEVENTY

Blackstone's captains and Killbere had muffled their horse's hooves and during the fight led them out of the château's rear gate. Leading them silently on foot in the darkness, they had flanked de Soissons's men and waited in the gulley that lay to one side beyond the walls, a plan prepared in case the routiers attacked. Will Longdon had taken every second archer from their places on the rampart and had skirted the château on the blind side to where the routiers were gathered. They waited in line, backs against the wall, out of sight, held fast by the wall's deep shadows.

As la Griffe's skinners spurred their horses, Jack Halfpenny's archers on the ramparts waited until they were 250 yards from where Blackstone stood facing them. And then they loosed. Twenty-five archers would cause little damage to a large body of men, but their yard-long shafts from the walls were joined by Longdon's twenty-five hidden bowmen shooting into the horsemen's flanks. Horses went down, men fell, pierced from the hailstorm plummeting from the night sky. The double-edged attack from the bowmen threw the riders into confusion. They wheeled their mounts, barging each other in their panic, driving them away from Blackstone and the château towards the only route open to them unencumbered by their dead and dying. They rode straight into the waiting ranks of Killbere's men who rose from the depression like demons from the underworld blocking their escape route.

Terrel had had no choice but to ride with Killbere and John

Jacob after Blackstone's squire had dragged him from the stables.

'No man shirks his duty tonight,' Killbere had told him.

Caught up in the fury of their attack, fright and survival instinct drove Terrel headlong when Killbere's line peeled away as captains led their men into the fray. He had gone too far. He was alone. La Griffe's men swirled about him. Terrel viciously yanked the reins and spurred his horse's flanks in his desperation to escape. He would ride back through the ranks. Head for the village. Anywhere was better than this screaming terror. His horse veered into Killbere's path as the knight was being attacked by two horsemen, one either side. Sir Gilbert's shield looked ready to give way under the onslaught. In its panic Terrel's horse barged the attacker as Terrel instinctively swung his sword in a killing arc. It severed the attacker's arm. Killbere rammed his sword point into the other man's armpit.

'With me!' Killbere yelled to Terrel, who had inadvertently saved Killbere's life in his escape attempt. The surge of horses behind Killbere forced Terrel's mount to turn despite his efforts to stop it. There was nothing he could do to stop being hurled into the slaughter.

Stragglers at the back of la Griffe's men were killed by the archers; others were driven apart by the attacking horsemen. Killbere and the men drove a wedge through the middle of the panicked routiers, forcing those on either side into pockets that were soon surrounded, where they were hacked and beaten to death. A few escaped into the night, but the bulk of la Griffe's killers met their end in the glimmering half-light as the braziers spluttered their last.

Blackstone remained encircled by the braziers. The dead lay scattered beyond him. Riderless horses ran wild or stood unmoving, some foundered, lame, struck by arrows. Cries from the wounded rose onto the night breeze, soon to fall silent as Blackstone's men went among them. This was no time for prisoners. Embers danced and swirled upwards, fleetingly released from the smouldering wood only to die quickly, obliterated by the night.

John Jacob left the killing ground when he saw Blackstone limp back towards the gates. The squire dismounted in time to stop Blackstone from falling. Blood ran freely down his arm and leg from his wounds.

'Steady, Sir Thomas. Rest your back against the wall while I get that piss pot off you.' He wasted no time trying to undo the straps that held the helm but carefully sliced through them with his knife and then lifted the suffocating helm free. He tossed it aside, keen to release Blackstone's gauntlets and blood knot that held Wolf Sword to his wrist. The squire's fingers were slippery with the blood soaking Blackstone's mail, their links biting into his wounds.

'We need to get your mail off, Sir Thomas. You're losing too much blood.'

Blackstone nodded, but put a restraining hand on John Jacob's arm. 'Let me see my son.'

His squire was about to argue, but knew better. 'Can you walk?'

Blackstone nodded. 'With help, John.'

The squire draped Blackstone's arm across his shoulders and edged the few yards to Henry's room. He pushed open the door and was met by an anxious-looking Gifford who had his sword ready for enemy intruders.

He sighed and lowered his blade. 'I heard the cries outside. I could not see which way the fight had gone.'

Blackstone leaned on the door frame. 'Master Gifford, my son?'

Gifford took in Blackstone's exhausted and wounded appearance, then gestured to where Blackstone had left him; sprawled on the floor covered with a blanket. 'He still sleeps, Sir Thomas. But another hour or so and I reckon he'll awake.'

'I'll face his anger then,' said Blackstone. 'And beg his forgiveness.'

Gifford looked at Blackstone's sweat-soaked hair and beard and the arm he cradled that dripped blood. 'I'd say he should be grateful, looking at how hard you fought, Sir Thomas.' He glanced at the sleeping Henry and then back to his father. 'But he won't be.'

Killbere greeted Master Alphonse as the steward and the three men-at-arms pulled up their mounts at the gates. Despite the darkness, torch-bearing peasants, who seemed to come from nowhere, crept from the forest and began scouring the dead for whatever might be of value.

Killbere held the old man's bridle and apologized on behalf of Blackstone, saying Henry had been wounded in the fight and naturally, as a father, he was concerned to be at his injured son's bedside.

'Sir Gilbert, please express to him my concern for his son,' said Master Alphonse.

'I will,' Killbere said, without offering an invitation for the Count's steward to come inside the walls.

The wily old steward had seen fighting men come and go through his master's castle for half a century, and as he glanced around Blackstone's seemingly unconcerned men while they tended to what looked to be mostly minor wounds, he sensed that their action had been planned before the night's killing.

'I will convey what I witnessed. That Jean de Soissons's men attacked and were beaten once he had been killed by

Henry Blackstone. I was concerned before the contest, but I see that Sir Thomas trained his son to fight like him.'

Killbere smiled. 'A willing pupil, Master Alphonse.'

The steward nodded. 'And a lucky one.'

There was no need to extend the charade. Did it matter who had killed the master swordsman? One less violent routier could only be a good thing. The old man bent down to grasp Killbere's outstretched hand.

Killbere felt the rough edge of folded parchment pressed into his palm.

Master Alphonse spoke softly. 'My master sends you this. He holds Sir Thomas and his men in high regard. The men with me should not hear of it.'

He turned his horse. One of the men-at-arms accompanying him leaned over his mount's withers. 'Sir Gilbert. I am Bernard de Lagny. My companions and I fought at Nájera for our master Louis of Anjou against you and your Prince. Fate placed us on the same road as Master Henry. I would be grateful if you would extend our good wishes to him. If our paths cross again I hope it will not be as enemies. We return to Paris now and shall report back to our King.'

He spurred his mount and the four horsemen took the route less obstructed by the fallen. As they cantered by, crows, roused from their nests by the peasants' torchlight, hopped, fluttered and settled, and then began to compete with the villagers to peck at the dead.

435

CHAPTER SEVENTY-ONE

Killbere tucked the secret note under his tunic. It was just as well the Count de Foix's steward left when he did. Before Master Alphonse and his escort were out of sight, a bedraggled Henry Blackstone, looking like a man who had drunk too much, burst out of his room. Hugh Gifford took a blow as he attempted to calm his enraged charge.

'Where is he?' Henry demanded loudly, too enraged for good sense to prevail in front of Blackstone's loyal men. 'Where is the man who calls himself my father?'

Meulon, Renfred and William Ashford were with their men attending to wounds as others stoked fires and stirred smoke-blackened pots, readying a meal. They turned at the young man's outburst.

'Calm yourself,' said Meulon. 'You have no right to be angry.'

Henry Blackstone stood like an encircled beast before the captains. Spittle flecked his lips; his eyes were wild. The effects of the wine and the numbing potion had not yet left him. 'I am cursed by his name! Now I am damned forever!'

Killbere stepped forward and raised a hand to calm him. 'That's enough, boy. Your father saved your life.'

Henry stupidly struck Killbere's hand aside. 'I am dishonoured!'

The words barely escaped his lips before Killbere slapped him hard. Despite being head and shoulders taller than the veteran knight, Henry went down, sprawling. Gifford and the others offered no helping hand to get him to his feet. Henry, dazed, unable to comprehend what had happened, glared.

Killbere pointed at him. 'You whimper like a mewling child at the teat. Stay down, gather your thoughts and settle your anger. If you stand and offer more insults I will beat you harder than you have ever been thrashed.'

Henry looked pathetic. His lip was split, his hair bedraggled. He dragged a hand across his face, saw the blood, and looked for a moment as though he was going to launch himself at Killbere. Meulon seemed to read his thoughts, stepped between them and offered his hand. 'You need to see your father, Henry,' he said gently.

Meulon's bulk was enough to stop any foolish action. Chastised, and ignoring the hand of friendship, Henry rolled away and got to his feet.

John Jacob pushed through the men gathered to witness the outburst.

Henry brushed the hair back from his face and spat bloodied phlegm, standing defiantly before the hard-faced men who stared at him.

'Henry,' said John Jacob. 'Trust me, your father needs you at his side.'

'And why should I trust you? You serve him and his deception. All of you!'

John Jacob edged closer, standing at Killbere's shoulder. 'Every man here has earned your trust. I protected you, your mother and your sister when we escaped to Avignon all those years ago. Have you forgotten that time? Sir Gilbert, Meulon, Will Longdon, Jack Halfpenny, Renfred and William Ashford: every man here is loyal to your father and every one of them saw you grow from a child into a man. There is not one among them who would not shield you from death. There is no shame, Henry. You are alive this morning because your father fought a man who was more skilled than himself.'

Henry's breathing calmed, but the burden he bore dug its claws deeper still. 'And I am still dishonoured.'

Killbere grunted. 'Men find honour when it suits them. We kill and maim to stay alive. If there's just cause, then we seek it out. There's the honour. Being true to your word depends who you give it to. And you gave no such vow to an arse-wipe like Jean de Soissons. There was no honour to be had in killing him. He was a sewer rat.'

'Where is my father? Why isn't he here now? Is he ashamed to face me?'

Killbere's face took on a look of weary resignation. He softened his tone. 'John, take him to his father.' The men parted as John Jacob lifted a lantern and led the aggrieved Henry through the men.

The squire stopped in front of an open-fronted store room. At first, Henry could not see clearly what was going on inside. He stepped closer, peering into the gloom. Will Longdon and Halfpenny had their back to him. They stood at the side of a flatbed cart, a trestle table at their side bearing a bucket of water, a wooden bowl and a fist-sized smooth stone. Jack Halfpenny held a raised lantern. Discarded bloodied rags lay at their feet.

'We staunched his wounds, but he's lost a lot of blood,' said John Jacob, hanging back as Henry edged sideways to see more clearly.

'You're casting shadow!' said Will Longdon without turning.

Henry shifted more to one side. His father lay, shoulders propped, on a bloodstained straw mattress. He was naked except for his braies. The height of the cart allowed Longdon to stand and attend to the injured Blackstone.

Henry had never seen his father bearing so many wounds. Or being so weakened by them. Blood sluiced and discoloured his torso.

Longdon smeared ground paste into one of Blackstone's wounds, scooped more from the bowl on the trestle table, pushed his fingers into a wicked-looking incision in Blackstone's leg and then dipped his hands into the bucket of water, drying them on a length of cloth.

Henry was confused by the scene in front of him. He muttered, 'Will... what are you doing?' Uncertainty about his father's injuries prompted the most obvious of questions.

Longdon spared him a glance and then went back to his ministrations. 'Old Jewish doctor showed us how to stop any poison getting in,' he said.

Longdon bent over the trestle table, lifted a threaded, curved needle and pressed it into another bowl. 'We stitch him with silk from the binding on our fletchings. Dip it into vinegar first, like the old man told us, and then we'll have your father back making life difficult for us all.' He squeezed a wound and pressed the needle into it. 'If my days as an archer ever end, I'll turn my hand to barber surgeon. Damned sight easier money to be made.'

Blackstone winced, but remained silent.

'Thomas, when you flinch I can't make a decent stitch.'

Blackstone gritted his teeth and gripped the cart's sides as Longdon pushed and pulled the needle through the gaping wound. He hissed, 'I've seen you mend a torn tunic. Damned thing never fitted again.'

Longdon kept his head down. 'The man was a hunchbacked dwarf. Nothing would have fitted. Jack, bring that lantern closer.'

Blackstone grunted as raw tissue was pulled tight.

'Give him potion to dull the pain,' said Henry with unconcealed anguish.

Longdon didn't look up. 'Aye, well, you had the last of what we had.'

Blackstone's uninjured arm snatched at Longdon's wrist. 'Dammit, Will, you stitch too deeply.'

Longdon sighed. 'I know, Thomas, and it grieves me to cause you hurt, but if I don't, the wound will split again. You've already torn the wound in your side wide open.'

Blackstone nodded and breathed deeply through the pain.

Longdon turned to Henry. 'Make yourself useful. Fetch more clean water.'

Henry stepped forward and reached for the bucket. Its water swirled with blood. He glanced at his gaunt-faced father, who gave him a reassuring nod.

Henry Blackstone quickened his pace to reach the well outside.

For a shuddering moment, it had felt as though his father was close to death.

CHAPTER SEVENTY-TWO

'The priest?' said Killbere.

Will Longdon nodded. 'He's lost a lot of blood. His heartbeat is slow. He slips in and out of consciousness. I can do no more. We've moved him to his quarters.'

'Dammit, Will, we've seen him on his deathbed before. He needs rest, food and wine. He's just sleeping. My God, we all slumber after a hard fight.'

Killbere saw the concern etched on the archer's face.

'All I'm saying is—'

'I know what you're saying!' Killbere snapped, pulling him aside, eager to keep anyone else from hearing the archer's concerns. Fighting men's morale could plummet when their war leader died, and Thomas Blackstone had been on the battlefield since he was a boy. Legends forged in battle inspired men to do extraordinary things. And the legend that was the King's Master of War was too damned important to die. Not now.

Killbere took a moment. He shrugged. 'Thomas is no priest-lover. He's blessed by the Silver Wheel Goddess. He's a creature of nature. A chanting priest hovering could turn any man away from thoughts of heaven. At least the devil takes you without ceremony.'

'So what do we do?' said Longdon.

'Has Thomas asked for the priest?'

'No.'

'There you have it. He has no desire for one, and is not intending to die.'

'We can't be sure, though, Sir Gilbert.'

'No one can be certain of anything. Death comes to us all, Will. We have all faced the grim reaper and spat in his eye. Let's stay close to Thomas and wait.'

Will Longdon nodded. 'All right. Do we tell the others?'

'No. I'll wager John Jacob will see things as they are, given he's Thomas's shadow, but he's wise enough to know when to remain silent. I'll go and see Thomas for myself. You've done well. See to your own men.'

Killbere let Will Longdon merge back into his company of archers and then made his way towards Blackstone's room. John Jacob sat on a barrel cleaning Wolf Sword. Killbere knew it to be a means of taking his mind off Blackstone's injuries. If he wiped that honed blade any longer, it would dazzle the sun. Hugh Gifford sat back against the wall sharpening his knife. He got quickly to his feet when he saw Killbere.

'Sir Gilbert.'

'Is Henry in there?'

'Aye. He's calmed himself down since he saw his father's wounds.'

'Damned fool, that lad. Let's hope he's learned a lesson.'

'His pride is wounded. He doesn't want to be seen a coward.'

'No one here thinks that. Have you spoken to him, John?'

'I told him as much – and much good it did me.'

Gifford pushed his knife into his scabbard. 'He's young. We all were once.'

'I'm too old to remember,' said Killbere. He hesitated as Gifford reached for the door latch. 'You're staying with Henry?'

'I've not been released from my duty, Sir Gilbert. Only Warwick can do that at the behest of the King.'

The door creaked open. Henry sat on a stool next to his

father's cot. The room was barely lit. A couple of candles and a small window were the only source of light. Killbere recognized Will Longdon's anxiety. Thomas Blackstone's face was gaunt, almost bloodless. He lay, eyes closed, his chest barely rising and falling. Despite the poor light Killbere could see Henry's red-rimmed eyes. He had quickly wiped a sleeve across them when the door opened.

'Henry, I'll sit with him for a while. Go and get some food.'

'No, I'll stay.'

'You do no good here except to cause yourself grief.'

'I'm not hungry.'

'Listen to me. You have a man loyal to you standing in the cold. He is your responsibility. Give him a reason to do his duty. Ask him to get food and drink. Go and stand with the men. Talk about the fight. Let them see you. Cowering in here is not the place to be. They will be concerned to hear about your father. It's important their spirits are not dampened. You understand?'

Henry nodded.

'When you lead men, you need to keep their despair at bay. That's what a leader does. Can you do that? For them? Your friends?'

It was easy to see Henry's reluctance to leave his father, but Killbere's gentle persuasion and reasoning convinced him.

'I'll call for you if there's any cause for alarm. You have my word. Remember what I said about the men.'

As Henry passed Killbere, the veteran said, 'I'm sorry I struck you.'

Henry nodded. 'I deserved it.'

'Yes, you did.' He patted his shoulder and closed the door behind him.

Killbere pulled the stool closer to Blackstone. He squeezed out a cloth from the bowl at the side of the bed and dabbed

Blackstone's face. His friend did not respond. Killbere looked over his shoulder as if checking there was no one else within earshot. There couldn't be as he was the only person in the room, but the news he had to give Blackstone was for his ears alone.

Killbere hunched forward closer to Blackstone's face. 'The men fought well, Thomas. Hard and fast. Even that scoundrel Terrel. Damned if he didn't save me. We lost only three men and some wounded. It was a rout. Thomas, if you can hear me, give me a sign. I beg you.' Killbere waited but there was no flicker of movement behind Blackstone's closed eyes. Killbere pressed on, hoping the urgency of the matter would reach into the darkness that entrapped his friend. 'Thomas, I have a note from Gaston Phoebus. He relays a message to you. I was obliged to read it. For that I apologize, my friend, but there is an urgency to it.' Killbere waited again for some response, but Blackstone's eyes remained shut, his breathing so shallow that Killbere lowered his ear to Blackstone's lips. Uncertainty gripped him. Thomas Blackstone was more dead than alive. He shuffled the stool nearer to the cot so that his face was closer to Blackstone's ear. 'Thomas. Fate has played a trick on us. The Italian priest, Torellini, was in England to see the King and then the Prince. There will be no money for them from the Bardi bank and another war with the French will surely come.' Killbere stared in desperation at his friend who lay so unresponsive. He unfolded the letter as if to show it to Blackstone. 'But there *is* gold that does not belong to the bank. *That* is the information relayed by the priest. We are commanded by the King to abandon Trastámara and seize it.' Killbere waited. There was still no reaction… until Blackstone gave a soft exhalation. As if a final breath had left his body. Tears stung Killbere's eyes. His voice was strangled with despair. 'Thomas… Thomas… for pity's sake, hear me…

hear me.' He wiped a hand across his face, clearing tears and snot from his beard.

There was no response.

'Damn you, Thomas, you cannot die. The King orders you to save his ailing son and the ruin and defeat that awaits him.' Killbere forced his words from a choking heart through gritted teeth. 'You-cannot-disobey-the-King.'

Killbere stared hard at his friend. It was over. And he knew it. He covered his friend's cold hand with his own. 'God bless you, Thomas.'

He pushed the stool back momentarily, but started as a fierce grip clasped his wrist. Blackstone's eyes opened. His voice was a determined whisper.

'Where is this gold?'

AUTHOR'S NOTES

When Edward, Prince of Wales and Aquitaine, launched his offensive across the Pyrenees to put the King of Castile and León back on his throne, he gathered an army of professional soldiers of fortune. His entourage consisted of the noblemen of Aquitaine and his brother, John of Gaunt, who had sailed from England with five hundred soldiers, most of whom were mounted archers. The renowned Knight of the Garter, John Chandos, brought together notorious routier captains, as well as the Englishman Sir John Calveley. He and Chandos had served Don Pedro's enemy, Henry of Trastámara, and put him on the throne the previous year. Fighting wars was purely a business opportunity. How else were men to be paid? Now, these two stalwart knights returned to serve the Prince and the English Crown.

The Prince of Wales's army consisted of Gascons, Bretons and Englishmen with those Castilians still loyal to the exiled King Don Pedro. It was an army of between 8,000 and 10,000 men, similar in size to that which the Prince had commanded when he fought and beat the French army at Poitiers. But to re-place Don Pedro on his throne they had to cross the Pyrenees through the narrow pass of Roncesvalles.

Henry of Trastámara had seasoned French and Breton commanders, among them Marshal Arnoul d'Audrehem and Bertrand du Guesclin: experienced men who knew how to fight the English. Trastámara had even received advice from the French King to harass the English, to wear them down with lightning-fast attacks, something he did with great success, until that fateful day when he was provoked to stand his ground, much to the despair of his commanders.

The Battle of Nájera was a great military victory for Prince Edward but it had emptied his Treasury and the costs of the war were never repaid as promised by Don Pedro. During the ransoming of the prisoners Don Pedro came across a nobleman once loyal to him. In a fit of rage he stabbed the man to death. I used this recorded incident in my fictional account of Don Pedro killing Don Fernando Ferrandes of Castile.

Over the previous years, the Prince's lavish lifestyle at his palaces in Bordeaux and Angoulême had already consumed the funds he needed to pay the fighting men. In England, his father Edward III permitted no monies to be sent from the English Treasury. Aquitaine had to be self-sufficient. It was, in many respects – despite the Prince's renowned extravagance – a shortsighted approach, given that the duchy was scarcely able to produce sufficient revenue in peacetime. The Prince of Wales, like many a hard-pressed householder in the modern age, remortgaged his lands in England to raise capital. When he returned to Bordeaux after Don Pedro was reinstated he had no choice but to start raising taxes and that led to the local lords turning to the French King for his support.

The tide was turning for English dominance in France.

ACKNOWLEDGEMENTS

I always like to hear from my readers and I am continually appreciative of their ongoing support. Their generous comments on social media are valued and appreciated, as are their reviews on sites such as Amazon and Goodreads. Enormous thanks to Isobel Dixon, James Pusey and everyone at Blake Friedmann Literary Agency, who continue to create new foreign markets and readers for Thomas Blackstone's adventures. My editor Richenda Todd's skill at working diligently through the text making astute observations and suggestions is second to none. My publisher Nic Cheetham and his team's enthusiasm at Head of Zeus/Bloomsbury keep the books' momentum going forward.

I am grateful to you all.

David Gilman
Devonshire
2023

ABOUT THE AUTHOR

DAVID GILMAN has enjoyed many careers, including paratrooper, firefighter, and photographer. An award-winning author and screenwriter, he is the author of the critically acclaimed Master of War series of historical novels, and was shortlisted for the Wilbur Smith Adventure Writing Prize for The Last Horseman. He was longlisted for the same prize for *The Englishman*, the first book featuring ex-French Foreign Legionnaire Dan Raglan. David lives in Devon.

Follow David on @davidgilmanuk,
www.davidgilman.com, and on Facebook
at davidgilman.author.